"Thank you for [...] alone."

He reached across the table and his big hand engulfed hers, warming some of the cold spots she'd had inside. "There's no way I'd leave you alone, Lexie. I know what it's like to be alone with grief and I don't want that for you."

As she looked into his soft gray eyes, she wanted him. She wanted the warmth of his body wrapped around hers. She needed him to keep the horror at bay.

"Come to bed with me, Nick. Come to bed and make love to me."

His eyes flared wide at her words. "Lexie, that's probably not a good idea tonight. You're grieving and you aren't thinking straight and the last thing I'd want to do is take advantage of you."

"You wouldn't be. I know you've already had your Cupid arrow, Nick. This isn't about love, it's about need." She got up from the table. "I need to be held. I need to feel alive. I need you, Nick."

CARLA CASSIDY

SCENE OF THE CRIME: WIDOW CREEK

™ **Harlequin**®

TORONTO NEW YORK LONDON
AMSTERDAM PARIS SYDNEY HAMBURG
STOCKHOLM ATHENS TOKYO MILAN MADRID
PRAGUE WARSAW BUDAPEST AUCKLAND

To Valerie Francis

For Sundays and girl talk and all your support! For laughter and jewelry and a little touch of sanity in my life. All I can say is thanks!

Recycling programs
for this product may
not exist in your area.

ISBN-13: 978-0-373-74622-4

SCENE OF THE CRIME: WIDOW CREEK

Copyright © 2011 by Carla Bracale

ABOUT THE AUTHOR

Carla Cassidy is an award-winning author who has written more than fifty novels for Harlequin Books. In 1995, she won Best Silhouette Romance from *RT Book Reviews* for *Anything for Danny*. In 1998, she also won a Career Achievement Award for Best Innovative Series from *RT Book Reviews*.

Carla believes the only thing better than curling up with a good book to read is sitting down at the computer with a good story to write. She's looking forward to writing many more books and bringing hours of pleasure to readers.

Books by Carla Cassidy

CAST OF CHARACTERS

Lexie Forbes—She'd come to Widow Creek seeking her missing twin sister but instead had found danger…and more.

Nick Walker—Was he friend or foe to Lexie?

Lana Forbes—Lexie's missing twin. Had she walked away from her life or stumbled onto something malevolent in the small town?

Gary Wendell—Was the chief of police a good guy or somebody who would do anything to protect the secrets of his town?

Bo Richards—A handsome rancher who dated Lana. Was he the last person to see her alive? And was he responsible for her death?

Clay Cole—A tough guy with an attitude. What did he know, if anything, about what had happened to Lana?

Chapter One

Lexie Forbes rarely left her job at the Kansas City FBI field office early, but on this Friday afternoon she knocked off work at three and headed toward her car in the parking lot. There was nothing pressing on her desk, just the usual cons and perverts for her to chase down. But she'd awakened that morning with a vague sense of anxiety that she hadn't quite been able to shake off.

She knew the source of the anxiety—her twin sister, Lauren. They were extremely close and spoke on the phone to each other at least once or twice a day, but for the past two days Lexie had been unable to get hold of her sister.

As she walked through the parking lot, the first fallen autumn leaves swirled around her feet and a cool breeze danced unexpected goose bumps along her arms.

She reached her car, unlocked it and then slid in behind the wheel. She'd just put the key in and started the engine when it struck, an excruciating pain that slammed into the back of her head with such force it momentarily stole her breath away.

It was there only a moment and then gone, leaving her gasping for air and holding on to the steering wheel with clenched fingers.

"Whoa," she finally breathed. What was that all about? It had felt like a bomb had detonated in the base of her brain. With a shaky hand she reached up and adjusted the rearview mirror so she could look at her reflection.

She wasn't sure what she expected to see, but the woman who stared back at her looked the same as always. Short, light brown, spiked hair with a vivid pink streak, black-rimmed glasses nearly hiding green eyes and no blood or missing skull from that sharp pain.

Adjusting the mirror back where it belonged, her thoughts once again shot to her sister and the anxiety swelled bigger and tighter in her chest. There had been a time several years ago when Lexie had suffered from inexplicable arm pain for a couple of hours. Later she'd discovered that Lauren had broken her arm. It had been one of those crazy twin things that nobody understood and that only happened occasionally.

Had Lauren hit her head? Had Lexie just experienced her twin's pain? She dismissed the idea. Each and every pain Lexie suffered wasn't tied to her twin sister.

As she pulled out of the parking lot she decided that if she didn't get hold of Lauren when she got to her apartment, then a road trip was definitely in order.

Four months ago Lauren had realized her dream and bought six acres of land in a small town about an hour and a half from the Kansas City area. Over the last couple of years she'd become an established dog breeder and trainer and had wanted enough property to expand her business.

Lexie had helped her move but hadn't been back to visit since that time. It was definitely past time for a trip to see her sister. She had the weekend open and this was a perfect opportunity for a surprise visit.

Once Lexie got home to her small apartment she tried her sister again, both on her landline and on her cell phone. When she still didn't get an answer she packed a bag, locked the apartment door and headed toward the small Kansas town of Widow Creek.

It was a pleasant drive. Traffic was light, and once she left the city she enjoyed the country scenery. Her favorite oldies played on the radio and she sang along until she reached the city limits of the small town.

It was just after five when she pulled up in front of her sister's place. The ranch-style farmhouse looked warm and inviting with pots of colorful flowers and a wicker rocking chair on the porch.

She got out of the car and gazed around. She'd forgotten that the place was a bit isolated, with only one other house visible in the distance. Aware of the sound of barking dogs, she walked to the side of the house where a large fenced area contained four young German shepherds.

They all raced to the fence with youthful pup eagerness, stepping on each other in an effort to get closer to her. She might have laughed at their antics if she didn't see that their food and water bowls were empty.

Lauren would never allow any of her dogs to go without food and water. The disquiet that had simmered inside her for the past two days now roared into full-bloom alarm.

She left the dog pen and hurried to the front door where she knocked. "Lauren? Lauren, are you in there? It's me." She waited only a moment and when no answer came she pulled out her keys and used the one that Lauren had given her on moving day.

Visions of her sister filled her head. Maybe she'd slipped in the shower and hurt herself to the point she couldn't get to a phone. Or maybe she was in bed, deathly ill, and couldn't rouse herself enough to make a call for help.

She unlocked the door and then pulled her gun and held it steady in her hand as she shoved the door open with her foot. Even though Lexie's job with the FBI consisted of her sitting in a small cubicle in front of a computer, she'd been trained to be proficient with her weapon.

As she entered the small foyer the first thing she noticed was that the house smelled slightly musty, as if it had been closed up for too long.

There was a low woof and Zeus greeted her. The old German shepherd ran to her like she was his new best friend. He sat on the floor at her feet and released a low, mournful whine.

Lexie dropped her gun back into her purse. There was no way anybody threatening could be in the house without Zeus letting her know.

"Hey, boy." She crouched down and scrubbed the dog behind his ears. "Hey, buddy, where's your mama?"

Zeus closed his eyes and released what sounded like a contented sigh as she continued to scratch behind his ears. She finally stood up and walked into the kitchen, then worried all over again when she saw that Zeus's food and water bowls were also empty.

She checked the rest of the house and confirmed that nobody was home, then returned to the kitchen and got food and water for Zeus. He attacked the food as if he were starving.

As Lexie watched him eat, her heart beat a rhythm of dread. What was going on here? Where was Lauren? Her dogs were her family and there was no way she'd leave them like this.

When she'd walked through the house she'd seen nothing amiss, no sign of trouble. The rooms were all neat and tidy, just the way Lauren always kept them.

The last time she'd talked to her sister had been Tuesday evening and Lauren hadn't mentioned going anywhere. Lauren almost never traveled because she didn't like leaving the care of the dogs to anyone else.

As Zeus finished his meal, Lexie stared out the back window where there were several outbuildings and beyond them an expanse of thick woods.

Was Lauren out there somewhere? Had she taken a walk, somehow fallen and hurt herself and been unable to summon help? She grabbed the leash that hung on a hook by the back door and then called to Zeus.

If Lauren was out there somewhere surely Zeus would find her. Lauren had gotten the dog when he was eight weeks old and he was now nine. No matter how many other dogs passed through Lauren's life, she and Zeus had always had a special bond.

Moments later, with Zeus on the leash, Lexie stepped out the back door and headed toward the outbuildings. Zeus bounded ahead on the length of leash she gave him as she tried to tamp down the overwhelming sense of dread that grew stronger with each minute that passed.

Her dread increased as she opened the door of the detached garage and found Lauren's truck inside. Where could she be without her vehicle?

Next she checked the first large shed, which held a variety of items Lauren used for her various training sessions. There were poles and jumps, risers and items used for agility training. Unfortunately, there was no Lauren.

She moved to the second, smaller shed and discovered it held only gardening tools. She told herself not to jump to any conclusions, but it was hard not to with the knot of fear that pressed tight in her chest.

The woods. It was the only place she had left to check. She looked at her watch. Almost six. She'd maybe get two good hours in before darkness began to fall and made a search impossible.

She took off with Zeus in tow and within minutes was surrounded by tall trees and thick brush. "Lauren!" she called every few steps and then stopped and listened for any kind of answering reply. But there was nothing except the sound of Zeus crunching leaves beneath his big paws.

"Zeus, find your mommy," she commanded the dog.

He barked and danced in place, as if unsure what she wanted from him. They walked for what seemed like an eternity until she finally reached a rocky creek bed with just a trickle of water running in it. She sank down on the edge, Zeus at her side and looked around with a sense of failure as she rested.

Darkness was slamming down with a swiftness that was disheartening. She'd done a cursory check of all the property and Zeus had never given an indication that his master might be near.

"Where are you, Lauren?" She had a bad feeling. None of this was right and she couldn't imagine any scenario that would allow any of this to make sense.

Lauren was definitely not the type to just take off somewhere with no thought to her dogs, no thought for Lexie. Something was terribly wrong.

She pulled herself up from the creek bank and headed back to the house. Maybe by now Lauren had returned. Or perhaps a friend had picked her up for shopping or dinner out and they hadn't returned yet. Of course that wouldn't explain why she hadn't answered Lexie's phone calls since Tuesday night.

The shadows of night had begun to cling to the house as Lexie reentered through the back door. For the first time in her life she hated to see nightfall. She removed Zeus from the leash and then went into Lauren's bedroom and stood staring at the neatly made bed.

The room breathed the essence of Lauren. It was infused with warmth from the peach and navy ruffled bedspread to the photo of the two sisters hugging on the nightstand. A faint scent of the orange blossom lotion that Lauren loved lingered in the air, intensifying Lexie's overwhelming sense of confusion and worry.

She thought back to the last phone conversation she'd had with her sister but couldn't think of anything Lauren had said that might explain her absence here. Lauren had talked about the dogs, about how excited she was about the growth of her business, but she hadn't mentioned going anywhere for any extended period of time.

There was absolutely no reason to believe

that she'd been missing since that phone conversation, Lexie told herself. She might have left the house that morning for some sort of day trip and hadn't realized the dogs were out of water.

The fact that the house smelled like it had been closed up for a couple of days didn't mean anything either. Maybe she was only thinking bad thoughts because of her job. As an FBI agent she was trained to look at the worst-case scenario.

An unmistakable sound came from behind her—the slide and click of a bullet being chambered in a shotgun. She froze as her heart nearly stopped beating.

"Who the hell are you and what are you doing in Lauren's bedroom?" The deep male voice was calm but held a steely edge.

She raised her hands above her head and slowly turned. He stood in the threshold of the bedroom. With his dark hair and gunmetal gray eyes, he was a hot hunk in a pair of tight jeans and a navy pullover. And he had the business end of a shotgun pointed directly at her heart.

NICK WALKER SLOWLY LOWERED the shotgun as he recognized the woman standing before him as the same one in the picture with Lauren on the nightstand.

"You're Lexie," he said as some of the tension ebbed from him.

Even though she and Lauren were identical twins it was obvious Lexie had gone to some extremes to find her own identity. Lauren wore contacts while the woman standing before him wore oversized black-rimmed glasses that almost hid the beauty of her bright green eyes. Lauren's hair was shoulder-length and Lexie's was short and spiked and sporting an unexpected pink streak.

Nick was surprised to feel a small kick of attraction in the pit of his stomach, something he'd never felt for his friend and neighbor, Lauren.

"The real question is who in the hell are you and what are you doing in Lauren's bedroom?" she asked, her chin lifted and eyes narrowed.

"I'm Nick Walker and I live next door. Why don't we both get out of Lauren's bedroom and go into the kitchen where we can talk."

He didn't wait for her response but rather turned and left the bedroom. During the past four months he and Lauren had become good friends and in that time she'd spoken often of her twin sister.

He knew that Lexie worked for the cyber-crime unit with the FBI in Kansas City, that Lauren worried that Lexie had a better relationship with her computer than with any real people and that the twins had been raised by their father who had passed away five years ago.

He leaned his shotgun against the kitchen wall and then sat at the round oak table. She came into the kitchen holding a handgun and wearing a scowl.

"Now you can answer some more of my questions," she said as she eased down into the chair opposite him.

"There's no need for your gun," he replied easily. "I'm on your side."

"I don't know that yet," she countered. "What are you doing here and how did you get inside?"

"Lauren and I exchanged keys to our homes about a month after she moved in here. Since neither of us have family here, we thought it would be a good idea in case of emergency. I let myself in when I saw the unfamiliar car out front and I knew that Lauren wasn't home."

Lexie stared at him unblinking. Under normal circumstances the length of time of the eye contact would have bordered on inappropriate, but he told himself these weren't normal circumstances. "Where is she?" There was a faint whisper of fear in her voice.

"I don't know. I haven't seen her since Tuesday. She's been working with my dog and I came here late afternoon on Wednesday for my usual session and she wasn't here."

He tried not to notice the scent of her, a clean fresh smell coupled with a hint of sweet, blooming flowers. God, he didn't remember the last time he'd noticed the scent of a woman.

He consciously focused back on the issue at hand. "I realized that it didn't look like the dogs in the yard had been fed and watered, so I took care of them and then left. Same thing happened yesterday. I was worried that maybe she was sick, so I used my key to come inside. I fed and watered Zeus and the dogs outside and then went back home."

He frowned thoughtfully. "I haven't known your sister for very long, but this felt out of character for her. I was worried, and then tonight when I realized somebody was in the house, I decided to come in and investigate."

He didn't feel it was necessary to tell her that when he'd seen that pink streak in her hair before she'd completely turned around to face him, he'd thought she was one of the teenagers of the town taking advantage of Lauren's absence for an opportunity for a little party or a bit of theft.

"This is definitely out of character for Lauren," she said and finally laid her gun down on the table next to her. "What's your relationship with her? Romantic?"

"Not at all," he replied. "Over the last couple of months Lauren and I have become good friends, but nothing more than that."

"Her truck is in the garage."

It took him a second to adjust to the leap in topic and her words sent a vague sense of uneasiness through him. "I didn't know that."

She nodded. "I checked out the property. Zeus and I walked it looking for her, but needless to say we didn't find her." She stood abruptly. "Thank you for looking out for things here."

It was an obvious dismissal and Nick stood

and grabbed his shotgun as she started out of the kitchen. He followed just behind her and tried not to notice the cute shape of her butt in her tight jeans.

What was wrong with him? He was far too conscious of Lexie Forbes's attractiveness and it made him more than a little bit uncomfortable.

Maybe part of the problem was even though he knew Lauren and Lexie were identical twins, the woman in front of him seemed more vibrant and much prettier than her sister.

"So, what's your next move?" he asked as they reached the front door.

She frowned. "First thing in the morning if she doesn't come home or I don't hear from her, I'll head into town and file a missing persons report at the police station."

"Don't expect much from the local authorities," he replied, remembering a time when he'd filed his own missing person's report and nothing had been done until it was too late.

She looked at him sharply. "Why? Is there a problem?"

"I went to high school with Gary Wendall, the chief of police. He tends toward big talk and little action." Nick's stomach knotted at thoughts of Wendall, who had been damned little help when Nick had needed him most.

"I'll file the report and then I'm going to ask questions and see if I can find out who might have last seen Lauren and when. I spoke to her Tuesday night so I know she was here and fine then."

She looked up at him and in the depths of her pretty green eyes he saw fear. "She's all I have. I have to find her," she said, her voice husky with emotion.

He had a crazy sudden impulse to pull her into his arms, to assure her that everything was going to be just fine. Instead he opened up the door, flipped on the outside porch light and then stepped out.

She followed him, her gaze automatically scanning the area as if hoping her sister would suddenly appear in the illuminated spill of the high-powered beam of light.

"I'd like it if you'd keep me informed," he said and then frowned. "I should have given you my cell phone number."

"Give it to me now," she replied.

"You don't have any place to write it down," he protested.

"I'll remember it."

Although dubious, he rattled off the number. When he was finished she nodded. "I'll let you know if I find out anything or if she turns up here."

"I'd appreciate it. I guess I'll talk to you soon." He stepped off the porch, and as she murmured a goodbye he headed for his pickup in the driveway.

When he got into the truck, he gazed at her once again. Lexie Forbes affected him like no other woman had in a very long time.

Despite the circumstances of their meeting he was surprised to realize what he'd felt for her was a momentary flare of desire.

He shook his head and started his truck, focusing his thoughts back on the missing Lauren. There was no question that mutual loneliness had forged their friendship over the last couple of months. She'd been new in town, hadn't known anyone, and he'd been mired in grief for so long he'd become isolated from everyone else.

Lauren had been easy to talk to, pleasant to be around, but he'd told Lexie the truth when he'd said there had been nothing romantic between them.

There would never be romance in Nick's life again. He'd had his one great love with tragic results. His heart would forever remain unavailable to any other woman on the face of the earth.

He headed down the road to the farmhouse that no longer felt like home, but was rather just a place to sleep and eat, a place to exist.

That's all he'd been doing for a long time—existing and marking time. Lauren had definitely helped pass the time, especially the evening hours after dinner and before bedtime.

Still, as he thought of Lauren he was filled with a sense of dread, that somehow history was repeating itself. He couldn't stop thinking that the last time a woman had disappeared for a couple of days she'd wound up dead in a motel room.

Chapter Two

The night had been endless.

Before going to bed Lexie had found a local phone book and called the hospital and the clinics in the area, but none of them would admit to having Lauren as a patient. Surely if she was in the hospital somebody would have called Lexie by now. Lexie was listed as Lauren's emergency contact.

The only thing that made Lexie feel a little bit better was that she couldn't find Lauren's purse or her cell phone in the house. She could only assume Lauren had those items with her wherever she was.

Still, by the time morning had come Lexie's eyes felt gritty from lack of sleep. She had tried to rest in the guest room, but had finally ended up on the sofa with Zeus on the floor next to her.

Every sound the house had made through

the night, every creak and whisper shot her up with the hope that it might be Lauren returning home. At 5:00 a.m. she finally gave up any pretense of sleep and went into the spare bedroom that Lauren used as an office.

She powered up the computer on the desk. Knowing that Lauren used Zeus20 as a password, she checked the email to see if there was anything that might explain her sister's absence.

Most of the correspondence was business related, emails from potential customers asking about her dogs and her training. Others were from past customers catching Lauren up on news of some of the dogs she'd trained.

She also checked the history to see where Lauren might have gone on the internet, but found nothing that might yield a clue as to what had happened to her.

She drained her coffee cup and then began a search of the desk. A stack of file folders in a plastic holder drew her attention and she pulled them out to see what they contained.

They were contracts signed by the people whose dogs Lauren was training. There was one signed by Nick, who had been bringing his dog for obedience training.

Her head filled with a vision of the man she'd met the night before. Hot body, sensual lips and a hint of compassion in his bedroom eyes—the man could definitely be an unwanted distraction if she allowed it.

She focused back on the folders, surprised to discover that one of them contained a contract for Lauren to provide the Topeka Police Department with two drug-sniffing dogs.

She leaned back in the desk chair as a surge of pride mingled with surprise. She'd known that Lauren had wanted to get into the training of working dogs, especially for law enforcement and handicapped people. From the signed contract, Lexie assumed that Lauren was truly on the way to making a name for herself, on her way to achieving her dreams.

It was almost seven when she finished in Lauren's office and took a quick shower. She dressed in a pair of jeans and a neon pink blouse decorated with an abundance of sequins and then returned to the kitchen to pour herself another cup of coffee.

As soon as it was late enough she was heading into town. Her first stop was going to be the police station to file a missing persons report, and then she planned on talking to everyone and anyone to pin down the last time her sister had been seen.

The fear that had been inside her hadn't dissipated, but rather thrummed like a sick energy inside her chest. Throughout the long night she'd tried calling Lauren's cell phone over and over again but it had always gone directly to voice mail. Finally by that morning she'd gotten the message that Lauren's voice mail was full.

Zeus walked over to her and laid his big head on her knee, gazing up at her as if asking her why his mommy wasn't there. "I know, baby. I miss her, too."

Zeus barked and raced away from her as a knock fell on the door. Lexie jumped out of her chair and grabbed her gun from her purse. She knew she was probably overreacting, but she had no idea what to expect, was definitely out of her comfort zone.

When she got to the front door she saw Nick standing on the porch. "What are you doing here?" she asked without preamble as she opened the screen door.

"I thought you could use a friendly face

when you go into town this morning." He stepped past her and into the foyer, then turned back to look at her expectantly.

She wouldn't have thought it possible but the man was better looking in the light of day than he'd been the night before. Once again he wore a pair of jeans that looked custom-made for his long legs and narrow hips. His gray long-sleeved pullover clung to his broad shoulders and perfectly matched the hue of his eyes.

"That's not necessary," she said and tried to ignore the ridiculous flutter that went off in the pit of her stomach. This man and her reaction to him were the last things she needed right now. All she wanted, all she needed, was her sister.

"I know Sheriff Wendall. It would probably work to your benefit if I'm with you. And, if you want to ask questions of the people in Widow Creek you'll find that they don't take kindly to strangers."

"Why is that?"

He looked at her in surprise. "I don't know. I guess because we're a small town and we've always looked after our own. Lexie, I was born and raised here—people know me. They trust me and that means they'll talk to me. You're a big-city woman with…uh…" His voice trailed off.

"A pink streak in my hair," she jumped in to finish his sentence. "And it was purple before that." She raised her chin as if to challenge him to say anything derogatory.

"And I'm sure it looked as charming as the pink," he replied.

She eyed him dubiously. What was his story? Why the offer to help her? Was he just a nice guy or had his relationship with Lauren been something deeper than a friendship? She wasn't sure she trusted him, but what he'd said about getting answers made sense. People would probably talk to him much quicker than they would to her.

"Don't you have a wife or somebody at home who might not want you wasting your time with me?" she asked.

"No wife, no girlfriend, just livestock," he replied. "And a little miniature schnauzer puppy who is probably chewing on my best pair of boots as we speak." He smiled then and the warmth and attractiveness of it fired a crazy flame deep inside Lexie.

She ignored it. Any woman would have to

be dead not to find Nick Walker extremely hot, but Lexie had learned about hot men and cold hearts the hard way. And, besides, she had a sister to find.

"If you want to tag along, then I'd appreciate your help," she finally agreed. "Just let me get my purse and I'll be ready to go."

She went back into the guest room where she'd left her things and grabbed her purse. Before leaving the room she checked to make sure her gun was inside. Right now she believed Nick was probably okay, but in her line of work she didn't take anything for granted. She'd travel with her gun in her purse while she was here in Widow Creek.

Minutes later they were in her car and heading into the heart of the small town. The first thing Lexie noticed when they reached Main Street was that Widow Creek was a town obviously dying a slow death.

Half of the storefronts along the two-block main drag were boarded up. The ones that were still opened looked worn and faded, as if it was nothing more than sheer hope keeping them alive.

A half a dozen cars were parked in front of the Cowboy Corral, either attesting to good food or the fact that there was no place else to go to eat and spend a little time among friends.

"The police station is up ahead," Nick said, breaking the silence that had filled the car on the drive from Lauren's place. Lexie wasn't good at small talk and Nick seemed at ease with the quiet. "It's that two-story brick building," he said, pointing to it.

Lexie pulled into a parking spot in front of the station, cut her engine and then turned to look at the man in the passenger seat. "Before we go in there, are you sure you don't want to tell me anything else about your relationship with Lauren?"

His dark eyebrows rose in surprise. "I already told you about my relationship with her. We had become good friends."

"And nothing more?"

"Nothing more," he said firmly.

"Then why are you helping me?"

"I don't know what kind of world you live in with your FBI work, Lexie, but in my world when a friend goes missing you do whatever you can to help find her." He opened the car door and got out.

Lexie hurriedly followed and before they

got to the door she grabbed him by the arm. "I think it would be best if we don't mention what I do for a living," she said. It had been her experience that people didn't talk freely to an FBI agent, that they would be more likely to talk to a worried sister. Small-town law enforcement was known to be rather hostile to FBI agents. The last thing she wanted was to upset the police chief when she needed his help. "If anybody asks, I do web design for a living."

He nodded. "Okay, but you know it's possible Lauren mentioned to others here in town what you do for a living. I knew."

She considered what he said. "Then we'll just play it by ear, but I don't intend to volunteer any information about myself unless it's absolutely necessary."

As they walked through the door of the police station Lexie's fear for her sister spiked nearly out of control. What could have happened to her? Where could she be?

Filing an official missing persons report suddenly made Lauren's disappearance more real, far more frightening. For the first time since they'd left the house Lexie was grateful that Nick was beside her. Even though she didn't know him well, his presence made her feel not quite so all alone.

"Hey, Carol," he greeted the woman behind the receptionist desk.

"Nick!" The pretty blonde looked up from her computer and offered him an inviting smile that definitely spoke of feminine interest. Her gaze slid over Lexie, the calculating look of a woman checking out her competition. She obviously wasn't concerned by what she saw. She dismissed Lexie with a flick of her false lashes.

Nick returned the smile and gestured toward the closed office door behind her desk. "Is Gary in?"

"Should be on his second donut by now," she replied wryly. "You can go on in."

Lexie followed behind Nick as he approached the closed office door and knocked. A deep voice indicated they could come in.

Chief of Police Gary Wendall sat at the desk, but rose as they entered. He looked to be in his early thirties, with blond military-short hair and a fit physique. "Nick, it's been a while," he said, and in his words Lexie thought she heard a touch of tension. The two men shook hands and then Wendall looked at Lexie.

"Chief Wendall, I'm Lexie Forbes. I'm here about my sister, Lauren Forbes."

"Ah, our very own dog whisperer," Wendall said with a nod. "What about her?"

"She's missing." Sudden emotion filled Lexie's chest and she had to swallow hard against it.

Wendall motioned them into the chairs in front of his desk and then sat down. "What do you mean she's missing?"

"I spoke to her Tuesday night on the phone, but I couldn't get hold of her Wednesday or Thursday," Lexie explained. "Finally yesterday evening I decided to drive out to her place. She's not there and I don't think she's been there since Tuesday. Her dogs were left unattended and that's not like her. Something has happened. Something is terribly wrong."

"Whoa, let's not jump to conclusions," Wendall exclaimed, lines cutting into his tanned forehead. "She's a grown woman. There's no law that says she can't take off for a couple of days without checking in with anyone."

Lexie shook her head. "She wouldn't do

that, and even if she did she'd answer my phone calls. We talk to each other every day. This is unusual for her…for us. I want to file a missing persons report. She's been missing more than forty-eight hours. I need you to investigate her disappearance."

Wendall's gaze flickered from Lexie to Nick. "What's your role in all this?"

"I'm Lauren's friend and I'm concerned, and I'm here to support Lexie," Nick replied. His voice held a coolness that definitely chilled the air in the room.

"You aren't stirring things up because of your own history?" Wendall asked with a lift of one of his blond eyebrows.

Lexie looked at Nick and saw the tightening of his jaw as his eyes went flat. "One thing has nothing to do with the other," he replied tersely.

There was obviously some personal history between the two men, but Lexie didn't care about that right now. All she cared about was finding her sister.

"Will you look into this?" she asked Wendall. "Start an official investigation?"

"I'll see what I can do," Wendall replied. "Are you staying out at Lauren's place?"

Lexie nodded. "I'll be there until she's found." She gave him her cell phone number and then walked toward the door. There was nothing more to be done here. She wanted to get outside and walk the streets, talk to the people in town and see if anyone had seen or spoken to Lauren since Tuesday.

"I'll keep in touch," Chief Wendall said as she and Nick reached the door. "You know your sister always had a bunch of men hanging around her place. Maybe she took off with one of them and didn't want you knowing about her personal affairs," Wendall said.

Lexie stiffened and stared at him. At that moment she decided she didn't like him very much. He made it sound like Lauren was some kind of a whore. "I'm sure you're going to question whatever men were hanging out there to see what they know about my sister's disappearance," she replied.

She was surprised when Nick firmly took hold of her elbow, as if to offer support, as they left the office. What equally surprised her was how she responded to his touch—viscerally, like a not-completely-unpleasant punch in the stomach.

As they left the building he dropped his

hand to his side and she drew a breath of relief. She didn't want some crazy attraction to Nick complicating things. The last thing she wanted in her life was a man. She just wanted to find her sister alive and well, and then get back to her so-called life in Kansas City.

"I never saw a bunch of men hanging out at Lauren's," Nick said when they were back in her car. "And I drove by her place at least once a day going to and from town. But she mentioned to me that she was kind of seeing Bo Richards."

"Bo Richards?" Lexie turned in her seat to look at Nick. "Who is he?"

"He's a local rancher, a nice guy. He spends a lot of time in the mornings at the café. Maybe we can talk to him there," Nick replied.

"And Lauren was seeing him romantically?" Lexie frowned. Her sister hadn't mentioned anything to her about a romance in her life and they'd always talked about everything, including their love lives.

"They had just started dating. From what Lauren told me it wasn't real serious yet. I think they'd met for lunch or dinner a couple of times."

Lexie checked her watch and then looked down the street at the café. It was still early. Hopefully they'd find him there. "Then I want to talk to him." She started the car, but before backing out she turned to look at Nick once again. "There's some history between you and Wendall?"

Darkness filled his eyes and his jaw tightened once again. "Yeah, old history."

"Want to tell me about it?" she asked.

"No." The single word snapped out of him with a finality that brooked no further questions and made Lexie wonder what kind of secrets Nick Walker had in his life.

IN THE SHORT DISTANCE between the police station and the Cowboy Corral, painful memories cascaded through Nick's head. His chest tightened with thoughts of the three days that he'd been unable to get in contact with Danielle. His body remembered intimately the alarm it had felt when he'd realized nobody had seen her during that time and the horror of ultimately finding her dead in that motel room.

His stomach clenched and a slight nausea rose up in him as the memories continued to play in his head. He'd known something was wrong—that something was terribly wrong.

It had taken him months to finally accept that she'd committed suicide, but before coming to that acceptance he'd gone around and around with Wendall.

The chief of police had dismissed Nick's concerns and refused to begin any kind of investigation into Danielle's disappearance despite Nick pressing for one. There was part of Nick that had never quite forgiven Gary Wendall for that.

He consciously shoved the memories aside as Lexie parked in front of the café. There was absolutely no reason to believe Lauren's disappearance was in any way connected to Danielle's tragic death, but he couldn't shake the feeling that Lexie was destined for the same kind of heartbreak he'd suffered.

Still suffered.

He willed away all thoughts of Danielle as they got out of the car. Lexie appeared small and achingly vulnerable as she hesitated outside the door to wait for him to catch up with her.

A surge of unexpected protectiveness filled Nick's chest. It was crazy, he scarcely knew Lexie except for what Lauren had told him about her. There was no reason for him to be emotionally vested in the drama going on in her life, and yet for some reason he was definitely involved.

He told himself it had nothing to do with the beauty of her long-lashed green eyes behind those ridiculously large glasses, nothing to do with the fact that she intrigued him more than a little bit. Rather he tried to convince himself his interest in all this had everything to do with finding a woman who had become a good friend.

The minute they stepped into the café, every head in the place turned to look at them. "I guess pink streaks in a person's hair isn't that common here," Lexie muttered beneath her breath as she sidled closer to him.

"Don't worry, the only ones who bite have no teeth," he replied.

She looked up at him and smiled. It was the first real smile he'd seen from her and it nearly stole his breath away. Bright and beautiful, it transformed her features into something more than pretty, something warm and inviting.

"Come on, I'm hankering for some of Mabel's fried potatoes and eggs." He took her beneath her elbow and led her to a booth, surprised to realize she was shaking slightly.

Lauren had told him that her sister didn't do well in crowds. He knew the effort she was putting forth was because of her love and concern for her sister. It only made him more determined to support her through whatever happened next.

She paused before sitting down and looked around at the other diners. "I thought we'd just ask some questions. I didn't plan on actually having a meal."

"Did you eat breakfast this morning?" he asked.

"I never eat breakfast," she replied.

"And you've never had a missing sister before," he said and pointed to the booth. "Besides, you'll get more answers to questions if we finesse them out of people."

She frowned as if she had no idea what he was talking about, but slid into the booth and picked up the menu. She stared at it only a minute and then tossed it aside. "I feel like

I'm wasting time here. Breakfast isn't important. Finding Lauren is all that matters." Her voice held a wealth of frustration and impatience.

"You have to eat," he replied, understanding the urgency that was racing through her. "And you have to trust me." He looked up as the waitress appeared at their table. "Hey, Marge, how's it going?" he asked the older woman who had been waitressing at the café since he'd been a little boy.

"Like it's always gone. My feet hurt, my back is killing me and nobody tips worth a damn in this place." She flashed him a grin that set the deep wrinkles in her face dancing.

"Has Bo been in today?" he asked.

"Bo? No, in fact, I haven't seen him for a couple of days." Her gaze slid to Lexie. "Why? Is there a problem?"

"No, no problem," he replied hurriedly. "Marge, this is Lauren Forbes's sister, Lexie."

Marge nodded. "I can see the resemblance."

"When was the last time you saw Lauren?" Lexie asked.

Marge looked back at Nick, her eyes narrowed. "What's going on, Nick?"

Nick could feel Lexie's frustration growing

by the second, but he ignored her. "Lexie's in town to visit her sister, but Lauren seems to have gone missing and we're trying to hunt her down. Has she been in lately?"

Marge frowned. "I think she was in Monday for lunch, but I haven't seen her since then. Now, what can I get for the two of you?"

They ordered and once Marge left the table Lexie released a deep sigh. "That was no help. We need to question everyone in here, see who saw Lauren when."

"Just sit tight. Trust me when I tell you before we finish our breakfast you'll have spoken to everyone in this place." He could tell that she didn't believe him but she settled back in the booth, took her glasses off and rubbed at her eyes. "Not much sleep last night?" he asked sympathetically.

Her eyes were the most amazing shade of green with just enough shadow in them to be slightly mysterious. "I don't think I slept much more than an hour through the whole night." She slid the glasses back on. "I just can't wrap my head around this." Her gaze held a hint of vulnerability as she looked at him. "I'm scared."

He could tell what the confession cost her

by the way her gaze skittered away from his and from the telltale pulse of a delicate vein in her neck. Before he could respond Jim Caskie ambled by the table to say hello to Nick.

It was just as he'd suspected—as they ate their breakfast almost everyone who was dining in the café found a reason to stop by and say hello. Lexie merely picked at her eggs and nibbled on toast, more interested in what people had to say than in the meal in front of her.

Nick knew the people of Widow Creek were leery of strangers, but he also knew they were a curious bunch. And Lexie, with the pink streak in her hair and her pink sequined blouse definitely sparked plenty of curiosity.

The one thing that didn't happen was answers. Nobody had seen Lauren since Monday, at least nobody who would admit to it. And nobody had seen Bo for the past couple of days. This information eased some of Nick's concern.

Even the most levelheaded women occasionally went crazy over a man. It was possible the two had gone off together for a romantic tryst and Lauren had just forgotten to make arrangements for her dogs or had wound up being gone longer than she'd initially planned.

"Do you know where Bo lives?" Lexie asked the minute they were back in her car.

"Yeah, you want to go by there?" He wasn't surprised when she nodded her head.

After giving her directions, he tried to think of something, anything, he could tell her that might ease some of the tension that rode her slender shoulders and darkened her eyes.

"So, Lauren told me you're something of a computer geek," he finally said, wanting to connect with her on a more personal level. "What exactly is it that you do?"

"I work for the cybercrime unit for the FBI. Mostly I hunt down cybercriminals, those who are invading home computers to steal identities, and I try to find the source behind thousands of scams that people receive via email."

"Sounds fascinating."

She flashed him a quick glance. "Most people would find it pretty boring, but I like it. I'm comfortable working with a computer. It's predictable. I type in code and I know what's going to happen."

"Unlike people, who can be unpredictable," he observed.

"Exactly." She chewed her bottom lip and for just a minute he wondered what it would be like to taste her mouth with his. The thought flashed in his head with a shock. He had no business even thinking such thoughts. What was wrong with him? He hadn't entertained such a thought about a woman in years.

She was here to find her sister and nothing more. In any case, he was mentally and emotionally unavailable to any woman when it came to his heart.

Still, he grudgingly admitted that perhaps his momentary fantasy about the taste of her mouth meant that he wasn't quite as dead as he'd believed himself to be.

They pulled up in front of Bo's place and she cut the engine as she stared at the neat two-story house before them. The front door was closed and there were no vehicles around. "Looks like nobody is home," he said.

"You can wait here. I'll go find out." She got out of the car and walked toward the front door.

Nick remained in the car, his gaze following the slight sway of her hips. Okay, he could admit to himself that he was sexually attracted to her. There was no real explanation for the immediate physical chemistry he felt toward her.

Of course, it had been almost two years since he'd been with a woman. Maybe this was just his body's way of reminding him that he was a healthy thirty-three-year-old man who had been alone for too long. In any case, it wasn't something he intended to act upon, just a curious surprise that reminded him that he was very much alive.

He watched as Lexie knocked on the front door several times, then moved to peek through the living room windows and finally returned to the car.

"He's not here. Maybe she did go off with him for a couple of days," she said.

"Women have been known to momentarily lose their minds for love," he replied.

"Not me," she replied darkly. "Not ever."

She started the car and pulled out of the driveway. "I'm going back into town to ask more questions, but I'll be glad to drop you off at your place. I'm sure you have better things to do than spend the day with me."

"Actually, I don't." There was nothing for

him at home except the endless silence and loneliness that had gnawed at his heart for the past year. "If two of us are asking questions then we can get it done in half the time."

She eyed him for a long moment and then shrugged. "Suit yourself."

The remainder of the ride back into town was silent. Nick couldn't begin to guess what she was thinking. He didn't know her well enough, but he was surprised to realize that he wished he did.

They stayed in town throughout the afternoon, drifting into stores, stopping people on the streets and asking about Lauren. By five o'clock it was clear that Lauren hadn't been seen by anyone since Tuesday.

Nick still held out hope that she and Bo had taken off on some sort of romantic connection, but he could see with each minute that passed that Lexie was growing more distraught.

She nibbled on her lower lip and looked tense enough to shatter if anyone would reach out and touch her. He finally called a halt. "It's time to go home, Lexie," he said. "You've done all you can do for today and you're only getting the same answers over and over again."

For a moment he thought she was going to protest, but then her shoulders fell and she nodded wearily. "You're right. It's been a long day and we aren't getting anywhere."

Once again she was quiet on the ride back to Lauren's and Nick wished he had some encouraging words to give her. But there was no question that Lauren's disappearance was troubling. As the day had worn on his hope that she'd gone off with Bo had faded. If that was the case, then why hadn't she returned Lexie's phone calls? Why didn't she answer her cell phone? Surely she'd know that Lexie would be worried sick.

They had gotten one piece of information from one of Bo's neighbors who told them that Bo had mentioned visiting some family in Tulsa, Oklahoma. If Bo was with family in Oklahoma, then where was Lauren? The whole thing was growing more and more troubling with each minute that passed.

"Thanks for your help today," Lexie said as she pulled up next to his truck in Lauren's driveway. She stared at the house as if dreading going inside.

"Look, we haven't eaten since breakfast. Why don't I take you out to dinner?"

She turned to look at him. "Why would you want to do that?"

He shrugged. "Because I need to eat. You need to eat and we might as well eat together. Why don't I pick you up in an hour?"

She turned and looked at the house again, a frown pulling together her delicately arched eyebrows. "I have a bad feeling about this, Nick. I don't think she's ever coming home."

He reached across the seat and took her hand in his. "You can't lose hope already," he said softly. "Maybe she took off with Bo and her cell phone went dead. That would explain her not answering your calls." Her hand felt small in his grasp.

She stared at him as if desperate to believe his words. "Maybe you're right," she finally conceded. She pulled her hand from his. "I guess I'll see you in an hour."

They both got out of her car and Nick stood by his truck and watched her walk to the house. There was no question that something about Lexie touched him in a place where nobody had touched him in a very long time.

There was an awkwardness about her that

he found oddly charming. The pink streak in her hair spoke of a woman seeking attention and yet he'd never seen a woman who appeared more uncomfortable with any attention she garnered.

As he got into his truck he wondered what in the hell he was doing. He'd spent the day with her and now had invited her to dinner, as if he couldn't get enough of her company.

And yet he knew nothing could come of his attraction to her. She'd given him no indication that she felt the same kind of attraction to him that he did for her, and even if she did he wouldn't follow through on it.

He'd had the one great love of his life and he'd blown it and the consequences had been devastating. He was responsible for his wife's suicide, and he'd never allow himself to get close to a woman again.

Chapter Three

She shouldn't have agreed to dinner, Lexie thought as she entered the house. She shouldn't have agreed to dinner with *him*. Nick Walker definitely made her slightly nervous, although she'd been grateful for his presence during the long day.

Still, she should have thanked him for his time and let it go at that. She didn't need the distraction of spending time with a man who made her just a little bit breathless when he gazed at her, a man who made her feel a strange mix of both anxiety and anticipation.

And yet she didn't consider calling him to tell him to forget dinner. She had to eat and she'd rather do it someplace else, anyplace else instead of in the horrible quiet of Lauren's kitchen.

Before she did anything else she checked the answering machine in Lauren's office to see if any calls had come in throughout the day. There was only one from somebody who had apparently stopped by for their appointment with Lauren while Lexie and Nick had been out. The woman, who said her name was Anna, only said that Precious had missed seeing Lauren and asked that Lauren call to reschedule the training session.

Lexie vaguely remembered that when she'd looked through the folder of contracts there had been one signed by an Anna. She made a mental note to contact the woman the next day and let her know that, at least at the moment, Lauren wasn't available for taking appointments.

Zeus followed Lexie to the bathroom where she quickly took off her clothes and stepped into the shower. As she stood beneath the warm spray, her thoughts whirled over what they'd learned that day, which had been darned little.

She still hoped they would discover that Lauren had gone off someplace with Bo Richards and that she'd return home any minute, feeling guilty and sheepish at causing so much unwarranted worry. Maybe she'd made arrangements for somebody to take care of the dogs in her absence and whomever she'd hired had just blown off the job.

She got out of the shower and changed into a clean pair of jeans and a Kelly-green lightweight sweater. Zeus sat at her feet and watched as she applied a light coating of both mascara and lipstick. As she finished with her hair and turned away from the mirror he whined, as if protesting the fact that she was leaving him again.

She checked her watch and realized she had another twenty minutes before Nick would be back to get her. "Come on, baby, let's see if I can find you a treat," she said to the big dog, who followed close at her heels as she went into the kitchen.

She rummaged in the cabinets until she found a bag of pepperoni dog treats. Zeus woofed his approval and she tossed it to him, laughing as he caught it midair.

He ate it and then headed for the doggy door cut into the kitchen wall that led to the fenced in backyard. She moved to the window and watched as the dog romped around in the grass next to the other fenced area and then lifted his leg against a bush.

As much as she wanted to believe that her

sister had taken off someplace, it just didn't feel right. Zeus was her baby and Lexie couldn't imagine Lauren just taking off for days and leaving him behind. She would have at least made arrangements for him to be fed and watered by somebody she trusted to do the job.

The ring of the doorbell pulled her from her thoughts. Nervous energy danced in her stomach as she hurried out of the kitchen to the front door.

Nick had showered and changed as well. He wore jeans and a long-sleeved gray dress shirt and, as if his physical attractiveness wasn't enough, he smelled like clean, crisp cologne mixed with the faint residual scent of shaving cream.

"Ready?" he asked.

She nodded. "Just let me grab my purse."

Her heart hammered with inexplicable quickness as she got her purse from the kitchen counter and then rejoined him at the front door. "Ready," she said, knowing that Zeus would return to the house through the doggy door.

The evening was cool as they walked to his car. A slight breeze stirred the autumn leaves on the trees, forcing some of them to drift down to the ground.

Although in her heart for some reason she trusted Nick, in her head she wasn't sure who she could trust. She was comforted by the fact that her purse held her gun and she wouldn't be afraid to use it if things somehow went bad.

"There aren't many eating choices in Widow Creek so I thought we'd drive the twenty minutes to Casey's Corner. It's a slightly bigger town and has a great Italian place," he said as they pulled out of the driveway.

"Sounds fine," she agreed. She wasn't really hungry, hadn't had an appetite since she'd discovered that Lauren was missing, but she knew she had to eat to keep up her strength.

For a few minutes they rode in silence. Lexie stared out the window at the encroaching evening shadows and anxiety pressed tight against her chest. She couldn't believe another night was about to fall without her knowing if Lauren was okay.

"I just can't imagine what's happened to her," she said as much to herself as to him.

"I keep thinking maybe she's been hit over the head and is lying someplace needing me to find her."

He gave her a curious glance. "Why would you think that?"

She hesitated, knowing he would probably think she was crazy for what she was about to say. "Friday, when I got into my car after work to go home, I was struck with a blinding head pain." She raised a hand to the back of her head, remembering that violent, momentary slice of pain. "It was there only a moment and then gone and I immediately wondered if maybe Lauren had gotten hurt."

She dropped her hand back to her lap as a laugh of embarrassment escaped her. "It's kind of a twin thing. One time Lauren broke her arm and I knew it before she told me because I felt her pain in my arm. Another time I broke my little toe and she called me to see what I'd done because her foot hurt." She laughed again without any real humor. "I know it sounds crazy."

"Not really, I saw a documentary one night about twins and the special bond they share. Must have been interesting growing up. Did you two pretend to be each other? Try to fool people?"

Lexie cast her gaze back out the window, her thoughts taking her backward in time. "No, never. From the very beginning, even though we were identical twins, we had completely different personalities. Lauren is an extrovert and I've always been painfully shy. I could have never made anyone believe that I was her."

She turned to look at him, trying not to notice how handsome he looked with the last gasp of the sun lighting his features. "When we started high school there was Lauren and then there was the other twin. Nobody could remember my name, nobody really knew who I was. That's when I decided to go Goth."

He gave her an amused smile. "So you dressed in black, wore heavy makeup and spouted tragic poetry."

She returned his smile. "Something like that."

"And did that help the other kids get to know you better?"

"Not really. I went from being the 'other' twin to being the weird twin." It all seemed so silly now, but at the time high school had been the most painful experience Lexie thought she'd ever live through. "It wasn't until I was in college that I realized it was okay to embrace my quirkiness, to be a little different than everyone else."

"We're all quirky in one way or another. Some of us just show it more than others."

"You don't look quirky to me," she observed.

He grinned. "Ah, but looks can be deceiving. I sleep in my socks."

"That's not quirky, that's nerdy," she replied and then gasped at her own words.

He laughed. "That's what I like about you, Lexie. I have a feeling you always speak what's on your mind. And you're right, it is nerdy, but I always have nice warm feet."

She averted her gaze back out the window and tried to cast out the vision of her in his bed, his warm feet against hers, slowly warming her body from her toes upward.

By that time they had reached the town of Casey's Corner. It appeared to be a big sister of Widow Creek. The business area stretched over three short blocks and there were only a couple of empty storefronts.

He pulled up in front of Mama's Italian

Garden and as he parked she realized that the conversation they'd shared on the drive had momentarily taken her mind off Lauren. She suspected that's what he'd intended and a warm gratefulness swelled in her chest.

It took only minutes for them to be seated at a table for two in the restaurant. It was a typical Italian setting, with red-and-white checkered tablecloths, a little candle flickering in the center of the table and a very limited wine list displayed between the salt and pepper shakers.

As Lexie picked up a menu her stomach rumbled with sudden hunger. Maybe it was the aroma of rich tomato sauce and fresh herbs that wafted in the air, or perhaps it was the conversation they'd shared that had relaxed her a bit on the drive to the restaurant.

"I eat here fairly often and can tell you that pretty much anything on the menu is good," Nick said.

She was acutely conscious of his nearness at the small, intimate table. His eyes glowed almost silver in the candlelight and she found herself wondering what his lips might taste like.

She snapped her focus down to the menu,

wondering if the stress of everything was making her lose her mind. She'd given up on men almost six months ago when she'd discovered that the man she'd believed was "the one" turned out to be "the rat."

Michael Andrews had been a smooth-talking, hot-looking guy who had swept Lexie off her feet and away from her computer. They'd met through a mutual friend and they'd dated for six months. Lexie had thought they were moving toward an engagement, but instead she'd found out that Michael had a woman on the side, a cute, bubbly blonde who was all the things that Lexie wasn't, that Lexie would never be.

"Face it, Lexie," he had said. "You're a little bit weird. It was fun for a while but I wouldn't want a steady diet of it."

She'd mentally dug a hole and buried her hopes for happily-ever-after in it and had returned to a social life that involved cyberfriends who didn't have the capacity to hurt her.

Nick reminded her just a little bit of Michael. Maybe because he was good-looking and seemed to know exactly what she wanted to hear when she wanted to hear it.

The waitress appeared at their table and Nick ordered lasagna while Lexie opted for the manicotti. "Lauren told me the two of you were raised by your father," he said once the waitress had departed.

She nodded. "Our mom died in a car accident when we were four. Dad was devastated, but he rose to the challenge of raising us." A pang of grief touched her heart as she thought of her dad. He'd been her rock and she missed him desperately.

"He didn't remarry?" Nick asked.

"No." She picked up her water glass and took a drink, then continued, "He told us that mom was his one great love and he had no desire to be with anyone else."

"Ah, the one arrow theory."

She looked at him curiously. "One arrow theory?"

"Some people believe that Cupid has one true arrow for everyone. If you're lucky when that arrow hits you, you're with your soul mate and you're together and happy for the rest of your life."

"That's a nice theory, but it doesn't account for Cupid's misfires," she said dryly.

His eyes sparkled with a light that threatened to draw her into their depths. "But if you believe in the one arrow theory, Cupid doesn't misfire, and people often misinterpret and think it's a real arrow that has struck their heart. I assume from your comment that you haven't been struck by Cupid's magic arrow yet."

Lexie thought about her relationship with Michael. Had she truly been in love with him? She'd certainly thought so at the time, but since their parting of ways, she had become equally certain that Michael hadn't been her soul mate. In the very depths of her heart, she wasn't sure there was a soul mate for her on the face of the earth.

"No," she finally replied. "I don't think Cupid's arrow has connected with me."

The conversation was interrupted by the arrival of the waitress with their orders. The food looked delicious and tasted just as good. "So, you said you grew up in Widow Creek. Have you always ranched?" she asked after enjoying several bites.

"Always," he replied. "The house where I live was my parents'. They decided to enjoy early retirement in Florida and so I bought the place from them. I thought it would be nice for my kids to be raised in the same house where I'd had such happiness."

"But you don't have a wife so I'm assuming there are no children yet."

His eyes darkened, the twinkling silver lights in the center dousing like candle flames that had been blown out. "I had a wife and almost had a child but then everything exploded apart."

Lexie stared at him as grief stole over his handsome features. She set down her fork, the food in front of her temporarily forgotten. "What happened?"

For a moment he stared down at his plate as if lost in thought, and when he looked up at her again some of the grief had passed and weariness lined his face. "I was twenty-five when I married my high school sweetheart and we moved to my parents' ranch to start our lives together. Danielle and I were a perfect couple. I worked the ranch and she worked in the mayor's office and things were terrific. After a couple of years of marriage we decided it was time to start a family. It took almost three years for Danielle to get pregnant. We were so excited when it finally happened."

He paused and took a sip of his water. Lexie felt a tightness in her chest. She knew something bad was coming and even though she'd only known him for a day her heart already ached for him.

As he placed his glass back on the table she noticed his fingers trembled slightly. "When Danielle was eight months pregnant she went in for her usual checkup and the doctor couldn't hear the baby's heartbeat. The doctor decided she needed to deliver immediately so Danielle was hospitalized and labor was induced. Ten hours later she delivered a beautiful stillborn baby girl."

Lexie released a small gasp. "I'm so sorry." She fought the impulse to reach across the table and take his hand in hers. "Did they know what caused it?"

He shook his head. "One of those tragic medical mysteries." He straightened his shoulders. "Anyway, I took Danielle and we went home to get on with our lives." He eyed Lexie intently, beseechingly. "She was so depressed, and I tried to do everything in my power to be supportive, but it seemed like no matter what I did or said it was wrong. After six months she told me she needed some space and she moved into an apartment in town."

"So, you not only lost your child, but your wife as well," Lexie said, working to speak around the lump in her throat.

He leaned back in the chair and released a deep sigh. "Actually, four months after the separation we began to see each other again."

For a moment his features lifted and a small smile curved his lips. "It was just like old times and we started talking about a reconciliation. She seemed to have moved past her grief and was ready to start living again." The smile dropped from his lips. "And then she disappeared."

"Disappeared?" Lexie's heart slammed into her ribs. Was he implying that there was some sort of connection between his ex-wife and her sister?

"She was gone for three days and during that time I went to Gary Wendall to file a missing persons report." His eyes darkened with a steely light. "And he basically told me the same thing he told you, that it wasn't a crime for a grown woman to take off. He also told me that everyone knew Danielle and I had a troubled history and she'd left me and maybe she just didn't want to be found by me. But I knew something was terribly wrong. Three days later her body was found in a motel room."

Once again a small gasp escaped Lexie, but before she could say anything he continued. "She had a fatal gunshot wound to her head and it was officially ruled a suicide."

Lexie searched his face. "But you didn't believe the official ruling."

His shoulders slumped slightly. "Initially no. I didn't believe that Danielle would take her own life. She didn't believe in suicide. She thought it was a mortal sin. Before she disappeared she'd had the old spark of life back in her eyes, had made me believe that we still had a chance together. I told Gary my concerns, insisted he launch a full-blown investigation into her death, but he dismissed me. Everyone knew how depressed she had been and there was absolutely no evidence to prove it was anything but a suicide. Eventually I realized Gary was probably right, that I just hadn't seen how depressed Danielle still was and she'd finally decided to end it."

Lexie had no words. The depth of his tragedy left her utterly speechless. He leaned forward and gave a small laugh. "Terrible dinner conversation. I don't know why I decided to share that with you."

"When did all this happen?" She finally found her voice.

"Danielle died a little over a year ago." He picked up his fork once again and gestured toward her plate. "I hope I didn't completely kill your appetite."

"Maybe just a little," she admitted. She picked up her own fork, her gaze lingering on his face, on the deep gray of his eyes. "Was Danielle your one true Cupid's arrow?"

"Yeah, she was. What we had doesn't come twice in a lifetime. As far as love is concerned, I'm done. But, I found your sister to be a good friend. We spent a lot of evenings together sitting on her front porch and just talking about life."

Despite her worry about Lauren and the sad conversation they'd just shared, Lexie couldn't help the smile that curved her lips. "There's nothing Lauren likes better than sitting around and talking about life. She analyzes and speculates and ruminates about everything."

"And you don't?"

She shrugged. "Life is what it is and talking about it rarely changes things."

"You are very different from your sister."

She smiled. "I think I've subconsciously worked hard to be different from her. That's the way I've found my own identity apart from the twin thing." Her smile faltered and she looked down at her plate. The idea of something happening to Lauren scared her not only because she loved her sister more than anyone else on the planet, but also because she was afraid that if Lauren was gone, somehow she would disappear as well.

Lauren was the mirror Lexie used to see her own reflection. If that mirror disappeared then Lexie wasn't sure who she would be anymore.

For the rest of the meal light conversation prevailed. Nick entertained her with stories of his childhood, making her laugh as he related wrestling with calves and saddle breaking a particularly stubborn horse.

He had a wonderful sense of humor and she found it sad that he'd decided he'd had his one great love and wouldn't be looking for another. She had a feeling he would have been a wonderful husband and a terrific father.

"Widow Creek was a great place to grow up," he said as they lingered over dessert. "It was a place where people didn't lock their doors and there was no fear. If you were a kid and did something wrong, half a dozen people would threaten to tell your folks and you knew they would because everyone knew everyone else."

"Sounds like a nice way to grow up."

"It was, but unfortunately Widow Creek has changed with the downswing of the economy. People have moved away to find work, kids no longer return to the town after college but rather choose to make their homes someplace else." He shrugged. "Guess it's happening all over. We're losing our small towns."

By the time they had finished their dessert and were on their way home, her thoughts returned to her sister. "I just can't imagine where Lauren could be," she said thoughtfully.

"Maybe you should bring in some of your FBI friends," he suggested.

"I wish I could. Unfortunately this isn't an FBI matter. It's a matter for the local law enforcement agency." She frowned. "She isn't the type to make enemies, I can't imagine anyone wanting to hurt her."

"I can't either," he agreed. "She didn't know a whole lot of people but she seemed well liked by everyone she did know." He glanced over and to her surprise reached out and lightly touched the back of her hand. "Maybe we'll have the answer when Bo gets back in town."

He pulled his hand back but not before the touch shot a tiny spark and then a wave of heat through her. She tried to ignore her response and breathed a sigh of relief when he pulled up outside Lauren's house.

The house was dark and unwelcoming. She'd forgotten to turn on any lights before she left. A fierce disappointment roared through her as she realized the dark house also implied that Lauren hadn't come home while they'd been out at the restaurant.

"You want me to come in with you?" he asked, as if sensing her uneasiness.

She drew a deep breath. She was uneasy entering the dark house alone, but she was equally uneasy in spending another minute with him. She was far too conscious of him as a man, acutely aware of some crazy attraction she felt toward him.

"No, I'm fine." She opened the car door. "Thanks again for all your time and help today. And thanks for the wonderful meal." She started to get out of the car but paused when he called her name.

"Whatever you need, Lexie. I just want you to know that I'm here to help in whatever way I can."

"I appreciate it, Nick." With a final good-bye she left the car and walked up to the silent, dark house. She fumbled in her purse for the keys, unlocked the front door and then turned on the porch light and waved to Nick.

He finally pulled out of the driveway as Zeus greeted her at the door. "Hi, baby," she said as she scratched the dog behind his ears. He followed her through the house as she turned on lights, her concern for her sister renewing itself with each flip of a switch.

Tomorrow was Sunday, the day she should return to Kansas City to be ready to go back to work on Monday. But there was no way she was leaving here without answers.

She made a call to her supervisor, letting him know that beginning Monday she would be taking some vacation days. Throughout her career with the FBI she'd rarely taken days off for illness or anything else, so her supervisor assured her it wasn't a problem.

Even though it wasn't quite nine o'clock, Lexie went into the guest bedroom and changed into her nightgown. She decided she didn't want to sleep in the bedroom. She was mentally and physically exhausted and hated that she felt so helpless.

She turned off all the lights in the house except the lamp on the end table next to the sofa and then turned on the television. Zeus circled the floor beside the sofa and then finally flopped down with an audible sigh.

She was way too wound up to go directly to sleep. Worries about Lauren battled with thoughts about Nick, thoughts like what it would feel like to stand in the warmth of his arms, how his mouth would feel pressed hotly, tightly against her own.

Foolish thoughts, she told herself. The last thing she needed in her life was any kind of a hookup with a man who had already told her he'd had his one Cupid arrow and was finished with love. Besides, all she really needed from Nick was his help in finding Lauren.

The dogs woke her, their raucous barking pulling her from a sleep she hadn't realized had claimed her. She shot straight up and grabbed her purse from the coffee table. Her fingers closed around the gun as she rose from the sofa, nerves jangling as the dogs outside in the pen continued to go crazy.

A glance at the clock on the bookcase let her know it was almost two. Zeus was no longer on the floor next to her and as she got up off the sofa her heart banged a frantic rhythm of inexplicable fear.

Instead of going to the front of the house to look out, she went into Lauren's bedroom, knowing that from her sister's window she could see the fenced dog area that ran from the side of the house to the backyard.

In the moonlight she could see that the dogs were at the back of the property, growling and jumping wildly at the fence. She quickly left the bedroom and went to the back door in the kitchen where Zeus stood in front of the door, his hackles raised as deep rumbles issued from his throat.

A cold sweat chilled her; her fingers were damp on the gun. What was out there? Who was out there? Her heart thundered loudly in her ears.

Was it nothing more than a raccoon or a squirrel that had set off the dogs, or was it a person—somebody who might have had something to do with Lauren's disappearance?

She froze as she thought she saw a shadow move from tree to tree in the wooded area beyond the fence. Her heart seemed to stop beating. It wasn't a four-legged creature she'd thought she'd seen. It had been a creature of the two-legged variety. It had been a person.

The dogs stopped barking.

Lexie found the abrupt silence as chilling as the noise. She watched as the dogs drifted away from the fence, as if no longer interested in whatever or whoever had been there.

Zeus released a low growl and then looked up at Lexie with a wag of his tail. He nosed her hand, as if seeking reassurance. "Good boy," she murmured and absently patted his head, her gaze still locked on the woods. The behavior of the dogs indicated to her that whoever had been out there was now gone, but that didn't stop the frantic beat of her heart or the fear that raged through her.

Who had been out there at this time of night? Did the person know what happened to Lauren? She checked to make sure the back door was locked then left the kitchen with Zeus at her side.

Her heart still banged against her ribs as she went through the house, checking doors and windows to make sure everything was locked up tight. Had she only imagined the large shadow moving silently in the night?

Lexie had never considered herself the kind of woman to indulge in flights of fancy or wild imaginings. The real question was: If somebody had been out there, what did they want?

As she sat back on the sofa, she fought a chill that invaded through to her very bones. As if to punctuate her dark thoughts, Zeus released a mournful whine.

Chapter Four

It had taken Nick a long time to go to sleep the night before. He'd been reluctant to call an end to his time with Lexie. She made him feel more alive than he had in a very long time.

He liked the directness of her gaze, the fact that she spoke what was on her mind and seemed not to possess an internal censor. Hell, if he were perfectly honest with himself he'd even admit that he liked the pink streak in her light brown hair.

He sensed a depth of loneliness inside her that called to something deep inside him, but by the time he'd made it home from her house, he was also feeling something else—the heavy weight of guilt.

He now rolled over in his bed and stared at the framed photo on the nightstand next to him. Early morning sunshine poured through the window, making it easy for him to see the picture of the wife he'd lost. Danielle's soft brown eyes seemed to be staring right at him, holding the faintest hint of accusation.

When he'd gotten ready for bed the night before with a desire for Lexie still simmering inside him, he'd gotten the photo of his wife out of the drawer and had placed it there to remind himself that he'd already had his one great love, that somehow, someway he'd managed to screw that up so badly his wife had taken her own life rather than face the rest of her days with him.

She'd killed herself because he'd been unable to give her what she needed, because he hadn't been man enough to take care of her in the way she'd wanted. Somehow, someway, he'd done it all wrong.

He got out of bed before the maudlin thoughts could fully take hold. The sun was up and it was time for him to get started with the morning chores.

The minute his feet hit the floor, Taz, his schnauzer pup, jumped on his toes like a furry ninja who had hidden beneath the bed for the sneak attack.

"Good morning to you, too," he said as he leaned down and scratched Taz behind his ears. The dog barked, his round brown eyes holding more than a hint of mischief.

It took Nick only minutes to pull on a pair of old jeans and a long-sleeved shirt. After a quick cup of coffee he put the leash on Taz and headed outside.

He'd gotten the dog almost four months ago when the silence of the house had been too much to bear. Taz certainly filled the house with energy and had been a loving and often humorous companion. But the little pooch was also incredibly stubborn and had never heard a command he really wanted to obey, which was why Nick had been taking the little guy to Lauren for some basic obedience training.

Once Taz had done his morning business and was back in the house, Nick headed to the barn, his thoughts not on the woman who had been giving Taz obedience lessons, but rather on her sister.

He had to let it go. He'd done what he could to help Lexie and now he needed to step back from the whole situation...from her. There was nothing more he could do to help her find her sister and she was stirring up things inside him that both made him uncomfortable and a little bit excited.

The fact that he didn't want to back away from her made it all the more important that he did. He had nothing to offer any woman. He'd already shown himself to be lacking as a husband and he didn't want to chance trying it again.

But he couldn't ignore the tension just beneath the surface between them, a tension he recognized as physical attraction. He thought she was aware of it, too. He'd seen it in her eyes, the recognition of sparks between them.

As he worked to do the morning chores, he recognized that much of the joy he'd once felt on this land had died with Danielle. Even though it was his childhood home, it had come to represent a failure of the worst kind.

He was supposed to live here with Danielle and fill the house with children. They had been meant to grow old together in this house, but somehow he'd let her down.

It was almost ten when he returned to the house, took a fast shower and then made himself some breakfast. Taz sat at his feet, hoping for a crumb to be dropped on the floor. Nick tossed him a little piece of toast and laughed as he gobbled it up practically midair. Nick had just finished eating and had carried his plate to the dishwasher when his phone rang.

He couldn't control the sudden leap of his heart as he wondered if the caller might be Lexie. Instead it was Marge from the restaurant. "Hey, Nick. You were in here asking about Bo Richards and I just thought I'd let you know he's back in town. He's here in the restaurant and just ordered his breakfast."

"Thanks, Marge, I appreciate the heads-up." He hung up but stared at the phone. Less than an hour ago he'd decided to back away from Lexie and her missing sister, and yet he couldn't ignore the fact that he had information that might be vital to Lexie's investigation.

It was quite possible that Lauren was home now, dropped off by Bo on his way back into town. It was also possible she'd never been with Bo to begin with, and Lexie was anxious for a lead, any lead that might give her information about her missing sister.

His indecision snapped and he picked up the phone with an eagerness that would have unsettled him if he'd given himself enough time to really think about it. Lexie answered on the second ring and instantly he heard the depth of exhaustion in her voice.

"I just heard that Bo Richards is at the restaurant in town. If I pick you up now we should be able to get there before he's finished eating," he said.

"I'll be waiting," she replied without hesitation.

Nick tried to tamp down the anticipation that filled him as he grabbed his car keys and then left the house. He told himself that it was simply the possibility of getting some answers from Bo that filled him with anticipation, but he knew in the very center of his heart that it was also because he was going to spend some more time with the woman who unsettled him in a pleasant way.

She was standing on the porch when he pulled up and as he watched she hurried to his truck. She was dressed in a pair of jeans that hugged her slender legs and a bright yellow long-sleeved blouse that made her look fresh and vibrant.

However, as she slid into the passenger seat and he got a look at her eyes, she looked less fresh and more tired. "Bad night, huh?" he asked as he pulled away from Lauren's place.

"The worst yet." She fastened her seat belt and leaned back. "At two this morning somebody was skulking around outside the fence in the backyard."

Nick nearly braked the truck in the middle of the road as he snapped his gaze to her. "Did you see who it was?"

She shook her head. "It was too dark. The dogs barking woke me and all I could see was a shadow moving from tree to tree."

Nick frowned. "It was a human shadow?"

"Definitely."

"Who would be outside at that time of night?"

"That's what I'd like to know. After that it was really hard for me to go back to sleep again. I stayed on the sofa with my gun in my hand, expecting something bad to happen, but nothing did. And now what worries me more than anything is, if Bo Richards is back in town then where is Lauren?"

"Maybe he dropped her off someplace," he offered, although he knew his words were totally lame.

"Yeah, maybe," she said without enthusiasm. "Or maybe Bo and Lauren had some sort of a fight and he killed her and dumped her body on the way to wherever he was going."

Once again Nick fought his impulse to brake at the shock of her words. He found it impossible to even imagine that Bo Richards was capable of murdering a woman, yet he had to remind himself that Lexie didn't know Bo.

"I've got to tell you, I can't imagine Bo being some kind of a killer. He's always seemed to be a nice, even-tempered man who everybody likes," he said. "He's lived here for years and never had any trouble with anyone."

"Yeah, but on the surface Ted Bundy was a nice, pleasant man, too," she replied darkly.

He felt her tension as he pulled up in front of the café. "That's Bo's truck," he said and pointed to the red vehicle two parking spaces from theirs.

As they got out she hurried to the door, as if unable to wait another second to speak to the man she hoped would have some answers about her sister. Nick hurried after her, his heart beating with the rhythm of her anxiety.

Bo sat alone at a booth near the back, a newspaper spread out on the table next to his plate. Nick motioned to Lexie to indicate him and together they wove through the tables to the booth where he sat.

As they reached him, he looked up and smiled. "Hey, Nick." He eyes widened as he gazed at Lexie. "And you have got to be Lauren's sister. Please, sit." He gestured to the seat across from him.

"No, thanks. We just want to ask you a couple of questions," Nick replied.

"Where's my sister?" Lexie blurted. "Where's Lauren?"

Bo lowered the fork he held in his hand and frowned at her. "What do you mean? I would guess she's at home. I just got back into town a little while ago and haven't had a chance to talk to her yet."

"She's been missing since you left town," Nick said.

Bo stared at Nick and then at Lexie. "What do you mean, missing?"

Bo was either a stellar actor or he was as genuinely confused as he looked, Nick thought. "Nobody has seen or heard from Lauren since Tuesday. She left the dogs un- cared for and nobody has been able to get in touch with her. We thought maybe she was with you."

"With me? No. I spoke to her Tuesday night before I left town, but I went to visit my parents in Tulsa and my relationship with Lauren hadn't progressed to the point where I felt comfortable taking her with me." He looked at Lexie once again. "We'd just started seeing each other. We haven't had time to get really serious, although I certainly find her company pleasant and would like to keep seeing her."

"Maybe she wanted you to take her with you and you had a fight," Lexie said. She nearly vibrated with energy and Nick realized how desperately she'd hoped Bo would have all the answers.

"Lauren didn't mention wanting to go with me and we had no fight," Bo protested. "You really think I had something to do with Lauren missing? That's crazy."

"When exactly did you leave town, Mr. Richards?" Lexie asked. Her voice trembled slightly and Nick had the feeling she was on the verge of snapping, like a rubber band pulled far too tight.

"My plan was to leave early Wednesday morning, but I was ready to go by around eight Tuesday night and so I went ahead and took off. Have you talked to Gary Wendall about all this?" Bo asked.

"We filed a missing persons report." Nick was aware that they'd garnered the interest of several other people in the café.

He took Lexie by the elbow, knowing that they'd learn nothing more here, but she pulled her arm away from his and stepped closer to the booth.

"Is there anyone who can substantiate your claim that you left here on Tuesday and what time you arrived in Tulsa?" she asked.

"My parents can tell you what time I got there Tuesday night." Bo dug into his pocket and pulled out his wallet. "I even have a gas receipt that will show you that I was on the road to Tulsa Tuesday night." He pulled out a receipt and held it out to Lexie.

Nick noticed that her fingers trembled as she took it from him and stared at it. "Look," Bo continued, "I don't know what to tell you about your sister, but whatever has happened to her, I had absolutely nothing to do with it."

Lexie stared at Bo for several long, agonizing seconds, then handed him back his receipt and looked up at Nick. Her eyes behind the dark-rimmed glasses were large and luminous with barely suppressed emotion. "Let's go," she said. She didn't wait for Nick, but hurried toward the door.

"Nick, I swear I have no idea what's going on with Lauren," Bo exclaimed. "Everything was fine with her when I spoke to her on the phone Tuesday evening before I left town. I'd never do anything to hurt her. I like her!"

Nick nodded and glanced toward the door where Lexie had disappeared from his sight. "Thanks, Bo."

"Let me know what you find out. Now I'm worried," Bo said.

"Will do," Nick replied and then left the booth, eager to catch up with Lexie.

As he stepped outside, he didn't see her either waiting for him outside the door or standing by his truck. He walked toward the truck and then spied her in the doorway of the vacant storefront next to the café.

She looked small and broken, leaning her back against the window with her shoulders hunched slightly forward. She'd taken off her glasses and held them in one trembling hand. As he approached her, his heart squeezed tight in his chest.

"I didn't realize how much I'd hoped that

she was with Bo until now." The tightness in her voice let him know that she was precariously close to losing it. "I believe him. I don't think he had anything to do with Lauren's disappearance." A sob escaped her lips. "Where's my sister, Nick? What's happened to Lauren?"

He could stand it no longer. He closed the short distance between them and took her into his arms. She stood stiff and unyielding for a long moment and then melted against him as she began to weep in earnest.

Although his intent was to simply comfort her, he was acutely aware of the press of her breasts against his chest and of the clean, sweet scent of her that filled his head.

She cried for several minutes. When she finally stopped she didn't move from his arms, but rather remained in his embrace.

She slowly raised her head and looked up at him and her trembling lips seemed to beg him to cover them with his own.

Before he could think, before he could even question his own intent, he lowered his mouth to hers. Hot and sweet, her mouth opened beneath his as he tightened his arms around her.

A greediness filled Nick as his tongue

danced with hers. He wanted more of her than a simple kiss. He wanted to feel the weight of her breasts in his palms, her naked legs wrapped with his.

These thoughts stunned him. He wasn't sure who backed away, him or her, but suddenly they stepped back from each other and her gaze held his. In the depth of her bright green eyes he saw a myriad of emotions—shock and embarrassment, but also more than a small flicker of desire.

"I'm sorry," he said, breaking the awkward silence that hung heavily in the air.

"Please, don't apologize. I wanted you to kiss me." She broke the eye contact and slid her glasses back in place. "And now I'd like you to take me back to Lauren's."

Whatever had flared inside her to want him to kiss her was obviously gone as she headed toward his truck. Nick followed behind her, trying to figure out what had just happened between them.

He frowned and forced any thoughts of the kiss out of his head. Instead his thoughts turned to Lauren. He couldn't help but feel that something bad had happened to her.

He had the terrible feeling that heartache

and grief were in Lexie's near future and that she was going to need somebody here to lean on. He just had to figure out if he wanted to be her strength or if it was better for the both of them if he completely distanced himself from her.

THE KISS HAD SHAKEN HER almost as much as talking to Bo. By the time Nick had dropped her off at Lauren's place, Lexie was a bundle of screaming nerves.

If she didn't get an answer about Lauren soon she was going to explode. And if she'd spent another minute in Nick's company she felt as if she might blow up as well.

She sank down on the sofa with Zeus at her feet and thought about the man who had just dropped her off. She felt a wild chemistry with him, one that she'd never felt with Michael. It scared her more than just a little bit. She didn't want to feel that way about any man. Nick Walker had heartbreaker written all over him and she'd do well to remember that.

Besides, even though Nick had kissed her like he'd meant it, he'd also made it clear that he'd had his one arrow and had no intention of ever falling in love again. She was smart enough to know that a kiss had nothing to do with love. Nick could want her in his bed, but he'd told her that his heart was closed for business.

Besides, even if he ever changed his mind about loving again, he was the kind of man who would choose a traditional kind of woman, not a woman like Lexie.

And I'm just here in town until I can find Lauren, she thought. She had a job to return to, an apartment and a life that had nothing to do with Widow Creek.

Unable to sit still another minute, she got up off the sofa and grabbed her car keys. She couldn't just sit around here and do nothing. Deciding to go back into town and ask more people about the last time they'd seen Lauren, she left the house.

The sun was warm as it cast through the autumn-colored leaves of the trees she passed. Both Lexie and Lauren had always loved fall. It had definitely been their favorite season, but now Lexie couldn't take pleasure in its beauty.

There was a huge lump in her chest that she knew wouldn't go away until she found her sister. *Surely if she were dead I'd know it,* Lexie thought. *Surely being identical twins I'd feel it if she were no longer on this earth.*

Or maybe she just wanted to believe that the twin connection was so strong she would know if Lauren had taken her last breath.

Before Nick had called her that morning she'd once again been on Lauren's computer, checking her sister's bank records. There had been no activity since the previous Sunday night when Lauren had paid some bills online.

Wherever her sister was, she wasn't tapping into any money source. Lauren didn't own a credit card. She was one of those smart people who had refused to succumb to the "buy now, pay later" mentality.

She'd also called the Anna who had left a message on Lauren's answering machine again. Although Lexie had spoken to the woman once before, she felt the need to check again and see if perhaps Lauren had called her about the missed appointment.

Anna Cartwell was a nice, elderly woman who had recently bought a poodle puppy. She'd told Lexie that Precious the puppy had already had one session with Lauren but when she'd shown up for her second session the day before, Lauren hadn't been home. She hadn't heard from Lauren but promised to call Lexie if she did hear from her.

And Lexie promised to let Anna know when Lauren would be available to reschedule an appointment for Precious. She just prayed there would be another appointment with Lauren for the poodle pup.

By the time Lexie parked on Main Street her heart was racing with the need to find something, anything that would lead to her sister.

She got out of her car and decided to once again hit all the stores and talk to the shopkeepers. Maybe there would be different people working than when she and Nick had last asked questions.

She started at one end of the block and it didn't take her long to work her way through all the businesses on that side of the street as she saw the same familiar faces in each place and knew they'd have nothing to give her.

In the feed store across the street an unfamiliar face greeted her as she walked through the door. Before when she and Nick had been here they had spoken to a teenage boy behind the counter.

"Can I help you?" the older woman wearing a Fred's Feed shop apron asked.

"I hope so," Lexie replied. "I'm trying to find out when the last time my sister was seen in town. Lauren Forbes?"

"Ah, I see the resemblance," the woman replied with a smile. "Lauren's a regular customer. Let's see, the last time she was in was last Wednesday, she picked up some doggy vitamins she'd ordered."

"Are you sure it was Wednesday?" Lexie asked in surprise.

"Had to be. I didn't work Tuesday or Thursday of last week and if I remember right she came in just before noon."

"Did she say anything about going out of town or anything like that?"

The woman shook her head. "No, she just picked up what she'd ordered and then left."

Lexie thanked the woman and as she left the store she realized that if Bo had been telling the truth about leaving town on Tuesday night then this news was confirmation that Lauren had been alive and well when he'd left.

So, what had happened to Lauren after she'd left the feed store? She'd apparently made it back home, parked her car in the garage and then what? Had somebody been waiting in the garage for her?

Lexie stood just outside the store on the sidewalk and looked around, but there was nothing in sight to give her a clue as to what might have happened when her sister had left Fred's Feed.

She hadn't heard from Gary Wendall, so she headed toward the police station. She'd almost reached the building when she felt the strange sensation of somebody watching her.

Glancing over her shoulder she saw a tall, dark-haired man leaning against one of the vacant storefronts across the street. Even from the distance between them she could see a livid scar that raked down the left side of his face.

His intent gaze seemed to reach across the distance and the hair on the nape of her neck rose in response. Who was he and why was he staring at her so strangely? It was definitely creeping her out.

She quickened her steps and breathed a sigh of relief as she entered the police station. The receptionist ushered her into the office where Gary sat behind his desk.

"Ms. Forbes," he said as he rose from his chair to greet her.

"Chief Wendall, I was wondering if you had any news for me about my sister."

"Please, have a seat, and call me Gary," he said.

Lexie sank down in the chair opposite his desk and nodded. "And you can call me Lexie," she replied. "Now, about my sister's case…"

"Unfortunately, so far I have nothing to offer you," Gary said as he sat back at his desk. "I've contacted the hospital and checked with the morgue and thankfully she isn't in either of those places. I've got a couple of my men asking questions around town but so far we've come up empty. I figured we'd give it until the end of today and then launch a full-blown investigation."

"Why wait?" Lexie countered. She felt as if every minute was of the essence. In another couple of days it would be a full week that Lauren had been gone.

"If this was a child or a minor missing I'd have my men all over it, but this is a grown woman and there is absolutely no sign of foul play."

"How do you know that?" she asked, trying to keep the edge out of her voice. "You haven't even come out to the house to look around." Lexie was aware that despite her efforts her voice was filled with her frustration. The man was an ass, an incompetent ass at that.

"You told me you were staying out at Lauren's place. I figured if something looked odd there you'd have told me by now. I was planning on bringing a couple of men out later today to take a look around. Will you be there around four this afternoon?"

"I'll make it a point to be there," she replied and stood. There was nothing more here for her. She could only hope that maybe Gary and his men might see something she'd missed at the house, something that would provide some answers. "I'll see you around four at Lauren's," she said.

As she left the office she told herself that Gary was probably doing what any law enforcement man would do in this situation. Just because he hadn't come up with any answers yet didn't mean he was an incompetent ass.

She just wanted somebody beating the bushes, turning over rocks and doing a house-to-house search. She just wanted somebody to find her sister.

As she left the police station she saw the dark-haired man just across the street, and once again he stared at her in a way that made her distinctly uncomfortable.

Who was he? And why did he appear to be watching her? Had he waited for her to come out of the police station? What could he possibly want, and if he wanted something then why didn't he approach her?

She got into her car and pulled away as she checked her rearview mirror. To her surprise she saw the man get into a big, black pickup and follow after her.

As she headed toward Lauren's place she divided her attention between the road and her rearview mirror and the truck behind her. He didn't drive too close to her, but the fact that he was there at all caused a rivulet of anxiety to dredge through her.

Was he the person who had been outside of Lauren's house in the middle of the night? Why had he been staring at her? What did he want from her? His presence felt threatening.

The fear spiked as she drew closer to Lauren's place. She didn't want to go there where she would be all alone and he might follow her into the driveway.

Instead when she reached Nick's driveway she pulled in, hoping that he was home. As she made the turn a glance in her mirror let her know the pickup had zoomed on. She parked in front of the attractive two-story house and breathed a deep sigh of relief as Nick stepped out on his front porch.

She got out of the car, surprised to feel her legs slightly shaky beneath her. "Sorry to bother you," she said as she approached where he stood on the porch. She gave a quick glance back at the road and then looked back at him.

"Problems?" he asked.

"A guy in town kind of freaked me out and when I got into my car to drive home, he followed me. I decided to pull in here instead of going on to Lauren's." She was surprised by how shaky she felt about the whole situation. Although the man hadn't really done anything bad, she'd definitely felt threatened.

"Come on in," he opened the front door and she swept past him and into the foyer of the home.

Almost immediately her feet were attacked by a little black ball of fur. "Taz, no!" Nick said.

"What have we here?" Lexie leaned down and picked up the puppy who then attempted to lavish her face with kisses. Lexie laughed, the fear that had gripped her momentarily impossible to maintain with the wiggling warmth of the affectionate dog in her arms.

"That is the dog from hell," Nick said, but his affection for the little pooch was evident in his voice. "Come on into the kitchen."

She placed the dog on the floor and then followed him through a large living room. Her first impression was of a room rarely used. The furniture was overstuffed and looked comfortable, but there was nothing to give the room a real sense of home.

She followed Nick into a large, airy kitchen, and it was in here she felt his presence. A coffee mug sat on the table along with the morning paper. A handful of pocket change and his keys were on the counter along with several dog treats.

"Have a seat," he said. "Want something to drink?"

She shook her head. "No, I'm fine." She sat at the table and Taz collapsed at her feet, as if he'd completely exhausted himself in his exuberant greeting of her.

Nick sat across from her, his gray eyes narrowed slightly. "So, tell me what happened."

"I think maybe I overreacted," she said, suddenly feeling rather foolish. "I went back into town to see if there was anyone working in the stores who we didn't question before. I found a woman in the feed store that told me Lauren had been in on Wednesday to pick up some supplies."

Nick leaned back in his chair. "So, she was okay after Bo left town on Tuesday night."

"Apparently," Lexie agreed. "Anyway, when I left the feed store I noticed a man standing across the street who seemed to be staring at me."

She felt the hairs at the nape of her neck lift as she remembered him. "Even though it made me uncomfortable, I walked down the street to the sheriff's office because I wanted an update from him on the case. When I came out the same man had moved to stand across the street from the police station and he was staring at me once again. When I got in my car to go back to Lauren's, he jumped in his truck and followed me. I got freaked out and so I pulled in here instead of going home."

There was no way she could explain that for a moment what she'd felt wafting off the man had been something bad…something evil.

A frown had swept over Nick's features and had deepened with each word that she said. "This guy, what did he look like?"

"Tall with big shoulders and dark hair, and he had a scar down one cheek."

"Clay Cole," Nick announced. "He's my age, not married and a pseudo-rancher who lives on the north side of town."

"A pseudo-rancher? What does that mean?" she asked curiously.

"He says he's a rancher and he's got a big spread, but he spends more time in the local bars than he does working his land. That's how he got that scar on his face, in a bar brawl. He got cut up with a broken beer bottle."

"Why would he be staring at me so intently? Why would he follow me?"

Nick shoved back from the table and stood. "Why don't we go ask him?"

Lexie stared up at him in surprise. "You mean go to his house?"

"Why not? I figure if you want answers, go directly to the horse's mouth, so to speak. Clay occasionally gets a snootful of booze and picks fights, but when he's sober he's always been an okay kind of guy."

Lexie got up from the table and once again her legs felt slightly shaky. She'd like to get some answers from Clay Cole, but the idea of confronting him face-to-face sent a small shiver of apprehension through her. She couldn't help feeling that somehow she and Nick were getting deeper into something dangerous…she just wasn't sure what it was.

Chapter Five

What Nick hoped to do by taking her out to Clay's was ease some of the anxiety he felt rolling off her. As they passed Lauren's place he saw her look, maybe hoping to see Lauren standing out by the dog pen or mowing the lawn.

He heard the faint sigh of disappointment that released from her as they passed on by and he wished he could say something to ease her worries.

He liked the idea that she'd felt threatened and had come to his place. It meant she trusted him. He was surprised by how much he wanted her to trust him, to depend on him if she was scared.

"I feel bad taking up so much of your time," she finally said, breaking the silence that had descended between them from the moment they'd gotten into his car.

"Over the last year I've had way too much time on my hands," he replied. It was true, since Danielle's death he'd come precariously close to falling into a depression, into wallowing in self-pity. If nothing else Lexie had forced him to look outside of himself, outside of his own heartache, and no matter what happened between them from here on out he would forever be grateful to her for that.

Unfortunately, he didn't know what had happened to Lauren. He couldn't give her a happy ending where her sister was concerned, and it was a fact that his optimism about finding her alive and well was beginning to fade away.

He could only hope that Lexie was strong enough to survive whatever the future held for her. And if she couldn't be strong enough on her own, then he hoped he could be strong for her.

"What did Gary have to say about the case?" he asked.

A frown of irritation crept across her forehead. "Nothing much. He's got his men asking questions and he'd checked the hospital and morgue. He's supposed to be at Lauren's at around four to take a look around there."

"What's he hope to find?"

She shrugged her slender shoulders. "I don't know. Maybe something I missed. Maybe a cluc that I've overlooked." She clenched her fingers together in her lap. "I just want him to be doing something." She flashed him a quick glance. "I want everyone to be doing something to help find her."

How well Nick knew that feeling. "In the days that Danielle was missing I felt as if I was the only person on earth who cared about her, the only person who was worried about her. I've never felt as alone as I did in those three long days."

He glanced at Lexie and she smiled at him, that warm open smile that made his heart do a crazy dance in his chest. "I'd feel like that now if it wasn't for you."

She broke the eye contact and cast her gaze out the side window and once again Nick wished he could say something that would take the sadness out of her eyes.

He had no idea why Clay would have been staring at Lexie enough to make her feel uncomfortable. He couldn't imagine why Clay would have followed her out of town, but he intended to find out. He hadn't forgotten that somebody had been outside of Lauren's place in the middle of the night.

Had it been Clay? And if so, what had he been doing out there? What had he wanted? Nick had known Clay almost all his life, the two had gone to school together from kindergarten to graduation from high school.

Clay wasn't the brightest bulb in the package; he had a reputation for being lazy and liked his beer more than most. But Nick couldn't imagine why he'd have any reason to make Lexie uncomfortable or why he might follow her.

When they pulled up in front of Clay's sad-looking ranch house his truck was parked in the driveway, letting them know he was home.

Nick didn't expect any trouble, but he could feel Lexie's tension as they got out of the car. Clay had definitely spooked her and Nick wanted to know why. It made no sense and Nick wasn't comfortable with things that didn't make sense.

Clay's house didn't breathe of prosperity, but rather, like many of the businesses in town, gave the impression of just barely hanging on.

The white paint had weathered to a dull gray and wood rot was evident around all of the windows. What had once been dark blue shutters were faded and hung askance.

There were several outbuildings in the distance, a barn that looked as tired as the house and a metal gardening shed that looked fairly new and sturdy.

Clay answered on the second knock and was obviously surprised to see them. "Hey, Nick, what's up?"

"Mind if we come in and speak with you?" Nick asked.

"Course not." Clay opened the screen door to allow them into the house.

Nick had never been inside Clay's home before and he was surprised by the lush living room and all that it contained. A rich leather sofa and recliner chair made the perfect place to sit to watch the flat-screen television, which was the biggest Nick had ever seen.

Several of the latest game systems sat on the floor next to the wall where the television was mounted and a state-of-the-art computer was on a nearby desk. Clay might not be putting any money into the outside of his place, but it was obvious he was spending it for his own entertainment and comfort.

"Clay, this is Lauren Forbes's sister, Lexie," Nick said.

"And I want to know why you were staring at me earlier when I was in town." Lexie said without preamble. *So much for finesse,* Nick thought. Lexie was nothing if not direct.

Clay rocked back on his heels and grinned at her. "You noticed that, huh? To be honest, I ain't never seen nobody with pink hair before. Besides, I think you're kinda cute."

Lexie's cheeks flamed with color and Nick had a sudden impulse to throw his arm around Lexie's shoulder and say, "mine," which was ridiculous. She wasn't *his* and he had no intention of making her his.

"You made her nervous, Clay," he said. "She's here in town looking for her sister."

"And nothing else," Lexie said, a hint of pink lingering on her cheeks.

"Yeah, I heard Lauren had gone missing and you two have been in town asking questions about her," Clay said. "I guess you haven't found her yet?"

"Do you know my sister?" Lexie asked.

"Sure, I've seen her around town," Clay replied. "But I didn't really talk to her or nothing like that. I heard through the grapevine that she was seeing Bo Richards."

Nick nodded. "Yeah, we've talked to Bo, but he doesn't know what happened to her."

Clay shrugged his massive shoulders. "Sorry I can't help you." He looked at Lexie and raised a hand to run a finger down his scar. "And sorry I made you nervous. I didn't know it was a crime to gawk at a pretty lady."

"Well, thanks for your time," Nick said. He could tell that Clay was making Lexie uncomfortable even now and Nick wanted nothing more than to get her out of there. He grabbed Lexie by the arm and drew her back to the door.

"Let me know if I can do anything to help," Clay said.

"Don't hold your breath," Lexie muttered as they walked toward the car.

"He's a piece of work," Nick said to Lexie as he backed out of the driveway.

She nibbled on her lower lip, as if trying to work out something in her mind. "Occasionally I've seen a man look at me with what I thought was interest, but that's definitely not how I felt when Clay looked at me." She turned and gazed at him. "The looks from Clay felt darker, filled with a malevolence of some kind." She released a small, embarrassed laugh. "Maybe I'm going crazy. Maybe I'm just imagining things and starting to see boogeymen everywhere."

Nick started the engine with a smile. "Somehow you don't strike me as the type of woman to go that crazy."

"The ranching business must be really lucrative," she said as Nick pulled away from the house. "Did you see all the toys he had inside?"

"Yeah, I'd like to know how a rancher who never seems to get his hands dirty makes the kind of money to afford all that," Nick replied.

"Maybe he's got family money."

Nick laughed and shook his head. "I knew Clay's parents. His father was a drunk and his mother worked long hours at the café. There's no way there was any big money in that family."

"Maybe he works harder than you think he does."

"Maybe," Nick conceded. There was no

way he could know what exactly Clay did to earn money or to judge how he spent what he had. He also couldn't really know just how many hours Clay spent actually working his land.

"The main thing is I never heard Lauren mention anything about Clay. He has no dogs so I can't imagine that they would have interacted in any way."

"If that's the way he comes on to women, then it's no wonder he's single," Lexie said with a touch of disdain. "There's just something a little creepy about him."

"I'm glad that you don't think there's anything creepy about me," he replied. Was he actually flirting with her?

"Nothing creepy that I've noticed yet," she returned with a smile.

"You have plans for dinner?"

"I haven't thought that far ahead," she admitted. "It probably depends on how thorough Gary and his men are at Lauren's house. If they're there late, then I'll just grab a sandwich or something."

He was surprised by the little wave of disappointment that fluttered through him. He wouldn't have minded sharing another meal with her, spending more time with her.

It wasn't like she was an arrow to his heart, he told himself. She was just a distraction from his own loneliness, a woman he enjoyed spending time with for now.

As they started past Lauren's place she sat up straight in the seat. "Turn in," she exclaimed.

He whirled the steering wheel to make the turn into the driveway and saw what had grabbed her attention. Gary Wendall's official car was there, along with several other vehicles.

"He must have decided to come early," she said with a glance at her wristwatch.

As they drew closer Nick felt a tightness spring to his chest. He recognized one of the men who stood next to Wendall. It was Roger Wiley, the town coroner.

There would be only one reason for Roger to be here. *No.* The word whispered inside his brain as he pulled the car to a halt and glanced over at Lexie.

She didn't know Roger but she must have seen something on Gary's grim face for she released a little gasp as she got out of the car. Nick hurried after her, instinctively not wanting her to face the next few minutes alone.

"What's going on?" she asked.

Her voice sounded tight, as if she needed to cough. Nick's heart constricted tight in his chest as he took her hand in his and stared at Gary, dreading what was about to come.

"I'm afraid I have some bad news," he began.

Her hand squeezed Nick's painfully tight. "No." The word was a faint whisper of denial from her lips.

At that moment several officers appeared on the edge of the wooded area in the distance. They stood as if awaiting further orders and it was at that moment that Nick realized they must have found Lauren somewhere in the woods.

Lexie must have noticed the officers as well. "No," she said, this time louder and more firmly, as if by that single word alone she could change the course of fate.

"It looks like she must have slipped on the bank of the stream and hit her head," Gary began.

Before he could say another word Lexie yanked her hand from Nick's and took off running.

LEXIE RACED TOWARD the woods, her heart pounding so fast it ached in her chest and she couldn't catch her breath. It had to be a mistake. It couldn't be Lauren. Gary Wendall was wrong. Somehow, someway he had to be wrong!

Even as those thoughts shot through her brain, tears blurred her vision and denial surged up inside her. *Not Lauren. Oh God, please not Lauren.*

There was no ambulance. If she'd been hurt then shouldn't there have been some emergency vehicles standing by? This thought caused the pressure in her chest to intensify.

She flew by the officers, somehow feeling that if she got to Lauren quickly enough she could make everything okay. She had to make everything okay. Anything else was unacceptable.

However, in the depths of her soul she knew it wasn't going to be okay. Nothing would ever be okay again. She saw another officer in the distance and she ran toward him, her heart pounding so fast, so loud she could hear nothing else.

Make it be a mistake. Please, make it be a mistake, a voice screamed inside her head. She saw her then, Lauren, on her back on the bank of the little stream. It was obvious she was dead and the grief that sliced through Lexie at the sight of her sister crashed her down to her knees.

A high, keening cry escaped from her as she buried her face in her hands and began to weep. There was nothing else in the world but her grief. She was lost in it, immersed to the point that nothing else mattered, nothing else existed.

Lauren was gone. She would never fulfill all the dreams she'd had. She'd never train her working dogs. She'd never get married and have children.

They'd had a plan, the two of them. Lexie was supposed to be Lauren's maid of honor at her wedding and Lauren was going to be Lexie's. They'd planned it since they were little girls, had talked about how their husbands would have to be best friends and their children would grow up as loving, caring cousins.

Now none of it would happen. Lauren was gone.

And Lexie would never hear her twin's voice again. She'd never have that special close relationship with anyone. She was alone…alone in the world and this thought only made her cry harder.

By the time Nick's hand gently touched her shoulder her tears were all spent and she was blessedly numb. He pulled her up and into his arms and she stood in his embrace in an endless fog that kept everything at bay.

She had no idea how long they stood together. It seemed like a minute. It seemed like an eternity. "Come on," he finally said softly. "I'll take you back to the house."

Yes, she needed to leave this place. She didn't want to look at her sister again. She didn't want to remember Lauren broken and lifeless.

Like an obedient child she nodded, wanting nothing more than to go to sleep and wake up to realize this had all been a dream, a terrible nightmare, and Lauren was still alive and was going to appear any minute now laughing and joking about the silly trick she'd played on them all.

As they reached the house Wendall approached her, his face somber. "My condolences," he said.

The words meant nothing to her. She had retreated to a place inside her mind where nothing was real, nothing could hurt her. She nodded vaguely to the chief and then Nick took her into the house where Zeus greeted them with a happy bark.

The dogs. Oh God, who was going to love Lauren's dogs? Who was going to take care of them now that Lauren was gone? The grief surged up once again, threatening to bring her out of her cocoon of numbness.

She shoved the thoughts and the emotions away and allowed Nick to lead her into the guest bedroom. Gently he maneuvered her so that she was seated on the edge of the bed. He knelt down and took off her shoes and her only feeling was a vague gratefulness that, at least for now, somebody else was in charge.

He forced her to her feet once again, but only long enough to pull down the covers on the bed. She crawled in and closed her eyes, wanting the sweet escape of sleep. Nick's lips pressed softly against her forehead at the same time he took off her glasses and set them on the nightstand.

"Rest," he whispered and then he was gone.

Gone. Lauren was gone forever. She'd slipped and fallen on the bank of the stream and hit her head. Vaguely Lexie remembered the excruciating pain that had lanced through her skull on the day she'd gotten into her car and decided to drive to Widow Creek.

Had it been at that precise moment that Lauren had fallen, that her spirit had left her body? Had she felt her sister's death and not realized it at the time?

Something niggled at the back of Lexie's brain, something she couldn't quite bring into focus but knew was important. What was it?

She squeezed her eyes more tightly closed and tried to focus on what it was that bothered her, but the gut-wrenching sorrow got in the way. She finally fell asleep and found the sweet oblivion she wanted.

She came awake with a small gasp, her heart pounding furiously. She'd been dreaming and in her dream Lauren had been telling her goodbye and Lexie had been begging her sister not to leave her.

Tears burned at her eyes and she quickly

squeezed them closed again, wanting to reclaim the dream, to have just one more minute with her sister.

But as the last of the dream filtered away and her heartbeat slowed to a more natural rhythm, she knew she wouldn't go back to sleep. The pain of her loss crashed back in. Her heart cried her sister's name. Her grief tasted bitter in the back of her throat and she knew the taste would be with her for a long time to come.

She realized it was quite late. The room was dark and the house was quiet. She rolled over on her side and looked at the illuminated hands on the clock. After one.

Her eyes adjusted to the darkness and she realized she wasn't alone. In the faint moonlight that drifted in through the window she saw Nick asleep in the chair in the corner of the room.

Her heart expanded as she remembered his gentle kiss as she'd drifted off to sleep, as she realized he hadn't left her alone while she'd slept. He'd been right there with her through the dark hours.

She had no idea what kind wind of fate had blown him into her life, but at the moment she was grateful that he was here with her. Unfortunately his presence did nothing to lessen the grief that spiked through her.

She wanted to go back to sleep again and dream of Lauren and this time she wanted to convince her sister not to go. But of course she knew this was a foolish wish that would never come true.

She must have made a noise for Nick's eyes opened, glittering silver in the semidarkness. "Lexie, are you okay?" His voice was soft and filled with a compassion that squeezed the air in her lungs.

"I guess I have to be," she replied as she reluctantly sat up.

"Are you hungry?"

It didn't feel right to think about food, but she had to admit she felt empty inside. "Maybe a little," she finally said.

Nick got out of the chair. "Why don't you come into the kitchen and I'll fix you something to eat?"

"I'll be right in," she replied.

As he left the bedroom Lexie rolled over on her back and stared unseeing at the ceiling. Lauren was gone and all the tears in the world wouldn't bring her back. *Somehow, someway*

Lexie was going to have to find the strength to go on all alone.

She got out of the bed, grabbed her glasses from the nightstand and went into the bathroom to wash her face. She stared at her reflection for a long moment. Her eyes were slightly swollen and her hair was slightly lopsided from sleep, but none of those things really entered her mind as she gazed at herself.

Her twin was dead. The person who had kept Lexie centered, the person who had defined her was gone. For a moment the woman in the mirror appeared to be a stranger. Who was she without her twin?

She washed her face and raked her fingers through her hair and then left the bathroom and headed for the kitchen.

Nick stood at the stove in his stocking feet. Several strips of bacon were beginning to sizzle in a skillet. He gestured her toward the table. "Sit and tell me that you don't hate cheese omelets."

"I don't hate cheese omelets," she repeated dutifully. She eased down at the table, finding it hard to breathe.

"This should all be ready in just few minutes."

She frowned. "I feel guilty even thinking about food right now."

"I know, but you have to eat. Grief doesn't fill you up. Trust me, I know." He flipped the slices of bacon and moved to the refrigerator.

She remembered his own personal tragedy and knew he probably understood the emotions that simmered just beneath the surface in her, emotions she didn't want to tap into because she knew they'd only make everything worse. Lauren would want her to be strong, and somehow, someway she had to find the strength to move ahead.

"Where did they take her?" she asked.

"Forrester's Funeral Home in town." Nick cracked a couple of eggs in a bowl. "You have a lot of decisions to make in the next couple of days."

"I know," she replied and stifled the deep sigh of grief that tried to escape from her. They were decisions she didn't even want to think about right now. She already knew that Lauren's will indicated that she left all her worldly possessions to Lexie, as Lexie's did to Lauren. The two sisters had gone to an attorney's office to have the official documents drawn up a year ago.

Tomorrow would be soon enough to think of all the things that needed to be done. The last things she would ever do for her sister in this lifetime.

She watched as he took up the bacon and then scrambled the eggs in a bowl for the omelet. He moved with the ease of a man comfortable in the kitchen. And why wouldn't he be? For the past year he'd been alone, cooking his own meals, consoling himself when he was sad.

He'd been where she was and she found that thought oddly comforting. He'd survived his tragedy and she'd survive this, too. She'd survive for the sister she'd loved.

When he set the plate in front of her any appetite she thought she might have had was gone. "Eat," he commanded firmly as he sat in the chair next to hers. "The days ahead are going to be difficult ones. You have to eat to keep up your strength."

Dutifully she picked up the fork and forced herself to tackle the omelet. "She'll want to be buried here," she said between bites. "Even though she'd only lived here four months she felt like this was home."

"The Widow Creek Cemetery is a beautiful place," he said softly. "It's where Danielle and my daughter are buried."

"Do you visit their graves often?" she asked curiously. It was so much easier to focus on his tragedy instead of her own.

"Occasionally. Danielle refused to go to our baby's grave but I went by myself a lot during the first few months after we lost her. And after Danielle's death, I visited the cemetery every day for the first couple of months." He frowned. "I think I believed that if I spent enough time there eventually I'd come to understand what happened, what went so wrong."

"And did you?"

He gave her a sad smile and shook his head. "No, and after those couple of months I realized I had two choices. I could crawl right into that grave with her or I could get back to the business of living. Needless to say, I decided to go on living."

Lexie looked down at her plate, surprised to realize she'd eaten everything on it. She looked back at Nick and a deep gratitude swept through her. "Thank you for not leaving me alone."

He reached across the table and his big hand engulfed hers, warming some of the cold spots she had inside. "There's no way I'd leave you alone, Lexie. I know what it's like to be alone with grief and I don't want that for you."

As she looked into his soft gray eyes, she wanted him. She wanted the warmth of his body wrapped around hers. She needed him to keep the horror at bay.

"Come to bed with me, Nick. Come to bed and make love to me."

His eyes flared wide at her words. "Lexie, that's probably not a good idea tonight. You're grieving and you aren't thinking straight and the last thing I'd want to do is take advantage of you."

"You wouldn't be. I know you've already had your Cupid's arrow, Nick. This isn't about love, it's about need." She got up from the table. "I need to be held. I need to feel alive. I need you, Nick."

She turned and left the kitchen, knowing with a woman's instinct that he would follow, knowing he would give her what she needed.

He would never marry her and he would never be in love with her, but he did desire her. She'd tasted his desire in the single kiss they had shared. She'd seen it occasionally sparkling in his eyes over the last two days.

When she got to the bedroom she didn't hesitate. Once again she felt as if she'd been wrapped in a layer of cotton that numbed all of her senses.

She'd just taken off her T-shirt when Nick appeared in the doorway and her need to be held, to feel something other than the wild grief that simmered just beneath the surface, raced through her.

He remained in the doorway, as if afraid to cross the threshold into the bedroom. As she stepped out of her jeans and then took her glasses off and set them on the nightstand she felt no shame about what she was about to do.

She was going into this with her eyes open, knowing that what they were about to share had nothing to do with promises or forever, it was just something to get her through the agonizingly long night.

When she was clad only in her bra and panties, she walked over to where he stood, opened her arms to him and whispered his name. He came to her then and wrapped her in his arms.

Closing her eyes, she reveled in the strength his arms contained, the warmth of their bodies together that shot through her and stole away an edge of the numbness.

He held her close enough that she could feel that he was aroused and she knew she hadn't been wrong about him desiring her. He might not be hers for forever, but he could be hers for the night. And at the moment that was more than enough for her.

His lips warmed her forehead in a surprisingly chaste kiss. "Go to bed, Lexie," he said in a soft voice. "Get a good night's sleep."

She raised her face to look at him. "I don't want to sleep. I want you. Don't worry, my mind isn't fuzzy with grief. I know exactly what I'm doing and I know exactly what I want."

She took a small step back from him and began to unbutton his shirt. He stood frozen, with all of his muscles tensed, but he didn't stop her. When his shirt was unfastened she pushed it off his broad shoulders and that seemed to snap the inertia that had gripped him.

This time when his lips found her, they

took her mouth with a fiery intent that stole her breath away. She wrapped her arms around his neck and pulled him close...closer still.

His tongue tasted hers and she nipped at his lower lip. She didn't want tenderness, rather she wanted wild and abandoned, hard and frenzied, mind-numbing sex.

She broke the kiss and reached behind her and unfastened her bra. It fell to the floor and she turned and slid into the bed. In the moonlight she watched as he took off his pants and then, clad only in a pair of black boxers and his dark socks, he froze by the side of the bed.

"I don't have protection," he said.

"I'm on the Pill," she replied. "I don't sleep around, Nick, and I know you don't either. I trust you if you trust me." There was no worry in her mind as he, too, slid beneath the sheets and once again took her in his arms.

His mouth found hers in a kiss that sparked her numb senses to life. She wanted to lose herself in him, forget the day that had passed and not think about the days to come. She wanted just this moment to exist.

His mouth left hers and blazed a trail of fire down her throat as his hands covered her bare breasts. Her nipples tightened and rose in response to the heat of his hands and she closed her eyes and gave herself to the sweet sensations his touch evoked.

When his mouth covered one of her nipples she tangled her hands in his hair. His tongue lightly flicked the taut bud and she wanted more, wanted harder, needed faster.

Reaching her hand between them, she stroked the hard length of him on top of his boxers and then plucked impatiently at the material.

"Slow, Lexie," he whispered against her breast.

"I don't want slow," she protested.

He raised his head and looked at her, his eyes pools of glitter. She sensed his smile rather than saw it. "I know exactly what you want, exactly what you need. Believe me, we're going to get there...eventually."

His words shot a new wildness through her. She rolled away from him and tore off her panties, unwilling to wait for eventually.

But he remained in control, stroking her body in slow, languid caresses that made her want to scream for release. His hands seemed to be everywhere, whispering the length of her body, lingering on her inner thigh and smoothing across the flat of her lower stomach.

He seemed determined to keep her mindless with need, lingering in a state of limbo of trembling desire without fulfillment.

Finally his fingers found the center of her and as he touched her there she gasped and moaned his name. There was no thoughts of anything but him and the sweet sensations that rushed through her. When he began to apply pressure, she arched to meet him as she felt the rush of her release. And then it was on her, trembling through her with a force that left her breathless.

It was only then that he kicked off his boxers and moved on top of her. She grabbed his buttocks as he entered her, but he refused to move his hips. Instead he remained still except for dipping his head down to capture her lips in a tender kiss.

As the kiss ended she released a half sob, half moan and he began to thrust into her. She loved the feel of him, both his skin against hers and the way he filled her up so completely.

He gave her fast and furious and he gave

her slow and tender and she was lost in him, breathing him in as he took possession of her.

He kissed her so hard he growled into her mouth and then moved his lips like butterfly wings against hers. The hard and fast followed by the tender and slow sent her spiraling again and this time when she came he moaned her name as his own release shuddered through him.

He sagged against her, their breaths coming in quick gasps that finally began to slow. He softly whispered her name as he pulled her close against him. And when their heartbeats were back to normal, when the rush of the release waned, tears burned once again at Lexie's eyes.

The tears weren't just for her sister, but also because she knew Nick was a one arrow man and he'd had his great love. The tears were because no matter what she and Nick had just shared, no matter how wonderful it had been, ultimately Lexie was all alone in the world.

Chapter Six

It was a gray, cloudy morning as Nick sat at Lauren's kitchen table and sipped from a cup of coffee. He stared out the window and absently watched the chilly autumn wind whip the trees and leaves flutter to the ground amid the assault.

However, his thoughts weren't on the turn in the weather, but rather on the woman who still slept in the bedroom. He had no illusions about what had happened the night before. She hadn't come at him with love or any real passion, but rather with a frantic need to keep her grief at bay.

He'd been in her shoes. In the days and weeks after Danielle's death he'd wanted to lose himself, to find some sort of oblivion that would take the bitter taste of grief out of his mouth. For about a week after Danielle's death he'd found his escape in the bottom of a bottle, and he knew last night Lexie had found hers, at least for a brief time, in his arms.

He frowned and took another drink from the mug. There were a million things he should be doing at the moment. Although Taz was proficient at using the doggy door to go out in the dog run to do his business, there was no telling what the little rascal had found to tear up while Nick had been gone.

There were morning chores to do and yet he felt as if the most important chore he had was to be here for Lexie. He knew when she woke up the jagged edges of her grief would be with her once again, poking and prodding and making her half-crazy with loss. He didn't want her to be alone.

Or was it possible that *he* didn't want to be alone?

He shoved this disturbing thought out of his head. This wasn't about him. He knew there were any number of women in town who would be happy to keep him company. Since Danielle's death several of the single women in town had come on to him with a vengeance, but none of them had touched him like Lexie.

She was getting to him in a way nobody had since Danielle. He didn't want to do it again. He didn't want a woman depending on him for anything. He didn't want to try again. He couldn't stand the idea of failing again.

Of course, it was just a matter of days now and Lexie would be gone. Once Lauren had been buried there was nothing to keep her here.

He'd just refilled his coffee cup and sat down again in the chair when Lexie came into the room. She'd apparently showered and dressed for the day in a pair of jeans and a long-sleeved pink knit blouse.

She wore her grief like an open wound on her face. Behind her thick-rimmed glasses her eyes were swollen and her face was lined as if she hadn't slept for days.

She nodded to him and went directly to the coffeemaker on the counter. He said nothing, deciding to let her take the lead. She didn't speak until she had her coffee and was seated across from him at the table.

"If I wasn't such a selfish person I would insist that you go home," she said as she raised her cup to her lips. "I'm sure you have plenty of things to take care of there."

"I do," he admitted. "But I thought maybe after you have your coffee we could head over to my place for breakfast and I can take care of some of the morning chores."

"Or I could just stay here and let you get on with your life." She took a sip of her coffee and eyed him cautiously over the rim of the cup.

"Is that what you want?" he asked.

"Not really." She lowered her cup back to the table with a sigh. "I just don't feel like being alone right now."

"And I don't intend to leave you alone."

She picked up her cup and took another sip, and when she finished she tilted her head to the side and held his gaze. "I can't imagine why Lauren wasn't madly in love with you. You're handsome and smart and such a nice man."

He smiled, ridiculously pleased by the compliments. "There's no accounting for chemistry between two people. There just weren't any romantic sparks between me and Lauren. Besides, Lauren knew the score. She knew I wasn't looking for anyone in my life." He wasn't sure if that was a reminder to Lexie or a reminder to himself that he was unavailable for love.

She nodded and cast her gaze out the window. "Looks like rain," she said.

"Yeah, according to the weather report I heard this morning it's supposed to rain off and on over the next couple of days." The weather would only make things more difficult for her, he thought. Dismal and cold only added another layer of pain to somebody suffering from grief.

She finished her coffee and got up to carry her cup to the sink. "Whenever you're ready to go to your place, I'm ready."

Within minutes they were in his car and headed to his house. Lexie was quiet and he didn't attempt to engage her in conversation.

He knew there were no words he could give her that would take away the pain of her loss. It was only recently that his ache of loss over Danielle had diminished to a manageable level.

When they reached his place Taz greeted them at the door with a happy dance around their feet. For the first time in the past twenty-four hours a smile danced across Lexie's face as she picked up the squirming dog.

"Hey, little guy," she said as she hugged him close to her chest. Taz responded by licking the underside of her chin with enthusiasm.

"Make yourself at home," Nick said. "I'm going to head out to the barn and get some things taken care of."

"I'll be fine," she assured him.

Eventually she would be fine, he thought as he headed out of the house. She'd bury her sister and then get back to her life in Kansas City. Eventually he and Widow Creek would be just a distant memory that she only revisited occasionally in her mind. He was surprised that this thought made him sad.

It took him over an hour to finish up his chores. Nick kept a herd of cattle in the pastures beyond the barn, but he also had several horses and needed to check their water supply and feed. Most of his money came from the cattle and crops he grew in other pastures. Still, there were always things that needed to be done to keep the place running smoothly. When he returned to the house he found Lexie on the sofa with a sleeping Taz in her lap.

She smiled as he entered. "He finally wore himself out," she said.

"Tell the truth, he finally wore you down," Nick replied.

"Maybe a little of both." Her smile fell. "I need to figure out what I'm going to do with Lauren's dogs."

He sat on the sofa next to her. "There are several other dog breeders in the area. Maybe we can contact them and one of them will be interested in taking the dogs."

She nodded. "All of them except Zeus. I'm not sure what I'll do with him, but I definitely don't want him going to a stranger."

"I could take him," Nick offered. "He likes me and I have plenty of room for him. Besides, maybe he can teach Taz some good manners."

Gratitude filled Lexie. If she did take the old dog herself she'd have a problem with the landlord, as she lived in a no-pets apartment. She would have had to find a new place to live that allowed pets.

It felt right for Nick to have Zeus. She knew Zeus would be happy here. "Thanks," she said simply.

He nodded. "And I'll place some calls about the other dogs and see if we can find them a good home. Now, are you ready for something to eat?"

They ate breakfast at Nick's, and then returned to Lauren's house. Lexie got on the phone to the funeral home to make the necessary arrangements for Lauren and Nick used his cell phone to make calls to the local dog breeders in the area.

Lauren's funeral had been arranged for Wednesday morning and on Thursday a breeder from a nearby town was coming out to look at the dogs.

With the business taken care of, Lexie sat at the table and stared out at the woods where her sister had been found. Nick sat across from her, wishing he could think of something to take her sorrow away. But he knew that nothing in the world he could come up with could sweep that emotion away from her. It was going to take time for Lexie to heal from this. Hell, it had been a year since Danielle had been found in that motel room and there were still days when the pain felt fresh.

"I want to take a walk," she said suddenly.

"A walk? A walk where?" he asked curiously.

She pointed toward the woods. "There."

"Oh, Lexie, honey, I don't think that's such a good idea," he protested. Aside from the fact that it was a miserable day, nothing good could come from her walking the area where her sister had tragically died.

Her chin thrust forward. "It's something I need to do, Nick." A frown swooped across her forehead. "I can't tell you why, but I need to go there. Something's bothering me. I'm just not sure what it is yet."

Nick stifled a sigh. He couldn't imagine what it was that was bothering her, and the scene of Lauren's death could only upset her even more. "You sure you don't want to wait until another day?" he asked.

"I want to do it now," she replied.

"If that's what you feel like you need to do then let's take a walk," he finally said, deciding he probably couldn't talk her out of it anyway.

"When we drove in here yesterday and saw all the men—I feel like everything after that happened in a fog," she said as they pulled on jackets and stepped out the back door.

Maybe she needed to go back to assure herself that it was all real, that all the tragedy of the day before had really happened, Nick thought.

"It was a rough day, Lexie," he replied. "Probably one of the worst you'll ever experience in your entire life."

"I know," she replied.

The dead leaves crunched beneath their feet and he sensed Lexie pulling into herself, preparing for the scene of her sister's accident. The sky overhead had grown darker as the day had gone on, as if reflecting Lexie's grief in the gathering dark clouds.

There was a fine mist in the air, as if the clouds hadn't decided yet whether to move on or release a torrent of rain. Nick just wanted for Lexie to do whatever it was she needed to do quickly so both of them could get in before the rain began in earnest.

As they drew closer to the thick grove of trees, her footsteps slowed as if dread was weighing her down. "You don't have to do this, Lexie," he said softly.

"No, I have to," she replied firmly. She stopped and looked at him in obvious confusion. "Something is bothering me. It's been bothering since Lauren was found. I swear Friday evening when I got here and couldn't find Lauren, Zeus and I went completely through these woods."

She broke eye contact with him and looked forward, a frown cutting a vertical line down her forehead. "I told you that everything was a blur yesterday. You need to show me exactly where Lauren was found."

Now she had him curious. "This way," he said and together they began walking again. When they reached the trees he led her along the creek to a rocky area and pointed to the opposite side of the bank. "She was there." He tried not to remember the agonizing cries that had come from Lexie when she'd seen her sister.

Lexie stood frozen and followed the direction of his finger with her gaze. For a long moment she didn't even appear to be breathing as she concentrated on the place where her sister had died.

"She couldn't have been there," she finally said. She reached out and grabbed him by the arm. "Are you sure? Are you positive that it was that exact spot?" Her fingers clenched tight, biting through the material of his lightweight jacket sleeve.

Nick frowned and looked around the area,

wanting to be sure of what he was telling her before he spoke again. "Positive," he finally replied. "I remember that fallen tree branch up ahead. She was right there." He looked at Lexie once again. "Why? What's wrong?"

She dropped her hand from his arm. "I sat right there." She pointed down the creek bed, her eyes narrowed behind her glasses. "I sat right on that big rock with Zeus next to me the first night I got here."

She took several steps forward, her body vibrating with barely suppressed energy. "We would have seen her if she'd been there. Zeus would have found her or at least would have sensed her presence in the area. I knew something was bothering me last night before I went to sleep, but I couldn't put my finger on it. That's what was bothering me. Lauren couldn't have slipped and fallen the way they said she did at the time they said she did. If she had I would have found her Friday night."

Nick walked to her side and looked at her in confusion. "What are you saying, Lexie?"

She stared at him with those big, beautiful eyes. "I'm saying that she must have been killed and then moved here to make it look like an accident. I'm saying that my sister was murdered."

She didn't wait for his response but instead turned and headed back to the house.

LEXIE FELT AS IF SHE WERE on fire as she headed back to the house. Her brain screamed with troubling thoughts that shifted around and around like nebulous shadows, seeking some kind of logical explanation for what didn't make sense.

She was vaguely aware of Nick following behind her as she entered the house, yanked off her jacket and then stood in the center of the kitchen, unsure of what she should do next.

"Lexie, sit down," Nick said as he took off his own jacket. "Tell me what's going on in your head."

She looked at him helplessly, then sank down at the table. He sat next to her, the familiar scent of him momentarily slicing through the chaos in her mind.

If she hadn't been in such a fog of grief the evening before when Lauren had first been found she would have realized that something was wrong...something was very wrong about the whole situation.

Nick's gray eyes gazed at her in confusion and for just a moment she wanted to fall into their depths, lose herself once again in the warmth and comfort of his arms and forget the bad feeling that now threatened to embrace her.

She shoved that desire away, knowing that it was just a convenient and very temporary escape from the questions that now clawed at her.

"There's no way that sometime on Wednesday or Thursday Lauren fell and hit her head and died there on that creek bank, because if she had I would have found her body there Friday night. I think Lauren was killed someplace else and then moved there." She wondered if he thought her grief was making her crazy.

"Nick, I'm telling you she wasn't there Friday night. I walked that entire area. Zeus and I searched for her. She wasn't there and nobody can make me believe otherwise."

He frowned. "But if what you say is true, then Gary Wendall would have had to know about it, he'd have to be a part of it. Gary is lazy and maybe more than a little incompetent, but I can't imagine that he'd kill a woman or know somebody who did and then conspire to make her death look like an accident. And in any case why would he or anyone else want Lauren dead?"

Lexie blew out a sigh. "I don't know." She took off her glasses and rubbed at her eyes, wondering if her grief was, indeed, making her crazy. Who on earth would want to harm her sister? Lauren had been kind and generous and Lexie couldn't remember anyone ever having a beef of any kind with her.

"If you really believe that, then what do you intend to do about it?" he asked.

"The first thing I'm going to do is get back in touch with the funeral home and tell them I want a complete autopsy on Lauren. I want to know if the head wound that killed her was from a slip and fall or from blunt force trauma."

"And if you find out it was blunt force trauma?"

A well of strength rose up inside her, strength born from the love of her sister. "Then I'll find out who is responsible for killing my sister and I'll make them pay for their crime." It was a promise not just to herself but to Lauren.

Unfortunately the call to the funeral home was too late. Lauren had already been embalmed and her wounds cleaned up in a way that would remove any evidence they might have gained from an autopsy.

Lexie was bitterly disappointed at the news, knowing that the best evidence of foul play had been washed away. She decided not to speak to Sheriff Wendall about her suspicions, at least not yet.

For one thing, she wasn't sure what she believed, and in any case she didn't want to give him a heads-up that she had any doubts about how Lauren had died.

But for the next two rainy days the doubts only grew bigger. If Lauren had died an accidental death, then why was her body moved to the creek bed? Lexie would swear under oath that Lauren hadn't been there on the night she and Zeus had walked the property. So, who had placed her there after death?

The rain that had poured down had washed away any evidence that might have been left at the scene. Footprints would be gone, as would any blood spatter pattern there that might prove or disprove Lauren's fall.

During those two days Nick scarcely left her alone. They spent their hours together talking about theories that made no sense, grieving for Lauren and discussing their lives before they'd met.

Nick talked a little bit about Danielle, who had been the president of their high school student council and a cheerleader.

Lexie found herself telling him about Michael the rat, although she certainly didn't confess to him the hurtful things Michael had said to her when he'd broken up with her.

Each night Lexie insisted Nick go home while she remained at Lauren's. Making love with Nick had been wonderful and Lexie knew if they stayed under one roof for the night it would happen again and she couldn't let that happen.

It would only make things more difficult for her when she left, and eventually she would go back to her home, back to her life.

Nick had heartbreak written all over him and her heart was already shattered enough by Lauren's death. He'd told her he wasn't looking for love again in his life, but even if he was she knew he'd choose some pretty blonde who didn't have a pink streak in her hair, somebody who was socially more adept than Lexie would ever be.

Michael had made it clear to Lexie that she lacked in areas that would make her a companion, a lover for life, and it was a lesson she'd never forgotten.

The morning of Lauren's funeral the sun finally reappeared and shone brilliantly. Lexie stood at the kitchen window sipping coffee with her head filled with thoughts of her sister.

She remembered the two of them playing as children, how supportive Lauren had been in high school when Lexie couldn't find a place where she belonged. Lauren had always tried to include Lexie in her group of friends, had encouraged Lexie to break out of her shyness and make friends of her own.

Bits and pieces of lives shared fluttered through Lexie's mind, alternately filling her with both happiness and tears of sorrow.

While she knew her grief would be with her for a very long time, over the past two days a resignation had slowly washed over her, a weary acceptance that Lauren was truly gone.

But along with the grief she had a fierce determination burning in her soul, the determination to somehow find out the truth about Lauren's death. If somebody had killed her, then Lexie wanted that person in prison for the rest of his or her life.

A knock on her door let her know Nick had arrived to take her to the graveside service she'd arranged. He looked amazingly handsome in a black suit and white shirt, and the first thing he did when he stepped through the door was take her in his arms and wrap her in a bear hug.

She closed her eyes and allowed the warmth of him to invade her soul.

What was she going to do when it was time to leave Widow Creek? Time to leave Nick? She didn't even want to think about that right now. He'd become her staff to lean on, her anchor in a storm-tossed sea. Eventually she'd have to regain her strength and stop depending on him, but at least for today she was grateful to have him by her side.

"You ready for this?" he asked when he

finally released her. "It's going to be a tough day."

"I know. I guess I'm as ready as I can be under the circumstances," she replied.

"You look nice," he observed.

"Thanks." She nervously smoothed a hand down the thighs of her black slacks and was grateful she'd packed a black-and-white blouse to go with them. She checked her wristwatch. "I guess we should probably go."

"It's about that time," he agreed. She grabbed her purse and together they left the house.

As she slid into the passenger seat she hoped that along with saying goodbye to Lauren at the funeral she'd get some answers as to who might be responsible for her murder.

Widow Creek might be Nick's hometown, but Lexie believed that at the moment the small town was hiding a murderer and she was determined to do anything in her power to bring that person out in the open.

Chapter Seven

"I don't imagine there will be too many people there," she said as Nick pulled his car out of the driveway and onto the road that led into town. "Lauren wasn't here long enough to make a lot of friends."

"At least the sun is shining," he replied. "It rained something fierce on the day I buried Danielle. It was like the sky cried all the tears that I couldn't release."

She glanced over at him. "I hope this doesn't bring back too many painful memories of that day for you."

He cast her a warm smile. "I'll be fine, Lexie. I'm just here to help you get through a tough day."

And it was a tough day. Lexie was surprised by the amount of people who came to pay their respects. She was also surprised to discover that the tears she'd shed on the night that Lauren's body had been found hadn't been the only ones she had to release.

As the minister spoke of the sorrow of the people of Widow Creek who hadn't gotten the opportunity to know Lauren, to share in her life, deep sobs escaped from Lexie as she was reminded of all the things she'd never share with her twin sister.

Nick kept an arm firmly around her shoulder and she leaned weakly into him as she said her final goodbye to her twin. When the service was over and the crowd began to disperse, Lexie tensed as Gary Wendall ambled up to her and Nick.

"It was a nice service," he said as he pulled his hat off his head. "It was good to see so many people turn out."

"Yes, even though my sister was here only a short time, it appears she made some friends," Lexie replied around the lump in her throat.

Gary put his hat back on his head and rocked back on his heels. "I suppose you'll be heading back to Kansas City now that this is all said and done."

"On the contrary, I have no intention of going anywhere until I find out who killed my sister." Lexie hadn't meant to tell him what was on her mind, but as she blurted out the words she watched Gary's face carefully.

His eyes narrowed slightly. "What are you talking about?"

"Somebody whacked my sister over the head and then put her body on that creek bed sometime between the time I arrived at the ranch and when you found her body. I'm not leaving Widow Creek until I have some answers."

Gary flicked a derisive glance to Nick. "You've obviously been spending too much time with him. I hope you two are very happy with your conspiracy theories, but there was nothing to indicate that anyone murdered your sister." Gary released a deep sigh. "Look, Miss Forbes, grief does terrible things to people. If I thought for one minute this was anything other than a tragic accident, I'd be conducting a full-blown investigation. Go home, Lexie. Go home and get on with your life and let your sister rest in peace." He didn't wait for Lexie's response, but instead turned on his heels and headed to his car parked in the distance.

"Come on, let's head back to Lauren's," Nick said.

"You want to visit Danielle and your daughter's graves while we're here?" she asked.

"No, I'm good," he replied and wrapped an arm around her shoulder. "Let's just get out of here."

"You said that in the first few days after Danielle was found you didn't believe that she'd committed suicide," Lexie said when they were back in Nick's car.

"That's right," Nick agreed. "I was definitely into conspiracy theories then. I wondered if somebody had kidnapped Danielle, taken her to that motel, killed her and then staged the scene to make it look like a suicide."

"Odd, isn't it? That two women went missing and have died in strange circumstances and the people closest to them believe both of their death scenes were staged."

Nick shot her a quick glance. "Odd, yes, but I can't imagine how we could possibly tie Lauren's death to Danielle's in any way. Danielle died long before Lauren even moved to town. One worked for the mayor's office and the other was a dog breeder. Trying to connect the two is definitely an impossible stretch."

Unless they'd both run into the same killer, she thought, but she didn't say the thought aloud. Instead she nodded and looked out the passenger window thoughtfully. "I can't figure out if Gary Wendall is a good guy or a bad guy."

"I've never thought of him as a bad guy. Lazy, yes, but definitely not bad. You know, if what you think is true about Lauren, it's possible that Gary knows nothing about it, that her body was moved there by somebody else altogether before he and his men showed up. Maybe the shadow man you saw in the night is responsible."

The shadow man. Lexie's stomach muscles clenched tight. It was as good as any description for the person she'd thought had been on Lauren's property. Had it been at that moment that he'd been moving Lauren's body to the creek bed, the night that the dogs had gone crazy?

How she wished she would have grabbed her gun and left the house. How she wished she would have gone outside to investigate. She might have come face-to-face with the person who had killed her sister. *And you might have been killed, too,* a little voice whispered.

Nick turned into Lauren's driveway. "In any case, you're probably going to be too busy for the rest of the day to think much about anything."

She looked at him in surprise. "Why?"

"If I know this town there are two things that bring everyone all together, the fall festival and death. Trust me, by the time this evening comes you're going to have a lot of company and more food in the house than you could eat in a month."

He was right. Within an hour, people began to arrive, bringing with them condolences and covered dishes.

Lexie was overwhelmed by the people and the food that kept coming throughout the afternoon. She found herself staying close to Nick, depending on him to introduce the people she hadn't met and to aid her in the social interactions she'd always found difficult.

Lexie met the woman who had trimmed Lauren's hair while she'd been living here and Anna, who had been bringing her poodle for obedience lesions. The man who'd fixed the brakes on Lauren's car a month before introduced himself and then self-consciously drifted away.

Lexie couldn't help but look at each person with an edge of suspicion at the same time she fought the grief that bubbled far too near the surface.

Bo Richards showed up, his sorrow evident on his handsome features as he first shook Nick's hand and then smiled sadly at Lexie. "I wish I would have taken your sister with me to meet my parents," he said to Lexie. "If she'd gone with me then maybe this horrible thing wouldn't have happened to her."

"We can't know that for sure," Lexie replied. But, armed with the belief that her sister had been murdered, she continued to watch Bo as he walked away and disappeared into the throng of people in the kitchen.

Had he left town on Tuesday night only to return the next day or night, kill Lauren and then return to his parents' home? Was it possible he'd wanted more from Lauren than she'd been willing to give? Or had Lauren wanted to take their relationship to the next level and Bo had grown tired of her?

As far as Lexie was concerned everyone was a suspect, everyone except Nick. He was the only person she trusted in this godforsaken town.

It was growing dark outside when a middle-aged man in a well-cut suit approached her. "Ms. Forbes, I'm Vincent Caldwell, the mayor of Widow Creek." He took Lexie's hand in his. "I just wanted to tell you how very sorry I am about what happened to your sister. I know she would have been a vital part of this little town had this tragedy not happened."

His eyes were a warm blue and as he squeezed her hand sympathetically, Lexie once again felt the burn of tears in her eyes.

Nick was right there beside her, swooping an arm around her shoulder in obvious support. "Vincent, thanks for coming," he said to the mayor. "What's made this even more difficult for Lexie is that we have some doubts as to what really happened to Lauren to cause her death."

Vincent released Lexie's hand and frowned. "What do you mean you have some doubts? I understood that this was a slip and fall, an accidental death." He looked at Nick and then back to Lexie. "Is there something I haven't been told about all this?"

"I think she was killed somewhere else and then moved to the place where her body was discovered," Lexie replied.

The mayor looked stunned. "Why would you think that?"

Lexie quickly explained about her searching the area on the night she'd arrived in Widow Creek and the fact that Lauren's body had not been there on that night. As she talked, the frown on the mayor's face grew deeper and deeper.

"Have you spoken to Gary Wendall about your concerns?" he asked when she was finished.

"He seems to think we've lost our minds," Nick replied, his voice laced with a touch of irritation.

"I'll talk to him. I certainly don't want a visitor to our town going away with these kinds of questions in her head." He smiled sympathetically at Lexie. "I'll certainly be in touch, Ms. Forbes."

By the time everyone had left Lexie felt totally wrung out. She and Nick worked side by side, wrapping up the leftover food and placing it in the refrigerator.

"You have enough green bean casseroles to feed a group of Pilgrims Thanksgiving dinner," he said as he put the last dish away.

"And I don't even like green bean casserole," she said. "Still, it was nice. So many people came. None of them knew me and a lot of them didn't really know Lauren, but they came out with food and sympathy."

"This town is dying a slow death, but it's not because of the heart of the people," Nick replied. "How about I make us some coffee and we sit in the living room for a little while before you send me home."

"That sounds good," she agreed, needing a little while to just chill before calling it a night. Minutes later Zeus followed them as they left the kitchen and carried their coffee into the living room.

Lexie sat on the sofa and Nick eased down in the nearby chair with Zeus at his feet. Lexie sipped her coffee and then set the mug on the coffee table and released a tired sigh.

"I hope this woman coming tomorrow wants to take the dogs," she said. "I want them to all find good homes."

"From what she told me on the phone she works with several animal rescue organizations so I have a good feeling about it," Nick replied. "Besides, the dogs are young and that's an advantage when it comes to placing them in a home."

Lexie reached for her coffee cup and cradled the warmth in her hands. "Maybe I'm wrong," she said softly.

"Wrong about what?" Nick looked at her in confusion.

"About Lauren being murdered, about her body being moved, about all of it. Maybe I didn't check that particular area of the creek. Maybe I'm just really confused." She'd gone over it and again in her mind and she was no longer sure what she believed anymore.

"What's changed your mind?"

"I don't know. I've just been thinking that maybe I've been suffering the same ailment that struck you when Danielle died, an overpowering denial and the need to make sense of a terrible tragedy."

She took another sip of her coffee. "Besides, if there was a crime committed, there's almost always a motive and I just can't come up with one in this case. I looked at every single person who showed up today and they all looked guilty to me."

"Even Anna with her poodle Precious?" he asked teasingly.

"She was the only one who didn't set off my radar," Lexie replied. She released a deep sigh. "I think I just have to make peace with the fact that Lauren slipped and fell and when Zeus and I checked the property on Friday night we weren't as thorough as I thought we were."

"I think what you need more than anything is to go to bed. It's been a long day and sleep is the best thing right now." Nick got up from his chair and walked over to Lexie.

Once again she thought about how wonderful it would be to fall into bed with him, to feel his body heat next to hers, to allow his desire to burn away all thought, all heartache, if only for a little while.

"You could stay here tonight with me if you want," she said, her gaze holding his intently.

His eyes flared molten silver as if he knew what she offered wasn't just a bed to sleep in, but rather a bed with her and a night of desire.

He pulled her to her feet and into the

warmth of his embrace. At that moment the front window exploded and the sound of gunfire filled the air.

Chapter Eight

Nick yanked Lexie to the floor as bullets smashed through the front window and riddled the opposite wall. Framed pictures crashed to the floor and Zeus barked uncontrollably and then ran out of the living room while Nick covered Lexie's body with his.

His heart beat frantically in his chest as he tried to wrap his brain around what was happening. He was vaguely aware of Lexie screaming beneath him, her shrill cries adding to the cacophony of chaos that surrounded him.

The melee lasted only a minute or two and then Nick heard a squeal of tires from outside and an abrupt silence reigned. He felt Lexie's heart against his own, beating a frantic rhythm of fear.

Her glasses had fallen off and her eyes were wide. "Are you okay?" he asked urgently and became aware of the dogs outside barking raucously.

She nodded. He rolled off her and went to the window, glass crunching underfoot. He looked outside but there was nothing to see. Whoever had made the sudden attack was now gone.

He turned back to look at Lexie and found her on her feet, her glasses back in place. "I changed my mind," she said. "I'm not all right. I'm angry." She brushed off the back of her jeans and then grabbed her purse off the coffee table and pulled out her gun. "I guess maybe somebody isn't happy with the questions I'm asking and wants me to leave town."

She was right. This was either a dangerous warning or somebody had just tried to kill them both. If they hadn't hit the floor when they had there was no question in his mind that one of them might have been seriously wounded or dead.

"We need to call Wendall," he said as she walked to the window to stand next to him.

"You do that," she replied. "And I'm going to stand right here. The next car or truck that pulls in front of this house better be an official patrol car with a cherry on top, otherwise I'm shooting first and asking questions later."

Nick had never seen her this way, so focused, so incredibly strong. Since he'd met her she'd appeared vulnerable and needy but now there was a fire in her eyes that made him realize she was much stronger than he'd initially given her credit for.

As he made the call to Chief Wendall, she remained at the window, not moving, gun pointed out toward the darkness. "Would you find Zeus and make sure he's locked up in a bedroom?" she asked when he'd finished with the call to Wendall. "I don't want him walking around in here and cutting up his paws."

As he went in search of the dog some of the shock of what they'd just been through began to wear off. She was right. Somebody wasn't happy with her…with them. Whether this had been a warning or an attempt to do actual harm, he couldn't know, but one thing was clear—something wasn't right in his hometown and it broke his heart.

He hadn't been sure what to believe about Lauren's death until this moment. All the questions Lexie had had about Lauren's death now seemed credible, not the crazy meanderings of somebody consumed by grief. There was more to Lauren's death that a simple slip and fall.

He found Zeus in the guest bedroom, hunkered down next to the bed. The dog raised his head and whimpered as Nick approached. "It's all right," Nick said as he scratched beneath the old boy's ears. "Everything's going to be fine."

It was easy to make that promise to a cowering dog, but as Nick left the bedroom and closed the door behind him, he wondered what in the hell was going on.

When he returned to the living room Lexie was still in the same position in front of the broken window, her back rigid with tension. "Something is very wrong here," she said.

He picked his way back across the glass-littered rug to stand next to her once again. "I know." The admission was difficult for him. This was his hometown. These were people he thought he knew, people he'd always thought he could trust.

"Any theories?"

"None," he replied. "Maybe now it's time you call in the FBI."

She shook her head. "Right now all we

have is a death ruled accidental and a random shooting in a small town, nothing that rises to the standard of FBI involvement."

"At least let Gary know that you're an FBI agent. If nothing else it might shake him up enough to do a more thorough investigation into all this," he replied.

"I'm just not ready to let him know about my job yet. Besides, what I do for a living shouldn't make any difference in how hard he works on his investigation. He should work hard whether I'm an FBI agent or a waitress." She frowned. "If I had some proof that Chief Wendall was dirty, that the local law enforcement agency was corrupt, then I might be able to make a case to get the FBI involved." She straightened her back as the swirling red light on the top of Gary's car came into view. "And it appears the man of the hour has arrived."

"You didn't see the make or model of the vehicle they were driving?" Gary asked minutes later as he surveyed the damage in the living room.

"Unfortunately we were too busy diving for cover," Lexie replied.

"Looks like it was buckshot," Gary observed. "Who have you two managed to stir up?"

"We might have upset Clay Cole," Nick said.

"What did you do to Clay?" Gary asked with a frown.

Nick looked at Lexie, then back at Gary. "Lexie thought he was following her around in town. He made her feel uncomfortable so we went out to his place to have a talk with him. Maybe he took exception to us calling him out."

Gary's frown deepened. "Clay isn't really the type to do something like this. If he has a problem with you he comes at your face in the daylight, not sneaking under the cover of darkness, but I'll certainly check him out. There's also the possibility that it was kids. Last month when old Henry Riley was in the hospital his barn got all shot up and I suspected a couple of kids then."

"Maybe I should contact some of my associates and see if they're willing to come out here and help you with your investigation," Lexie said with a quick glance at Nick.

"Your associates?" Gary looked at her with interest.

"Lexie's an FBI agent," Nick said, oddly satisfied by the stunned surprise on Gary's face.

Gary stared at Lexie. "Is that true?" She nodded and he rocked back on his heels. "Look, this is a local matter, there's no need to get anyone else involved." He took a step closer to Lexie. "I know you feel like I didn't do my job where your sister was concerned, but I did everything in my power under the circumstances. Now I intend to do everything in my power to find out who's responsible for this and what's going on. If after I do my investigative work you still feel like you need to call in somebody else, then by all means do so."

"I just want some answers," Lexie replied. "Why would somebody do something like this? It's obvious somebody wanted to either warn me or kill me and I want to know why."

"So do I," Gary said grimly. "This is Widow Creek, not Chicago and I won't tolerate drive-by shootings and such nonsense in my town. I've got a couple of kids I want to talk to about this and I'll also talk to Clay.

I definitely intend to get to the bottom of things."

Nick wondered if he'd underestimated Gary. He certainly seemed to be taking this issue seriously. "I'm going to take Lexie to my place for the rest of the night," he said and steeled himself for a protest from her, but she said nothing.

"We'll need to board up this window," Gary said and once again looked at Lexie. "I don't want the missing window to be an open invitation for somebody to come in and steal. You know if your sister had any ply-wood anywhere?"

"I think I remember seeing some in the garage," she replied.

Gary looked at Nick. "Why don't we go take a look and see what we can use."

Together the two men left the house and headed for the garage. "I'm hoping this is just a case of maybe some teenagers who thought the house was empty and decided to have a little fun," Gary said. "But I gotta tell you, Nick. I've got a bad feeling about this."

"That makes three of us," Nick replied as he opened the garage door. He flipped on the light and saw that behind Lauren's car was a stack of plywood that could be used to cover the broken window.

"I'll admit I didn't jump on the fact that Lauren was missing as fast as I should have," Gary said. He leaned against the bumper of the car. "Hell, she was a grown woman and I figured if she didn't want to be found by her sister it was her choice. But when we found her body on the creek bed there was no question in my mind about what had happened, about how she had died." He rubbed his forehead as if he had the beginning of a headache. "Now, I'm going to have to rethink this whole thing, see what I missed and try to figure out what in the hell is going on around here."

For the first time in days Nick felt a bit of relief flood through him. He'd much rather have Gary on their side than thinking he and Lexie were a couple of conspiracy nuts.

"Nick, I probably wasn't the most sensitive man when your wife died and I've always been sorry about the way things wound up between us."

The apology shocked Nick. He knew how proud Gary was and the effort it cost him to say the words that had just fallen out of his mouth. "Water under the bridge," Nick replied gruffly. "Come on, let's get the window boarded up and then hopefully you can find out who in this town decided to pop off several rounds tonight," Nick said.

It took twenty minutes for the plywood to be put into place and then with Gary gone Nick and Lexie got to work cleaning up the broken glass.

"I hate to impose on you by staying at your house," she said, breaking the silence that had lingered between them since Gary had left.

"Nonsense, I have plenty of room and I wouldn't feel comfortable with you staying here alone after this," he replied. "Gary apologized to me out in the garage for the way he handled things when Danielle disappeared."

"That was big of him."

"It was," he agreed. "I definitely think he wants to find out who is responsible for this."

"I just feel like we're missing something." She leaned on the broom, her brow wrinkled in thought. "If Lauren's death was nothing more than an accident, then why would my presence here make somebody nervous enough to shoot up the house?"

"You're assigning a motive to the shooting that we don't know for sure is true," he replied. "It could have been bored teenagers out for a little rowdy fun who thought Lauren's house would be empty."

"You're right," she said and began to sweep using more force than necessary. "I'm just so frustrated."

"I know. Maybe by morning Gary will have some answers for us." Even as he said the words he didn't believe them and he had a feeling Lexie didn't believe them either.

It was almost nine o'clock when they finally left Lauren's place and headed to Nick's. Lexie had packed her things in a small suitcase that was loaded in the backseat along with Zeus, his food and water bowls and a huge bag of dog food.

Lexie had once again fallen silent and Nick didn't know what to say, what to do to bring her out of the shell she'd crawled into.

There was no question that he was worried about what had happened tonight. One of those bullets could have easily found either one of them. Who had shot the gun? What had they hoped to accomplish? Had it simply been some of the wild teenagers in town or had it been something darker...more dangerous? He shoved these thoughts aside as he pulled into his driveway.

When they got into his house the first thing they did was introduce Zeus to Taz. The little pooch raced around Zeus's legs until Zeus gave a warning growl. Taz hunkered down in front of the bigger dog, properly chastised.

Nick led Lexie to one of the guest rooms, wishing instead that she would warm his bed for the night, wanting a repeat of the lovemaking they'd shared before.

But he had a feeling that it had been emotional trauma and nothing more that had driven her into his arms on the night that Lauren's body had been found.

"Make yourself at home," he said as she placed her suitcase on the floor next to the bed. "The bathroom is across the hall, and if you need anything just let me know."

He suddenly realized he wanted her to need him. He wanted her to sleep with him because she wanted him more than any other man on the face of the earth. He wanted her driven by passion and desire and nothing more and it scared the hell out of him. He murmured a quick good-night, leaving her alone, and went back downstairs.

He checked that the doors were all locked and was surprised to find Taz curled up tight against Zeus's side in front of the fireplace. It looked like the two were going to be best buddies. Good. He wanted Zeus to have a home here. It was the least he could do in honor of the friend he'd lost and her sister.

When he climbed the stairs once again and got into his bedroom he sat on the edge of the bed and picked up the photo of Danielle from the nightstand. She had definitely been his one arrow. He'd loved her as deeply as a man could ever love a woman.

When they'd lost their baby he'd tried to be strong for her, thinking she needed his stoic strength, his broad shoulders. Then she'd accused him of not caring, of not grieving deeply and hard enough for the child they'd lost. He'd been unable to give her what she needed from him and there was a dark place in his heart that believed that was ultimately what had led to her suicide.

There was no question his feelings for Lexie were deepening with every moment he spent with her, but could he trust himself to try to be everything for a woman again?

He'd already been there, done that and failed miserably.

He realized that as much as he desired Lexie, as much as he wanted only good things for her, he would never be willing to step up and try to have a long-term relationship with another woman.

LEXIE AWOKE WITH THE SUN streaming through the windows in Nick's guest room. She remained laying in bed, her mind flittering over the events of the night and dreading those to come.

Today the breeder was coming to take the rest of Lauren's dogs. Eventually she'd have to arrange for the sale of the house, and then there would be nothing left to mark the fact that Lauren had ever lived here in Widow Creek.

Lauren had come here with such high hopes, so excited to finally have the space, the perfect place and the opportunity to achieve her dreams. She'd been charmed by the small town, had raved about the people she was meeting each time she and Lexie had spoken on the phone.

Lauren had never mentioned anyone making

her feel uncomfortable or scared in her new home. She'd only had positive things to say about Widow Creek.

Unexpected tears burned at Lexie's eyes, and she knew they weren't only tears for Lauren, but were also tears for herself. She knew she was offbeat, considered different by most people, but Lauren had always understood her. Lauren knew of her innate shyness, of her awkwardness when in a group of people. Lauren understood all that pieces that made up Lexie and now Lauren was gone forever.

She rolled over on her back and after wiping the tears away with the back of her hand, reached for her glasses on the nightstand. She put them on and as her thoughts once again turned to the night before a slow burn set off in her stomach.

There was something rotten in Widow Creek. She had no idea what it was or how deeply embedded the rot was, but there was no question in her mind that something was wrong here.

Had Lauren been murdered? The gunfire of the night before certainly made her believe that her presence here in town asking questions about her sister had made somebody very nervous. It was just too coincidental and Lexie didn't believe in that kind of coincidence.

Her thoughts turned to Nick. If she allowed herself, she realized she could be more than half-crazy about him. He was solid as a rock and sometimes when he looked at her she felt a shiver inside, a shiver of need, of want that she'd never felt before.

She would have liked nothing better than to crawl into his bed last night, but she'd also known it would be a mistake on her part.

With a sigh she rolled out of bed, grabbed clean clothes for the day and then darted across the hallway to the bathroom. She took a quick shower, used a squeeze of gel to spike her hair and then went in search of Nick.

She followed the scent of fresh-brewed coffee down the stairs to the kitchen, but instead of finding him there she found a note from him letting her know he was outside doing morning chores.

Both Taz and Zeus greeted her and after lots of scratching behind all ears, the two dogs stretched out on the kitchen floor side by side. Lexie looked at the big dog that Lauren had loved and once again her heart squeezed tight with pain.

Zeus would be happy here with Nick, she told herself. He already looked as if he'd made friends with the young pup next to him. Lauren would definitely be okay with this arrangement and Lexie found some peace at that thought.

She poured herself a cup of coffee and then, too restless to sit, she wandered back into the living room. This was a house meant for a family and as she thought about the baby and wife that Nick had lost her heart found a new ache, this time for him.

Lexie hadn't ever really had her heart broken. Oh, she'd thought at the time that Michael Andrews had broken it, but with time and distance away from his betrayal, she'd realized it hadn't been love that had driven her into his arms, only an intense loneliness.

He'd confirmed to her something that she'd always known deep in her heart—the fact that she was an outsider and would never have a real place that she belonged. Oh, she was good for a change of pace, a little walk on the weird side, but when it came to choosing somebody for a long-term relationship, Lexie would always be the one left behind for a more traditional woman.

She found herself climbing the stairs to the bedrooms and going past the room where she'd slept. She knew she was being nosy, but she wanted to see Nick's room.

The master suite was at the end of the hallway. She stood in the doorway and breathed in the scent of him that lingered in the air. She'd always felt safe and secure because she was an FBI agent and carried a gun, but there was no question that Nick made her feel safe and secure in a much different, more provocative kind of way.

She stared at the bed with its rumpled white sheets. The sheets would smell of him, perhaps still retain some of his body heat and there was nothing more she wanted at that moment than to climb in and close her eyes and wait for him to come back into the house and find her there.

Her gaze fell on the photograph on the nightstand and as she gazed at the attractive blonde woman her impulse to crawl into his bed died a sudden death.

Danielle.

His one arrow.

She was a pretty blonde with a bright smile. Her hair fell to her shoulders in soft waves and she was clad in a very proper dress in a mute shade of gold.

Nick had told her that Danielle had been a traditional kind of woman, one who enjoyed working as secretary for the mayor but also loved to bake cookies and work the social events the town offered.

Lexie was the antithesis of Danielle. She worked a job that put her in contact with criminals, wouldn't know how to bake a cookie that didn't come in a plastic tube and wanted to crawl out of her skin when surrounded by too many people.

The photo was a physical reminder to Lexie that Nick's heart had already been taken and that he didn't believe he had any part of his heart left to give to another.

Maybe he was helping her because he hadn't been able to help his wife. Maybe if he could be what Lexie needed him to be to get through this rough time, it would assuage some of the guilt she knew he felt over his wife's suicide. She wanted that for him. It would be nice if when she left this godforsaken place at least one of them would have complete peace.

She shoved these troubling thoughts to the back of her mind and hurried back down the stairs. She had just sat at the table when he came in the back door, bringing with him fresh autumn-scented air and a warm smile.

"I see you found the coffee," he said as he shrugged out of his jacket, exposing a revolver shoved into his waistband. He saw her look of surprise as he pulled out the revolver and laid it on the countertop. "Don't worry, I'm licensed to carry. After last night I decided I'd rather be armed and dangerous than unarmed and helpless."

"You're a smart man, Nick Walker," she replied dryly.

He poured himself a cup of coffee and joined her at the table. "Did you sleep okay?"

"Surprisingly well, given the events of the night," she replied. She took a sip of her coffee and tried not to notice how hot he looked in his jeans and tight, long-sleeved pullover. She didn't want to fall victim of his bedroom eyes and lose herself in a fantasy that would never come true.

"Want some breakfast?" he asked.

"No, coffee is fine for now," she replied.

"Want to talk about last night?"

"Until we have more information there isn't much to talk about," she countered. "Before we leave to meet the breeder I'm going to call my boss, Director Andrew Grimes, and let him know what's been happening here. I also need to tell him that I'm taking off some additional time until I'm satisfied with the investigation into Lauren's death."

"I'd like you to stay here with me until you decide to leave town. I definitely believe in the old adage that there's safety in numbers."

She didn't think it was a great idea, but Lexie also wasn't a fool. She recognized that she'd be safer if she was here with him rather than all alone at Lauren's place.

"If it's not too much of an imposition," she replied.

Again he flashed her that smile that warmed every cold inch that might linger in her body. "You're always worried about it being an imposition and you know it isn't. I like having you here. This house has been silent for far too long." He got up from the table. "And now I'm going to rustle me up some breakfast and then it will be time to head over to Lauren's to meet with the breeder."

He talked her into eating pancakes with him and once they cleaned up the mess it was time to head back to Lauren's place. The sight of the plywood where glass should have been in the front window sprang the terror of those few minutes of gunfire back into Lexie's brain.

It had been nothing short of a miracle that neither she nor Nick had been seriously hurt. What the shooting had done was lit a fire inside her to get to the bottom of things.

As they got out of the car the dogs in the pen at the side of the house greeted them with raucous barks of excitement. "Why don't I take care of feeding and watering the pups and you head inside and relax until Linetta gets here," Nick said.

Lexie nodded her agreement and they parted ways, Nick heading to the dog pen and Lexie stepping inside the house. With the front window boarded up the living room was dark. She flipped on a light and looked around and for a moment felt the aching absence of her sister.

She walked over to a bookcase where

dozens of figurines of dogs were displayed. She found the German shepherd that Lauren had bought on the day she'd gotten Zeus.

Lexie picked it up and carried it into the kitchen where she wrapped it in a paper towel and then put it in her purse. It was just a cheap, silly piece of ceramic, but it had been Lauren's prized possession and it was the only thing Lexie wanted from this house.

She'd arrange for a local charity to take most of the items and then would list the place with a Realtor in the area. Hopefully it would sell quickly and Lexie wouldn't have to worry about being out of town with a vacant property to worry about.

She sat at the table and fought against a wave of sadness that threatened to overwhelm her. Funny in a sad kind of way that an entire lifetime could be packed up in boxes and given away to charity, she thought.

At least she didn't have to give up her memories of the sister she had loved. She only wished she and Lauren had taken time to make more memories with each other.

She had no time for sadness anymore. She needed to figure out why somebody had driven up the night before and fired bullets into the front window. She needed to know for certain if Lauren had really slipped and fallen to her death or if foul play had been involved.

Nick came into the kitchen. "All taken care of," he said as he went to the sink to wash his hands. Once he was finished he joined her at the table.

"I'm not weak," she said, and saw the momentary confusion that shadowed his eyes. She winced inwardly, aware that she should have prefaced her statement in some way. As usual her form of communication was awkward.

"I never thought you were," he replied.

She took off her glasses and leaned back in the chair. "I'm strong and decisive when I'm in front of a computer. I'm respected at work and I do a good job. I'm perfectly capable of taking care of myself and have never needed much from anyone."

"Why are you telling me this?"

She picked up her glasses and put them back on. "I just need you to understand that I'm not some weak, pathetic woman who needs a white knight to ride to her rescue."

He smiled at her. "Do I really look like a

white knight? And keep in mind I do wear socks to bed every night."

"I just don't want to be your redemption."

He sat back in his chair and looked at her in confusion. "Lexie, what are you talking about?"

"Your wife. I'm talking about Danielle. I know you somehow blame yourself for her death." She saw his eyes darken and knew she'd touched a nerve. "I just don't want you to be here with me because you somehow feel that if you help me it will be your key to salvation."

"You obviously think too much. I'm here because I liked Lauren and more importantly because I like you. It's no more or less complicated than that."

At that moment the dogs outside began to bark, signaling the arrival of the breeder. Both Lexie and Nick got up to go outside to greet her.

Linetta Stone was built like a professional football tackle. Her short gray hair was tightly permed as if she had neither the time nor the inclination to deal with it. She was clad in a red flannel shirt and a pair of worn jeans and looked like a woman who didn't take crap from anyone.

As she climbed out of her truck her gaze was sharp and darted in all directions as if seeking any source of trouble that might come her way.

"Morning," she finally said.

Introductions were made and a hint of softness lit her eyes as she shook Lexie's hand. "Sorry to hear about your sister," she said. She rocked back on her heels and once again swept the area. "I have to admit, I was a little reluctant to drive in here, but I did a search on your sister and everything seemed to look legit."

"Why were you reluctant?" Nick asked.

"Widow Creek has a bit of a reputation. I thought it might be some sort of a scam. You know, where I get out here and somebody hits me over the head and takes any money I might have with me." She barked a laugh. "Although the joke would be on them, only thing I have in my wallet is my driver's license and an old picture of Blue, the first dog I ever owned."

"Why would you worry about somebody knocking you over the head?" Lexie asked.

"Drug fiends," Linetta said in a lowered voice. "This town is full of them."

Lexie looked at the older woman in surprise. "What kind of drugs?"

"Rumor has it Widow Creek is the place to come if you want meth. They make it and sell it out of their bathrooms, their sheds, their closets."

"Who does? Who makes it and sells it?" Lexie asked. Her mind boggled at this new piece of information.

Linetta's big shoulders moved up and down in a shrug. "I don't know who. It's just rumors. I heard it from my grandkid. He's sixteen and he's been told I'll take off a stripe of his hide if I ever hear he was in or around Widow Creek. Now, let's go take a look at those dogs."

As Lexie followed her to the pen her mind worked to digest what she'd just heard. Was it possible there was a major meth operation here in Widow Creek?

She knew enough about the making of methamphetamine to know that it could be manufactured in a bathroom or in a shed. The ingredients were easily obtained and it certainly didn't take a chemistry degree to put them all together. But here in Widow Creek? Wouldn't Nick have heard rumors about such a thing?

It didn't take long for Linetta to leave the pen and return to where Nick and Lexie awaited her. "They're terrific. They have friendly personalities and their overall health looks to be good. I'm sure I can find homes for all of them with no problems."

Minutes later Lexie watched as Nick and Linetta loaded the dogs into the cages waiting in the back of the breeder's truck. When the final dog was loaded and Linetta waved a goodbye and got into the truck, Lexie felt as if the last pieces of her sister were driving away from the house.

Nick looped an arm around her shoulder and she leaned against him and watched until the truck disappeared from sight. "You ready to head back to my place?" he asked.

She nodded and stepped away from him, her mind still working to process what she'd just learned from Linetta. It wasn't until she got into Nick's pickup that pieces began to fit together in her mind.

A rush of adrenaline filled her as Nick started the engine. "Did you know that

Lauren was about to start training drug-sniffing dogs?"

"No, I didn't know that," he replied. He fastened his seat belt and then turned to look at her. "I seem to be asking you this all the time, but what are you thinking?"

"I'm thinking I might have just stumbled upon a motive for murder," she replied and watched his eyes widen in surprise.

Chapter Nine

"Think about it," Lexie said. "There's a big drug operation going on in the area and the people behind it discover that my sister is about to start training drug-sniffing dogs."

They were back in Nick's kitchen and seated at his table. Zeus was sleeping at Lexie's feet and Taz was chewing on a rawhide treat.

"And maybe the people in charge of the operation saw Lauren's newest venture as a threat to their business," Nick replied. "The last thing they'd want is a drug-sniffing dog running around town alerting on people and places. What this theory doesn't tell us is who is responsible...and it is just a theory," he reminded her.

She looked more alive than she had since the discovery of Lauren's body. Her green eyes snapped with life and a wild energy radiated from her, an energy that called to him, that made him want to sweep her into his arms and carry her up the stairs and into his bedroom.

Instead he tried to keep his mind focused on the conversation at hand. "But, it's the first real theory we've come up with," she replied. "And now what we need to do is prove or disprove it."

He frowned. "And how exactly do you intend to go about doing that?"

"I need to spend some more time in town, ask some subtle questions and see what kind of answers I get."

He gave her a wry grin. "You aren't exactly the subtle type, Lexie. I just don't want you to stir up somebody who decides to take pot-shots at us in the night again. The next time they might get lucky and actually hit one or both of us."

As much as he liked her, there was no doubt in his mind that, if what she believed was true, her style of asking questions would put a very large target on her back. Lexie was about as subtle as a pit bull.

Her cheeks grew pink. "You're right. But if I just hang out in town I should at least be able to tell if somebody is using or not. People using meth aren't able to fly under the radar very well."

"Euphoria, paranoia, acne, sores, weight loss, a lack of personal hygiene." He smiled as she looked at him in surprise. "Don't worry, I learned everything I know about it from a documentary on television. I like documentaries—it's one of those nerdy things about me. You know, we could ask Gary what kind of a problem drug use is in the town."

She shook her head. "I'd rather keep this to ourselves for the time being."

"You still don't trust Gary?" he asked.

Her beautiful green eyes held his in a gaze he felt pierce clear through to his heart. "The only person I have left in the world that I trust without question right now is you, Nick."

In that moment Nick felt as if he'd been given a precious gift. He had a feeling Lexie wasn't a woman who trusted easily, and the fact that she trusted him made him want to jump up and grab the moon for her if that's what she needed.

"So, what's the game plan, Agent Forbes?" he asked.

She gave him a tight smile. "I'm thinking

we go to the café for dinner tonight and then maybe find out if we can figure out where the young people hang out when the sun goes down. If anyone knows if there are drugs available here in Widow Creek it's probably going to be the teenagers."

Nick leaned back in his chair, a slow burn of anxiety beginning in his gut. "If what you think is true, then these people are very dangerous. They've killed Lauren and could have killed both of us."

She narrowed her eyes slightly. "So, does that mean you want out? Nick, I'd certainly understand if you do. This isn't your battle to fight."

"Of course it's my battle. This is my town." It was the easy answer, but the truth of the matter was it had become his battle the moment his mouth had taken hers on the night they'd made love. It had become his battle when he'd held her in his arms as she'd cried over her sister's death.

"I think maybe I'll take a little nap, if you don't mind," she said as she pushed back from the table. "It's been kind of a stressful morning."

"Go on, get some rest," he replied. "We'll talk about everything else later."

As she disappeared from the kitchen Nick remained seated in his chair. He realized that saying goodbye to Lauren's dogs had been more difficult for her than she'd let on.

It had been the same for him when he'd donated Danielle's clothing and shoes to a local charity. It had been almost six months after her death and he'd thought he was ready, but folding the clothes and placing them in boxes, picking up the shoes and remembering when she'd worn them last had slammed his grief back into him in a way he hadn't expected.

His mind shifted back to his conversation with Lexie. Drugs in Widow Creek? Nick didn't want to believe it, but during the past year he hadn't spent a lot of time in town. He'd isolated himself too much, he realized. He'd pulled his grief around him and wallowed in it and it was past time he changed that.

It was time he find out what was going on in his hometown, time he stop isolating himself and truly integrate himself back into life in Widow Creek.

Every town probably had a drug problem

of sorts, but Nick knew from the documentary he'd watched that meth had become the scourge of small-town America. Meth labs were dangerous not only because of the drug they produced, but also because of the chemicals needed to make that drug.

He got up from the table and went up the stairs. He passed the guest room where Lexie had gone. The door was closed and he hoped she was resting peacefully. Between the funeral yesterday and the shooting and then giving the dogs away today, she had to be emotionally exhausted.

He went on into his bedroom and instantly saw the photo of Danielle on his nightstand. As always his heart squeezed at the sight of her, but this time his grief wasn't the cutting, breath-stealing force it had always been. It was simply the ache of loss that was natural after saying goodbye to a loved one.

Was his desire to help Lexie his need to somehow find some sort of redemption as she'd suggested? Did he believe that in being there for Lexie he could mitigate some of the guilt he felt about Danielle?

He didn't believe it. The minute he'd seen Lexie she had touched him in a way he hadn't been touched in a very long time. That night that he'd met her in Lauren's house it should have been easy for him to walk away from her, but he'd been unable to do so.

Her awkwardness drew him, her quirky little smile warmed him and there were moments now when he couldn't imagine what his life would be like when she was gone.

But he knew he couldn't think that way. Lexie didn't belong here. She had her life, her work in Kansas City. Once she had the answers she needed to find peace, she would be gone. And besides, he had already made the decision that he was destined to live here alone.

Zeus came running into the room, chased by the rascal Taz. Both dogs stopped in their tracks at the sight of him, as if they were two kids caught with their hands in the cookie jar. Deciding they both could use a run outside, he placed the picture of Danielle in the nightstand drawer and then left the bedroom and headed downstairs, the dogs close at his heels.

He sat on the deck and watched the two dogs frolic in the fallen leaves and went over things in his mind. He didn't know what to believe about Lauren's death and the drug angle. All he knew was that he was in this until the end…even though he knew that in the end he would have to tell Lexie goodbye.

It was almost six o'clock when Nick and Lexie left the house to go into town for dinner. She'd awakened an hour earlier and had showered and changed, but had been unusually quiet since leaving the bedroom.

"You should be starving," he said once they were in the truck and headed into Widow Creek. "You slept through lunch and you didn't do much more than pick at your breakfast."

"I wasn't sleeping the whole time. I called my boss and checked in with him and then called a friend of mine, a fellow agent, Amberly Nightsong, and yes, I am a little bit hungry, but I'd rather get information than food."

"Let's hope we get both," Nick replied.

They fell silent once again and not for the first time Nick wished he could get inside her head, see what she was thinking, know exactly what she was feeling.

When had it happened? When in the course of the five days since he'd met her had her thoughts become so important to him? When had his need to know everything about her become so intense?

She remained quiet through their meal at the Cowboy Corral, eating very little and instead keeping her attention focused on the other diners.

Nick saw nobody that he thought might be under the influence of drugs. He also saw none of the teenagers of the town inside the restaurant.

"You might try eating some of that food instead of moving it around on your plate," he said.

She looked down at the chicken-fried steak dinner she'd ordered and then up at him. "You're food obsessed."

He smiled. "And you don't eat enough to keep a bird alive."

"That's not true. I can eat my weight in hot wings."

He laughed. "I'd like to see that."

"I should probably warn you, it usually involves a six-pack of beer at the same time." Her smile fell and once again her gaze darted around the room.

"You know, we might have more luck tomorrow night," he said as they lingered over coffee. "It's Thursday night and school is in session. It's doubtful any of the teens would be out late tonight doing illegal activities. We'd probably have better luck tomorrow or Saturday night."

"That makes sense," she agreed reluctantly. She picked up her cup and took a sip. "Maybe Linetta Stone's rumors were just that, silly rumors with no fact." Her voice held a weariness of spirit that reached inside him and squeezed his heart.

"Lexie, just because we didn't find what we were looking for in a two-hour meal on a Thursday night doesn't mean that what we're looking for isn't here."

"You're right," she replied and sat up straighter in her chair. "I'm just impatient. Lauren used to tell me all the time that unlike my computer where things happen with the click of the mouse, real life requires more patience."

"We'll come back tomorrow night," he promised. "And the night after that and the night after that. We'll do this however long it takes for you to get some peace of mind. And after we eat dinner if we don't see anybody who might give us some answers we'll drive around town and find out where the kids all hang out."

"Where did you hang out when you were a teenager?" she asked when they were in his truck and headed back to his house.

"When I was young there was a bowling alley and a movie theater and most weekends that's where all the kids gathered. But both of those businesses closed down years ago. What about you? Where did you hang out?" he asked, hoping to steer the conversation away from drugs and Lauren's death at least for a few minutes.

"I didn't hang out a lot when I was a teenager. Occasionally Lauren would twist my arm and I'd reluctantly go with her and some of her friends to a pizza place where a lot of the kids hung out. As I'm sure you've noticed, I'm not at my best in a crowd, so I didn't go often. I spent a lot of time with my dad," she replied.

"What was he like?" He cast her a quick glance and saw the softening of her features as she thought of her father.

"He was the best," she replied. "He took us fishing and painted our fingernails. He baked cookies for school functions and taught us how to play basketball. He was both mom and dad to us and did a good job at being both. He knew I struggled with my shyness, with my awkwardness, but he always made me feel special. When he died I knew I'd lost my best champion."

"There hasn't been any other important man in your life?"

She gazed out the side window. "Only Michael, and I already told you about him." She turned back to look at him. "I thought he might be my one real Cupid's arrow, but he was just a silly misfire."

She sat up straighter in the seat as he pulled into his drive. "I just wish I knew whether we were onto something here or if we're just spinning our wheels."

"Hopefully we'll know by the end of the weekend," he replied. "If we take each troubling incident separately they don't add up to much. You saw somebody in the back of Lauren's place lurking in the middle of the night right before her body was found. You believe that Lauren's body was placed on the creek bed long after she was killed. Somebody shot up Lauren's place. When you add them altogether and throw in a drug angle, it's all more than troubling. It feels criminal."

"So, you don't think I'm crazy?" she asked.

"Definitely not," he replied as he pulled up in front of his house.

As they walked inside Taz and Zeus greeted them with happy barks. Nick tried not to think about how right it felt for Lexie to be by his side, tried not to notice how the house filled with her very presence.

It was going to be hard for him when she went back to Kansas City. The house would once again radiate with the emptiness that had become all too familiar over the last year of his life. Dogs were great companions, but they didn't quite take the place of human beings.

"You want some more coffee?" he asked as they went into the kitchen. "I could make a pot."

"No thanks. I drank enough coffee for one day."

"How about a glass of wine?"

She hesitated a moment and then nodded. "Sure, that would be great. White if you have it."

"I do," he replied. "Why don't you make

yourself comfortable in the living room and I'll bring it to you."

"Sounds like a plan." She left the kitchen with the dogs trailing at her heels.

Nick poured them each a glass of wine and then carried it into the living room where she was seated on the sofa. He handed her a glass and then sank down next to her.

Throughout the evening he'd been acutely aware of her on a physical level. He'd found the familiar scent of her intoxicating and couldn't help but notice the way her green sweater hugged her breasts.

It had been difficult for him to keep his mind on the reason they had been in the café, difficult to keep his mind away from the night they'd made love.

He wanted her again. He wanted to taste her lips, feel the warmth of her naked in his arms. It was more than a simple want, it was a growing need that was getting more and more difficult to ignore.

"Tell me about the fall festival," she said. She took off her glasses and set them on the coffee table and then leaned back against the sofa cushion. "You mentioned it was one of

the things that brought the whole town together."

"It's always the first week in November.
The stores close down for the day and Main
Street becomes a playground for everyone.
The mayor's office provides a bean feast with
pots of beans and corn bread. There are pie-
eating contests and carnival rides and something to bring a smile to everyone's faces."

"Sounds wonderful," she replied.

"It's definitely small town at its best." He
stared down into his wine glass, recognizing
that in all probability when the fall festival
in less than a month occurred Lexie would
be long gone. "Maybe you could come back
here for the festival."

"Maybe," she agreed, but he had a feeling
they both knew that it was doubtful that once
she left she'd ever return to Widow Creek,
except occasionally to visit her sister's grave.

"More wine?" he asked as he noticed her
glass was empty.

"Maybe just a little."

He got up from the sofa and returned to the
kitchen for the bottle and used the opportunity to attempt to tamp down the desire that

seemed to be building to mammoth proportions as the night continued.

He returned to the living room and any efforts he thought he'd made to get control of his hormones vanished. He felt like a nervous teenager out with the prettiest cheerleader, desperate to make a move on her, but afraid at the same time.

He poured her wine and set the bottle on the table, then leaned back and smiled at her. "You look pretty tonight. You should wear green more often."

She smiled self-consciously and reached for her glasses. "Thanks. You look very nice yourself." She put her glasses back on, took a sip of her wine and then ran her tongue over her top lip.

The desire that had been simmering inside him all night long exploded into a flame. "Lexie." Her name escaped his lips of its own volition. He set his glass on the coffee table and then reached out and removed hers from her hand and placed it next to his.

Her eyes widened behind her glasses, as if she knew his intent. He wrapped his hand around the back of her neck and gently pulled her toward him.

Chapter Ten

His mouth was hot against hers and tasted of wine and a heady intoxication flooded through her veins. He was an assault on every one of her senses. The familiar scent of him filled her head, the heat of his mouth warmed her to her toes and when he reached to embrace her she allowed him to pull her closer... closer still.

She wanted him like she needed her next breath, desperately, viscerally. And ultimately it was the depth of her want of him that forced her away from him and to her feet.

"Nick, we can't do this anymore." Her own breathlessness surprised her. "I don't want you to kiss me anymore." Her gaze fled to the furthest corner of the room.

"I'm sorry," he replied. "I...I guess I got my signals crossed."

Her cheeks flushed pink. "No, I've probably been giving off mixed signals to you." She pulled off her glasses and rubbed her eyes as unexpected tears stung. "I want you, Nick, but I just don't think it's a good idea for us to be intimate again. I'll be leaving here as soon as I get some answers and I've never been good with casual sex." *Or goodbyes*, she thought.

"It didn't seem casual to me," he replied, his eyes dark and enigmatic.

"But we both know that's what it was," she replied. She hesitated a beat, giving him an opportunity to make her believe otherwise. When he didn't say anything she released a deep sigh.

"I think I'll just call it a night," she said and although she put her glasses back on her eyes didn't quite meet his. "I'll just see you in the morning."

She felt as if this had been a defining moment, that something had happened that had forever changed things between them.

What had changed was that the little bit of hope Lexie hadn't even realized she'd entertained in her heart about Nick had just died. It had been the hope that his heart might be capable of realizing love for a second time in his life, the hope that he might be falling in love with her.

She had to tell him goodbye.

Lexie sat on the edge of the bed in the guest bedroom and knew she had to get away from Nick. She was in love with him. It had crept upon her insidiously, without warning. It had been fed not only by his warm smile and sense of humor, but also by his seemingly easy acceptance of all that she was as a woman—and of all that she wasn't.

She had to get out before things went any deeper. Already it was going to pierce her very core to have to tell him goodbye.

With this thought in mind she grabbed her cell phone out of her purse and made a call. When she hung up after having a long conversation with her friend and coworker Amberly Nightsong, she waited for the sense of relief to flood through her. But there was no relief, only sadness as she realized it was time for her to make some changes.

It was just her luck, to fall in love with a man who was emotionally unavailable. First Michael the jerk, and then Nick, a man who had known a love so great it was apparently enough to last him a lifetime despite the fact that the woman he loved was dead.

She couldn't even be mad at Nick. He'd warned her from the very beginning that he'd had his one arrow shot in the heart and wasn't looking for another. It was her own fault for being foolish enough to fall in love with him.

She changed into her nightgown and got into bed, her heart as heavy as a stone. In the very depths of her soul she'd always worried that she'd been destined to be alone, to never really know the wonder of a man's love. She squeezed her eyes tightly closed as tears once again burned.

There had been moments when she'd thought she'd felt love from Nick, when his eyes had glowed with emotion, when his kiss had tasted of not just desire, but of something deeper, something more profound. She'd been a fool.

Time and distance, that what's she needed. She wasn't ready to leave Widow Creek, but it was time she left Nick Walker and gave herself time to heal.

The next morning she carried her suitcase down to the kitchen where she found Nick seated at the table eating a muffin and drinking a cup of coffee. As usual both dogs were at his feet, looking perfectly content to relax in the sunshine that drifted in through the window.

"Good morning," he said and looked pointedly at her suitcase. "Going somewhere?"

"I'm checking into the local motel this morning," she said.

He looked at her in surprise and got out of his chair. "Lexie, if this is about what happened last night—"

"It is…and it isn't," she interrupted him. "Nick, you've given me enough of your time and energy. I appreciate everything you've done for me and all the support you've given me, but this really isn't your battle and it's time I move on."

"Lexie, I don't want you to be alone. I don't think it's safe," he protested.

"I won't be alone," she assured him. "An FBI friend of mine is meeting me at the motel this afternoon. She's going to stay with me for a couple of days. It's better this way, Nick. Better for both of us."

He looked as if he wanted to protest but after a moment he simply nodded. "I guess there's nothing I can say to change your mind." She shook her head and he continued, "Then just know that I'm here for you if you need me."

Although this was exactly what she wanted to hear from him, she couldn't help the small flutter of disappointment that he hadn't tried to change her mind, hadn't insisted that she stay here with him.

"Want to stick around for some breakfast?" he asked.

Again she shook her head. "No, thanks. I'm just going to head on out and get settled in at the motel."

He walked toward her and she steeled herself for his nearness, afraid that somehow she might fall into the gray depths of his eyes and lose herself forever.

He placed his palms on either side of her face and stared deep into her eyes. "Call me, Lexie. Let me know what's going on. Let me know that you're okay. It's important to me, okay?"

His touch made her ache and she fought against the need to lean into him, to feel his arms embrace her one last time. She stepped back and he dropped his hands to his sides.

"I will," she agreed. "And you'll take good care of Zeus?"

"Of course, he's part of my family now."

She thought about how happy she would be to be part of his family and this propelled her out of the kitchen and toward the front door. She was aware of Nick following right behind her, but when she reached the door she didn't stop. She didn't want any long goodbyes. She just wanted to get gone, away from his concerned eyes, away from the scent of him that smelled so much like home.

She didn't stop walking until she reached her car. She opened the door, threw her suitcase in the backseat and only then did she turn to look at him. "Thanks again, Nick."

"Keep in touch, Lexie."

"I will." She slid into the seat, closed her door and started the engine. She refused to look in her rearview mirror as she pulled away. She was afraid that one more glimpse of him might make her cry, and that would be foolish.

She hadn't even cried when Michael had left her and they had dated off and on for months. It was crazy that in six days Nick had managed to get so deep into her heart.

But there was no happy ending and she knew the best thing she could do was cast him out of her thoughts and hope that eventually her heart would forget him.

She checked into the Stop and Sleep Motel, the only such establishment of its kind in the small town. The room held two double beds covered in gold spreads and the gold shag rug on the floor was obviously the original. She might have found it depressing, but she knew when Amberly arrived the decor couldn't matter.

She sat on the bed and thought of the gorgeous Native American woman who would be arriving in the next couple of hours. Amberly worked as a profiler. She was also the single mother of a four-year-old named Max and she and her ex-husband shared custody of the little boy.

Lexie and Amberly had struck up a friendship a little over a year ago. She not only told wonderful stories from her Cherokee grandmother, but she understood all of Lexie's quirks and seemed to accept them.

Amberly arrived just after noon. Her butt-length black hair was pulled back in a careless chignon and eyes as dark as tar pits snapped with energy as she carried in her suitcase.

"Nothing like a little road trip to get the juices flowing," she said as she gave Lexie a hug. She stepped back from her and frowned. "You look like you've been beaten up with a tired stick."

Lexie smiled. "It's good to see you, too."

"I'm so sorry about Lauren."

Lexie's heart constricted in her chest as she nodded. "Sit down and let me tell you about everything that's happened."

It took nearly two hours for Lexie to share with Amberly everything that had happened since she'd arrived in Widow Creek. "But I really didn't invite you here to get involved in my investigation. I just didn't want to stay here in the motel by myself and I knew I'd enjoy your company for a couple of days."

"I'm interested in your theory of what's going on here, but I'm equally interested in this Nick Walker," Amberly said when Lexie was finished.

"Why?" Lexie asked in surprise.

"Because he obviously means something to you. It's evident every time you say his name. You get a soft, gooey look in your eyes."

Lexie felt her face fill with heat. "I do not," she exclaimed and then released a sigh. "In any case it doesn't matter. He's a widower still very much tied to his dead wife." As she told Amberly about Danielle's suicide she tried not to allow her emotions full rein.

"My grandmother would say that the moon god has captured his heart and refuses to let it go to find love again."

"Is that an old Cherokee legend?" Lexie asked.

Amberly flashed a bright smile. "No, that's a Granny Nightsong legend. She was an expert at making things up to fit any circumstance."

Lexie grinned at her. "I would have loved your granny. How are things at work?" Lexie asked in an attempt to keep the conversation away from Nick.

"Slow, which is good."

"And how's Max?"

Again the beautiful smile swept over Amberly's features. "He's the most amazing kid on the face of the earth."

"And what about men? Are you seeing anyone?"

Amberly shook her head. "Right now I

have a good relationship with John, I have Max and I have my work and that's all I need. Besides, I've pretty much decided no dating until Max is older."

"Have you ever thought about you and John getting back together?" Lexie asked. She knew John and Amberly had been married for three years and had divorced when Max was two, but they seemed to share a special bond that hadn't been broken by the divorce.

"John and I were meant to be best friends, not lovers," she replied.

The two women stayed in the motel room catching up with each other until dinnertime, then headed for the café for their evening meal and to check out the locals.

"I give this place another two or three years and it will be a ghost town," Amberly observed as Lexie drove down Main Street. "It looks like it is already dead and nobody has mentioned it to the people who have remained."

"Just another victim of the bad economy," Lexie said as she pulled into a parking place in front of the café.

"Like so many other small towns," Amberly replied. "It's sad, isn't it? Mayberry towns are dying every day and soon there won't be any left."

As they walked into the busy café Lexie couldn't help but remember the meals she'd eaten here with Nick and she mentally cursed herself for allowing him to get too close, for allowing herself to fall so hard for a man so wrong for her.

She saw the table of teenagers as soon as they were seated in a nearby booth. There were four of them, two boys and two girls, and as the waitress took their orders it was evident by the expression on her face that she found them both rude and obnoxious.

What Lexie couldn't discern from her distance from the four is if it was just normal teenage rebelliousness or something else.

"You know, it's possible the people using in this town aren't teenagers at all. Meth use crosses age, economic and social boundaries," Amberly said softly. "It's the scourge of the earth as far as I'm concerned."

"I'm just hoping we find somebody who is using and can get them to answer some questions," Lexie replied.

Amberly laughed. "You're going to ask them who their source is and they're just going to answer you? That's a little naive, Lexie."

"I didn't say I thought they would answer me, but it doesn't hurt to ask. When I do identify somebody I think is using then I intend to watch them day and night. Eventually they'll take me to their source," Lexie explained.

Amberly leaned forward, her eyes coals of intensity. "Lexie, you're sure what you're doing here? Are you sure you aren't seeing boogeymen in an effort to explain a senseless tragedy?"

"It wasn't imaginary boogeymen who shot up Lauren's place," Lexie replied.

"True, but didn't the chief of police mention that there had been other instances of kids shooting at houses and barns?"

"Yes, but that doesn't explain that Lauren's body wasn't on that rocky shore when I first arrived here and checked." She released a sigh of frustration. "Amberly, have you ever had a gut instinct that you can't dismiss? That's what I feel…that something isn't right here and Lauren got into somebody's way. The drug angle is the only thing that halfway makes sense."

At that moment the waitress arrived to take

their orders. When the meal arrived Lexie picked at the food and kept her focus on the four teenagers. One of the males, dark-haired and slightly unkempt, looked spun, as if he'd been up for days. He scratched his belly and picked at his face and a rush of adrenaline filled Lexie as the four got up and headed to the cashier.

"I've got a live one. You wait here and I'll be right back," she said to Amberly. Before her friend could protest, Lexie slid out of the booth and followed the teens outside.

"Hey," she called after them. The four of them turned as a unit.

"Hey yourself," the dark-haired boy said and then snickered as if he'd been remarkably clever. Up close Lexie could see the acne-like sores that covered his jaw and hovered around his mouth. *Definitely a meth-head,* she thought.

"Cool hair," one of the girls said with a friendly smile.

"Thanks. By the way, I'm Lexie Forbes. I'm new here in Widow Creek."

"And my name is Jimmy Carter," meth-head replied.

The girl with him poked him with her

elbow. "Don't be stupid. He's Jimmy all right, but he's not Jimmy Carter, he's Jimmy Morano." The girl went on to introduce the others and then frowned at Lexie. "Was there something you wanted?"

"I was just wondering what people did for fun around here," Lexie replied. "Any private clubs where you can find something a little more fun than booze?"

Instantly she knew she'd pushed too fast, too hard. Jimmy's eyes narrowed. "What are you, some kind of a narc?"

Lexie forced a silly grin. "Duh, do I look like a narc?" she countered. She allowed the grin to fall. "Look, my sister just died and I'm stuck in this small town until I can sell her house. I can party like a rock star in Kansas City, but I need something now to make me feel better."

"Then go see your doctor," Jimmy replied. He turned on his heels. "Come on, let's get out of here."

As he walked away with two of the others, the girl who had been with him looked at Lexie, her eyes dark and slightly frightened. "You'd be better off going back to Kansas

City to party. You don't want to ask too many questions here in Widow Creek."

Before Lexie could say anything else, the girl whirled around and ran after her friends. As Lexie watched the four head down the sidewalk she knew with a certainty that Jimmy Morano, aka Jimmy Carter, and his girlfriend were her key to solving the mystery of Lauren's death.

All she had to figure out was how to make them cooperate with her before the people in charge got wind that she was onto them and tried to shut her up permanently.

NICK HAD THOUGHT the silence of the house after Danielle had moved out was bad, but the deafening silence that Lexie had left behind was a hundred times worse.

All day Saturday Nick felt her absence in a way he hadn't expected. It rang in the hallways of his house, seeped through the living room and into the kitchen like a gray fog.

He caught up on chores, played with the dogs and wondered what Lexie was doing, if she were eating properly. He worried about that. In his short experience with her, she didn't eat when she needed to. She needed somebody watching over her, making sure she was getting proper nutrition.

Not your job, he reminded himself again and again. She didn't need him to take care of her, she was perfectly capable of taking care of herself.

Still, by dinnertime that night he broke down and called her cell phone, which resulted in a brief, awkward conversation with her assuring him she was just fine.

By five on Sunday night he was sick of his own company and decided to head into town for dinner. The truth of the matter was the café was the only place in town to eat and he was hoping to see Lexie and her friend there.

Disappointment fluttered through him as he walked in and looked around. There was no sign of Lexie, but he told himself it was still relatively early for dinner. He took a stool at the counter and smiled at Marge.

"What's up?" he asked.

"My blood pressure," she replied with a wry grin. "What's up with you? I see you've lost your little sidekick. Did she go back where she came from?"

"No, she's still here in town. She's staying

with a friend. So, what's the special of the day?"

Nick had just finished his burger and fries when they walked in and his heart leapt at the sight of her. Lexie was clad in her usual pair of jeans and wore a purple, sequined long-sleeved T-shirt that hugged her curves like a lover. She was with a tall, attractive Native American woman.

In that first initial glimpse of him a smile of what appeared to be unadulterated joy burst over her features, a smile that quickly tempered into something less.

They nodded to each other and then she and her friend walked toward the back where a booth had become available. It wasn't enough. He realized just seeing her wasn't enough to fill him up.

He waited until they'd given their order to the waitress and then he got up off his stool and walked to their booth. "Hi, Nick. This is my friend, Amberly Nightsong," Lexie said.

"Amberly, nice to meet you," he replied.

"Nick, why don't you join us," Amberly said with a friendly smile.

"I've already eaten, but maybe I could sit for a cup of coffee," he agreed. He slid in next to Lexie, breathed in her familiar scent and tried not to notice how she tensed with his nearness.

"Lexie has told me all about you, Nick," Amberly said.

"And you're still willing to let me sit here with you," he said jokingly.

"I've told her what a support you've been to me," Lexie replied.

"And I appreciate you taking care of my friend," Amberly said.

"It's been my pleasure." In fact, it had been more than his pleasure. Lexie had brought him back to life, filled him with an excitement that had been missing for too long. "Have you managed to find out anything in the last two days?" he asked in a lowered voice.

He tried to stay focused on what Lexie told him about Jimmy Morano instead of dwelling on how much he wanted to take her back to his house, how much he'd like to wake up in the morning with her back under his roof.

"I know the Morano family. George works at the post office and his wife, Sarah, works at the grocery store. Jimmy is their only child.

They'd be appalled if he's gotten himself hooked up in some drug scheme."

"Amberly and I have been following him since Friday night, but so far he hasn't led us anywhere interesting," Lexie said. "But if he's like any meth-head, it won't be long and he'll be contacting his source for a score. When he does I'll have another piece of the puzzle."

"Are you sure it isn't time to take your suspicions to Gary?" he asked.

"Gary?" Amberly looked at Lexie. "Who's Gary?"

"Chief of Police Gary Wendall. And, no, I'm not ready to take this to him," Lexie replied. "I'm not convinced he's completely innocent in whatever is going on in this town."

"I just don't want to see you doing all this alone," Nick said.

"I'm not alone. I have Amberly with me," she replied.

Silence reigned and in that silence Nick realized he was making Lexie uncomfortable. At that moment the waitress arrived with their orders and Nick slid out of the booth. "I'll just leave you two alone to enjoy your meal."

"I thought you were going to have coffee," Amberly protested.

"Nah, I'd better be on my way." He looked at Lexie and was shocked by the wave of sadness that suddenly hit him.

Something had broken between them. When he'd kissed her that last time he could have sworn she'd answered the kiss with a sweet longing. He'd been certain that she wanted him as badly as he wanted her. But she had been right to halt the kiss, to stop whatever might follow.

He stepped out of the café and into the evening autumn air, and a deep depression settled over his shoulders as he headed toward his truck.

He told himself it was for the best, that he had nothing to offer her except a temporary passion. He knew they had been getting in too deep with each other and it was probably a good thing she'd not only called a halt to another night of passion, but also had moved out of his house.

He got into his truck and leaned his head back before starting the engine. She'd blown into Widow Creek, pink hair, sparkly shirts and all, and had turned his life upside down.

Her escape from his last kiss had felt oddly

like a goodbye. What shocked him more than anything was how much he didn't want to tell her goodbye.

Chapter Eleven

"He's hot," Amberly said.

The two women were back in the motel room and in their beds. Lexie didn't pretend not to know exactly who her friend was talking about. "Yes, he is, but that doesn't matter. He's unavailable."

"Such a shame. Still, he looked at you like he wanted to gobble you up for dessert."

"I didn't say he was sexually unavailable," Lexie said dryly. "He's just emotionally unable to move forward in another relationship."

Her heart squeezed tight in her chest. The last person she wanted to talk about at the moment was Nick. The sight of him in the café had been almost more than she'd been able to bear. And when he'd slid in next to her in the booth she'd wanted nothing more than to melt against him in utter surrender.

"I can't believe we're no closer to finding out who Jimmy's source for drugs is," Lexie said in an attempt to change the subject. She rolled over on her side in her bed and looked at Amberly in the bed next to her.

"Maybe Jimmy wasn't tweaking when we saw him Friday night. Maybe he's just a hyper kid with bad skin who isn't fond of good hygiene."

"Maybe, but he looked like he was tweaking to me," Lexie replied.

"Lexie, we followed that kid through the weekend and he didn't do anything more exciting than pick his nose when he thought nobody was looking."

It was true. They'd shadowed Jimmy Morano as he'd left his house on Saturday morning, raked leaves at a neighbor's house for two hours and then hung out with friends in front of an empty store lot. Today had been much the same with them tailing Jimmy as he did nothing out of the ordinary for a teenager. He'd gone to church with his parents then had played a game of tag football with a bunch of other kids in an empty lot and finally had returned home.

Lexie released a deep sigh. To make matters worse, a few minutes earlier Amberly had received a call and needed to return to Kansas City the next day.

Thoughts of Nick once again filled Lexie's mind, just as they had every other minute since she'd left his house.

He haunted her in ways she'd never been haunted before, invading her dreams when she slept and filling her head with memories of their time together.

Driven by grief and need she'd slept with him and now she found herself wishing she'd made love to him one last time with only her love for him driving her into his arms.

Besides seeing him in the café that evening he'd called her the day before, resulting in a brief conversation that had made her feel bereft when they'd hung up. The mere sound of his voice had caused her heart to ache.

"So, what are you going to do about Nick?" Amberly asked, as if she'd been able to read Lexie's thoughts.

Lexie rolled over on her back and stared up at the ceiling. "Nothing. There's nothing to do. He has no desire to be with another woman and, besides, I wouldn't be right for him anyway."

"And why is that?"

Once again Lexie turned to face her friend. "Aside from the fact that he lives and works here and I live and work in Kansas City, Nick is a small-town, traditional kind of man. He'd never really consider a long-term relationship with an offbeat woman like me."

"Lexie, you're the only person who thinks you're offbeat. That's the identity you gave yourself to be different than Lauren. The truth is you're no more offbeat than any other person on this planet."

"You aren't offbeat," Lexie protested.

"The hell I'm not," Amberly exclaimed. "I'll only sleep on the left side of the bed. I make Max wear a necklace and I worry that if he ever loses it or it comes off his neck something bad will happen. I only like mac and cheese if it's burnt and I'm addicted to red licorice. We all have little quirks that others find a little strange."

"But Michael told me I was too weird for him when he broke up with me," Lexie reminded her.

"Lexie, Michael was a dirtbag. He would have tried to convince you that you were an alien if it served his own selfish needs."

A giggle escaped Lexie and for the next hour the two talked about every dreadful date they'd ever been on. It was only when Amberly fell asleep that Lexie's thoughts once again went to Nick and tears burned behind her eyelids.

Maybe she should just leave Widow Creek tomorrow when Amberly left. Maybe she should just accept Lauren's death as an accident and get back to her life in Kansas City.

It wasn't her job to clean up any problems that might exist in Widow Creek. It wasn't her duty to try to do Gary's job. She could go to him with all her suspicions, lay it out on the table and then leave town.

But the next morning she was more determined than ever to get to the bottom of the case. "Call me if you need anything," Amberly said as she got into her car to leave. "And don't try to be a hero. If you need backup, ask for it."

Lexie watched as Amberly's car disappeared down the highway and then she went back into her motel room. Jimmy would be at school until three that afternoon so there was really nothing she could do in the meantime.

She still believed he was her ticket to finding out who was the source for the drugs.

She tried not to think about the fact that she was truly on her own now in a town where she didn't know who to trust. At three o'clock she was parked down the street from Jimmy's house, waiting for the teen to get home from school.

Maybe today would be the day the kid would lead her someplace where she could get a handle on who might be selling drugs in Widow Creek. Once she had that person in her sights she could work up the chain of command to find the person behind it all, the person she believed was ultimately responsible for Lauren's death.

Unless you're making this all up, a little voice whispered in the back of her brain. As long as she was thinking about drug connections and nefarious characters, she wasn't thinking about Lauren and she wasn't thinking about Nick.

It could be argued that there was a logical explanation for everything that had happened. Lauren really could have slipped and fallen to her death on the rocks by the creek and Lexie simply hadn't seen her body on the night she'd searched.

The shooting could be nothing more than stupid teenagers performing a daring drive-by at the house of a dead woman and that Linetta Stone could have passed on nothing more than malicious gossip.

She sat up straighter in her seat as the high school bus lumbered into view. And maybe Jimmy Morano really was just a teenage kid with bad hygiene and acne.

Maybe her mind had subconsciously tied all these things together in a big bow of desperation so that she'd have something to focus on other than the grief that was never far from the surface. Not to mention the loneliness that she knew awaited her when she finally went back home.

She watched as Jimmy got off the bus with what looked like a younger girl. The two didn't talk and Jimmy made a direct beeline to his house while the girl walked in the opposite direction.

Lexie settled back in her seat, knowing it might be hours before he left his house again…hours when she'd have nothing to do but think.

And as always, when she had a minute to herself, she thought of Nick. She'd spent most of the day trying to convince herself that she didn't really love him, that her feelings for him had gotten confused because of her fear and grief about Lauren.

But no matter how hard she tried to convince herself that what she felt for Nick wasn't love, but rather some combination of gratitude and friendship, she couldn't.

She knew what was in her heart, what was in her soul, and she knew it was the kind of love she'd always dreamed of, the kind that might have lasted a lifetime if given a chance to flourish.

But she was no match against a dead woman who had been perfect in every way for him. She couldn't battle the guilt that would keep Nick a victim, tied to a tragedy that would forever resonate in his soul.

She sat up straighter in her seat as a car pulled into Jimmy's driveway. She couldn't tell who was driving from the distance she was parked away from the house, but Jimmy came running out of the front door and hopped into the passenger seat.

As the car backed out of the driveway Lexie

started the engine of her own vehicle. She waited until the car she intended to follow turned right on Main Street and then she put her car into gear.

Tailing somebody without discovery in a town the size of Widow Creek wasn't an easy feat. There were rarely enough cars on the road to get lost in a crowd. It would have been much easier in Kansas City where the traffic was busy.

Still, she got lucky. When she turned onto Main Street there were two cars between her and her quarry, making it easy for her to keep some distance.

It was possible they were headed to another friend's house, or just taking a drive. She told herself not to get excited, that this might just be another exercise in futility.

She slowed a bit as she lost one of the cars between them, not wanting to draw any attention to herself. Hopefully the two boys in the car weren't savvy enough to worry about anyone tailing them. Besides, the road was straight and she had no trouble keeping the vehicle in sight.

A burst of adrenaline torched through her as the car left the city limits, heading in the direction of Nick's place and Lauren's house. Where were they going?

They passed both Lauren's and Nick's houses and continued on. Then, to her stunned surprise, they turned into the lane that she knew led to Clay Cole's place.

She drove on past, her heart pounding a million beats a minute. Clay Cole. Of course, why hadn't she and Nick thought of him?

The expensive furnishings, the plethora of toys and electronics inside his house all spoke of money to spare, money that Nick didn't think came from Clay's ranching efforts. Was it possible that the money came from selling drugs?

She found a place to ease her car off the road and parked, adrenaline spiking through her as she realized she might be getting closer to identifying the person who had killed her sister.

Once she'd parked, she pulled her cell phone from her purse.

Lexie wasn't a fool. She knew she was teetering on dangerous ground and she suddenly realized she wanted somebody to know what she was doing and where she was. The only person she knew to call was Nick.

She was aware of the fact that she'd been fairly cool to him the night before and as the phone rang a second time she hoped he wasn't avoiding her calls.

He answered on the third ring, his voice slightly breathless. "I just had the dogs out for a run," he said. "It's good to hear your voice, Lexie."

Her heart squeezed tight, but she kept focused on the reason for the call. "I just wanted somebody to know that I followed Jimmy Morano and one of his friends as they drove out of town a little while ago."

"Lexie, where are you? Where's Amberly? Is she with you?" His voice was low and vibrated with sudden tension.

"Actually she was called back to Kansas City this morning and I'm sitting in my car just down the road from Clay Cole's place. I'm parked in a grove of trees so nobody can see I'm here from the house."

"You should have called me when she left town. Get out of there, Lexie. You shouldn't be out there all alone. Come on back here to my place and we'll sort it all out here."

"Don't worry. Nobody knows I'm here and I'm not unarmed," she assured him. Her mind whirled with a million thoughts a minute. "I'm just going to sit tight for a little while and see if the boys come right out. When I get to your place we need to do a little computer research on Clay Cole's finances. We should have seen the red flags when we saw the inside of his house."

"Just get out of there," Nick exclaimed.

"I'll call you back when I'm leaving. Give me thirty minutes or so." She didn't wait for his response, but ended the call and dropped her phone back into her purse.

She wasn't about to do what he'd asked. This might be the first real break they got. She felt perfectly secure in her car with her gun in her purse next to her.

She tapped her fingers impatiently on the steering wheel, trying to decide what to do next. It was possible the boys had gone to Clay's to play some of his games, to just hang out in there where the electronics were nothing short of amazing.

She rolled down her window and tried to listen for any sounds coming from the direction of the house. If there was something screwy with Clay's finances, she'd find it. That's what she did; that was part of her expertise. She could make a computer dance and sing with personal information about somebody if she wanted.

She should have done some computer work the day that she and Nick had seen the inside of Clay's house, when they had first speculated about the source of his money. She cursed the fact that while both of them had marveled at the things he owned, neither of them had thought about checking it out further.

Was this just another wild goose chase? Was she targeting the wrong kid, chasing the wrong motive? It was possible that Clay made enough money ranching to buy his toys. It had been evident that he wasn't spending much on the maintenance of the exterior of his home.

After several more minutes passed she began to doubt what she was doing here. She wasn't about to confront Clay Cole all alone. That would be the height of foolishness. She really wasn't going to learn anything even when the kids came out of his house.

The best thing she could do now was get to her computer and do some digging into Clay Cole's life. It was time to get out of here.

She moved her hand to her keys but just before she could crank the engine the barrel of a gun pressed hard against the side of her head.

"Well, well, if it ain't the pretty pink-haired woman sticking her nose in where it don't belong." Clay's deep voice filled her with horror as she shot a glance at her purse with her gun inside.

"Whoa, if I were you I wouldn't move a muscle that I don't tell you to move. Now, nice and easy, get out of the car. If you make a wrong move I'll blow your brains out, and trust me, I'm a man of my word."

NICK PACED THE FLOOR of his living room waiting for Lexie to call and tell him she was on her way to his place. He fought the desire to jump in his car and head to Clay's, afraid if he did she'd show up here, afraid that he might miss a call from her. He didn't think she had the number to his cell. Any time she'd called him it had always been on his landline.

When twenty minutes had passed and she still hadn't shown up or called him back and he couldn't stand it any longer, he called her on her cell phone. When the call went directly to her voice mail a sick panic slithered through him.

He had no reason to believe that anything was wrong or that she was in any kind of real trouble, but he couldn't stop the alarms ringing in his head.

He was afraid to call Gary Wendall for backup. He still wasn't sure the lawman could be trusted. But as the minutes continued to click off, he recognized he had to do something. By the time forty minutes had passed and she still hadn't shown up and still wasn't answering her phone, he'd made a decision.

He grabbed his gun and was headed to the front door when he paused, his mind racing. He felt the same way he had when Danielle had told him she was leaving him...helpless and afraid that somehow he hadn't done enough.

He never wanted to feel that way again. He pulled his cell phone from his pocket and got the number to the FBI field office in Kansas City. When he connected with the office he asked to speak to Director Grimes.

"I think one of your agents is in trouble," he said when the man got on the phone. He quickly explained the situation and was glad to realize that apparently Lexie had already told her boss much of what had been happening.

"Is there law enforcement there that you can trust?" Grimes asked.

Nick hesitated only a moment. "No."

"I'll get agents there as quickly as I can," Grimes replied.

Nick gave him Clay's address. "That's where she was the last time I talked to her, but I don't intend to wait for the cavalry," he exclaimed. "I'm headed there now." He ended the call and headed out the door. He got into his truck and roared out of his driveway, recriminations firing through him.

He shouldn't have waited so long to call Grimes. He should have left for Clay's the minute she'd called and told him she was there.

He hadn't done enough.

The words thundered in his head, a repeat of what he'd heard for months after Danielle had been found dead. He'd somehow let her down, he thought, but it wasn't Danielle who filled his mind, it was Lexie.

Maybe she was fine and just hadn't answered his calls. Things had definitely gone awkward between them. Maybe she'd instantly regretted calling him in the first place and had simply left Clay's and gone back to her motel.

No, she wouldn't do that. She knew him well enough to know that he'd worry and she would never do that to him. Something was wrong, dammit.

He'd pushed her too hard, wanted her too much. That's what had run her out of his house and into danger all alone. If something happened to Lexie he didn't know if he could survive it. She was in his heart so deep that he felt that if something happened to her it would stop beating altogether.

As he got closer to Clay's place his mind began to work scenarios. He couldn't go in guns blazing; he had no idea what he might be walking into or who he might be facing.

He looked for Lexie's car when he got close to Clay's, but didn't find it parked anywhere along the road. Had she left the area? Was she maybe on his way back to his place? He frowned and dismissed the idea. She hadn't been in town long enough to know all the back roads. If she'd been on his way to his house he would have met her.

He parked his car about a mile away from Clay's house behind a grove of trees on Old Man Johnson's property. Before he left the car he pulled his cell phone from his pocket and tried one last call to Lexie's cell phone. Once again it went directly to her voice mail.

A tight tension coiled in his belly. He had no plan as he left his car. He had no idea what he intended to do, but rather moved on instinct.

This was the last place she had been and he wouldn't be satisfied until he'd checked every inch of Clay's place to assure himself that she wasn't there.

He approached Clay's house from the back, using the cover of trees to assess the situation. Unfortunately there was nothing to see. There was no sign of life anywhere.

With a frown he decided to check the outbuildings first and if he didn't find Lexie somewhere soon he'd take the chance and knock on Clay's door, insist the man show him every room in the house.

What worried him was that if she wasn't here, then he was wasting precious time. But the truth of the matter was if she wasn't here he wouldn't know where else to look.

Thankfully Clay's property was overgrown and unkempt, allowing Nick to use the cover of brush and trees to make his way to the detached garage.

His heart thundered with anxiety as he approached the building. *Lexie, where are you?* He felt the same sickening sense of danger that he'd felt when Danielle had first disappeared, the horrifying sense that something was desperately wrong.

Peering into one of the filthy garage windows, Nick's pounding heart seemed to crash to a halt. Inside, nestled next to Clay's big pickup, was Lexie's car.

Along with a renewed, nearly crippling guilt that gripped him came a rage he'd never known before, a rage directed at Clay and whoever else was a participant in this.

Nick's fingers tightened on the butt of his gun. If he found out that Clay had hurt Lexie, Nick had no doubt that he could kill the man.

From his vantage point it looked as if Lexie's car was empty, but he needed to get inside the garage to know for sure. He crept around to the opposite side of the building and found a side door unlocked.

He slid inside, his heart once again crashing in his chest as he approached her car. The interior was empty but her keys hung from the ignition.

He stared at the trunk, afraid to open it, afraid not to. He leaned into the driver side and popped the trunk latch and then, with feet that felt like lead, he approached the trunk.

It was ajar only an inch, not enough for him to see if she was inside. Tears burned in his eyes and a lump in his throat made it almost impossible to breathe as he pulled up the trunk lid.

A gasp of relief exploded out of him. She wasn't there, but her purse was. The sight of her purse sent him into a new panic.

She was here.

And she was in desperate trouble.

Now all he had to do was find her and pray that he wasn't already too late.

Chapter Twelve

Lexie twisted and turned her wrists, attempting to break free of the rope that held her captive. Her hands were tied behind her back, and her ankles were trussed together as well, making it impossible for her to escape from the shed where Clay had stuck her.

As if the ropes that bound her weren't enough, he'd duct-taped her mouth closed as well. She was trapped, unable to scream for help and unable to help herself.

Leaning her head back against the metal structure, she fought against the tears that begged to be released, knowing that crying would solve nothing.

She'd been stupid. She should have never followed Jimmy Morano on her own. She should have never trusted that just because she was an FBI agent and carried a gun she wasn't making a huge mistake.

She'd gone off half-cocked like the Lone Ranger, her only thought trying to find somebody to blame for her sister's death. Now she had the face of at least one of the bad guys emblazoned in her brain. Clay Cole. But in identifying Cole, she'd also put herself in imminent danger.

What she hoped for was that Nick would worry when she hadn't called him again and would come looking for her. What she really hoped was that he wouldn't show up here without a plan and find himself in trouble as well.

But what frightened her more than anything was that she knew that if she didn't survive this, Nick would find a way to blame himself and she knew he'd never recover. It didn't matter that he didn't love her, she would still be, in his mind, another woman he'd somehow let down.

She squeezed her eyes closed and thought about Danielle. She had no idea exactly what had transpired between Nick and Danielle when they'd lost their baby, but there was no doubt in her mind that Nick had done everything humanly possible to support the woman he loved.

Whatever forces had driven Danielle to commit suicide, Lexie couldn't imagine that Nick had been one of them. All thoughts of Nick and Danielle jumped from her mind as she heard approaching footsteps.

The shed door creaked open and Clay walked in. He leaned against the opened door and grinned at her. "I'd ask you if you were uncomfortable, but I can tell by looking at you that you are," he said. "Unfortunately it's going to be a little while before something happens. I've got to wait for the boss man to show up and tell me exactly what he wants to do with you."

Lexie stared at him through narrowed eyes.

He laughed. "Now I understand that expression 'if looks could kill.'" He sobered. "It's a damn shame, really. A pretty girl like you finding yourself in this mess. You should have buried your sister and hightailed it back to Kansas City. You should have never started sticking your nose in things that don't concern you."

He shoved himself off the door. "Your sister, she was going to be trouble, that's for sure. We had to arrange that little accident for her before she started training dogs that would screw up everything we're doing."

They'd killed her. Just as Lexie had suspected, they'd killed Lauren. As grief and rage exploded through her, she fought her ropes, struggling to get free so she could kill him. Sobs welled up in her throat, strangled from release by the duct tape across her mouth as the ropes held tight.

"It was the same thing with Nick's wife," he continued. Lexie froze and once again stared at him. "She had a habit of sticking her nose in where it didn't belong. She was way too curious about things for her own good."

He offered her a self-satisfied smile. "That was a piece of work if I do say so myself," he said. "The way I staged that scene so that everybody would believe she'd blown her own brains out. It was genius and it didn't hurt that she had a history of depression."

Nick. Oh, Nick, Lexie's heart cried. He'd carried the burden so long of Danielle's death and the truth was she hadn't committed suicide, but had been brutally murdered.

The next thing that chilled her blood was the knowledge that Clay had already killed two women. There was absolutely no reason to believe that she was going to suffer any different fate. Clay wasn't going to let her just walk out of this shed with the promise that she'd hightail it out of town.

A deep, shuddering chill worked through her as she realized Widow Creek wasn't just going to claim her sister's life, but her own as well.

NICK SAGGED TO THE GROUND behind the shed, overwhelmed with a myriad of emotions as he heard Clay's words. She hadn't killed herself! Danielle hadn't taken her own life. That meant she hadn't given up on them; she hadn't given up on Nick. She'd planned on getting back with him, expected to continue to build a life together.

He'd been about to check out the barn in the distance when he'd seen Clay leave the house and enter the small shed. He'd made his way to the back of it in time to hear everything that the man had said to Lexie.

Tears once again burned in his eyes, this time for the woman he'd loved, for the woman he'd believed he'd somehow let down. The tears were quickly followed by a rage like he'd never known before. They'd already stolen from him one woman he loved. He would not let them take another.

What worried him was that the whole time Clay had been talking, Lexie hadn't made a sound. Was she hurt? Was she unable to make a sound because she was injured? Weak?

There was only one person in there with Lexie and Clay wouldn't be expecting Nick, especially Nick with a gun. He pulled himself up and was about to round the side of the shed when he heard a car door slam shut.

He pressed against the back of the shed so that he wouldn't be in sight of whoever was coming. The boss, that's what Clay had said. He'd been waiting for the boss to arrive.

Footsteps approached, heavy and crunching dead leaves. Gary Wendall? Was it possible the chief of police was the Mr. Big behind everything?

Nick's heart beat so furiously he found it difficult to draw a full breath. He was afraid to ease around the corner and see who was coming, afraid that he might be seen and the last hope to save Lexie would be gone.

Instead he placed his ear against the side of the shed, knowing he'd be able to hear whatever was going on inside. "Clay, take that duct tape off her mouth so we can have a civilized conversation here."

Stunned surprise filled Nick as he recognized the voice. Mayor Vincent Caldwell. So, the rot in Widow Creek had gone all the way to the top.

"You bastard, you killed my sister. You killed Nick's wife." Lexie's voice was strong and filled with emotion and the sound of it shot a rivulet of relief through Nick.

"You have become quite a nuisance, Ms. Forbes," Vincent said. "I'm trying to keep a town alive here and sometimes the individual has to be sacrificed for the good of the people."

"You're nothing more than a drug dealer," Lexie exclaimed.

"I'm doing what I have to do in order to keep this town functioning. Do you have any idea what it costs for snow removal each year? For trash pickup? Do you know what it takes to keep a town functioning? This isn't just about selling drugs, it's about our very survival here in Widow Creek."

"Is Gary Wendall one of your henchmen? Does he sell meth in his spare time?" Lexie asked.

Vincent laughed. "Gary Wendall is a lazy buffoon. Unfortunately he's a straight arrow so we've had to work around him. Fortunately for us it's been pretty easy to get around him."

Nick found some comfort in the fact that Gary hadn't been a part of Danielle's death, that he wasn't a part of the madness that had gripped this town. Still it was small comfort because Nick now had two men to get through in order to save Lexie.

"You're insane," Lexie exclaimed. "You think snow removal is worth two women's lives? You really want me to believe that you're so noble and just doing this to save the town and not lining your own pockets in the process?"

"Of course I'm lining my own pockets," Vincent said, speaking as if talking to a mentally challenged person. "But, I'm also taking care of my people…the good people of Widow Creek."

Nick wanted to burst inside. His natural instinct to protect Lexie surged up inside him. The element of surprise would be on his side, but a voice of reason reminded him that he didn't know if Clay and Vincent were armed.

Lexie could be shot in the blink of an eye

and then nothing else would matter in the world. *Patience,* he told himself. He had to be patient and wait for the perfect opportunity to act. He just prayed that opportunity would come before all was lost.

LEXIE FINALLY HAD her answers. Lauren had been murdered along with Nick's wife over a year ago to protect a drug operation. The rage that filled her as she looked at Clay and Vincent nearly blinded her. Beneath the rage was a pounding terror as she recognized she was going to die here in this shed.

She had no idea where Nick was, or if he were even looking for her. Maybe he was still at his place, waiting for her to call, wondering if she would really call him.

"What about Jimmy Morano? Is he in on this?" she asked.

"He's just a stupid kid who takes care of selling to the teenagers around town. Unfortunately, he likes to use more than he likes to sell," Clay replied.

"So, it was you who shot at us at Lauren's place?" she asked Clay.

"Yeah, it was me." Clay clapped his hand on Vincent's shoulder. "The boss here, he doesn't get his hands dirty. He leaves that kind of work to me."

Vincent moved away from him, as if disliking Clay's touch. "You should have taken the warning, Ms. Forbes, and left town. Now we not only have you as a problem, but we also have Nick."

"There's no reason to hurt him," she said quickly. "He doesn't know anything. He was just helping me, but he thought I was crazy when I told him Lauren had been murdered." She couldn't stand the idea of them harming Nick. The very thought squeezed her heart so tight in her chest she could scarcely draw a breath.

"We'll figure out how to deal with Nick later," Vincent said. "In the meantime take her out to the field and kill her. Make sure you bury her body where it won't be found."

Terror thundered in Lexie's head. She wanted to beg for her life, but she knew it wouldn't do any good. Had Danielle begged for her life? Had Lauren?

"I'm going back to the office," Vincent continued. "We'll figure out what to do with her car later this evening. Call me when you're finished here."

As he left the shed a new panic seared through Lexie. "Clay, let me go," she said as tears sprang to her eyes. "I'll head back to Kansas City and you'll never hear from me again."

"Sorry, no can do." Clay grabbed the roll of duct tape and tore off a piece. "You really believe I can just let you walk out of here? I'm afraid, Ms. Pink Hair, that you need to disappear permanently."

He slapped the duct tape back over her mouth and then cut the rope that bound her ankles and yanked her to her feet. She fought the rope that still held her wrists, desperate to get free, to at least have a fighting chance to save herself, but it was no use.

"Knock it off," Clay said with irritation as she tried to body slam into him. He held her arm painfully tight and pulled her toward the door.

Clay took one step outside and halted as Nick pressed the barrel of his gun against his temple. Lexie's heart jumped with relief as Clay released his hold on her. She sidled next to Nick, her heart crashing a million beats a minute against her chest.

"What are you going to do now, big guy?

Shoot me?" Clay asked derisively. "You don't have it in you."

Lexie wanted to scream at Nick not to fire, that Vincent might still be on the property and would hear the shot and she knew he was just as dangerous as Clay.

"You're right, I don't have it in me," Nick replied. He crashed the butt of the gun into the back of Clay's head and at the same time swung his fist into Clay's stomach. Clay crumbled to the ground with a moan.

Nick then turned to Lexie, his gray eyes filled with fire. "Come on, let's get the hell out of here."

He yanked the duct tape off her mouth and grabbed her elbow and then motioned across the field. "That way," he said.

She'd been in the shed long enough that the shadows of night were beginning to fall as they took off running. With her arms tied behind her back she found it difficult to run, but with the flame of survival burning bright inside, she gave it all she had.

They hadn't gone far when they heard Clay shout. "Dammit, I should have shot him," Nick exclaimed as they hit the cover of a grove of trees.

"Where's your car?" Lexie asked between gasps as she tried to catch her breath.

"On the other side of them," he said grimly as Vincent and Clay came into view.

Lexie cursed the fact that her hands were tied behind her back, that she didn't have a gun and couldn't help Nick defend against an assault.

Clay fired, the bullet chipping bark off the tree in front of where Nick and Lexie stood. Vincent fired as well, his shot going slightly left, but Lexie knew the closer the men approached the more accurate their shots would be.

Nick answered with a shot, at the same time scanning the area for an escape route.

"We need to split up," Lexie exclaimed. "We'll have a better chance of one of us getting out of here alive."

"No!" Nick's voice was stronger, more firm than she'd ever heard it before. "No, we stay together."

"Then we'd better move," she said, "because Clay is getting closer and Vincent has disappeared." She looked behind them, worried when she realized the grove of trees that sheltered them was small and it was probable that Vincent was now attempting to come up behind them. If he succeeded, they would never make it out of this grove alive.

And she desperately wanted to live. In the days just following Lauren's death she hadn't been so sure that she could go on. In the days since she'd realized she loved Nick and would never be able to have him forever, she'd lost some of her love of life. But it was back now, screaming through her.

She wanted to survive this and she wanted Nick to survive. It didn't matter that he didn't love her as she loved him, all that mattered was that they both escaped.

Nick fired at Clay once again, forcing Clay to hit the ground. At the same time the sound of a helicopter overhead drew Lexie's attention upward.

The helicopter was the kind used by the FBI for hostage rescue. Her heart soared as she realized help had arrived. The clearing behind Clay filled with men.

"Down on the ground. Get down on the ground," the men yelled at Clay. "Hands over your head."

Harsh voices had never sounded so sweet to Lexie's ears.

"We're here," Nick called to the advancing men. He raised his hands above his head to show them his gun and to indicate he wasn't a threat.

At that moment a gun banged and Lexie gasped as her body was pierced with an excruciating pain that stole her breath. She turned toward Nick, her mouth working but no words coming out.

He smiled at her and she tried to smile back but tears blurred her vision. The raw pain inside her clawed at her. She couldn't breathe and she wondered why she couldn't take in any air. She felt herself falling...falling. The autumn leaves around her began to spin in her head, a kaleidoscope of orange and red and finally black.

Chapter Thirteen

As Lexie hit the ground, Nick screamed to the men in the field as he fell to his knees by her side. In his peripheral vision he caught a glimpse of Vincent Caldwell in the brush behind them.

Nick didn't hesitate. He pulled his gun and fired at the man. There was no satisfaction as Vincent fell, screaming as he grabbed his thigh.

Nick threw his gun to the ground as he placed a finger on Lexie's neck, seeking a pulse, praying for a pulse. The shouts of the men and the whoop of helicopter blades overhead faded to silence as Nick leaned close to Lexie and whispered fervently.

"You have to be all right, Lexie. Open your eyes and talk to me. For God's sake, just tell me you're going to be all right."

She didn't move. Her eyes didn't magically open and there was no indication that she could hear him as he pled with her to be okay. He didn't realize he was crying until a man in a SWAT uniform touched him on the shoulder. "We have to fix her," Nick said, his voice half-strangled by emotion.

"We're going to do that," the man said as he pulled Nick to his feet. "Step back and let us take care of her."

As several men with a stretcher took over, Nick looked around him in shock. The helicopter had landed in the middle of Clay's field and Clay was in custody. Several of the men had run to Vincent, who was screaming and writhing on the ground.

It was surreal...and Nick felt as if he were moving in a fog. It was only when the men tending to Lexie began to carry her out that the fog dissipated. "Where are you taking her?" he asked, his heart pounding frantically in his chest as he saw how still, how pale she looked.

"The nearest hospital," one of the men replied.

As Nick ran after them, he realized he was in love with Lexie. His love for her roared through him with a force than nearly dropped him to his knees.

Cupid had found him twice in a lifetime. Now all he had to do was pray that she survived so he could tell her that he loved her.

He was just about to his car when a man called his name. "I'm Director Grimes," the man said as he approached Nick. "And I want to thank you for calling to let us know one of our agents was in trouble."

"She's still in trouble," Nick replied around the lump of emotion that nearly clogged his throat.

Grimes nodded. "We'll be taking things over here in Widow Creek. There will be a full investigation by us, not by the locals, and we'll see to it that this place is cleaned up."

Nick didn't care about the town. He didn't give a damn if the whole place blew up, all he cared about was getting to the hospital and finding out about Lexie.

"I've got to go," he said and without waiting another minute he got into his car and tore off toward the Widow Creek Hospital.

He knew now that Danielle hadn't committed suicide, that he hadn't let her down, but even if he hadn't known that his love for Lexie couldn't have been denied another minute.

If he'd never known about Danielle he would have taken a chance on loving Lexie, on hoping that they could build a life together.

Why hadn't he realized sooner? He'd been so mired in his past that he hadn't been able to look toward a future, and now it might be too late.

No! No, don't think that way, he told himself. *She has to be all right. She has to be!* He couldn't lose her. He refused to allow fate to take away another woman that he loved.

He screeched into the hospital parking lot and raced toward the emergency entrance. Several of the FBI agents were there, apparently also awaiting word on Lexie's condition.

"She's in surgery," one of them told Nick. "And so is Vincent Caldwell. He's having his leg repaired." He gave Nick a small smile. "Too bad you didn't aim a little higher."

"I didn't aim at all," Nick admitted. "I was blinded by rage when I realized he'd shot Lexie. I just fired at him instinctively. Was she conscious when you brought her in?"

The man shook his head. "No, she never regained consciousness." He gestured toward one of the chairs in the waiting room. "You might as well have a seat. I have a feeling it's going to be a very long night."

Nick sat in the chair, his heart heavier than it had ever been in his life. Danielle had been stolen from him and at the time he'd thought he'd never get over it, that he'd never survive.

Then Lexie had come into his life. Lexie with her warm smile and pink hair. She'd wiggled right into his heart and the idea of burying another woman that he loved nearly shattered him.

All he could do now was wait through the dark, endless night and see if fate would once again rip love away from him.

CONSCIOUSNESS CAME LIKE a soft whisper in her ear, tugging her reluctantly from sweet dreams. She'd awakened several times before only to succumb to the darkness within seconds. This time consciousness remained, although she kept her eyes closed as she assessed her condition.

She was in a small amount of pain, but nothing like the pain that had ripped through her the last couple of times she'd tried to awaken.

She knew Vincent Caldwell had shot her, but she had no memory of anything after that bullet had struck. Wiggling her fingers and toes, relief swooped through her. Whatever her injuries, everything seemed to be working okay.

Without opening her eyes she knew she was in a hospital, she could tell by the smell, by the noises that came from someplace in the distance.

She'd survived. Lauren was dead, Nick was nothing more than a fantasy, but the important thing was that Lexie had survived. As soon as she was well enough she'd go back to Kansas City, immerse herself in her work and try to find some kind of happiness that was meaningful.

That's what Lauren would have wanted for her—happiness. And as a tribute to her twin she would find a way to be happy. She finally ventured a peek at her surroundings, unsurprised to find herself in a hospital bed.

Morning sunshine streamed through the windows and she was surprised by the sight of Nick slumped down in a chair, sound asleep.

Had he been there all night? Her heart

ached as she gazed at him, memorizing his handsome features for when she was back in Kansas City and feeling all alone. She would remember being held in the warmth of his arms, the fire of his lips against hers and the magic of their lovemaking for a very long time to come. The memories would both warm her and fill her with sadness.

His eyes snapped open and for a moment they were filled with a soft sleepiness that made her want to lose herself in their depths.

"You're awake," he said as he sat up and raked a hand through his hair. "How are you feeling?"

"Stiff, sore and lucky to be alive," she replied. "How long have I been out of it?"

"Three days." He got out of his chair and moved to the side of her bed.

"Three days!" She stared at him, stunned by the passage of time. "What's the damage?"

"I hope you didn't like your spleen." He stood close enough to her that she could smell the scent of him, the scent that would forever haunt her with the memory of love.

"Nah, I've never been much of a spleen person," she replied.

"You were so lucky. The bullet managed

to miss every vital organ and your spine. It caught a rib and deflected into the spleen but stopped there. I imagine you'll be out of here soon, but according to Director Grimes you won't be going back to work for a little while. He's put you on medical leave."

"Who called in the cavalry?" she asked.

"I did. When you weren't answering my phone calls and you hadn't called me back, I panicked. I called Director Grimes and told him he had an agent in trouble." He rocked back on his heels and gave her the smile that shot heat through her. "I guess they take that kind of thing very seriously."

"Thank goodness. So, what's happened to Clay and Vincent?"

"Vincent is in a hospital room down the hall under armed guards. He suffered an unfortunate incident with my gun and will walk with a limp in the prison yard. The FBI and DEA have taken over the town. Clay's barn was filled with enough chemicals to make meth for the next year. Vincent was arrogant enough to keep a file on his computer that had names of mules, places they were selling and other financial information about the operation. According to your coworkers, it wasn't a huge bust, but it was a substantial one."

"And so it's over and the guilty will pay." She studied his features and her love for him pressed tight against her chest, hurting her as deeply as the bullet that had pierced through her. "At least you should feel some peace that Danielle didn't commit suicide," she said softly.

"I am relieved over that, but I'm not at peace." He took a step closer to her and reached out and touched a strand of her hair, the strand she knew was bright pink.

"I've been a fool, Lexie, a fool trapped by a ridiculous one arrow theory that got shot all to hell the moment I laid eyes on you."

His eyes glittered with a light that shone through Lexie, heating her with the whisper of possibility. But she was afraid to hope, afraid that somehow whatever he felt for her now was simply a fleeting thing that would fade with time.

"I love you, Lexie, and I don't want to let you go," he said.

His words torched joy through her, but it was a joy tempered with harsh reality. They'd both been through such an emotional wringer.

Surely he was just confused about his feelings.

"Nick, I'm in love with you, but I don't think I'm the kind of woman you want in your life forever." Pain lanced through her, a pain that had nothing to do with her physical condition.

Before he could reply Gary Wendall walked into the room. "Well, it's good to see you coming around," he said to Lexie as she used the button to raise the head of her bed a little bit. "I owe the two of you a huge apology."

He jammed his hands into his pockets and frowned. "I didn't know. I didn't have a clue about the drugs. Oh, I was aware that we had a little drug issue with some of the teenagers, but I never dreamed what Clay and Vincent and some of the others were involved in anything like this. Anyway, just wanted to stop by and let you both know I'm turning in my badge. If Widow Creek survives this scandal somebody else will be in charge of law enforcement."

"Chief Wendall, I don't think either Nick or I expect your resignation," Lexie said.

He shook his head. "I don't want it any

other way. I got too complacent, too lazy. The fact that there was a drug operation taking place right under my nose and I didn't smell it lets me know I need to get out. Anyway, I just wanted to apologize to you both for not taking your concerns about your loved ones more seriously."

IIe didn't wait for a reply, just turned quickly and left the room. "He's not a bad man," Lexie said. "He just wasn't a good chief of police."

Tension pressed tight in her chest as she remembered the conversation they'd been having before Gary had come into the room.

"Now, where were we?" Nick asked as he approached the side of her bed again.

"I was telling you that I'm not the right woman for you," she replied, her heart beating with a heavy dread.

"And why is that?" His gaze held hers intently as he leaned closer.

"I have pink hair," she blurted out miserably.

"I know, and I'd love you if you had green hair with purple stripes," he replied.

"I spent my whole life trying to be different

from Lauren and now that she's gone I don't know who I am anymore."

His eyes were a soft gray. "Allow me to introduce you to you. Lexie, you're bright and funny and sometimes when I look at you my love for you gets so tight in my chest I can hardly breathe. You're loyal and loving and I can't imagine not having you in my life."

Lexie's heart swelled at his words. She liked who she saw reflected in his eyes, and deep down she knew she *was* that woman, the woman who could love him for a lifetime, the woman who had become his second arrow.

"Oh, Nick, I wasn't expecting you," she said as happy tears burned in her eyes.

He grinned at her. "You weren't expecting a splenectomy either, but here we are."

She laughed and then sobered. "So, where do we go from here?"

"I thought maybe you'd like to recuperate at my place and then when you're well enough we'll pack up the dogs and my belongings and head to Kansas City."

She looked at him in surprise. "You'd do that for me? You'd move from here?"

"Don't you get it? I'd follow you to the ends of the earth. I'm ready to start over, Lexie, and I know how important your job is to you. I want to be your husband and I want to be the father of your children. Tell me you want that, too."

"I do. I want that, Nick." Happiness soared through her as he leaned down and gently kissed her lips.

"Then it's settled," he said as he straightened. "The nerd has found his mate."

Lexie laughed, knowing that she'd finally found the man who understood her, the man who got her quirks and found them charming. He was the man of her dreams and now he was hers. She knew their future would be filled with happiness and love and that the socks on his feet in bed would warm hers forever.

* * * * *

continued . . .

Berkley Sensation Titles by Alissa Johnson

NEARLY A LADY
AN UNEXPECTED GENTLEMAN

An Unexpected Gentleman

Alissa Johnson

BERKLEY SENSATION, NEW YORK

THE BERKLEY PUBLISHING GROUP
Published by the Penguin Group
Penguin Group (USA) Inc.
375 Hudson Street, New York, New York 10014, USA
Penguin Group (Canada), 90 Eglinton Avenue East, Suite 700, Toronto, Ontario M4P 2Y3, Canada
(a division of Pearson Penguin Canada Inc.)
Penguin Books Ltd., 80 Strand, London WC2R 0RL, England
Penguin Group Ireland, 25 St. Stephen's Green, Dublin 2, Ireland (a division of Penguin Books Ltd.)
Penguin Group (Australia), 250 Camberwell Road, Camberwell, Victoria 3124, Australia
(a division of Pearson Australia Group Pty. Ltd.)
Penguin Books India Pvt. Ltd., 11 Community Centre, Panchsheel Park, New Delhi—110 017, India
Penguin Group (NZ), 67 Apollo Drive, Rosedale, Auckland 0632, New Zealand
(a division of Pearson New Zealand Ltd.)
Penguin Books (South Africa) (Pty.) Ltd., 24 Sturdee Avenue, Rosebank, Johannesburg 2196,
South Africa

Penguin Books Ltd., Registered Offices: 80 Strand, London WC2R 0RL, England

AN UNEXPECTED GENTLEMAN

A Berkley Sensation Book / published by arrangement with the author

PRINTING HISTORY
Berkley Sensation mass-market edition / December 2011

Copyright © 2011 by Alissa Johnson.
Excerpt from *Practically Wicked* by Alissa Johnson copyright © by Alissa Johnson.
Cover art by Judy York.
Cover design by George Long.
Interior text design by Laura K. Corless.

ISBN: 978-0-425-24491-3

BERKLEY SENSATION®
Berkley Sensation Books are published by The Berkley Publishing Group,
a division of Penguin Group (USA) Inc.,
375 Hudson Street, New York, New York 10014.
BERKLEY SENSATION® is a registered trademark of Penguin Group (USA) Inc.
The "B" design is a trademark of Penguin Group (USA) Inc.

PRINTED IN THE UNITED STATES OF AMERICA

10 9 8 7 6 5 4 3 2 1

For Ralph E. Johnson, because even though
you'll probably never read this book,
you're still proud I wrote it.

Chapter 1

*M*iss Adelaide Ward was, by her own admission, a woman of unassuming aspirations.

In recent years, she had come to the conclusion that it was folly to seek more from life than what might reasonably be expected to materialize. And for an undowered spinster burdened with an eighteen-year-old sister, an infant nephew, a brother in debtors' prison, and seven-and-twenty years, what might reasonably be expected was very limited indeed.

She wanted a home, the company of those she loved, and the security of a reliable income. These were her dreams. They were few in number and simple in nature, but they were hers. She longed for them as any debutante might long to snare a peer, and she had fought for them as any officer might fight for glory on the battlefield.

It was with some disappointment, then, that on the very eve of seeing her efforts come to fruition, she found herself not emboldened with the thrill of imminent victory but battling fear, nerves, and the surprising weight of reluctance.

Tonight, Sir Robert Maxwell would propose. She was

certain of it. Fairly certain. It seemed a reasonable expectation. The courtship was reaching near to four months, which,
in her estimation, was an excessive amount of time to allo-
cate to romance. More significantly, Sir Robert had strongly
hinted at the possibility of a proposal should she attend Mrs.
Cress's house party. Well, she was in attendance and had
been for a fortnight. Surely, tonight, amidst the music and
drama of a masquerade ball, Sir Robert would present his
offer.

Mind you, Sir Robert had no great appreciation for
music, but he did seem to Adelaide to be inordinately fond
of dramatics.

"I don't care for dramatics," she muttered.

Her feet slowed in the hall that led from her guest chambers to the ballroom. At best guess, the distance between
the rooms required a thirty-second walk. She managed to
stretch the first twenty yards into a ten-minute exercise of
unproductive meandering. She stopped in front of the mirror to fuss with a rebellious lock of chestnut hair and wrin-
kle her small nose at the narrow features and light brown
eyes she'd inherited from her father. Eyes that had, she
could not help but note, begun to crease a bit at the corners.

A few feet later, she reached down to straighten her hem
and pull a bit of lint from the ivory silk of her sleeve. Then
she peeked into a room, fiddled with a vase, adjusted the
low bodice of her gown, and stopped again to examine an
oil painting . . . in minute detail, because art appreciation
was not something one ought to rush.

And between each pause in movement, she literally
dragged her feet. Her dancing slippers made a soft and
drawn-out *woooosht, woooosht, woooosht* against the polished wood floor with every step.

Annoyed by the sound, Adelaide stopped to pull off her
mask and fiddle with the feathers. This, she assured herself, was *not* another bid to stall. The mask required a considerable amount of fussing. She'd constructed the silly
piece herself, and having no experience with—nor any
apparent talent for—such an endeavor, she'd made a terri-

ble mess of the thing. The feathers were unevenly spaced, sticking out where they ought to be lying flat, and bent in several places.

Sir Robert was certain to take note of it. She could envision his reaction well. His pale blue eyes would go wide, right before they narrowed in a wince. Then he would cover the lapse of manners with a smile that was sure to display his perfect teeth to best advantage. *Then* he would pronounce her a *most charming creature* in that awful, condescending tone.

"I don't care for that tone," she muttered.

She rubbed an errant feather with the pad of her thumb while the lively strains of a waltz floated down the hall and the scent of candle wax tickled her nose.

It was only a tone, she told herself, a minor flaw in a man positively brimming with things to recommend him. He was handsome. He was fond of her.

He was in possession of five thousand pounds a year.

The mere thought of so much money lightened the worst of her nerves with visions of a happy future. Her sister, Isobel, could have a London season. Little George could have a proper nanny. Wolfgang's debts would be paid. And the lot of them would have a roof over their heads and no shortage of food on the table. It was her dream come true.

"Right."

Ignoring doubts that lingered, she replaced the mask, securing it with a double knot and an extra yank on the ribbons for good measure. She set her shoulders, took a single step forward . . . and nearly toppled to the floor when a deep voice sounded directly behind her.

"I'd not go just yet, if I were you."

She spun around so quickly, she dislodged her mask and tripped on the hem of her gown.

"Easy." The deep voice chuckled, and a large, warm hand wrapped around her arm, steadying her.

She caught a glimpse of dark blond hair and light eyes, and for one awful moment, she thought she had been caught dawdling in the hall by Sir Robert. But by the time she righted herself and straightened her mask, that fear had been replaced by an entirely new sort of discomfort.

The man was a stranger. He shared the same light coloring and uncommon height as Sir Robert, but that was where all similarities ended. There was an air of aristocratic softness about Sir Robert; his frame was elegantly long and thin, and his features were delicate, almost feminine. There was nothing even remotely delicate or feminine about the man before her. He wasn't long—he was tall, towering over her by more than half a foot. And he wasn't thin but athletically lean, the definition of muscle visible through his dark formal attire. He was handsome, without doubt, with broad shoulders and a thick head of hair that was more gold than blond. But his features were hard and sharp, from the square cut of his jaw to the blunt jut of his cheekbones. Even his eyes, green as new grass, had an edge about them.

He put her to mind of the drawings her sister had shown her of the sleek American lions. And that put her to mind of stalking. And *that* made her decidedly uneasy.

Her senses tingled, and her breath caught in her lungs.

She wasn't sure if she cared for the sensation or not.

"My apologies," he said quietly. His voice held the cadence of an English gentleman's, but there was a hint of Scotland in his pronunciation. "It was not my intention to startle you."

"Quite all right." She wanted to wince at how breathless she sounded. She cleared her throat instead and carefully withdrew her arm from his grasp. "I was woolgathering. Do excuse me."

She turned to leave, but he moved around, quick and smooth as you please, and blocked her path. "You shouldn't go just yet."

"Good heavens." The man even moved like a cat. "Why ever not?"

"Because you want to stay here."

He offered that outrageous statement with such remarkable sincerity that there could be no doubt of his jesting.

The act of silliness both stunned and intrigued her. He didn't look to be the sort of man who teased.

"That is the most ridiculous, not to mention presumptuous—"

"Very well, *I* want you to stay here." His lips curved up, crinkling the corners of his eyes. "It was unkind of you to make me say it."

She was surprised to find he had a charming smile. The sort that invited one to smile back. It did little to slow her racing pulse, but she liked it all the same.

She shook her head. "Who are you?"

"Connor Brice," he supplied, and he executed an eloquent bow.

She curtsied in return, then righted her mask when it slipped. "Miss Adelaide Ward."

"Yes, I know. Settle your feathers, Miss Ward."

"You've not ruffled them, Mr. Brice." She hoped he believed the lie.

"No, I meant . . ." He reached out and brushed the edge of her mask with his thumb. She swore she could feel his touch on the skin beneath. "Your feathers need smoothing. What are you meant to be, exactly?"

"Oh. Oh, drat." She reached up and pulled on the knot of ribbons at the back of her head. They refused to give. Sighing, she pulled the contraption over her coiffure and tried not to think of the damage she was doing. "A bird of prey."

"Ah." He grasped his hands behind his back, leaned down, and peered at the mask in her hands. "I thought perhaps you were aiming for disheveled wren."

The sound of her laughter filled the hall. She much preferred the gentle insult to the sort of compliment Sir Robert was sure to give. Mistakes were so much easier to accept when one was allowed to be amused by them.

"It's true," she agreed. "I look dreadful."

He straightened, and his green eyes swept over her frame in a frankly appraising manner that made her blush. "You're lovely."

"Thank you," she mumbled. And then, because she'd mumbled it at the mask instead of him, she forced herself to look up when she asked, "And where is your mask?"

"I don't have one."

"But it's a masquerade." Had a mask been optional? She wished someone had mentioned that earlier.

"There is more than one way for a man to hide himself." He gestured at a door she knew led to a small sitting room.

"Is that where you came from?" No wonder he'd been able to sneak up on her so quickly. "Whatever were you doing in there?"

"Avoiding a particular lady. What were you doing out here?"

She wanted to ask which lady, and why he'd broken his self-imposed exile to speak with her—she was hardly the most interesting person at the party—but she was too busy trying to arrive at a suitable excuse for her dallying to devise a subtle way to pry. In the end, she didn't have to come up with anything. He answered for her.

"You're avoiding a particular gentleman."

"I'm not."

"Sir Robert," he guessed, and he shrugged when she sucked in a small breath of surprise. "Your courtship is hardly a secret."

She hadn't thought it was fodder for gossip either. At least not in . . . wherever it was Mr. Brice was from.

"I'm not avoiding anyone."

"You are."

Since he seemed immovable on that point, she tried another.

"Perhaps it is Mr. Doolin," she said smartly. She did make a habit of steering clear of the elderly man and his wandering hands, so it wasn't a lie, per se, but more of an irrelevant truth.

He gave a small shake of his head. "It's Sir Robert you're not eager to see, and you were wise to drag your feet. Last I checked, he was lying in wait for you right on the other side of the ballroom doors."

Her mouth fell open, but it was several long seconds before she could make sound emerge.

"Sir Robert does not *lie in wait*. I am quite certain he is not to be found crouched behind the doors like an animal." It was a little discomfiting that she could, in fact, easily imagine the baron doing just that. More than once in the past, she'd felt as if his sudden appearance at her side had been something of an ambush.

She sniffed and, with what she thought was commendable loyalty, added, "He is a gentleman."

"Do you think?" Mr. Brice's smile wasn't inviting this time. It was mocking. "It is a constant source of amazement to me how little effort the man must exert to disguise his true nature. But then, the ton is ever ready to take a baron at his word and at his . . . five thousand pounds a year, I believe you said?"

Oh, dear heavens. She'd said that bit out loud?

Heat flooded her cheeks. This was awful. Perfectly dreadful. There was no excuse for having made such a comment. And yet she couldn't stop herself from attempting to provide one.

"I was only . . . What I meant by that is . . ." She told herself to give up the effort before she somehow made matters worse. "One cannot . . . There is no shame in marrying a man with an income."

And there it was . . . Worse.

Oh, damn.

Leave, leave now.

"Excuse me." She struggled to untie the ribbons of her mask. She'd put it on, go to the ball, and pray to every deity known to man that Mr. Brice's low opinion of Sir Robert kept the two men from speaking to each other, or about each other, or *near* each other, or . . .

"Allow me." Mr. Brice took the mask from her hands, his long fingers brushing across her skin.

"You're right," he said gently. "There is nothing wrong with making a practical match."

"Oh. Well." That was very understanding of him, she

thought with a sigh of relief. Then she wondered if he might expand on that understanding a little. "You'll not repeat what I said?"

"On my word." He pulled the knotted ribbons free and handed her the mask. "The true shame is that you're given no other choice."

Was he speaking of the lack of opportunity for women everywhere to make their way in the world, she wondered, or was he referring to her shortage of suitors? She would have asked him, but she was distracted when his gaze flew to something over her shoulder.

She heard it then . . . Footsteps. The sound was muffled and distant, still around the turn in the corridor, but it was growing louder and more distinct.

She winced and stifled the urge to swear. It wasn't uncommon for two guests to meet in the hall and share a few words in passing, but it was generally frowned upon for a young, unmarried lady to converse with a gentleman to whom she'd not been properly introduced. At seven-and-twenty, she was no longer considered a young lady, but that wouldn't stop Sir Robert from chiding her for not making the trip to the ballroom in the company of a maid.

She didn't care for his chiding.

"*Please*, do pretend we've not been speaking," she whispered and took a step to move around Mr. Brice. Perhaps, if she put a bit of distance between them . . .

Mr. Brice had another idea. He reached over and opened the door he'd emerged from earlier. "This would be easier."

"Yes, of course." Hiding seemed something of an over-reaction, but it was preferable to having a marriage proposal turn into a lecture.

She brushed past him into the dimly lighted room. The door closed behind her with a soft click of the latch, and she stood where she was for a moment, taking a deep breath to settle her racing heart. It was fortunate Mr. Brice had so quickly interpreted the cause of her discomfort. It was even more fortunate that Mr. Brice had thought to shield her presence while he sent the passing guest on his way. Quite considerate of him, really. Very nearly the act of a knight-errant.

Having never before been the object of a gentleman's chivalry, the thought brought a warm slide of pleasure and a small, secret smile. But both began to fade as the hairs on the back of her neck stood on end. She turned around slowly and found herself staring at the small ruby pin in Mr. Brice's crisp white cravat.

"*Good Lord,*" she gasped and stumbled back in retreat. "*What* do you think . . . ?"

Mr. Brice held a finger up to his lips, and she had no choice but to obediently snap her mouth shut. The unknown guest was approaching the door. She could hear his footsteps . . . or were they hers? She couldn't make out a click of a heel, and there was an odd rhythm to the gait, as if the person was shuffling down the hall.

The noise paused outside the door.

No. Oh, please, please don't.

She watched in mounting horror as Mr. Brice slowly extended his arm and took hold of the door handle. Surely he wasn't going to try to turn the key in the lock. *Surely* he wasn't stupid enough to open the door.

He wasn't. He kept perfectly still, his hand wrapped around the handle as if he meant to physically keep it from turning if necessary—which wouldn't seem *at all* suspicious to someone on the other side—until their uninvited guest resumed his leisurely stroll.

She let out a long, shaky sigh . . . then froze when the shuffling stopped and a loud creak issued from an old wooden bench not five yards down the hall.

He was stopping to rest. Who the devil actually used those benches to rest? An elderly guest, she realized, or a maid or footman neglecting their duties. It could be Mrs. Cress's mastiff, Otis, for all she knew. The dog was always about climbing on the furniture.

Adelaide bit her lip and clenched and unclenched her hands. What was she supposed to do now? She couldn't be seen leaving a dark room without causing raised brows . . .

But Mr. Brice could. Gentleman could get away with all sorts of suspicious behavior.

She waved her hand about to catch his attention, then pointed a finger at the door and mouthed the word "go" as clearly as possible.

Apparently, she wasn't clear enough. He gave a slow shake of his head.

She pressed her lips together in frustration and jabbed her finger more emphatically.

He shook his head again.

Idiot.

He lifted a finger and pointed behind her. *"Go."*

Glancing over her shoulder, she saw doors leading onto the terrace. The *dark* terrace that led down to the *dark* garden. The ballroom and lighted side of the terrace and garden were on the other side of the house.

She turned back with a scowl and shook her head.

He nodded.

She had the most ridiculous urge to shake her fist at him.

She fought it back. The silent battle of wills was getting them nowhere, and the longer they remained in the room, the greater the chance of discovery. With no other option left, she gave him a final resentful glare, then spun about and headed for the terrace doors.

The soft pad of his footsteps trailed behind her. Damn it all, he was following her. She would be in the garden, at night, with a complete stranger.

Without another thought, she grabbed a sturdy brass candlestick from the mantel. Instantly, he was beside her, his large hand covering hers on the candlestick. The scent of him filled her senses—the hint of soap on his skin, the light touch of starch on his clothes. His breath was warm and soft in her ear as he bent his head to whisper.

"It's the poker you want." His hand slid over hers until he grasped the top of the candlestick. He drew it away from her slowly and replaced it on the mantel without moving his mouth from her ear. "Longer reach."

She heard the edge of amusement in his voice and could

have cheerfully murdered him in that moment. At the very least, she would have liked to snatch the weapon back and take aim at his head. But ever the practical woman, she took the poker instead and slipped out the doors and into the garden.

Mr. Brice fell into step beside her. "There's a rarely used door around the back of the house. It opens to a short hall and stairwell that will lead you back upstairs."

"I know that." Her sister, Isobel, had an insatiable curiosity. She'd explored every inch of the house on their first day and then given a detail accounting of the building that evening. Adelaide made a mental note to apologize for the lecture she'd delivered to Isobel on the perils of snooping.

"Why are you following me?" she demanded.

"What sort of gentleman would allow a lady to traverse a dark garden alone?"

"The gentlemanly sort." Her eyes scanned the grounds for other guests, but their side of the garden was still and silent as a tomb. "Why on earth did you come into the room? You should have remained in the hall."

"*I* should have? Why not you?"

"Because . . . You opened the door. I assumed—"

"That I opened it for you? There's a fine bit of arrogance."

She tried to remember if he had motioned her inside the room or not and was forced to admit he hadn't. "Nevertheless, you should have remained outside once I had gone in."

"You were not the only person hoping to avoid a particular guest," he reminded her.

How was it she could be walking in a dark garden while carrying a fire poker and fearing for her future—all because of the man beside her—and still feel as if she needed to apologize for the circumstances?

She was not apologizing. Probably. She would reconsider the matter when she was safely back inside. For now, she needed to concentrate on the best route through the garden.

The single path before her split into three. The one to

the right went to the front of the house. The path to the left led to the back, but it wound about the flower beds close to the house. It was visible to anyone who happened to look outside. The path in the center led deeper into the garden where they would be shielded from view by a hedgerow. She could make her way to the back of the house from that path, but she hesitated at the thought of going further into the darkness with a near stranger for company.

"If I wanted to hurt you," Mr. Brice said conversationally, apparently aware of her line of thought, "I'd not have troubled to introduce myself first. Nor suggested a better choice of weapon."

Adelaide had to admit that he made a sound point. But, all the same, she readjusted her grip on the poker before setting off down the middle path.

Chapter 2

The trip through the garden began in silence. Adelaide steered them past sweetly scented flower beds and shrubs, a pretty stone fountain, and a small reflection pool that sparkled in the light of a full moon. The warm air was cooled by a soft breeze, and the occasional hum of music could be heard in the distance.

When they passed under a long arbor thick with climbing roses without incident, Adelaide let out a quiet breath and loosened her hold on the poker. If Mr. Brice was interested in assault, he could not have chosen a better spot than what essentially amounted to a long, dark tunnel. Evidently, he wasn't interested.

"May I speak now without sending you into a faint?" Mr. Brice inquired.

He'd been so quiet until now that the sudden intrusion of his voice sounded unnaturally loud in the stillness of the garden. She started a little and wished she hadn't.

"I'd not have fainted." She might well have swung the poker at him if he'd startled her before the arbor, but she wouldn't have fainted.

Flicking a glance at him, she saw he was striding along beside her with his hands behind his back, his long legs taking one step for her every two. He turned his head, caught her eye, and smiled amiably, looking for all the world as if they were out having a perfectly innocent, perfectly harmless evening stroll.

"You're being very cavalier about this," she muttered.

"I'm remaining calm," he corrected. "Would you prefer I panic?"

"No."

"Would you like me to distract you from your panic?"

"I am not panicking." Not yet, she added silently. If they didn't reach the end of the path soon, that might very well change.

"I'll distract you for my own amusement, then. Do you suppose there are more of us?"

"Us?"

"Refugees from the ball. People hiding amongst the roses and hyacinths."

They weren't taking refuge so much as they were trapped, but the image of guests scattered about the garden peeking out from behind the plants brought a reluctant smile.

"Hyacinths grow no higher than twelve to fourteen inches," she informed him. "And they're not in bloom."

"I imagine a few of the guests fancy themselves dainty enough. Sir Robert amongst them." He smiled at her scowl. "Twelve to fourteen inches. You've some interest in horticulture."

"Two insults in under a quarter hour. You've some interest in Sir Robert."

"Indeed, I do."

He didn't comment further, and she didn't ask him to explain. Mr. Brice's opinion of her suitor didn't concern her at present. Her primary focus was to find the safest, most expedient way through the garden and back to the house.

The path widened into a graveled clearing featuring several small iron benches with elaborate scrollwork. She rushed through the opening, eager to get to the other side where the end of the hedgerow marked the boundary of the garden. Once she rounded the corner, it would be but another forty or fifty yards of clear lawn to the house.

She stepped out from the small courtyard, careful to stay in the deep shadow of the hedges, and had just enough time to catch a glimpse of the open lawn and the house before Mr. Brice grabbed her arm and pulled her back.

"We've an obstacle."

He jerked his chin toward the house, and when she peeked around the bushes again, she saw the door she'd been hoping to use, and a heavyset man sitting on a bench not six feet away. Her premature relief died a swift and painful death.

"Oh, no." Oh, *damn*. She glared at the back of the man's head. They didn't have an obstacle. Obstacles could be gotten over or around with a bit of maneuvering. What they had was a blockade.

"Can he hear us?" she whispered.

"Not unless we shout."

That was something, anyway.

"Right." She worried her lip with her teeth. "Well . . . There are other doors. Other rooms."

"All leading to the main hall, the kitchen, or the servants' quarters," Mr. Brice reminded her. "You've a far better chance of returning undetected if you use that door."

"Not at present." She went back to biting her lip. "Perhaps . . . Go up there and . . . and ask to be shown to . . ." She had no idea to where a gentleman might wish to be shown. "To somewhere. The library."

A short pause. "Everyone knows where the library is."

"Then ask for something else. Just make him go away."

He leaned to look around the bushes. "I can't."

"Why not?"

"Because that"—he pointed toward the door and the man—"is Mr. Birch. He has known me for fifteen years and not believed a word to come out of my mouth for the last fourteen and a half. If I try to lead him into the house, he'll march straight for the garden."

She took a long, slow, deep breath through her nose and held it. She would not panic, nor would she shout at Mr. Brice, because neither response would bring her any closer to a solution.

He gave her a sheepish smile designed to charm. "Shall I apologize for a misspent youth?"

Rather than answer—and risk the temptation of punctuating her answer with the fire poker—she began to pace, a habit that always helped focus her thoughts and settle her nerves.

"He must be made to move. My absence will be noticed. A maid will be sent to my chambers. My sister will tell them I left—"

"It's a masquerade, Miss Ward." Mr. Brice settled his tall frame on one of the benches. "No one will know you're not amongst the guests."

"Sir Robert will know. You said he was waiting for me."

"He was. And now he probably isn't." He shrugged, looking very much at ease with the situation. The blighter. "The man has a remarkably short span of attention."

"You should go back inside, through the study, and—"

"I'll not leave you in the garden alone." He leaned against the back of the bench and stretched his legs out before him. "What if you should run across Sir Robert in the dark?"

"This is not a jest," she snapped. "Go *back* and—"

He held a hand up, cutting her off. "That last was a bid to make you smile, I admit, but I meant the first. This is a masquerade, Miss Ward. The house is crawling with revelers, gentlemen emboldened by an excess of drink and the anonymity afforded by their masks."

Again, he had a point. She'd never attended a masquerade before, but she'd heard her share of stories. Masquerade balls could be quite wild in nature. Several of the younger ladies at the house party had been denied participation by their chaperones.

Evidently, Mr. Brice was—in a roundabout and rather ineffectual way—attempting to be a gentleman. It was only fair she acknowledge his efforts.

"I appreciate your concern," she said at length. "And I apologize for being short with you."

To prove her sincerity, she propped the fire poker against the hedge and stepped away . . . But not too far away. She was apologetic, not stupid.

Mr. Brice nodded. "A very nice show of faith."

Pleased he thought so, she resumed her pacing, taking care to not walk too far from the poker.

There had to be another way to sneak into the house. There had to be a way to make the man move. There had to be a way to make Mr. Brice stop staring at her so she could *think* of a way to make the man move.

Nothing about the way Mr. Brice was watching her was overtly threatening. But everything about it was distracting. He was so very . . . present. His large frame looked out of place amongst the feminine benches and moonlit blooms. And yet he appeared perfectly at ease, perfectly content to sit still and silent and follow her every movement with those piercing green eyes.

She tried to put him out of her mind, but her body stubbornly refused to cooperate. Her pulse raced, and her skin grew over-warm under the silk of her gown. She gave brief consideration to walking a bit further into the garden so she could pace in solitude, before deciding he would only follow.

"May I make a suggestion?" He gestured to one of the benches across from him. "Have a seat. Settle your nerves. Our obstacle will bore of the night air soon enough. Another quarter hour at most. You'll be free to return to the ballroom, and Sir Robert will be none the wiser for your little adventure."

She shook her head. She couldn't sit still when she was anxious.

"Then again," he continued, "he might be a little wiser if you return looking as if you walked a half mile down the road."

"What?"

"Bit of breeze tonight," he said and pointed to her mask. "And you're kicking up a fair amount of dust."

She stopped and looked at her mask and her gown. The former was rapidly disintegrating into an unrecognizable mess of feathers and ribbons, and the latter was covered in a fine powder of dust.

"Oh, no," she whispered. Her heart sank. The gown could be shook or brushed out, but she'd never be able to repair the mask. And without a mask, she couldn't attend the ball. Without the ball, there would be no offer from Sir Robert. How had things gone so wrong so quickly?

Her voice shook. "What am I going to do?"

"You are going to sit," Mr. Brice told her gently. "And you are going to listen to reason."

If he had snapped at her, or ordered her to comply, she might have found the strength in anger to argue. But his soft tone drained the last of her fight. She nodded, but she didn't move her feet. She felt deflated, lost, and uncertain of herself.

Mr. Brice rose from his bench and walked to her. He slipped a finger under her chin and nudged until she looked up, meeting his eyes. There was kindness and warmth there, and the spark of something else, something she thought prudent to leave alone.

"I'll see you through this, Miss Ward." His rubbed his thumb lightly along her jaw. "Trust me."

She didn't trust him. She had no reason to believe him. And yet, as improbable as it seemed, she took comfort from his touch, reassurance from his words. When he took her by the elbow and led her to sit next to him on the bench, she followed without protest.

"You've not disappeared from the ball." He spoke over her head. She could feel his breath against her hair. "You simply haven't arrived yet. You'll concede there is a difference."

"Yes." There was a considerable difference, in fact. Her mind struggled out of its daze. It might have recovered faster if he'd not been sitting so close. The hard muscle of his thigh pressed against her leg, and the subtle scent of him surrounded her.

"There are a variety of excuses available to explain your tardiness," he continued. "I'll help you select one if you like, but I doubt you'll need it. I wager there are a half dozen ladies who've yet to arrive because they decided on a change of gown, or took exception to the way their maids arranged their coiffure. Do you imagine their tardiness will be questioned?"

"No, I suppose it won't."

"Neither will yours be. And as for this . . ." He drew the mask from her hands and set it aside. "Mrs. Cress is an experienced hostess. She'll have another you can borrow."

She nodded again, and her shoulders slumped in relief. She hadn't thought of that. "Yes, I suppose you're right."

"Here." He reached under his coat, produced a small flask, and handed it to her. "Have a sip. It will settle your nerves."

Wary, she took it from him and sniffed at the contents.

"Whiskey," her companion informed her.

Adelaide frowned, her first instinct to refuse. A lady did not partake of spirits. Then again, a lady also did not converse with a handsome gentleman in a dark garden while her suitor waited for her inside.

She took a long swallow. The liquid burned her throat and brought tears to her eyes. The last of her lethargy vanished.

"Oh, good heavens," she gasped.

"You've not had whiskey before," he guessed on a quiet laugh.

She shook her head and turned her face to blow out a short breath. She wondered a little that she didn't see flames.

"No." She resisted the urge to fan her mouth with her hand. "But my brother swears by the benefits of drink. Brandy, in particular. I thought there might be something to his claims."

"It has its uses. For the right ailment, and in the correct dosage."

She looked down at the flask. "What is the correct dosage?"

"Heart racing yet? Nerves still eating at you?"

"Rather."

"Then have a bit more."

She considered it. The burn had turned into a lovely warmth in her chest. She could have a glass of wine or two without feeling the effects. Surely she could have a few swallows of whiskey without losing her head.

She took another drink and sighed in pleasure when the warmth intensified. Curious to see if the sensation would continue, she drank again.

Oh, yes. That was very nice.

Mr. Brice took the flask from her hand. "I believe you've arrived at the optimal dosage."

"Hmm." He was probably right. She didn't feel drastically different save for the pleasant glow in her belly. But she did sense a lightness begin to settle over her, as if the whiskey was wrapping the sharp edge of her fear in cotton batting. "I should have thought of having a drink before leaving my room. I'd not have been so inclined to stall in the hall."

"And you'd have missed this fine adventure."

She gave a delicate snort. "I'm not in need of an adventure. I'm in need of a way to get back into the house."

"What if you didn't have to go back?"

She frowned in confusion. "Beg your pardon?"

"Suppose you had your own five thousand pounds a year," Mr. Brice explained. "Suppose you could be anywhere you liked, doing anything you wanted at this moment. Where would you be?"

She shook her head and found it wobbled a bit on her neck. "What is the point of such an exercise?"

"It's merely a way to pass the time," he said lightly. "For example, I would be at home, in my favorite chair in the library. I would have a book in one hand and a snifter of brandy in the other. There would be a hound at my feet and a roaring fire in the hearth."

"It's too warm for a fire," she pointed out.

"It would also be winter. Now you."

Oh, well, if he was asking where she would rather be at the moment, that was simple enough to answer. "I should like to be at home as well, with my nephew and—"

"No," he cut in. "You're thinking too small, Adelaide. May I call you Adelaide?"

She knew she ought to refuse, but there seemed to be some sort of disconnect between her common sense and her mouth, because what she said was, "Certainly."

"Excellent." He nodded. "You're imagining the common, Adelaide, the mundane."

"It's very nearly what you said."

"Yes, but the small and mundane are new to me. I wish for them now because I've already experienced the significant and unusual. Wouldn't you rather be in London, or Bath, or sailing across the channel on your way to Florence?"

Fascinated, she shifted in her seat to better face him. "Have you been all those places, Mr. Brice?"

"Connor," he invited. "And, yes, I have."

She could scarcely imagine it. As a young girl, she'd dreamt of traveling. Her parents had met in Prussia, the country of her mother's birth. They'd married two months later in Italy and spent the next year traveling the continent. Adelaide had listened to their tales of travel and whiled away hours imagining herself on the peaks of the Alps and playing in the waters of the Mediterranean. Her parents often spoke of returning with the family, but war and her mother's declining health had kept them from making the trip.

"I would not be averse to a voyage," she admitted.

"To where?"

She thought of going to France. Her parents had always expressed regret that they'd been unable to enter the country because of the Terror. She could visit it for them. It was an appealing sentiment. It was also mawkish and highly improbable. There were impractical dreams, and then there were impossible ones. France was most assuredly of the latter variety.

"It doesn't matter to where," she said with a shrug. "So long as it's new. Any place more than twenty miles from my home would suffice. I've never left Scotland." It was less than a half day's drive from her home to the border, and less than five miles from where she sat now, and yet she'd never made the trip.

"You'll have your chance after the wedding."

Her eyes flicked in the direction of the house. "I've not yet received a proposal."

"But you expect it."

There didn't seem a reason to deny it or play coy. "I do. I thought perhaps tonight."

"Where will you go?"

"For a bridal tour?" The pleasure of the game dimmed. "I won't go anywhere. Sir Robert does not care for travel."

"I see," he said. It was astounding, really, how much understanding could be conveyed in those two little words.

That sort of understanding made her uneasy. It was too similar to pity for her liking. She didn't want Connor to feel sorry for her, in part because it pricked her pride, but mostly because it was depressing to think that there might be good cause for sympathy—that a marriage to Sir Robert would, in fact, be a pitiable state of affairs.

"He has many other fine qualities," she blurted out.

If Connor was taken aback by the emphatic statement, it didn't show. His lips twitched. "I am agog to hear them."

"He is a baron," she reminded him.

"In possession of five thousand pounds a year. Yes, I know," he replied with a nod. Then he just sat there, obviously waiting for her to elaborate on Sir Robert's fine qualities. Which was unfortunate, because "he is a baron" was really all she had at the ready.

It took a full thirty seconds for her to think of something else. "He is considered handsome by the ladies."

"And do you agree?"

"Well . . ." She frowned, picturing him in her mind. Sir Robert brushed his hair forward in a severe manner, so that nearly every strand ran parallel to the ground. And he had a penchant for brightly colored waistcoats and overlarge cravat pins. "I think Sir Robert is, possibly, on occasion . . . much dressed."

"Much dressed," Connor echoed and ran his tongue along his teeth as if tasting the description. "That is very diplomatic."

"Diplomacy is a useful and admirable tool."

"Sometimes. Sometimes it's a crutch and a barrier." He bent his head to catch her gaze, and she saw the inviting light of humor in his eyes. "Sir Robert and I are not friends, Adelaide. He'll not hear of your opinion from me, nor believe a word of it, if he did. I wager you can't speak of it to your friends or your family. Why not speak of it to me?"

He made it sound so tempting, so simple. And perhaps it was. Why shouldn't she speak her mind, here where only the two of them would hear? Why not say aloud what she had always thought?

"He's rather like a parrot caught in a mighty tailwind."

Connor's deep laughter filled the courtyard.

Appalled, she slapped a hand to her mouth. Then made herself drop it when she realized she was mumbling behind her fingers.

"I didn't mean to say that. I should not have said that."

"I'm delighted you did."

"It was most unkind."

"Not at all. Unfortunate styles of hair and dress are easily remedied. Unkind would be to point out he has an oversized nose. Poor man can't do a thing about that."

"*You've* an oversized nose." Good heavens, what had come over her?

"You see? Very unkind." He tilted his head just a fraction to the side. "You're a little bit foxed, aren't you?"

"Certainly not." She gave the idea further consideration. "How does one know?"

"In this case, one is informed by an objective bystander. You're a little bit foxed."

That would certainly explain what had come over her, and why her thoughts seemed to flit about her head like hummingbirds arguing over a flower. Just as she thought one was settled, another buzzed it aside. She tried to work up a proper fret over this new dilemma but couldn't concentrate long enough to see it done.

She blew out a short breath and slumped back in her seat. "I can't see him like this."

"Sir Robert? Why not? You're tipsy, not inebriated."

"He doesn't approve of spirits."

There was a short pause before he spoke. "You must be joking."

She bobbed her head, realized that didn't make any sense, and shook it instead. "No. I am in earnest. He doesn't believe a lady should partake and is most adamant on the subject."

"The man's a hypocrite. He'll be three sheets to the wind before two. I wager he's already a sheet and a half there."

"A sheet and a half?" She laughed at the saying but didn't believe it to be true of Sir Robert. Oh, he enjoyed his wine, and she'd smelled spirits on him a time or two, but she'd never seen him lose his head. Not the way her brother did when he overindulged. She shook her head to dislodge the thought. She didn't want to think of her brother now. Or Sir Robert for that matter. She felt a little silly, a little reckless. She wanted to enjoy the sensations.

She leaned toward Connor and smiled at him. "And what am I?"

"Slightly foxed," he reminded her.

"Yes, but in keeping with the theme of sheets . . ." she prompted.

"Ah." He smiled back, that lovely, lovely smile she was certain she could stare at all evening. "You're embroidery."

She straightened. "That's not linen."

"But it's to be found on linen. It decorates. It adds value. It gives life to the tired and bland." He reached up and stroked her cheek with the back of his hand. "It makes the everyday extraordinary."

The warmth of his fingers sent a pleasant shiver along her skin.

"I think perhaps we've gone off topic," she whispered.

"Just on to one that makes you uncomfortable." His lips curved with amusement as he let his hand fall from her cheek. "Doesn't Sir Robert pay you compliments?"

"Yes." She wondered if it would be unforgivably forward if she asked him to return his hand.

"Tell me what he's said."

Connor's steady gaze and smile made it difficult to think. It took her several moments to come up with an example. "He has told me I have lovely eyes."

"They're passable. What else?"

"Passable?"

Humor danced in his eyes. "What else?"

Defensive now, she scowled at him. "He compared the color of my cheeks to rose petals."

"Fairly unoriginal of him. What else?"

She folded her arms over her chest. "I'm clever."

So help her God, if he contradicted *that* . . .

His lips twitched. "I believe you just made that up."

"I did not." She had made up the bit about her cheeks and the roses, though. "I bested Lady Penwright yesterday at a game of chess. Sir Robert was suitably impressed."

It was very nearly impossible to lose to Lady Penwright in a game of anything, but as Lady Penwright had never made mention of a Mr. Brice—and the lady did so like to make mention of handsome gentlemen—Adelaide felt it safe to assume Connor was familiar with neither the lady nor her lack of gaming skills.

Apparently, Connor wasn't concerned with either.

"He doesn't deserve you."

She blinked at the non sequitur. "I beg your pardon?"

"Sir Robert doesn't deserve you." He spoke quietly but clearly. The humor was gone from his features, replaced by an intensity she found alarming.

She stood and walked a few feet away, though whether she was trying to distance herself from him or from what he said, she couldn't tell. "A half hour's acquaintance is not a sufficient amount of time to make a judgment—"

"Uninspired flattery," he cut in. "A gentleman much dressed. A man afraid to travel. Disapproves—"

"I never said he was afraid."

"You don't want him," he said softly and rose from the bench.

"Of course I do."

"No. You want the security his income will provide." His eyes caught and held her gaze as he walked toward her. "You don't even like him."

It was mesmerizing, the way he moved. He closed the distance between them in the long, unhurried strides of a man confident in what he sought and convinced of his success in obtaining what he desired. She had ample opportunity to back away. But she couldn't move. She couldn't drag her eyes away.

"He's been very kind to me," she heard herself whisper.

"And that's enough for you, is it?" The light of the moon disappeared behind his tall form. "Kindness and an income?"

He was so close, she had to tilt her head back to see his shadowed face. "Yes."

"Don't you long for something more?"

Yes. "No."

A small smile tugged at his lips as he slipped an arm around her waist and pulled her close. "You do."

Her hands flew to his chest in a futile effort to create the illusion of space between them. She shook her head, or thought she shook her head. It was difficult to say. And it made very little difference either way. He simply pulled her closer, bent his head, and whispered against her lips.

"Sweetheart, everyone wants more."

And then he was kissing her, his mouth moving over hers in a series of soft brushes and tender caresses. He was so careful, so gentle, she could almost believe that he was unsure of her, that she had the option of pulling away. But the iron band of his arm around her waist told a different story. He wasn't unsure, merely patient. He kissed her with gentle demand, as if he meant to coax her into an inevitable submission. Even if it took all night.

The wait wasn't quite that long. The supple dance of his lips warmed her blood and drew a sigh from her mouth. Her limbs grew heavy and her head light. She leaned against him, feeling the hard beat of his heart against her palms and the strength of his large body through the barrier of their clothing.

His hand cupped her face, and his thumb brushed along her jaw to press lightly on her chin. She opened her mouth without thought, and his tongue darted inside for a taste.

She heard her own gasp, and the amused whisper against her mouth.

"Do you want more?"

In that moment, she wanted everything. She nodded and was rewarded with the feathery brush of his lips against her temple.

"Then don't see him tonight." He covered her mouth before she could answer, lingering just long enough to tease at that promise of more. "Don't see him."

"Yes," she whispered, stretching up for him when he pulled away.

He kept just out of reach. "Swear it."

"I swear." She was only vaguely aware of saying the words.

"Remember," he whispered. He pressed his lips to hers briefly, skimmed a hand along her cheek, and let her go.

Disoriented, she stood where she was as he backed two steps away. If she'd felt steadier on her feet, she might have followed him. Instead, she said the first thought that popped into her head.

"You said there was more. You promised—" She broke off and winced. Even tipsy and dazed, she knew when she was making a fool of herself.

Connor merely smiled. "You made a promise as well. Keep yours first."

"Oh." Something about that struck her as terribly unfair, but she wasn't willing to embarrass herself further by arguing. It seemed wise not to say anything at all, in fact. She'd never kissed a man before and hadn't the foggiest notion of what was expected of her now. Should she make polite conversation? Stare longingly into his eyes? Offer a quick farewell? The last seemed rather appealing, all of a sudden.

Connor leaned a bit to look around the hedge. "Our obstacle is gone."

"Oh. Well." What marvelous timing. Feeling equal parts dazed, awkward, and relieved, she forced her legs into cooperation and turned for the house. When she realized Connor wasn't following her, she turned back. "Are you coming?"

He shook his head. "I'll watch from here."

"Well," she said again, and feeling as if she ought to make some gesture, that one of them ought to do *something*, she smiled and gave a wobbly curtsy. "Good night, Connor."

"Sweet dreams, Adelaide."

He spoke the words like a caress, and Adelaide felt the warmth of them, and the heat of his gaze on her back, as she navigated her way across the lawn through the shadows. Her last thought before she opened the back door to the house was that the night had certainly not gone as expected.

Chapter 3

Connor strolled to the door after Adelaide went inside. The night, he decided, had gone mostly as planned. He leaned back against the cool stone of the house and took a moment to savor his success . . . and the lingering taste of Adelaide Ward on his tongue. He'd known she'd be sweet. The hint of tartness was a pleasant surprise.

He avoided surprises as a rule. Or, more accurately, he avoided being taken by surprise—catching other people off guard was an entirely different matter. In the case of Miss Ward, however, he was willing to be charmed by the unexpected.

He was willing to be all kinds of things with Miss Ward. Naked came to mind. For now, however, he'd settle for engaged. The challenge would be to convince her to settle for the same, but he would manage it. The lady's circumstances, courtesy of her degenerate brother, had already done half the work for him.

Wolfgang Ward had wasted the family fortune on a string of business ventures so risky they'd been little more than poorly conceived wagers. Rumor had it that Wolfgang's late wife was in part to blame for his choice of investments, but Connor hadn't found anything to substantiate the claim. Moreover, the bad gambles had continued on after the wife's death in childbirth.

That had been nearly two years ago. Wolfgang had been given ten months to celebrate the birth of his son and mourn the passing of his wife before he'd been hauled off to debtors' prison . . . where, unbeknownst to Adelaide at the time, he'd proceeded to procure his heaviest debt yet. The source and extent of that debt remained a mystery to her still.

Only a dark spot of providence had kept Wolfgang's sisters and his son from the poorhouse—a small inheritance to Adelaide and Isobel from a distant cousin. It wasn't enough to free Wolfgang from prison, but it was sufficient to keep the women and child housed and fed . . . for now. There couldn't be much left, and Wolfgang's creditors were clamoring to have what little remained. It wouldn't be long before they convinced the courts that with a woman was no place to leave an inheritance.

Adelaide was running out of time and money.

Connor smiled grimly. Fortunately for her, he had plenty of funds. Time, however, was a concern. He'd bought a day, maybe two, with tonight's little ruse. He needed more.

The fact that tonight had been a ruse caused Connor only passing discomfort. There was a time and place for a guilty conscience. Namely, when one has done something wrong. He didn't doubt for a second that he was in the right.

"What you scowling for, boy? Couldn't have gone better, you ask me."

Connor merely lifted a brow as Michael Birch appeared from around the corner of the house. The heavyset man rubbed his hands together in excitement as he limped his way over on a bad knee. Though edging past middle age, Michael's red hair retained its rich color, and his round face was as smooth as the day they'd met. Connor had been sixteen then, just as he'd told Adelaide. The rest he'd made up. It didn't take Michael six months to spot a liar. Deceit was the man's stock and trade.

"It went as planned," Connor said by way of a response.

Mostly as planned, he amended silently when the back door rattled and cracked open. Gregory O'Malley's ancient visage appeared in the space. His wrinkled and weathered face split into a wide grin. "What say you, lad? Will she be having you?"

"Eventually." Connor watched the old man emerge from the door. Gregory was spry for his age, but it was a toss-up as to which creaked more, the door hinges or the old man's bones. "Did you follow her?"

"Aye. It's straight to her chambers she went."

"You stopped outside the sitting room earlier." *That* hadn't been part of the plan. Gregory had been instructed to walk slowly down the hall, past the door, and take a seat on the bench.

"Sure and I did." There wasn't a whisper of regret in Gregory's voice. "A man's needing a spot of fun now and then. And a lass is needing something to think about."

"You're fortunate she didn't think of swooning."

Michael made a scoffing sound in the back of his throat. "Our girl's more spine than that."

She did, in fact, but neither of the men were in a position to know it. "You've never met her."

"Seen her, haven't I?" Michael countered. "Coming alone to visit her worthless brother in prison with a babe in her arms and naught but a prayer to protect her."

"Aye," Gregory agreed. "It's spine she has. She'll make a fine wife . . . You will be marrying the lass?"

Michael leaned toward Gregory. "He were scowling and brooding a minute ago."

"Worried? Our Connor?"

Connor gave them a facile smile. "I'm not worried. She agreed not to see Sir Robert tonight."

"And tomorrow?" Gregory asked.

"We'll see."

The two men exchanged looks but said nothing.

Connor debated how much to tell them. "The courtship is further along than I realized. She's expecting an offer."

"Well, there'll be time to woo her after the banns are read," Michael said at length. "Not final till they've paid a visit to the vicar."

"And the marriage bed," Gregory added.

Because the image of Adelaide and Sir Robert sharing a bed turned his stomach, Connor pushed the thought, and the subject, aside.

"It's no simple matter for a lady to break an engagement with a baron." He straightened from the wall. "And Miss Ward is a bird-in-the-hand sort."

Michael looked to Gregory. "Well, here's hoping she agrees to marry him tonight, then."

Gregory nodded sagely. "Aye."

The logic of that escaped Connor.

"Why?" he asked Michael.

"She'll have broken her promise to you, won't she have? And the sort of woman willing to break a promise now is the same sort who'll break a promise later. But if she keeps to her word now, and gives her word to Sir Robert later . . ." He trailed off, shared a look with Gregory, then offered Connor a bolstering smile and pat on the arm. "Well, with any luck, we'll find she's not to be trusted, eh?"

"She'll not break her promise."

"Then you're in a bit of a fix."

"Don't scare the boy." Gregory lowered his voice and leaned in a little. "Look here, lad. Used to be, if a man were wanting a particular lass to wife, he took her, and there was an end to the matter."

Connor gave the old man a bland look.

"He's not suggesting you steal the girl," Michael explained.

"I'd never be suggesting such a thing." Gregory looked suitably abashed. He sidled a little closer. ". . . But there *was* a time a man gave the notion a proper thinking over."

"I've thought it over." He'd had a fantasy or two that fell

along those lines, anyway. That was close enough. "The answer is no."

He started out across the lawn toward the line of trees beyond the garden. The men fell into step behind him.

"Told you it wouldn't work," Michael whispered.

"Boy's gone soft."

"No more'n a body expect, what with all your coddling."

"*My* coddling? Was it me who talked him out of shooting the bastard in Montserrat, I ask you? It was not."

Connor smiled at the exchange and let the sound of their bickering fade into the background of his mind. He was accustomed to their squabbles. Like the scrape and groan of a favorite old chair, he took pleasure and comfort in the familiar noise. He took strength of purpose as well. These men, who had once been his saviors and mentors, were now family. He owed them. He'd have been lost to the gutters of Boston if not for Michael and Gregory. And they'd have spent the last year of their lives as free men instead of caged in a prison cell if it hadn't been for him . . . and, in a more direct manner, Sir Robert.

If it was the last thing he did, Connor would see Sir Robert suffer the cost of his crimes.

Adelaide Ward would be the first payment.

*A*delaide wasn't any less tipsy by the time she stumbled her way into her room. She was, however, putting considerably more effort into pretending she was fully sober. She ran hands down her gown and tried to focus her thoughts. When that failed, she tried focusing her eyes instead.

Isobel was still up, reading a book in a chair by the window. They shared the same slight stature and finely boned features, but Isobel had their mother's dark blonde hair and a set of mild blue eyes that hid a stubborn, and oft-times impetuous, temperament.

Isobel flicked a narrowed glance at Adelaide before returning her attention to her book, neatly reminding Adelaide that they had argued before the ball.

"Is it done, then?" Isobel asked caustically. "Has the fair maiden sacrificed herself to the dragon and saved the kingdom?"

"No." Adelaide walked very carefully across the room, silently congratulated herself for not tripping, and tossed her mask on the bed. "The realm of Ward remains in peril."

"Sir Robert didn't ask?" Isobel looked up from her book, her hard expression replaced with one of confusion. "And you've returned?"

"I never went."

"But you've been gone an hour at least. Where have you been?" Isobel squinted. "And why are you so mussed?"

"In a sitting room. In the garden." She waved her hand about. "There was a breeze. I never made it to the ball."

"The garden?" Clearly intrigued, Isobel set her book aside and stood. "Whatever were you doing there?"

She tried, and failed, to come up with a suitable lie. "Avoiding Sir Robert."

"Oh! I knew it," Isobel cried with uninhibited delight. "I *knew* you would come to your senses."

"I've *lost* my senses."

"Rubbish. You had lost them, and now you've become reacquainted with them." Isobel crossed the room and patted Adelaide's arm with exaggerated sympathy. "Poor dear. I've heard the process can be quite disorienting. Having never lost my own, I can't . . ."

Isobel trailed off and sniffed. "You smell . . ." She leaned in and sniffed again. "Decidedly flammable."

"Oh, I . . . There was a sideboard . . . In the sitting room. I thought perhaps a sip to quell the nerves . . ."

"Are you drunk, Adelaide?" She sounded positively enamored of the idea.

"Absolutely not. I'm . . ." A bubble of laughter escaped. "Embroidered."

"Embroidered? What on earth does that mean?"

Adelaide shook her head and dragged her hands down her face with the irrational idea that it might wipe the stubborn smile from her face. "It means I've made an awful mess of things. Dear heavens, what have I done?"

"Made fine use of an hour by the looks of it."

Adelaide ignored that, slipped her shoes off, and began to pace between the bed and the door. She told herself to concentrate. She would figure a way out of the tangle she'd created. She would *think*, damn it.

"What in heaven's name was I thinking?" she muttered.

Certainly, she hadn't been considering her family, or Sir Robert, or the money she'd spent on a new ball gown. She frowned down at her skirts. It wasn't the finest silk or the most fashionable of cuts, but the dress was new, and its production had cost a pretty penny. She could have spent that money on new half boots for herself and Isobel. They were in desperate need of new boots. She should have used the money for something more practical.

"I should have gone to the ball," she muttered.

It was too late now. Even if she were not embroidered, even if she'd not made the promise to Connor, she'd be damned if she kissed one man in a garden and accepted a marriage proposal from another man in the same night. She liked to think she retained some measure of honor.

How long, she wondered, did one need to wait between kiss and proposal?

"A day or two?" She flicked a glance at Isobel who, accustomed to Adelaide's habit of pacing and speaking to herself, had taken a seat on the arm of the chair.

Isobel shrugged. "You do realize I haven't the foggiest notion what you're talking about."

"Of course I do." She'd just forgotten for a moment. Just as she'd forgotten how much she needed Sir Robert's income and how much she had spent on the ball gown.

"I suppose I could try to sell it," she murmured, but it seemed such a waste, and she was so weary of selling her possessions. Nearly everything of value her family owned had been pawned away for a fraction of its worth.

"It's not even been used, really." An idea occurred to

her. She stopped and grinned at Isobel. "You should use it."

"What's that?"

"You should go to the ball."

Isobel straightened from the chair, blue eyes sparking with eagerness. "Do you mean it?"

"There's no sense in letting the gown go to waste." She laughed as Isobel immediately began to struggle with the buttons on the back of her dress. "You'll have to procure a new mask from Mrs. Cress, however. Mine has perished."

Isobel threw a glance at the bed and grimaced. "May it rest in peace."

Feeling slightly better for having righted this one mistake at least, Adelaide brushed out her skirts and made the clumsy (on her part) exchange of gowns with Isobel. She sat Isobel at the vanity, made several maladroit attempts to do something with her sister's hair, then gave the task up to Isobel.

Isobel all but squirmed on the bench in her excitement. "Perhaps I'll meet the gentleman who purchased Ashbury Hall and he'll fall madly in love with me."

Adelaide thought of the vast and long-abandoned manor that sat just a few miles from their home. "We don't know the gentleman who purchased Ashbury Hall. We don't anyone wealthy enough to have purchased Ashbury Hall."

"But we might, by the end of the night."

It took a moment for Adelaide to recognize the glint in Isobel's eyes. "Right."

She strode to the bellpull and yanked.

Isobel frowned at her. "What are you doing?"

"You need a chaperone." She was tipsy, not unconscious.

"I don't," Isobel protested. "How am I to have fun with a chaperone looking over my shoulder?"

Rather than answer, Adelaide yanked the bellpull again. Harder.

"Oh, very well." Isobel gave a disgruntled huff and returned her attention to the mirror. "See if Lady Engsly is amenable. She's a cheerful sort, and she's not intimidated by your dragon."

"Sir Robert is *not*—"

"What shall I tell Mrs. Cress?"

Adelaide blinked at the blatant change of subject. "What shall you tell her about what?"

"You *are* tipsy." Isobel laughed. "How shall I explain your absence?"

"Oh." She tried to remember what excuse they had planned for Isobel's absence from the ball. It certainly hadn't been that the Ward sisters had been unable to afford the purchase of more than one ball gown. "Tell her I have the headache."

"I imagine there will be some truth to that in a few hours."

Adelaide took a seat on the bed and watched Isobel fuss over her appearance. She was such a pretty young woman. So full of life and hope and energy. But that life was stifled by poverty, and Adelaide knew all too well that, unless something changed, the hope would die before long.

"Isobel," she said and waited for their eyes to meet in the mirror. "Would it be so very terrible, having a wealthy baron for a brother?"

It was a long moment before Isobel spoke, and when she did, her voice was soft and filled with a sadness that tore at Adelaide's heart.

"I should adore a wealthy brother." She turned on the bench to face Adelaide. "But I don't want a martyr for a sister."

Adelaide digested that in silence. It was the last thing said between them in private that night, and the last thing Adelaide thought of before she closed her eyes and dreamed of dragons and maidens. And a knight with seductive green eyes and lips that tasted lightly of whiskey.

Chapter 4

$\mathcal{A}$ delaide rose the next morning with every intention of putting the events of the night before behind her. It was a remarkably easy decision to make, requiring only a brief reflection on what a fool she'd made of herself. Drinking whiskey, kissing strangers in a garden, promising to avoid her suitor—she could scarce believe her own behavior.

She could, however, take very good care not to repeat her mistakes. She would dress, go to breakfast, pay her attentions to Sir Robert, and otherwise pretend she had never met a man named Mr. Connor Brice.

She made good on the first and second intentions. She enjoyed less success with the third and fourth. Sir Robert was not present at breakfast, a detail she all but overlooked during her spectacular failure at ignoring the existence of Connor Brice.

He wasn't at breakfast either—she noticed this immediately—and she spent the next hour trying to figure how she might inquire after him without confessing to all that they'd met the night before.

She finally gave the effort up when Mrs. Cress stood from the table and suggested the guests join her for a stroll about the grounds. Adelaide demurred, claiming a lingering headache made her poor company. She added the lie to her ever-increasing list of sins. She hadn't a headache. She'd woke that morning feeling fit as ever. A small, welcomed, and undeserved blessing.

Her guilt increased when she slipped out one door of the breakfast room just as Sir Robert entered through another. She would speak with him soon, she told herself firmly . . . but not right now. First, she needed a long walk to settle her mind.

She briefly fooled herself into believing that it was fresh air and solitude she sought as she made her way through the garden, taking care to stay well away from the other guests.

It was such a lovely morning, after all. The late summer sun warmed her back while a light wind caught at her skirts and cooled her skin. All around her were the sights and sounds of a well-loved garden—the hum of bees amongst the asters, the tidy mounds of sweet william, and the lush and wild growth of an ancient climbing rose. She concentrated on each, doing her best to distract herself from thoughts of Connor Brice, but her best proved woefully inadequate.

Her mind was filled with thoughts of Connor. She wondered when she might see him again. She wondered *if* she might see him again. She wondered if he might kiss her again. She wondered how and when, exactly, she had become a shameless tart.

Disgusted with herself, she spun on her heel and began a determined march back the way she'd come. She would go to her room and stay there until dinner, or until Sir Robert requested her company. Whichever came first. She passed the rose and the sweet william, turned a corner, and there was Connor.

Her feet came to an abrupt halt. So did her heart, a split second before it started again with a painful thud.

He sat not six feet away, on a bench that had been unoc-
cupied on her first passing. Leaning back, with his long
legs stretched out before him, he looked relaxed, confident,
and even more handsome than she remembered. Probably,
it wasn't rational to think twelve hours was a sufficient
amount of time to have forgotten how someone looked. But
she wasn't inclined to think rationally at present, not while
the sun was weaving brighter strands of gold in his hair and
he was giving her that wonderfully inviting smile.

"I wondered if I might see you here," he murmured.

Too late, she realized that she should have been a little
less preoccupied with wondering when she might see him
and a little more concerned with what she ought to say to
him if she did.

Because what she did say—or croaked, to be accurate—
was, "Morning."

And, really, he was the first man she had ever kissed—
there had to be an infinite number of more eloquent state-
ments to croak than that.

He shifted his large frame, making room for her on the
bench. "Will you sit?"

She shouldn't. She really shouldn't. She did anyway and
felt like the proverbial moth to the flame.

"You weren't at breakfast." Though not a brilliant comment, she deemed it an improvement over her first attempt
at speech.

"I rose early." He turned his head at the sound of distant
laughter in the garden. "Why aren't you with the others?"

She shrugged, affecting a casual demeanor. "I'm not
fond of crowds, particularly. I prefer the quiet."

"Shall I leave you to your thoughts?"

"No. I'm not fond of solitude either." It occurred to her
that he might be angling for a polite way to be rid of her.
"Would you care to be alone? I didn't mean to impose—"

He tilted his head at her, full lips curved in amusement.
"Are we back to being shy with one another?"

"I don't mean to be." She plucked at an imaginary piece
of lint on her gown. "I don't know why I should be."

Well, yes, she did. She'd kissed him, an act that should make any decent young lady blush. And now she sat there making idle conversation as if the two of them were acquaintances merely passing the time. It was, in a word, awkward.

"I could fetch a glass of whiskey if you like," he offered. "Or a fire poker."

She stopped plucking and laughed. It was a relief to hear him speak so casually of their last meeting. Like poking fun at the pitiful condition of her mask the night before, acknowledging the obvious was far easier than dancing around it.

"That won't be necessary," she said primly. "Thank you."

"Are you certain? You were remarkably confident with a bit of drink in you and a weapon at hand."

"I cannot believe I was so ill behaved." She threw him a look of censure, but there was no heat in it. "I cannot believe you would be such a cad as to remind me."

"I liked you ill behaved." His mouth curved in the most wicked of grins. "I liked being a cad."

That, she decided, was much, much too casual. And dear heavens, that smile. It could tempt a woman to all manner of sins. It *had* tempted her to sin. She looked toward the house. "I should go. I shouldn't have—"

"I shouldn't have teased," he cut in gently. "I apologize."

She eyed him warily. "If I stay, will you promise to behave as a gentleman?"

"You have my word as a cad." He smiled again, but there was no wickedness, just a disarming silliness that eased her tension. "Tell me what you did after we parted last night. Was your tardiness noticed?"

"No." She hesitated, uncertain of how much she cared to admit. "I never went. My sister gave my excuses."

"Your sister, Isobel?"

She nodded and leapt at the chance to settle on a safe topic. "Yes. Isobel with an 'o.' " She laughed softly at his raised brows. "She often finds it necessary to make that distinction."

"Adelaide, Isobel with an 'o,' and Wolfgang, correct? An unusual set of names."

She stifled a cringe at the mention of her brother. Wolfgang's circumstances were public knowledge, but she'd rather hoped that knowledge had managed to slip by Connor.

"My mother was Prussian," she replied, setting her embarrassment aside—something she'd become all too adept at over the last year. "Her mother was Italian."

"But the best part of you is British."

She smiled at that. "My father liked to think so. He liked to say so as well, but only to nettle my mother."

His tone and expression turned gentle. "They didn't get on."

"Oh, they did," she assured him. "Very much. They liked to tease, that's all."

"A common way to show affection." He reached behind him, plucked a bright yellow flower, and held it out to her. "I believe this is another."

Flattered, she extended her hand to take the offering. "Thank you—"

He drew the token out of reach. "Do you know what it is?"

"Yes. It's *Helenium*, brought from the Americas." It was also known as sneezeweed, which she didn't see the benefit of mentioning.

"Do you have a favorite?"

"Flower?" She shook her head. "No, though I've a fondness for poppies."

"Poppies. I'll remember that and buy you a dozen."

She blushed with pleasure at the thought. She'd never received flowers from a gentleman, not even Sir Robert. "You can't. Buy them, I mean."

"Everything can be bought."

"But they won't last. They wither as soon as you cut them." For her, that was part of their appeal. Poppies couldn't be tamed in a vase or lost in a bouquet. "They have to be appreciated in the garden, just as they are."

He twirled the flower between long, elegant fingers. "Will this last?"

"For a time. Without the proper nutrients, everything will wither eventually."

"Until then," he said and handed her the bloom.

Their fingers met on the stem, and she remembered how those fingers had felt trailing across her cheek. The memory made her blush and pull the flower free with more force than she intended.

"Isobel paints them," she blurted out before remembering that Isobel no longer painted because they had long since run out of funds for supplies. "She has a tremendous talent for it. My father used to say that when I gardened, I created beauty for a season, and when my sister painted, she captured an essence of that beauty for eternity. He was a hopeless poet."

"Do poets come any other way?"

"Not that I'm aware of," she replied with a smile. She was glad she'd chosen to stay. It was so pleasant to sit with a man and make interesting conversation. She'd forgotten just how pleasant.

With Sir Robert, she listened. Or tried to listen, if one wished to be precise. The man wasn't a bore, exactly, but he was predictable and more than a little redundant. Always he spoke of his most recent acquisition for his stable, then his most recent purchase from the tailor, and finally his most recently acquired tidbit of gossip, which generally concerned an individual she had never met and knew nothing about. If she were very lucky, he would vary his routine with a complaint or two about his staff. Her contributions were limited to "oh, my" or "oh, yes" or "what a pity" at the appropriate pauses in conversation.

Sir Robert never asked her questions. He knew nothing of her family, her past, her likes or dislikes. She very much doubted he was aware of her interest in horticulture, or her sister's gift for art.

It was different with Connor. He made her laugh, made

her think, made her feel. He had learned more about her in less than twelve hours than Sir Robert had in four months.

The exchange reminded her of the lively debates and long, rambling talks she'd once shared with her father. He'd encouraged her to think for herself, to be an active participant in the conversation. She missed that, missed having a man speak with her rather than at her.

"Where are you?"

Connor's murmured question pulled her from her musings. She shook her head. She didn't want to think or talk about Sir Robert. Not this morning. Not just this minute. She didn't want to think about the years of mindless interaction ahead of her.

"I was woolgathering. Tell me what your family is like."

"My mother was Irish, and my father was a British gentleman with Scottish holdings."

She frowned a little. That was fairly nondescript. "Do you have siblings?"

"None I care to claim."

She thought at first that he might be jesting, but a quick search of his features showed no signs of humor.

"I have felt that way once or twice," she admitted. There had been days when she wanted nothing more than to renounce Wolfgang.

"About your brother," Connor guessed.

She nodded reluctantly. So much for the hope he'd not heard of Wolfgang's failings. "We were very fond of each other as children."

"But now . . ."

But now her brother sat in prison because of debts he'd accumulated through a combination of obstinacy and selfishness. And he would continue to sit there, unless she did something about it. Suddenly, the morning didn't seem quite so charming. The changing light, the warm air, the whisper of the breeze through leaves, it all seemed rather sad.

"I wish . . ."

"What do you wish?"

She wished she had Isobel's talent for capturing beauty.

She might have stolen a moment or two that morning and kept it for herself.

It was an impossible dream, an unreasonable expectation.

"I wish to return to the house." She rose and, before she could think better of it, asked, "Will you escort me?"

"I can't."

"Why not? There's nothing amiss with a lady and a gentleman taking a stroll from a garden in broad daylight." Particularly when there were no other guests about to see and comment.

"Not generally, no."

"I can't imagine any circumstance that would . . ." The most horrifying thought occurred to her. "Dear heavens, you're married."

"No. I haven't a wife, or a fiancée."

She blew out a short breath of relief. Her sins were many. She had no desire to add adultery to the list. "Then why—?"

"Because I haven't an invitation either."

"To come in from the garden?" She gave a small, perplexed laugh. "Don't be ridiculous."

"To be *in* the garden," he corrected.

The implications of that statement sank in slowly. "You jest."

He gave her a sheepish smile. "I'm afraid not. The lady I wished to avoid last night was your hostess."

"You . . . You're an *interloper*?" Oh, *good Lord*. No wonder he'd been hiding last night and missing that morning at breakfast. "Why would—?"

"To see you," he replied easily.

"We just . . . You can't . . . I have to go." She spun around and headed for the house at a pace just shy of an outright trot.

"Adelaide, wait." Connor caught up and fell into step beside her.

"You should have told me. You should have . . . Good Lord, you broke into the house."

"The door was open," he countered. "It was a ball. I'm not the first gentleman to invite himself to a ball. Happens all the time during the season. It's an accepted practice."

Having never participated in a London season, she had absolutely no idea if that was true.

"Accepted or not, it was wrong, and you ought to have told me—"

"I should have. Will you stop a moment so I can apologize properly?"

She shook her head. "Sir Robert will be looking for me."

And if he was not, she would begin looking for him. It was well past time she remembered why she had come to Mrs. Cress's house party.

"You can't marry him," Connor said gruffly.

"I haven't a choice," she admitted, hoping bluntness would put an end to the matter.

"You do. Marry me, instead."

"What?" She threw him an incredulous glance and increased her pace. "No."

"Why not?"

Why not? Was the man unhinged? "I've only just met you. We scarcely know each other."

"I'm one-and-thirty. I have all my teeth. I've never before proposed to a lady. And I have more money than Sir Robert."

"Those are not—"

"I've thought of nothing but you for months."

She stumbled to a stop under the rose arbor and spun to stare at him. "We met last night."

"I've seen you before, bringing your nephew to see his father. You passed by my window every Saturday."

She shook her head in patent disbelief. Though most of the people in her village of Banfries were familiar to her, she couldn't claim to have met everyone who resided in the four miles between her home and the prison. "You've watched me?"

"Just for those minutes I could see you."

She didn't know what to say to that. She didn't know what to feel about it. Should she be flattered? Unnerved? Offended? She rather thought she was all three, but they were buried under a mountain of astonishment.

Evidently interpreting her silence as encouragement, Connor smiled and reached for her hand. "Marry me, Adelaide."

In the absence of anything else to say, she settled for the obvious. "You're in earnest."

She couldn't believe he was in earnest. It was even more alarming that a small part of her was tempted to accept his offer. She knew almost nothing of Connor Brice except that he was willing to sneak into a party to which he was not invited and watch a woman through his window for months before speaking with her. He could be a drunkard. Or a consummate gambler. He could be a thief or a murderer. He could be all four.

She didn't love Sir Robert, but four months of courtship had afforded her some assurance of his character.

Those four months had also depleted much of her inheritance. She was out of time.

"I can't." The words felt thick and sour in her mouth. Her hand felt cold and empty when she pulled it away. "I'm sorry. I have to go."

Connor stepped in front of her, blocking her path. "Not to Sir Robert."

"He's a good man."

"Give me time to prove I'm a better man. Give me another day."

She shook her head. Every day she put off Sir Robert was a day her family's future remained in peril. The risk of offending Sir Robert was too real, the consequences too great.

"I'm offering another option," Connor pressed. "I'm giving you the chance to have something more than—"

"I don't need more. I don't want it." How easily the lie slipped from her tongue. "I want to secure what I have."

That, at least, was the truth.

A hardness settled over his face. "Is there nothing I can say to change your mind?"

"Nothing. I'm sorry." She stepped past him, only to have him catch her arm and spin her around again.

"Kiss me good-bye," he growled. "Give me that, at least."

He yanked her to him before she could think of denying him.

This kiss wasn't gentle. There was no coaxing or teasing or easy slide into warmth. His mouth slanted over hers and took it. His breath was hot, his scent as intoxicating as the whiskey she'd sampled the night before. The rasp of stubble against sensitive skin made her shiver. The skillful pressure of his lips and smooth glide of his tongue made her tremble.

His hand cupped the nape of her neck, angling her head to his liking . . . and hers.

The world spun away. And just as quickly righted itself when laughter erupted directly on the other side of the arbor.

Mrs. Cress. The tour. A wave of panic washed over her.

She froze, her mouth open an inch from Connor's lips.

Connor moved. In a single fluid motion, he pulled them both out from the shelter of the arbor and into full view of a dozen guests.

Which is precisely when her world begin to spin away once more, and this time, there would be no righting it.

Chapter 5

$\mathscr{A}$delaide was surrounded by a sea of wide eyes, gaping mouths, and a silence so absolute it was deafening.

She tore herself away from Connor and then stood there, as red-faced as any of the guests . . . with the possible exception of Sir Robert, whose skin wore scarlet blooms that were expanding with disconcerting speed.

Never in her life had she known such mortification, not even when she'd tossed up her accounts on the shoes of the vicar's son in front of the entire congregation. She'd been twelve then, old enough to know what mortification was, and still young enough to be certain she could die of the affliction.

Oh, how she wished she'd been right. Because in comparison to what she was facing now, ruining a young man's footwear was really but a slight embarrassment. And if there was ever a time a young lady ought to be able to die of shame, it was when half the guests of a house party, including her almost-fiancé, caught said lady tossing away her family's future in exchange for a kiss . . . from a near stranger.

A stranger who had compromised her *on purpose*.

"What have you done?" she whispered in a daze.

Connor's voice floated softly over her head. "I've saved you."

Thoughts of her own death were immediately replaced by visions of his. If there was ever a time a young lady ought to be able to get away with murder . . .

"You—"

The list of vile names she had on the tip of her tongue was lost in the sudden explosion of noise from the guests. They found their voices, all at once, and assailed her with a volley of questions and demands.

She stammered and rushed, trying to address them all at once.

"I demand an explanation!"

"You shall have one, Sir Robert. I—"

"Good heavens, child, what *were* you thinking?"

"If you would allow me to explain, Mrs. Cress. We—"

"La, I never expected it of Miss Ward."

She opened her mouth, then closed it. She had no response to that.

"Connor?" Lady Engsly, a pretty woman with kind blue eyes and dark hair, appeared in a small gap between the shoulders of two guests. It was another moment before her husband, the Marquess of Engsly, stepped aside and the rest of her became visible. "Connor? What on *earth* are you doing here?"

"Never mind that." Lady Engsly's sister-in-law, Lady Winnefred, fought her way to the front of the crowd, her amber eyes wide with fascination. "How did you get out of prison?"

Adelaide was sure she hadn't heard the young woman correctly. "What did . . . Prison?"

"Little Freddie," Connor drawled, "always so tactful."

She had heard correctly. It-hadn't seemed possible for things to become any worse . . . but there it was. She'd been compromised by an escaped convict.

"Prison?" The word was barely more than a squeak, but

it was a wonder she managed even that because, honestly—
Prison?!

Mrs. Cress gave Connor a quick looking over. "I do not recall issuing you an invitation, sir."

Connor returned her censure with an eloquent bow. "I beg your pardon, madam. I assumed Sir Robert's was extended to his family."

"We are *not* family," Sir Robert barked. Several heads, including Adelaide's, snapped from Connor's, to Sir Robert's, and back again.

"You're related?" someone asked.

"Absolutely not!" Sir Robert's face had gone from mottled to uniformly purple. Adelaide fully expected him to begin foaming at the mouth at any moment.

"Brother," Connor drawled, "you wound me."

"Brother?" She turned to Sir Robert. "You've an escaped convict for a brother?"

Not the most pertinent question at the moment, but it did a fair job of turning attention away from her . . . Until Mrs. Cress turned to her and said, "You have an escaped convict for a lover?"

"She does not," Connor said stiffly. He even looked a little offended on her behalf, which was rather nice. Surprising, but nice. "I was *released.*"

Oh, the rotter.

"This man is not my . . . my . . ." She couldn't even say it. Surely the guests could see that a lady incapable of even saying the word "lover" was highly unlikely to possess one. She looked from expectant face to expectant face. Apparently, they didn't see. "He is *not.* Mr. Brice took advantage of . . ." Of her willingness to sneak away into the garden to meet with him. "What I mean to say is . . . I was not expecting . . ." Only she *had* rather been hoping. "That is . . ."

Lady Engsly took pity on her. "Perhaps we should discuss this inside."

"There is nothing to discuss." Sir Robert stepped forward and slapped Connor across the face with his glove.

The challenge elicited gasps from several of the guests, a roll of the eyes from both Lady Engsly and Lady Winnefred, and—unless Adelaide was much mistaken—an amused snort from Lady Winnefred's husband, Lord Gideon.

Connor met the challenge with a long, chilling silence followed by the single most menacing smile Adelaide had ever seen.

"Name your weapon," he said at length. His tone was frigid, and he stared at Sir Robert as if he were imagining running the man through on the spot.

A shiver skittered along Adelaide's skin. This was not the Connor who had teased and laughed with her in the garden. This was not the kind gentleman who had patiently listened to her plans and dreams. This man was . . . Well, she had no idea who or what this man was, except terrifying.

Sir Robert paled, spluttered a moment, and finally managed a shaky, "That . . . is not how it is done."

"*You* pick the weapon," some idiot explained.

"Fists," Connor growled. "Nothing would give me greater pleasure than tearing you apart with my bare hands."

"Good gracious," someone breathed.

"Such brutality," someone else said with unmistakable relish. Adelaide guessed it was the same helpful idiot who had set Connor straight on the rules.

Sir Robert's swallow was audible. "That . . . is also not how it is done."

Lady Engsly appeared to be one of the few people present who was not morbidly enthralled by the scene.

"Oh, what stupidity," she said on a huff. "Duel, indeed."

Adelaide was inclined to agree. "Enough. There will be no duel." She wedged herself between the men and faced Connor. "Mr. Brice, this is not help—"

She broke off mid-word when Connor grasped her by the shoulders, lifted her off her feet, and simply set her aside . . . all without taking his eyes off Sir Robert. It was as if she didn't exist.

And all she could think was: Now? *Now*, he chose to pretend not to see her, when it wouldn't do either of them a speck of good? He couldn't have brushed her aside last night, this morning, five bloody minutes ago?

She heard Lord Engsly sigh a moment before he walked forward into her line of sight. He was an imposing figure, both as the highest-ranking member of the house party and as a man in his physical prime.

"Miss Ward is correct. There will be no duel," he announced.

Sir Robert immediately stepped back from Connor and began to replace his glove. "If you insist."

Every head in the group swiveled to Sir Robert in perfect unison, an unusual bit of choreography Adelaide was able to note by virtue of her eyes going very, very wide.

Insist? There had been no insisting. A hint of chiding, perhaps. A clear note of impatience. But nary a whisper of insistence.

"Well, that was very quick," someone commented.

"Instantaneous, really," Lady Winnefred said.

Mrs. Cress leaned toward her and whispered, "This does not bode well for you, my dear."

Indeed, it did not. A duel was out of the question, of course. It was illegal, immoral, and as Lady Engsly had pointed out, stupid. But there wasn't a soul present who would be willing to believe Sir Robert had capitulated for any of those reasons. Not now.

Sir Robert had backed down because he'd reconsidered the value of her honor. There would be no offer of marriage. No five thousand pounds a year. No secure future for her family.

Or perhaps he was simply a coward.

Please, please let him be a coward, she thought, and she immediately wondered if any woman before her had ever prayed for the existence of such a dreadful attribute in a bridegroom.

Had it come to this, then? Had she lost *all* sense of hope? Was marriage to a coward now the most advantageous match she could expect? She refused to believe it.

I am not pathetic.

I am not without worth.

I can do better for my family than this.

"I . . ." She began in a loud voice. All eyes turned to her, and she realized, belatedly, that she couldn't announce to all and sundry what she had been thinking. "Am . . . going inside."

And with that spectacularly feeble finish, she turned and strode toward the house without any clear idea of what she would do once she reached it. Go to her room, pack her things, leave for home, and wait there until it was time to go to the poorhouse. That was the best she could come up with at present.

She knew she was being followed by everyone, but it was only Lady Engsly and Lady Winnefred who made the effort to catch up with her. They flanked her like a pair of guards.

"There is a study off the library," Lady Engsly said. "May I suggest we—"

"I am going home." She kept her eyes on the house and increased her pace.

"I understand you're upset, Miss Ward," Lady Engsly said, "but it would be better for you, and your family, if you settled matters before you left."

The mention of family silenced the dissent on the tip of her tongue. A vision of George and Isobel formed in her mind. She couldn't imagine how such a mess could be settled, but she owed it to them to at least try.

"The study, then."

"A wise decision," Lady Engsly said placidly. "Our husbands will mediate on your behalf, if you like."

She threw a surprised glance at the lady. "They would do that?"

Lady Winnefred brushed impatiently at one of many light brown locks of hair that had slipped from their pins. "Yes, of course. They're quite fond of you."

Adelaide blinked at that admission. She hardly knew them, really. It was their wives with whom she'd begun to develop a friendship over the last few months. Adelaide said a small prayer of thanks for that friendship. Lady Engsly and Lady Winnefred were clever, sensible, and level-headed women. More, they were the only ladies who hadn't eyed her a moment ago like a temporarily amusing but ultimately pitiable creature. And the only two who weren't even now trailing behind her like starving dogs after raw meat.

"I would be grateful for their assistance."

She doubted the marquess and his brother would welcome the responsibility, but even reluctant interference was better than dealing with Connor and Sir Robert on her own.

Lady Winnefred nodded and sidled closer to speak in a low tone. "Perhaps you would like to slow your steps, so that your champions might keep pace."

If Adelaide had not already been shamefaced, she would have blushed. Lord Gideon was as fit as his brother, but an old war injury required the use of a cane. A quick glance over her shoulder told her he was keeping up well enough, but the pace couldn't be comfortable for him. Nor for Mrs. Cress, who also required the assistance of a walking stick.

She slowed down for Lord Gideon's sake. Mrs. Cress she would have been happy to leave behind.

Doing her best to ignore her audience, she pushed through a side door and turned her feet toward the study door.

Lady Winnefred caught her arm. "Wait a moment."

"What for?"

"Your pride, of course." She gestured at Lady Engsly, who'd stepped over to confer with Lord Engsly and Lord Gideon. "She'll only be a minute and then—"

Lord Engsly nodded and stepped away from his wife. "Mrs. Cress, would you be so kind as to take the guests . . . elsewhere?"

There was a murmur of discontent amongst the guests, and Mrs. Cress's round face scrunched in annoyance. Clearly, no one wished to miss the next chapter of the sordid tale. One didn't argue with a marquess, however, not even in one's own home. After a bit of cane thumping, a harrumph, and finally a heavy sigh of resignation, Mrs. Cress began to herd the disgruntled guests down the hall.

"The two of you as well," Lord Gideon told his wife and Lady Engsly.

"We shall leave that for Miss Ward to decide," Lady Engsly said.

Adelaide's immediate inclination was to make as many people as possible go away. She changed her mind, however, after looking over who would be left if the ladies were sent away—Lord Engsly, Lord Gideon, Connor, and Sir Robert. A marquess, the marquess's brother, the man who'd compromised her, and the man she'd betrayed.

"Oh, please, do stay."

Chapter 6

The study's dark paneling, slivered windows, and over-sized mahogany furniture gave Adelaide the impression she was walking into a crowded cave. Uncertain of what to do with herself, she stood in the middle of the room while Lady Engsly and Lady Winnefred took seats on a small settee, Lord Engsly and Lord Gideon positioned themselves in front of the desk, and Connor leaned a shoulder against a bookshelf.

Sir Robert stopped three feet inside the door.

"I would have a word with Miss Ward before we begin," he announced suddenly. "And I would have that word alone."

"No." The sharp refusal came from Connor.

"Miss Ward?" Lady Engsly prompted.

Adelaide considered it. She'd faced his censure in public; there was nothing to be gained by facing it in private as well.

"I would prefer we speak here."

Sir Robert sighed the sigh of an eternally beleaguered

man, but he didn't argue. He walked to the middle of the room, took her hand, and held it between his own.

"Miss Ward," he began, "you have my most sincere and abject apology."

"I beg your pardon?"

He nodded thoughtfully and patted her hand. "I have told you some of my family's story, but much of it . . . most of it, I kept hidden from you out of fear of disgrace. And now, my selfish reticence has put you in grave danger. This man"—he flicked an accusing glance at Connor—"is indeed, and to my family's eternal shame, an offspring of my father's."

"He's not cattle," Lady Winnefred muttered just loud enough for everyone in the room to hear.

Connor flashed a brief smile. "Thank you, Freddie."

"Don't talk to my wife," Lord Gideon ordered.

Sir Robert squeezed her hand. "Connor Brice is a most depraved individual. Until recently, however, he was safely removed from society."

"He had me tossed into prison for a crime I did not commit," Connor translated.

"His imprisonment was of his own doing," Sir Robert insisted. "He is a violent man, Miss Ward. And consumed with jealousy of me. His lowborn mother poisoned his mind with—"

"Mention my mother again," Connor said darkly, "and we'll be getting round to that duel after all."

Sir Robert cleared his throat but didn't respond to Connor. "He nurtures a bitter hatred of me. Nothing would give him more pleasure than to destroy all I hold dear."

"That's true," Connor agreed easily.

Sir Robert pretended to ignore him, but the new burgeoning flush of red on his neck betrayed the lie. "Knowing his nature and his capacity for cruelty, I kept watch over him during his incarceration. But his whereabouts were lost to me after his recent release. I—"

"What he means to say," Connor broke in, "is that he had half the prison guards in his pocket." He answered Sir

Robert's glare with a mocking curl of the lip. "Pity for you it wasn't the clever half."

The red expanded to Sir Robert's face. He spun on Connor. "You have *no* proof of such a—"

"You have no idea what I have proof of."

"I will see you—!"

"You were apologizing, Sir Robert?" Adelaide punctuated the quick interruption with a firm tug on Sir Robert's hand.

He looked to her, to Connor, and back again. "Right. Yes, of course. I beg your pardon." He took a deep breath, held it, and released. Adelaide was surprised to smell brandy. "I was apologizing because it is on my head that this . . . this *libertine*, this cad, this—"

Lady Engsly cut him off. "We have established your opinion of the gentleman, Sir Robert."

"Of course." Another long, dramatic breath. "What happened today is entirely my fault. I should have taken better care. I should have known he would seek out and attempt to injure what I hold of value. I failed to warn you, and I failed to protect you. I do, and shall always, regret this error bitterly. I can only beg your forgiveness now and plead for the opportunity to make amends."

This speech was met with silence by the group, with the exception of Connor, who muttered something that sounded rather like, *"Bravo."*

Adelaide was inclined to agree. It was a fine speech. Unfortunately, it also confirmed the suspicion that he was a coward.

"Allow me to make this right," Sir Robert continued. He cleared his throat in a dramatic, and regrettably affected, manner. And then he said, "My dear Miss Ward, I most humbly and arduously beg the honor of your hand in marriage."

She had the sudden urge to yank her hand free and run.

"Oh. Oh, I . . ." She looked around her with the vague and inexplicable notion that someone else might answer for her. "Er . . . Sir Robert . . ."

"Don't be a fool, Adelaide." Connor's voice was low and dangerous. It put the hair at the back of her neck on end.

Lady Engsly was not similarly affected. She leaned over and hissed at him, "She'd be a fool not to accept, thanks to you."

"She has other options."

"Not unless you've offered for her," Lady Engsly snapped. When he merely lifted a brow, she blinked and straightened in her chair. "Have you offered for her?"

"I have."

"Well, why didn't you say so?" Lady Engsly's transformation was instant. Her pretty face lit up with a smile, and she very nearly bounded off the settee. "That changes things considerably."

Bewildered, Adelaide could only stare and sputter a few halfhearted protests as Lady Engsly detached her from Sir Robert and ushered her toward the door.

"It seems you have quite a bit to consider, Miss Ward. I suspect a nice long lie-down will put everything into perspective. Come along, Freddie."

Adelaide tossed a dazed look over her shoulder as she was bustled out of the room. "I thought we were to settle things."

"We have," Lady Engsly assured her with a quick pat of the arm. "You received an offer of marriage. Two in fact. We'll leave the gentlemen to bicker over the details."

"Shouldn't she have some say in those details?" Lady Winnefred asked with a hint of indignation.

Adelaide nodded in enthusiastic agreement. If anyone was to be bickering, it ought to be her.

Lady Engsly stopped at the bottom of a back stairwell and turned to address Adelaide with the sort of gentle patience that put her to mind of a governess. "You have the only say that truly matters, Miss Ward. And you'll be pressured from both sides to make that say known as soon as possible. Do you want to face that pressure now, or do you want a bit of time to think the matter through?"

"Time," Adelaide replied without hesitation and wondered that she hadn't seen the wisdom in leaving for herself.

"Excellent. Freddie and I will spread the word that offers have been made. It won't silence the gossip, I'm afraid, but it will certainly temper the censure."

She wouldn't have seen the wisdom in that either. Her mind was so muddled, her emotions so turbulent, it was a miracle she was able to put two words together.

Adelaide looked at the two women before her and wondered what she would have done without their assistance today. Gone to her room without a much-needed proposal or accepted a proposal without much-needed consideration. Either might well have proved disastrous.

"Lady Engsly—"

"Lilly, dear. And Winnefred," she added with a quick look at her sister-in-law for agreement. "I should think we've come far enough in our friendship for given names."

Adelaide digested that silently for a moment. She wasn't sure what to say. She wasn't sure she could speak around the lump that formed in her throat. It had been so long since someone had offered to help, longer still since she'd had an offer of friendship. She couldn't find the words to express what it meant to receive both.

"I'm grateful," she managed at length. And because she couldn't think of a more adequate sentiment, she repeated it. "I'm so grateful."

*T*he abrupt departure of the ladies from the study left Connor in what most men might consider an unenviable position—facing the suitor and two champions of a compromised lady. Connor didn't mind the silent and tense atmosphere in the least. In fact, he took dark pleasure in ignoring the brothers and staring at Sir Robert until the man looked away, then shifted his feet, then squirmed, then caved.

"I will not remain in the same room with this libertine

a moment longer!" Sir Robert announced and bolted for the door.

The entire process took less than thirty seconds. Which—to give credit where credit was due—was a solid twenty seconds longer than Connor had anticipated. Sir Robert had held his ground in the garden longer than expected as well. Apparently, the baron had grown some sort of backbone over the years. Connor estimated his half brother to now be in possession of two, possibly three, full vertebrae.

Connor straightened from the bookshelf and gave a passing nod at Lord Engsly and Lord Gideon as he headed for the door. He felt under no particular obligation to speak with the men. He'd not invited them into the affair.

"A word, Mr. Brice."

Connor turned at the sound of Engsly's order and considered each man coolly and carefully.

He knew little of Lord Engsly, and he'd met Lord Gideon only once before—through the bars of a prison cell. Their wives, on the other hand, had been regular visitors to the prison. Before they'd come to their fortunes by way of their husbands, they'd scratched out a meager existence by, amongst other things, mending the clothes of officers and well-to-do prisoners.

But, despite their brief acquaintance, Connor was inclined to like Engsly and Lord Gideon. They had reputations for being levelheaded and fair-minded men. They were also known as men who were not above a bit of brawling when the occasion called for it. In that regard, he wasn't concerned about the marquess or his brother. He was, however, a little concerned about the marquess *and* his brother. Lord Engsly had speed. Lord Gideon had a sturdy cane and the strength to break it over a man's head. Connor had honed his fighting skills on the streets of Boston and thought he might be able to take the pair of them, but not without cost.

"Have your word, then."

"Where are you staying?" Engsly asked.

Lord Gideon answered for him. "He and his men are at the widow Dunbar's cottage."

"Spying on me, were you?" Connor inquired with a raised brow.

Lord Gideon's lips curved. "I had the sense to bribe the clever half."

Irritation bit at him. "You stand with Sir Robert?"

"I stand with my family," Lord Gideon corrected.

"Ah." That made more sense. "Thomas."

Thomas Brown. The boy who'd been tossed in the cell next to his. No more than twelve, and naïve with it. Connor had looked out for the lad until his release. Lord Gideon and Freddie had taken over after that.

"Worried I might lure him back into iniquity?" Connor asked with a smirk.

"Oddly enough, I was concerned you couldn't be trusted with an innocent."

"That is peculiar."

Lord Engsly took a step forward. "Did you force your attentions on Miss Ward?"

"I did not."

"Did you mislead her into thinking you were a member of this house party?"

"I never lied to her." About that, specifically.

"That was not the question."

Connor shrugged. "The ladies do like a bit of mystery."

"Was it your intention to compromise Miss Ward?"

"No." A half-truth. It hadn't been his intention when he'd begun, but it had certainly been his intention when he'd hauled Adelaide onto the path.

"And is it your purpose now to make her your wife?"

"Yes."

"To spite your brother."

"My reasons are immaterial."

"Miss Ward is apt to disagree."

Miss Ward was apt to want his head on a platter. But it couldn't be helped. "Miss Ward is free to marry Sir Robert if she chooses."

Connor was confident she wouldn't choose Sir Robert. But it would be helpful if her champions, and their wives, were not openly opposed to a match with himself. Which is why, despite his distaste for the conversation, he tolerated another round of questions from Lord Engsly.

Did he have a home and the means to support a wife and family? Did he have children of his own or a mistress tucked away somewhere? What, exactly, had begun the feud between the two brothers? Connor answered each in turn, feeling much as he had on the day he'd gone before the magistrate on charges of highway robbery. Yes, yes, no, no, and . . .

"None of your bleeding business. Now, if there's nothing else?" He didn't bother to wait for a reply before heading for the door. Their support would be advantageous, but it wasn't necessary. He was not obliged to go groveling for it.

"One more thing," Lord Gideon said softly. He'd been mostly silent during the questioning. Connor suspected he'd already been aware of more than half the answers. "A bit of advice. You would be wise to remember that my wife is fond of Miss Ward."

And Lord Gideon was madly in love with his wife. If she asked him to squash Connor like a bug, he'd not think twice before obliging her.

"Then Freddie and I have something in common," Connor replied. He didn't take offense at the implied threat, but he emphasized the use of Freddie, just a little, just enough to make the muscle in Lord Gideon's jaw pop.

It didn't quite make up for the inconvenience and insult of a half hour's interrogation, but it was gratifying nonetheless.

Chapter 7

Lilly and Winnefred left Adelaide at her door so that she might privately inform her sister what had occurred in the garden and study. Adelaide could only assume that the ladies expected Isobel's reaction to be most unpleasant. They couldn't have been more wrong.

Isobel's eyes grew round as saucers. Which, evidently, was not round enough to contain all her unholy glee. It spilled out into a voice bubbling over with mirth.

"A duel?"

"It is not amusing."

"It certainly is," Isobel countered and burst into fits of laughter. "I cannot believe it," she choked out. "My sister . . . My own eternally decorous sister . . . The subject of a duel." She let out a shaky breath and wiped tears from her eyes. "Oh, stop looking at me like that. Lord Engsly will put an end to it."

"He has already put an end to it," Adelaide muttered.

"There you are," she said, with a sweep of her hand. "You're not truly distressed by this, are you? It's not an ideal development, I grant. But if there is nothing you can do to change the situation, you might as well appreciate it. And you must admit . . . two men willing to die for you." She gave a lusty sigh. "That is flattering."

Perhaps it would have been, if Sir Robert hadn't been quite so eager to rethink the sacrifice. And if the rest of the morning hadn't been so mortifying.

"Well, who is this Mr. Brice?" Isobel demanded. "Why have you not told me of him before now?"

"I only just met the man." Too late, she realized the folly of that statement.

"Only just . . . And you were kissing him in the garden?"

Adelaide waited patiently for the next round of Isobel's laughter to subside. She wasn't feeling especially patient at the moment, but she was feeling grateful. Not every young lady would accept such dreadful news about her older sister with good humor.

"If you are finished?" she asked after a time.

Isobel lifted a finger and laughed a minute more. Finally, she gave a great sigh and nodded. "Oh, goodness . . . Has this Mr. Brice offered for you, then?"

"Yes, they both have."

"Two proposals, a compromise, and a duel. My, but you've been busy this morning." Isobel wiped her eyes again, then pursed her lips thoughtfully. "I think you should accept Mr. Brice."

"You don't know the man."

"Neither do you, by the sound of it," Isobel reminded with a smirk. "But we know Sir Robert, and—"

"Lady Engsly says I should take some time to think the matter through." Adelaide wasn't interested in hearing, yet again, her sister's opinion of Sir Robert.

"I like Lady Engsly," Isobel said, bobbing her head in agreement. "She's a sensible sort."

As Isobel's idea of sensible was to check for witnesses before engaging in all manner of inadvisable behavior, Adelaide could only stare at her sister in disbelief.

"I can appreciate a sensible mind," Isobel said in a defensive tone. "I like you, don't I? It's stodginess I can't abide."

Adelaide was saved from having to respond by a soft knock on the door. Lilly and Winnefred, she guessed. They had promised to return after they'd spoken to the guests.

"Are we interrupting?" Lilly asked when Adelaide opened the door.

She stepped back and waved them inside. "No, please come in."

Winnefred patted her arm as she passed, just as Lilly had earlier, only a bit more awkwardly and with more force than was strictly comfortable. Adelaide assumed Winnefred was either unaccustomed to delivering friendly overtures of a physical nature or unaware of her own strength.

Lilly paused inside the doorway. "We want you to know that our carriages are at your disposal."

Adelaide's heart sank. "Mrs. Cress has kicked me out."

"Good heavens no." Lilly led her to the foot of the bed where she settled them both. "Mrs. Cress is more apt to lock you in your chambers for the next fortnight than send you off. You are now her most interesting guest. She likes to gossip."

"She loves to gossip," Winnefred corrected. "She's not cruel, mind you. Merely dedicated."

Lilly gave Adelaide a sympathetic smile. "Others will not be so kind. To be frank, Adelaide, the proposals have kept you from outright ruin, but I fear things will become uncomfortable for you nonetheless."

Adelaide closed her eyes on a sigh. Lilly was right. Talk amongst the guests was sure to be open, rampant, and ugly. Worse, the questions and criticisms would spill over onto Isobel.

Do you suppose her sister is the same?

I hear she is most liberal in her opinions.

With her favors as well, no doubt.

Adelaide wasn't sure what was more galling, that they were now the center of such speculation, or that they had no choice but to flee from the insults.

"I should marry Sir Robert and be done with it."

Lilly shared a look with Winnefred. "I must be honest

with you, Miss Ward. I do not particularly care for Sir Robert."

"*We* do not care for Sir Robert," Winnefred amended.

"He strikes me as being rather duplicitous in nature," Lilly explained.

"You see?" Isobel chimed. "Sensible."

"Why have you not said so until now?" Adelaide asked. Granted, she'd met the ladies only a few months ago, but they'd grown sufficiently familiar with each other that distrust of her suitor might have been mentioned.

"I assumed you had similar reservations," Lilly explained. "But that circumstances were such that you'd no choice but to press ahead. Was I wrong?"

"No," she admitted softly. There had been reservations. She'd been late in acknowledging them, but they had been there.

Winnefred nodded. "Now, however, you have an alternative solution. You have Connor."

"I don't know that I like Mr. Brice any better."

"You looked to have liked him well enough in the garden," Winnefred commented.

"*Freddie,*" Lady Engsly chastised.

Adelaide gave a dismissive shake of her head. "It's only the truth. I did like him. Until he went out of his way to see we were discovered."

"Surely not," Lilly protested.

"Ask him yourself, if you like."

Lilly studied her a moment before speaking. "I can see that won't be necessary. Good heavens, did he say why?"

"Well, that's obvious," Isobel said. "He must be in love with her."

"We met last night."

"Last night?" This from both ladies.

Oh, dear.

"Passing in the hall," she explained lamely, and she tensed, waiting for Isobel to mention the sitting room, or the garden, or the whiskey.

Winnefred spoke first. "He's been aware of you for a lot

longer than that. He used to look for you to bring your nephew to the prison."

"Prison," Adelaide repeated. It was a cell window Connor had been watching her through. She groaned and covered her face with her hands.

"What was he imprisoned for?" Isobel asked.

"Highway robbery," Winnefred informed her.

Adelaide dropped her hands. "Good God."

"There was never any doubt of his innocence," Lilly assured her. "Connor might look fit for the job, but his men, I assure you, do not."

"He has men?"

Winnefred nodded. "Gregory, who I vow is one hundred, if he's a day. And Michael, who likely hasn't seated a horse in the last decade."

"Who brought the charges against them?" Isobel inquired.

"Sir Robert," Winnefred answered with obvious disgust. "Who happens to be old friends with the magistrate."

"How do you know all of this?" Adelaide asked.

Lilly looked uncomfortable with the question. "Well . . . Freddie and I had . . . on occasion . . . in the past . . . reason to visit the prison. We . . . That is . . ."

"Oh, for pity's sake, Lilly," Winnefred cut in impatiently. "She'll not judge. Lilly and I did a bit of sewing for coin. Connor was one of the prisoners who could afford to pay for mending. I'd not have paid particular attention to him, except that he shared the cell with Michael and Gregory— the most delightful gentlemen—and Thomas was in the next cell over. Connor took him under his wing."

"Thomas Brown? Your ward?" Adelaide shook her head. The boy was much too young to have been locked away with grown men.

Winnefred nodded. "He came to be with us after his release. But Connor and his men looked after him in prison. My husband took it upon himself to look into their affairs."

"And he discovered Sir Robert was their accuser," Isobel guessed.

"Yes, and that Connor's assets had been seized by the

courts. I asked my husband to intercede on Connor's behalf as repayment for the kindness he showed Thomas. It would appear Gideon had some success." She turned to Lilly. "Do you suppose the men are finished in the study? We should see what they've learned."

Lilly nodded but kept her gaze on Adelaide. "You will take the time to think? You'll not be rash, or choose out of anger?"

In a show of support, Isobel came to stand beside her. "My sister is nothing if not sensible . . . generally. She'll make the right decision."

Adelaide reached up to squeeze the hand Isobel placed on her shoulder.

"Then I'll not worry." Lilly bent to kiss Adelaide's cheek, then gestured to Winnefred. The pair left the room arm in arm.

Isobel blew out a long breath after their departure. "This is all very complicated."

Complicated, Adelaide decided, was too mild a word. It was an impossibly convoluted disaster, a hopeless tangle of questions and lies she had no choice but to try to unwind.

Slipping off her shoes, she rose from the bed and began to pace. Where did she begin? Compromises and duels, highway robbery, false imprisonment, and stolen fortunes. It was too much.

Her thoughts jumped about her head as wildly as the butterflies danced in her stomach. She felt off balance, just as she had after the whiskey, but there was nothing liberating in the experience. There was only dread, anger, and an abundance of confusion.

Why had Connor done it? Surely it wasn't merely to spite his brother. There were an infinite number of ways one could irritate a sibling. The vast majority of them did not require the ruin of an innocent bystander. Surely he wasn't so coldhearted, so cruel. There had to be a better explanation.

And if there wasn't, then there had to be retribution.

Determined, she crossed the room, threw open the wardrobe, and snatched her hooded cloak.

Isobel leapt up from her seat at the vanity. "Where are you going?"

"To speak with Mr. Brice."

"What? But you—"

"I want an explanation. I cannot decide what's to be done without an explanation."

"But you can't," Isobel insisted. "Even I know you cannot seek out a gentleman unattended."

"Really?" Adelaide clasped the cloak at her neck and gave her sister a bland look. "Why?"

"Because it . . . You would . . ." Isobel managed an expression that was both a grimace and sympathetic smile. "I suppose you can do most anything you want now."

And you as well, she thought. The ton was all too eager to spread the shame of one fallen woman onto every member of her family. "He'll answer for that."

Chapter 8

It took no time at all to discover where Connor was staying. The staff were all abuzz over the unfolding scandal. According to the maid Adelaide questioned, Jeffrey the footman had overhead Lord Gideon mention the widow Dunbar's cottage to his wife. The footman mentioned it to the housekeeper, and within twenty minutes, everyone knew.

Adelaide imagined it had taken half that time to spread the news of her ruin.

Rather than risk running into guests along the road, Adelaide slipped out the back of the house and followed a drover's trail into town.

The trip was scarcely more than a mile, an easy distance for one accustomed to walking. But in her haste, she'd forgotten to change into her half boots, and the thin soles of the slippers she wore now offered little protection from the rocky ground. The bottoms of her feet were stinging before she was halfway to town.

The discomfort only added to her roiling temper. By the time she reached her destination—the two-storied cottage

with green shutters and a tidy garden on the edge of town—
she felt positively murderous.

She strode to the door, gave it three solid knocks, and
waited for the housekeeper or maid to answer.

It was Connor who answered her summons, wearing
trousers, shirtsleeves, and an expression of mild surprise.

He flicked a glance over her shoulder. "Adelaide. Did
you come here alone?"

"Yes." She tipped her chin up and kept her eyes studi-
ously away from the open neck of his shirt. "Are you going
to allow me entrance, or shall we hold court on the street?"

He frowned slightly but stepped back to allow her inside.
She swept past him into a small foyer that opened into a
modest parlor dominated by an oversized settee and pair of
upholstered chairs.

"Does Lord Engsly know you've come?" Connor asked.

She unlatched her cloak and slipped it from her shoulders. "Lord Engsly is not my guardian."

His mouth curved up, but whether he was amused or
pleased by her statement, she couldn't say. Either way, it
annoyed her, and when he held his hand out for her cloak,
she took perverse satisfaction in shaking her head and
walking past him into the parlor without invitation.

Connor navigated the narrow path behind the settee and
retrieved a decanter and snifter from a built-in cupboard.

"You'll excuse the accommodations," he said conversationally. "Private rooms were difficult to come by on short
notice."

She stared at his profile as he poured his drink. On the
way there, she'd given some thought on how best to begin
the conversation. Ideally, it would start with a heartfelt apology from Connor, but he didn't appear inclined to oblige.

Nothing about Connor indicated he felt even a sliver of
regret. There was an insolent quality in the way he looked at
her, an irreverence in his tone when he spoke. He seemed to
her to be an altogether different man than the one she'd
known in the garden.

She briefly considered going with plan B, which was to

throttle him until he was very sorry indeed, but ultimately settled on plan C.

"Why?" she snapped. "Why have you done this?"

"To keep you out of Sir Robert's grasp." He held up the glass. "Drink?"

"What? *No*."

"Then have a seat."

"I'll stand."

"You've come for an explanation, haven't you?" He waited for her nod. "Then sit. It's a lengthy story, and I'd just as soon not stand for the telling of it." He smiled as he came around the settee. "It's been something of a trying day for me."

She reconsidered plan B but ultimately ground out, "How thoughtless of me," and took a seat on one of the chairs.

Connor sat across from her, leaned back against the cushions of the settee, and set his elbow on an armrest. "Comfortable?"

She responded with narrowed eyes.

"Excellent." He stretched his legs out before him. "My father, as you may have guessed, kept two homes. One with his wife and heir, and another, sixty miles away, with his mistress and son. The arrangement was not a secret. I was acknowledged at birth and raised as the well-loved son of a wealthy baron. My mother and I wanted for nothing— funds, education, my father's time and attention. All were to be had in abundance. We even enjoyed a limited taste of respectability in our little hamlet. My father made certain of it."

He paused to take a sip of his drink, and she almost filled the silence by proclaiming the baron a good man. But then she realized the baroness might have felt quite differently.

Connor's mouth curved. "You see the predicament. I cannot answer for my father's treatment of his wife and Sir Robert. I knew him only as the man who made my mother laugh and taught me how to hunt quail and seat a horse." He tapped his finger again. "We were happy."

"Sir Robert was not," she guessed.

"His mother certainly wasn't. And who's to blame her? Her husband's flagrant infidelity must have been a constant source of humiliation. She took her own life when I was thirteen."

"No, she drowned," Adelaide countered. Sir Robert had told her the story of his mother's death not three weeks ago. "She went for a walk along the banks of the estate's lake, slipped, hit her head—"

"She went for a walk *in* the estate's lake. The only rocks involved were the ones stuffed in the apron that was tied about her waist."

It was a horrific image. "You can't possibly know that."

"No, but Sir Robert could. It was he who found her."

That was worse. "He told you this?"

"Indeed. Two years after the fact, and two seconds before he hit me over the head with the butt of a pistol and delivered me into the hands of a press-gang."

He said it matter-of-factly, as if he were relating the story of someone else. She hoped he was. The alternative was unthinkable.

"I don't believe you. It is illegal to impress a boy under the age of eighteen." She felt foolish for the statement almost before she'd finished saying it. It was well known that a blind eye was often turned to infractions. The war had needed ships, and ships required able-bodied sailors.

"I don't believe Sir Robert would be capable of such a heinous deed," she added, lamely. "He's not a monster."

"Believe what you like. But the truth is, a carriage accident had taken my father and mother not six weeks earlier, and Sir Robert saw an opportunity to rid me of my inheritance and simultaneously rid Britain of a . . ." He glanced at the ceiling, remembering. " 'Murdering bastard son of a whore,' I believe he put it."

"Murdering?" She didn't want to believe that either.

A lazy shrug of one shoulder. "He holds me accountable for his mother's death."

"That is preposterous."

"Unjust at the very least. But by Sir Robert's reasoning, if I'd not been born, I'd not have been acknowledged, and if our father had not acknowledged me, he could have kept his mistress in secret and his mother would have remained blissfully unaware of her husband's philandering ways."

As she'd already used the word preposterous, Adelaide found herself at a loss for anything more to say. Her mind whirling, she rose from her seat without thought and began to pace. It was difficult to maneuver in the confines of the small parlor, but she found the space in front of the fireplace to be adequate.

Connor set his drink aside and cleared his throat. "Adelaide—"

She silenced him with an impatient shake of her head. She wanted the quiet to think. There was so much to absorb and consider. Too much. And why the devil did she have to do either? Even if Connor's story were true—and she wasn't altogether convinced that it was—she'd not been the one to toss him to a press-gang. Lord knew, she didn't have his lost inheritance.

She stopped and faced him. "Mr. Brice, I am sorry for . . . any unpleasantness you may have endured, and I am equally sorry that you and your brother should be so at odds, but this . . . none of this has anything to do with me."

"Unpleasantness," he repeated softly. "Do you have any idea what life is like for an impressed sailor? What it was like for a fifteen-year-old boy?"

"No, however—"

"A hell beyond your reckoning. It took me nearly a year to escape. Months more of sleeping in the gutters of Boston before I had a permanent roof over my head, and more than a decade before I amassed the wealth I needed to return to Scotland. I've waited half my life for my revenge."

"Revenge. You . . . All of this . . . *I* am your revenge?"

He stood up, slowly, and walked to her, a smiling golden

devil. "You are a prize, sweet. But not *the* prize. I've a long list of treats in store for my brother." He brushed the backs of his fingers along her jaw. "You're but the first order of business."

Her fingers curled into her palms at the callous words. She wanted to slap him. Never before had she been tempted to raise her hand to another human being. But, oh, how she wanted to now.

"You . . . selfish . . . arrogant . . ."

"Bastard?" he offered.

"Liar," she bit off. "I don't believe a word, not *one word* of your story."

"You've had more truth from me today than you would in a lifetime with Sir Robert." He bent his head and softly asked, "Would you like to know who owns your brother's final debt?"

"What has that to do with . . . ?" The insinuation seeped in slowly, like a thick poison into her blood. "Another lie," she whispered, but there was little conviction behind it.

"Ask him. Wolfgang's not half bad at keeping a secret, but he makes for a poor liar."

She shook her head, rejecting his words, even as she demanded, "Tell me what you've heard."

"It's for Wolfgang to tell you." He straightened with a small shrug. "You'll not believe it from me anyway."

Because he was right, and she detested that he should be right, she changed the subject. "You'd no right, *no right* to drag me and my family into an ugly feud with your brother."

"No, I didn't," he agreed easily. "And yet, it was the right thing to do."

She tried to speak through her fury but managed only a strangled sound in the back of her throat.

Connor had no trouble expressing himself. "Be reasonable, Adelaide," he cajoled. "Better yet, be unreasonable. Marry me and enact your own revenge. I've a fortune you can squander, homes you can burn to the ground—"

"Then where would I put my second family?" She spat. She was shocked at her own words. Shocked, and pleased.

His lips tucked down in a thoughtful frown. "I'm afraid I have to insist on fidelity."

"You *humiliated* me," she ground out.

His gaze skittered away for a split second before returning to hers. It was the smallest of movements, the stingiest hint of discomfort, but it was something. It was enough. She felt a burgeoning sense of power, of righteousness, of pure spleen.

"You humiliated my family. You tore my name to shreds and show not the slightest hint of shame now to be holding the remnants of it ransom. Do you think I care one jot for your insistence? You'll pay for what you've done. You'll pay dearly. And the punishment will be of *my* choosing."

He cocked his head at her. "Is that a yes?"

The sound that emerged from her throat was too strangled to pass for a true snarl. Out of insults, she snatched up her cloak, spun on her heel, and headed for the door.

"Adelaide."

His tone was soft and undemanding. The sudden change startled her into turning around.

He looked at her without smiling and spoke without humor. "Humiliating you was never my intention."

She absorbed that silently for a moment. "Is that an apology?"

"It is."

She didn't believe for a moment he was in earnest. The man changed his nature as if he were trying on a closet full of new coats. She didn't care for the cut of anything she saw at present.

She tipped her chin up and looked down the length of her nose. "How noble of you. Let us see how sorry you are after I'm done with you."

Pleased with what she felt was a very fine parting shot, she spun about again to leave.

"You've forgotten your shoes."

She stopped, felt the cool floor on her toes through her stockings, and grimaced. Damn and blast. She didn't remember even taking them off. Wiping her face void of any expression, she straightened her shoulders, turned about, again, and did her utmost to retain a regal appearance as she scanned the room for her misplaced footwear.

"Far side of the chair," Connor said easily. "Why did you take them off?"

It was a habit she developed years ago to keep her penchant for pacing from wearing out soles faster than she could afford to have them replaced. But no force in heaven, earth, or hell could have dragged that admission from her lips.

She crossed the room in silence instead, snatched up her slippers, and began to pull them on where she stood.

"Did you walk all the way here in those?"

It wasn't necessary to look at him to know he was scowling. She could hear it in his voice. She remained stubbornly silent, determined to be done, absolutely finished, conversing with the man.

"I'll take you back in my carriage," he decided.

Apparently, she wasn't finished. "No."

"I'll saddle a horse for you—"

She didn't know how to ride. "No."

"I can't allow you to walk about—"

"Allow? You forget, Mr. Brice, you are not my husband."

"Not yet."

She gave him a withering stare. "Do you really believe I would choose you over Sir Robert? That I would cast aside the affections of a perfect—"

"Coward?"

It only added to her anger that the same word had crossed her mind. "*Gentleman.* And bind myself to a man who wants me only as a means to render his brother miserable?"

"Sir Robert is miserable by nature. I would marry you to see him furious. He turns a glorious shade of purple."

"This is a jest to you." Disgusted, she marched out of the room.

Connor followed. "On the contrary, I take my revenge quite seriously. You ought to consider doing the same." He stepped in front of her and grinned. "Marry me, Adelaide. Render my life a living hell."

She shoved him aside, threw open the front door, and strode out.

The moment Adelaide disappeared, Connor let his smile fall. He retrieved a pair of pistols from the drawer of a small side table, then walked to the door that connected the parlor to a study. With a quick tug of the handle, he swung the door open. Gregory and Michael tumbled in from the other room, a stumbling mass of arms and legs. Connor took hold of the older man and let Michael fend for himself.

Michael caught himself on the windowsill, narrowly avoiding rapping his head against the glass pane. "Damn it, boy. Might give a man warning."

"A man might have better things to do than eavesdrop like an old hen." Connor let go of Gregory and held the pistols out. "Take these. Follow her back."

No one with a pair of eyes and an ounce of sense would mistake them for a pair of highwaymen. But two finer shots were not to be found in all of Scotland.

"No call for being short," Michael grumbled.

"Were you thinking we'd have let our lass walk home alone? On our way out the study door, we were." Gregory shook his head and took off across the room.

Michael caught up to him, grumbling. "First he's gone soft, now he's touchy as a teething babe."

"Sure and he is, on account of being sorry for bungling this business with the lass."

Connor rolled his eyes—teething babe, indeed—and resumed his seat as the front door opened and closed. Despite the belated apology to Adelaide, he wasn't all that sorry. He regretted she'd been hurt, but a compromising was a small slight compared to what she would have to contend with in a marriage to Sir Robert.

In this case, the end justified the means. Even when the

means involved infuriating Adelaide. In fact, he'd rather liked infuriating Adelaide. She was magnificent in her anger, an absolute pleasure to watch as those soft brown eyes turned molten with fury.

Connor rolled a knot out of his shoulders. It was possible he'd enjoyed the sight a hair too much. He hadn't intended to, but it had pricked at him to hear her make excuses for Sir Robert while she berated him. Even worse had been seeing the line of strain across her brow when he'd opened the door.

And so he'd poked at her for his own pleasure and because it was easier to see her anger than her fear. Undoubtedly, it would have been easier in the short term if he had soothed her temper with honeyed words.

There were a thousand easy lies that may, or may not, have served to appease her now . . . but would most certainly have enraged her later.

Adelaide was generous, and far too trusting for her own good, but she wasn't a fool. She might succumb to fine speeches and false flattery for a moment, but *only* for a moment. In the end, she was a woman who preferred an ugly reality to an attractive lie.

Let Sir Robert fill her ears with saccharine venom and see what good it did him. For that matter, let Sir Robert fill her ears with the truth and see what good *that* did him. It bloody well didn't matter what Sir Robert said now. After she spoke with her brother, the matter would be settled. Adelaide would become Mrs. Connor Brice.

She would be his. At last.

Suddenly restless, Connor rose and wandered into the study. There was a small wooden carving sitting on the desk—the perfect likeness of Adelaide as he'd known her through the bars of his cell window, with a child in her arms and the light of determination and courage on her face. Gregory had fashioned it out of oak with a small knife he'd paid a guard to smuggle in. Gregory had made a good half dozen carvings in prison and passed them off to Freddie to sell with the pretense that they'd needed the money. In truth, Gregory had been taken with Freddie and liked listening to the pretty lass exclaim over his skill.

So Freddie had sold the carving in the nearby village of Enscrum, and Connor had paid a guard to bring it back, with an extra coin to be certain the pretty lass remained none the wiser. In truth, they'd all been a little taken with Freddie.

Connor picked the carving up and turned it over in his hands. "Taken" did not begin to describe his reaction the first time he'd seen Adelaide.

He remembered that February day with perfectly clarity. After three months of being incarcerated, he'd glanced out the cell window with little expectation of seeing more than the depressingly familiar view of the frozen courtyard. But what he'd seen was Adelaide—standing in the bitter winter wind with her worn coat whipping about her ankles, and her arms wrapped protectively around an infant cocooned in a sea of blankets.

She'd stopped to speak with a guard and turned her face up when the guard pointed at the second floor of the debtors' wing.

Connor hadn't been able to see the color of her eyes. He hadn't known her name, where she'd come from, or why she was at the prison. But none of that seemed to matter. He'd experienced the most excruciating longing to reach out and touch, to brush the back of his hand against the cool silk of her wind-kissed cheeks, to draw her into the shelter of his coat and feel her grow warm in his arms.

He'd never before had such an immediate, visceral reaction to a woman. He'd known instant lust, even immediate fascination. But he'd never known such a hollow longing. He'd realized it was illogical, even embarrassing, but he'd reveled in every fantastical second, drinking in every inch of her until she nodded to the guard and disappeared into the prison.

He'd turned from the window then, disturbed that he should be so powerfully affected by a mere glimpse of a woman. That was the sort of maudlin nonsense to which other men, *lesser* men, succumbed. Dandies spoke of the angel they had seen from across a crowded ballroom. Poets waxed on about the captivating maiden they had spied from afar. Men of sound mind were not taken in by that sort of romantic rubbish.

He'd gone too long without the company of a woman, that was the trouble. Abstinence did terrible things, unnatural things, to a man's mind. And yet, twenty minutes later, he'd gone back to the window. And he'd gone back again and again—every Saturday for months, hoping for that next glimpse.

He'd built harmless fantasies around her when he'd thought her married . . . Mostly harmless . . . A man couldn't be blamed for the odd lurid thought. Once he was free and had access to all his funds, he would pay her husband's debts anonymously, and perhaps set something aside for the child.

When he'd learned her name and that she was coming to visit a wastrel brother, Connor decided he'd clear the debts and give Adelaide the home and income her brother was clearly incapable of providing. The notion of marriage was considered and rejected. He didn't want the responsibility of a wife distracting him from his quest for revenge. Perhaps after . . .

Then he'd heard of Sir Robert's courtship, and everything changed. There would be no anonymous donations. There would be no after. She would be his.

In the study, Connor set the carving back on the desk.

Adelaide Ward had always been his.

Chapter 9

The late summer sun beat down mercilessly on Adelaide as she made the return trip down the drover's trail. There wasn't a hint of chill in the air. And yet she felt cold down to her very bones.

A means to an end, that's all she was to Connor Brice.

She gathered her cloak around herself like fitted armor. She tried to do the same with her anger, but it slipped out of reach faster than she could grab hold, pushed aside by exhaustion and bitter disappointment. And the damn stinging of her feet.

"Damn and blast."

Abandoning the notion of reaching the relative sanctuary of her chambers as quickly as possible, she stopped to rest on a fallen log. She sat on it gingerly, thinking it would be just her luck to discover the center was rotted through *after* she took a seat.

It held. Which was more than could be said for her composure.

She pulled her right shoe off, glared at the thin, worn sole, then hurled it at a nearby tree with all her strength.

"Bloody . . . Damn . . . Hell . . ." Oh, how she wished she knew how to swear properly. "Bloody hell!"

And that was it. That was the last of her immediately available anger. Feeling the fight go out of her, she lowered her head to her hands and groaned.

She didn't cry. The tears were there, she could feel them pressing against the back of her eyes, and pooling into a heavy weight in the center of her chest, but she ignored both sensations. She had no right to feel sorry for herself. Her circumstances were as much her own doing as Connor's. The fact that he was a charlatan and a cheat did not excuse how readily she had succumbed to his charm and lies. She'd not come to the house party a naïve young girl fresh from the nursery. She was seven-and-twenty and, for all intents and purposes, the head of a household. She ought to have known better.

She ought to have done so many things differently.

The pressure in her chest built. She fought it back, lifted her head, and blew out a long, hard breath.

She was not, absolutely *not* going to make matters worse by indulging in a bout of tears. Crying would accomplish nothing more than to give her a red nose and stuffy head. And she needed a clear head to think.

There were choices to be made, steps to be taken, more questions that needed to be answered.

How long did she have to make a decision? Was there some sort of time limit? A day? Two? Could she put the decision off for a week? She had to put it off until she spoke with Wolfgang, at least.

As much as she hated to give credence to anything Connor said, she was forced to admit it was unlikely he'd imply Sir Robert knew something of Wolfgang's debt unless there was some truth to the accusation. He had nothing to gain by making an idle lie.

Sir Robert was connected to her brother's troubles. She couldn't decide on anything until she knew the details of that connection. She needed all the facts.

Good Lord, she wasn't sure she could stomach any more

facts. Already, she knew more about Sir Robert and Connor Brice than she cared to . . . No, that wasn't true. She didn't like what she'd learned, but she was better off for knowing. It was always better to be informed, wasn't it? Much better to enter marriage without an idealized perception of her bridegroom. There would be no rude awakening after the wedding, no unrealistic expectations guaranteed to end in bitter disappointment. Two days ago, she would have walked into marriage with Sir Robert blindly. Now she could choose her path with open eyes.

It was, arguably, the one bright spot in the entire black affair.

Brushing off her skirts, she rose from the log and hobbled over to fetch her shoe. She would concentrate on that bright spot and hope it was enough to illuminate each new step as she took it. Move forward, reevaluate footing, and move forward again—it was a prudent plan of action. Mountains were scaled one step at a time.

A strange sense of calm fell over her as she set aside her fears of the days and weeks to come and focused only on what needed to be done next.

Her spinning world narrowed down to a series of small, steady, and manageable tasks. She walked back to the house in a kind of daze. She spoke with Lilly and Winnefred, who assured her she could take a few days to make her decision. Then she helped Isobel pack, went to bed before dark, and rose at dawn to direct the loading of the carriage.

She spent the two-hour return trip staring blankly out the window, her only thought aside from her next step that she should have eaten something to settle the mild ache in her belly before leaving the house party.

Isobel slept, closing her eyes while they'd still been in Mrs. Cress's drive and not opening them again until the carriage came to a stop in front of the prison, four miles from their home.

Rumpled, eyes blurred with sleep, she glanced out the window and frowned. "Why are we here?"

"I need to speak with Wolfgang." Adelaide's voice sounded distant and dull in her head. "The carriage will take you home."

"I'll come with you. Or wait, if you prefer."

Adelaide shook her head and reached for the door handle. "Fetch George from Mrs. McFee. We've inconvenienced her long enough."

She hopped out of the carriage and hurried into the shadow of the looming stone building before Isobel could argue.

The prison was relatively new, built in the last decade to house an overflow of criminals from Edinburgh and an influx of French soldiers captured during the war. The first time Adelaide had visited her brother here, she'd been struck by the sheer size of the place, and the sense of gloom and despair that seemed to all but seep from its stones. She hardly noticed either anymore. Today, she passed through the gate and strode through the courtyard without paying heed to the towering walls or the few lethargic figures milling about in what scant sunlight could be found. She followed a guard down the long maze of halls without hearing the voices of inmates or noticing the smell of old straw and sweat.

Wolfgang had a private cell, courtesy of his position as a gentleman, and the few extra coins Adelaide had slipped to the appropriate official. She'd paid the bribe for George's sake and her own piece of mind. Neither she nor George needed to become acquainted with the other inmates.

The guard stopped outside Wolfgang's cell and pushed the door open for her in invitation. Debtors were free to move about their wing, take a bit of air, and exercise in the yard. Wolfgang rarely took advantage of the opportunity.

Stepping into the small, dark room, she watched as Wolfgang rose from a cot in the corner. As always, Adelaide was struck by how little he resembled the boy she'd once known. He'd been plump as a child, his features soft, round, and invariably lit with a grin.

She'd adored him then, the younger brother who could

tease her out of a pout with a jest and a smile. The carefree boy who had raced with her about their father's estate and enticed her into adventures in the fields and woods beyond.

It was difficult to see that boy in the man standing before her now. Wolfgang had grown gaunt, despite the extra food she brought each week. His face was haggard and drawn, with sharp angles and sunken eyes. They were less than two years apart in age, and yet he looked to have aged two decades beyond her.

"Are you going to come in properly," he asked, "or stand there gaping at me like a landed fish?"

"Wolfgang." She crossed the room and pressed a kiss to his cheek. The skin felt thin and rough from his night beard. "You need to shave."

"My valet's gone missing. What are you doing here? Shouldn't you be in—" He broke off, and his features lit with a rare smile. "You've come with news, haven't you? You brought Sir Robert up to scratch. Knew you would. I knew—"

"I've come to ask you a question."

He actually grinned at her. "If it's my permission to marry, you have it."

It had been so long since she'd seen him happy, she was almost tempted to hold her tongue and enjoy the all-but-forgotten pleasure. Almost. "Who holds your final debt?"

The moment of pleasure was lost. His face fell, and he groaned. "Not this again, Adelaide. We've gone over—"

"*Who*, Wolfgang?" She snapped at him. The calm of the last day was slowly wearing away. "Is it Sir Robert?"

Hooded eyes skittered away. "No, of course not."

Connor was right. Wolfgang was an abysmal liar. "Oh, God. How much?"

He pinched his lips together briefly before answering. "What does it matter?"

What sort of question was that? *"How much?"*

He turned to look out the window. There was a long moment of weighted silence before he gave her the answer under his breath.

"A thousand pounds."

She couldn't speak. She couldn't move.

A thousand pounds. It was far more than she had antic-ipated, three times the total of his other debts. They would never be able to repay such a sum.

"It's not my fault," Wolfgang snapped suddenly. He spun from the window, his face a heartbreaking mix of indigna-tion and poorly concealed guilt. "The ship was lost."

She shook her head at him and wished the numbness would return and swallow her whole. They were ruined, utterly ruined. "What ship?"

"The one carrying sugar from St. Lucia. Sir Robert swore we'd make a fortune."

"This was Sir Robert's idea?" Her mouth fell open. "You took . . . For pity's sake, Wolfgang, did it not occur to you to think carefully before accepting financial advice from a man who would loan money to someone in debtors' prison?"

"He said he would do it for you, that he wished to help the family."

"And you believed him?"

"Why wouldn't I have?" Wolfgang threw his hands up. "What did I have to lose? I was already here."

"You," she snapped. "*You* are here. Not your son, nor your sisters. How could you think so little of us? How could you allow Sir Robert to court me without informing me of his—"

"Sir Robert told me to say nothing."

"All the more reason you should have said *something*," she bit off.

"And have you turn your back on him?"

"As I should! You can't possibly expect me to have any-thing to do with him now."

Something like panic flashed across his features. "You must. You have to. It's the only way I'll ever be free of this place. If you marry Sir Robert, he'll pay my creditors and forgive what's owed to him."

"Did he tell you this?"

"Yes. Essentially," he amended. "He said he would see me freed once you were married."

"And encouraged you to promote the match." And Wolfgang had most certainly promoted the match, speaking of little else on their visits. Sir Robert this, Sir Robert that. It made her sick to think of it now.

"I didn't see the harm in it. You looked to be taken with him, and it's a sound match." He swore under his breath. "He'll not like that I've told you. He may not offer if—"

"Sir Robert has already offered. So has Mr. Brice."

"Who the devil is Mr. Brice?"

"A gentleman I met at the house party."

Wolfgang shook his head in dismissal. "I've never heard of him. You accepted Sir Robert's offer, of course."

"No. And I've no thought of doing so now." All this time, Sir Robert had been paying compliments to her with one tongue and threatening her brother with another. It turned her stomach.

"Don't be a fool. The man's a baron. You can't deny a baron."

"I can and shall."

"He'll not stand for it. You don't know him, Adelaide. You don't know what he's capable of."

A long, painful silence followed that statement. Adelaide watched as Wolfgang began to pace in short, quick strides across the room. There had been a time, when they were young, that she had found amusement in their sharing of that habit. But now, with every step he took, with every moment that passed, another joyful memory turned black. The implications of his words didn't occur to him. *She* didn't occur to him.

This was not the boy she loved. This was not the playmate of her youth.

"Is there something you would like to tell me about the man you would have me marry?" she asked thickly. Wolfgang appeared not to take notice. He offered her only an irritated shake of his head and continued on with his pacing, mumbling to himself about barons and debts and finding them all a way out of the damnable mess.

Adelaide had heard enough. She turned from him and headed for the door.

"I shall not bring George to see you . . . this Saturday." She'd almost said ever. But she wasn't sure if that would be punishing the father or the son.

"Why?" Wolfgang demanded at her back. "Where will you be?"

She couldn't bring herself to turn around and look at him. She wrenched the door open and strode into the hall with a parting shot over her shoulder.

"Planning a damn wedding."

Chapter 10

*A*delaide was spared the nearly four-mile walk home by accepting a ride on a cart from a passing farmer. After a time, the fresh air and rhythmic rocking served to clear her mind and settle her temper. Another step was completed. It had been painful, but necessary and productive. She'd gained the information she'd needed to make the most sensible choice.

Her next step was to formally accept Connor's offer. Some of Adelaide's burgeoning composure withered at the thought. Telling Connor he'd have his way wasn't going to be painful; it was going to be excruciating. And humiliating, and terrifying, and . . .

Her list was cut short when her home came into view and she spotted Sir Robert's carriage sitting in the drive.

Oh, blast.

He must have left the house party directly after her and Isobel. She wasn't ready to see him. She'd been building—or attempting to build—herself up to speak with Connor, not Sir Robert. What did she say to him? There were any number of things she *wanted* to say, but Wolfgang was right on at least one account. Sir Robert was a baron. He would take neither her rejection nor her censure lightly.

To give herself time to think, she bid the farmer to stop a ways from the house and walked the last few hundred yards of road slowly, her eyes soaking in the familiar surroundings.

Because the house and grounds were entailed, they were the only things her brother could not lose to debt. Wolfgang often bemoaned the inconvenience of owning property that couldn't be sold. Adelaide often said a prayer of thanks for the same thing.

She loved her home. Every square foot of brick and timber and every inch of land was filled with the cherished memories of her childhood.

The house had never been grand. It claimed but five bedrooms and two servants' quarters. There was no ballroom or orangery. The front parlor was small by ton standards, and the dining room could fit no more than twelve. Despite its modest proportions, however, the house had been tended and furnished as carefully as any grand manor. There hadn't been a door that squeaked, a fireplace that smoked, or a piece of furniture in need of repair or replacement.

That had changed in the years since her parents' deaths. They could no longer afford the staff needed to keep the house in good repair. Most of the chimneys were no longer safe to use, and half the doors couldn't be opened or closed without a good shove. Items of value had been sold to pay Wolfgang's mounting debt. Even most of her beloved flower garden had gone to seed or been turned over to make room for beets and turnips. Her mother's roses remained, but Adelaide rarely had the time and energy to do more than trim them back once a year, and cut the occasional flower that bloomed despite her neglect.

She stopped outside the front door, gathering her courage. The house had fallen to ruin before Sir Robert had come into their lives. He couldn't be held responsible for that, but he could damn well be held responsible for the absence of its master. Baron or not, he would answer for that.

Resolute, she opened the door and stepped inside. The foyer was small and in sight of half the downstairs when the parlor doors were open. They were open now, but the moment Adelaide entered, Isobel appeared, blocking her from view.

Isobel took her cloak and whispered in her ear, "He's in the parlor. I'll send him away if you like. Tell him you have the headache."

"Thank you, but no. Is George upstairs?" She waited for Isobel's confirmation. "Will you be certain he stays there, please?"

Isobel pressed her lips together but nodded. "If you need me, you've only to shout."

Adelaide almost laughed at that. For pity's sake, Sir Robert was a baron, not a one-man firing squad. And, really, if anyone ought to be feeling unnerved, it was him.

He didn't look unnerved in the least. The moment Isobel moved away, Adelaide saw Sir Robert standing in front of the settee, waiting for her. The vibrant yellow of his waistcoat clashed dreadfully with his hair and stood in stark contrast to the worn, faded colors of her grandmother's old carpet and settee. His confident and condescending air clashed with her temper. She wasn't sure how one could appear condescending, but Sir Robert always seemed to manage it.

He moved as if to take her hand and draw her into the room. "My dear Miss Ward."

She hurried forward of her own volition, hands gripped behind her back. "Sir Robert. You've returned early."

"Well, of course I have." His tone and expression turned chiding. "You left without word."

"My departure was expected."

"Darling girl, if we had arrived at an understanding before—"

"I would like to understand why you saw fit to extend a loan to my brother."

Sir Robert started at the question. And who could blame

him? It was far more blunt than she'd intended, but her patience was sorely tried. Besides, it was better to get what was sure to be an objectionable experience over and done with.

She tilted her head when he continued to stand there, looking flabbergasted. "Do you mean to deny it?"

Finally, he blinked and cleared his throat. "I do not." To this, he added a sniff of disapproval and an aside. "Wolfgang should not have brought you into it."

Oh, the nerve of the man. "You should not have brought yourself into my family's affairs."

"I would beg for the chance to explain."

Nothing about his tone or appearance lent itself to the notion of begging. He looked as sure of himself as he had when she'd walked into the room. And it was only out of a sense of fairness that Adelaide suppressed the urge to toss him from her home that very instant. Connor and her brother had been given an opportunity to make the accusations. Sir Robert had the right to mount a defense.

"Very well," she agreed. "If you've an explanation to give, I shall listen."

"Will you sit?"

She took a seat on the settee with reluctance and gave a muffled yelp when something hard poked her in the lower back. A quick reach between the cushions and she retrieved George's favorite wooden spoon.

Sir Robert stared at it. "Er . . ."

"My nephew fancies himself a percussionist." She gripped the spoon and silently dared Sir Robert to challenge the explanation. George was not yet two. He fancied digging in the dirt, the occasional foray into his own nose, and hitting things that made noise.

Sir Robert gave a strained smile. "Talented, is he?"

"Quite." She set the spoon aside. "You were explaining?"

"Right." He glanced at the spoon again, then away. "Right. It all began shortly after the start of our courtship. You received a small inheritance. A very small . . ." He trailed off at her incredulous look—was there a man in

Britain *not* sticking his nose into her business?—and had the decency to look abashed. "Forgive me, I took an interest in the well-being of the woman I intend to marry."

"You might have expressed that interest by asking instead of prying," she chided. And, oh, it was gratifying to use that tone of voice with him.

Sir Robert seemed not to hear her. "I was aware that the funds you received were sufficient to pay your brother's debts."

"They were." She'd actually paid two of them before discovering the futility of paying any.

Sir Robert nodded. "I also knew something of your brother, and I knew once he was released there would be nothing to stop him from returning to his old habits. I couldn't allow that to happen. I did what I thought best."

"You made the loan knowing he couldn't pay it back?"

"Certainly not." He hesitated, not looking all that certain. "I knew, however, that the investment was a considerable risk. My reasoning was, he would either earn a profit sufficient to keep him occupied until we wed, or he would remain in prison."

"Because of you."

A hint of impatience crossed his face. "What would you have had me do? Free him? Give him the opportunity to ruin you? Watch the woman I adore lose the little she has left? He would have spent that inheritance in a fortnight and left you with nothing."

"I'd not have given him the money to spend. I've more sense than that. And honestly, that is neither here nor there. You've lied to me."

"I never meant—"

"Did you not think to ask what I wished? Did it not occur to you to speak with me of this decision?"

A furrow worked between his brows. "Matters of a financial nature—"

"I have cared for the finances of my family for some time."

"You have performed the role of matriarch with aplomb.

No one can dismiss the steadfast loyalty and good sense you have shown in the care of your family. You are an exemplary woman, Miss Ward. Your accomplishments are to be lauded." He paused, and once again, his tone turned condescending. "But you are *only* a woman. You lead with your heart."

She wanted to lead with the broad head of the wooden spoon. "I am not a silly chit just come from the nursery, sir."

"I'd not have courted you these four months if you were," he replied with extreme patience. "Answer me this—if your inheritance had been sufficient to free your brother, would you have done so?"

"He's my brother." And most siblings searched for ways to bring their brothers out of prison, she thought, not put them in.

"With the heart," he repeated in a tone that made her feel like a foolish little girl. "Wolfgang would have petitioned the courts for what was left of your inheritance. You do know that."

The thought had occurred to her, but at the time, she'd retained some faith in her brother's loyalty and honesty. But that faith had been shaken. Would Wolfgang have respected the terms of their cousin's will? She honestly didn't know, and her uncertainty must have shown, because Sir Robert shook his head and pressed his advantage.

"Can you not see freeing your brother for the mistake it would have been?"

It troubled her that she could see it might have been a mistake. She hated that there existed the possibility that he was right.

Sir Robert sighed. "Perhaps it was my own mistake to have kept my involvement from you. But I can only claim the best of intentions."

It wasn't an apology, but it was an admittance of fault. She wondered how sincere that generosity was, and how deep it ran. "If I asked it of you, would you free him now?"

He shook his head. "When we marry. When I can protect you from his excesses."

Not all that deep, apparently. "But if—"

"Trust me, Adelaide. Trust me to do what is best for you and your family." He reached out and took her hand. "You need me, darling. Let us put this matter to rest."

She hesitated, then gave a distracted nod. There didn't seem any point in further argument. Sir Robert was not going to be persuaded that he was in the wrong. And though she wasn't ready to forgive his methods, she conceded that his intentions—however misguided—had been good. And really, wasn't it better that they should be able to part ways on civil terms?

"Excellent." Sir Robert said, a new cheer in his voice. "I'll have the banns posted immediately."

"What? *No.*"

She didn't mean to snap the refusal, or to yank her hand free of his, *or* to leap off the settee as if she'd been bitten in the backside, but she did all three.

Good Lord, that was not the matter she'd thought they were putting to rest.

Evidently, Sir Robert thought it was. He reared back, pale blue eyes going wide. "What the . . . What do you mean, no?"

"I thought we were agreeing to end our argument, not wed. Sir Robert, I am most dreadfully sorry—" Only, she wasn't, particularly. "But in light of all of this, I cannot marry—"

"You must marry." He rose from his seat, gripped his hands behind his back, and leaned toward her to impart in an excessively patient tone, "My dear, you have been compromised."

She clenched her jaw and prayed for patience of her own. For pity's sake, did he suspect her of having forgotten? Or somehow having overlooked that minor episode in the garden, and the one in the study, and the reason for her prompt departure? How ridiculous did he believe her to be?

"Miss Ward?"

"I was not compromised by you," she ground out.

He straightened, slowly. "You *cannot* be considering—"

"Lady Engsly suggested that I should consider all of my options, and that is what I've done. Mr. Brice has made a respectable offer, and—"

"There is *nothing* respectable about Connor Brice."

Very little, to be sure. And yet he was the wiser choice. Good heavens, how depressing. "Be that as it may, and whatever your opinion of Mr. Brice, he has—"

"You will not speak of him to me!"

Adelaide snapped her mouth shut, more out of shock than a willingness to obey.

Sir Robert looked to be on the very edge of control, and losing ground. His lips twisted. His skin grew red, and something dark and ugly clouded his eyes. When his hands curled into fists at his side, she took an instinctive step back. She'd never been the sole focus of his temper before. He'd been mildly put out with her in private, a little exasperated, but never truly angry. Even in the garden, it had been Connor who'd taken the brunt of Sir Robert's displeasure.

Her eyes darted to the wooden spoon. Sir Robert stood between her and it. She edged a little closer to the door.

She needn't have bothered. The storm passed as quickly as it had come. Sir Robert bowed his head and blew out a small, quiet breath. When he looked at her again, his color was returning to normal, his expression serene.

Good Lord, and she'd thought Connor mercurial. She wondered how the brothers would take the news that they had more in common than ancestry. Probably not well, and considering Sir Robert's appearance a moment ago, she wisely kept the observation to herself.

"My poor girl," Sir Robert intoned. "You have been through a trial, haven't you? And here I am, acting the heartless ogre, insisting on a forgiveness I've not yet earned."

Forgiveness? She wasn't certain if he was speaking of his failure to guard his brother, his failure to mention his involvement with Wolfgang's imprisonment, or his failure to treat her with a modicum of respect. At present, she didn't care. She just wanted him to leave. Her regrets could be sent in a letter.

Sir Robert surprised her yet again, by stepping forward and brushing her cheek with his fingers. She immediately reconsidered the necessity of a retreat. His hand was cool and gentle, yet her stomach turned in protest of the touch.

"I'll call on you tomorrow," he promised.

Oh, damn. "I'm afraid tomorrow will not be possible. I . . . I've only just arrived home, you see, and . . . and there are all manner of duties that went neglected in my absence. My nephew—"

"Yes. Yes, of course." He nodded in understanding. "You need a day or two to settle in. I shall call on you later in the week."

She offered a noncommittal "hmm" and curtsy and indulged in a long sigh of relief after he bowed and let himself out.

Another step completed, she thought. Well, another step *nearly* completed. She still needed to write the letter. But right now, she needed something else.

Anticipation sent a tingle along her skin as she crossed the room and climbed the stairs, careful to avoid the very center of the third step. It had a disconcerting tendency to bow in the middle.

Sailing straight past her room and Isobel's, she went to the open door of the nursery, and for the first time since leaving the house party, she smiled.

Oh, yes, this is what she'd needed—to see her twenty-two-month-old nephew fast asleep on his bed. George slept on his belly, with one arm caught under his chest and the other bent so that his fingers covered his face like a mask. He'd scooted down on the mattress, his head a solid foot from his pillow.

She ignored the urge to pick him up, straighten him out, and set him back on the pillow. He'd only wiggle back to where he was now.

Instead, she padded softly across the room and leaned over his sleeping form, soaking in the details of his face—

the long lashes against pink, round cheeks; the rosebud mouth and small, crescent scar from a lost battle with the corner of a windowsill. She brushed a hand over his soft curls, so blond they were almost ivory now, but they would darken with age, as they had for all the Ward children.

Bending down, she placed a kiss at his temple, and though she knew it was silly, she took a moment to breathe him in. There was no reason why he should smell different than her and Isobel. They lived in the same house, used the same soap, slept on the same linens. And yet . . . She breathed him in again. And yet there was something unique about him, something distinctively sweeter.

She straightened with a sigh.

This was why it was so important she make the right decisions. This was why she could not afford to make the wrong ones.

This was why she would marry a man she did not love.

Chapter 11

*A*delaide wrote the letter that very night but held off sending it the next day. Her reasons were varied but stemmed in part from the late-arising notion that it might be prudent to accept one offer—thereby authenticating its veracity—before rejecting the other. She rather thought ruination would be preferable to a marriage to Sir Robert, but her preferences came second to the needs of her family. The other—and possibly most influential—reason for delaying the letter was fear of Sir Robert reappearing on her doorstep to protest the rejection in person.

She had a day or two yet before he would call again. She'd send the letter tomorrow, or possibly the day after if—

"Are you constructing a sack?"

Adelaide pulled herself from her musings at the sound of Isobel's voice. They were sharing the broad window seat in the parlor, a sewing kit squeezed between them.

Though she'd used it as an excuse with Sir Robert, in truth, there was a great deal that needed her attention at home. And when Mrs. McFee had offered to take George for the morning, she and Isobel had taken advantage of the resulting quiet to fit in a spot of darning.

Isobel was down to four usable gowns. Adelaide was down to five, including the ball gown she hoped to sell and the blue dress she was wearing now.

Isobel set down a chemise and pointed to the gown Adelaide was holding. "You're sewing the hems together."

Adelaide looked down at the mess she'd made of her work. "Oh, dear."

"Only a stitch or two." Isobel handed her the stitch ripper and turned to look out the window. "There's a stranger coming down the drive in a phaeton."

Adelaide glanced over her shoulder then quickly vacated her seat. "That is Mr. Brice."

"Is it?" Suddenly fascinated with the view, Isobel set her darning aside without looking and squinted through the glass. "I can't make him out as yet. But it's a new phaeton. Quite stylish."

"I don't wish to see him this morning." She needed more time, just a few more hours to collect her thoughts, decide on a course of action, figure through . . . Oh, very well, she wanted a few more hours with her pride. "Would you send him away, please, Isobel? Tell him I'll be in this afternoon."

Isobel shrugged, pulled herself away from the window, and headed for the foyer. Accepting that as a yes, Adelaide followed her to the parlor doors and closed them behind her. She grimaced as the warped wood scraped loudly against the floor. The parlor doors had remained open for the last six months for that very reason. And because she hadn't the foggiest notion of how to fix the problem.

After considering and rejecting the idea of listening through the keyhole, she crossed the room and took a seat on the settee. She sat back against the cushions, then quickly righted herself again when the ancient wood frame groaned ominously—a new and unwelcomed sign of deterioration.

Oh, what she wouldn't give to go back fifteen years and tell her parents, no, she did not wish to learn how to paint and play the pianoforte. She would learn carpentry, estate management, and how to navigate a stock exchange. How different her life would be now.

She rolled her eyes at that bit of foolishness. One could not go back. And even if one could, one would probably be better served by going back a few weeks, declining an invitation to a certain house party, and making a bid for the carpenter's son.

Harold Autry hadn't the funds to pay her brother's debts, but at least her furniture wouldn't squeak.

Adelaide looked over at the muffled sound of Connor's voice coming from the foyer—then Isobel's, Connor's again, and then a long pause.

At length, a sliver of Isobel's slippered feet appeared beneath one of the parlor doors. The handle turned and the door gave way slowly and with a great deal of noise. Isobel squeezed inside the meager two feet she was able to access.

"Mr. Brice to see you, Adelaide."

Exasperated, Adelaide beckoned her inside with her hand and waited for Isobel to cross the room.

"I know Mr. Brice is here to see me," she whispered, flicking a glance at the open door. She shouldn't care if Connor overheard them, but the good manners that had been drilled in since birth were not easy to ignore. Especially when a young lady was sitting upon her grandmother's settee. "I thought you were going to send him away."

"I shall if you insist—" Isobel began in a normal voice.

"Shh!"

"Oh, for pity's sake." Isobel marched back to the parlor door, shoved it closed with two hard swings of her hip, then marched back again.

"I shall send him away if you insist," she repeated. "But first—I am to inform you that a façade of willingness to be courted might very well turn public opinion away from pity and condemnation."

Suddenly, she didn't much care if Connor could hear them. "I cannot fathom by what ridiculous twist of logic—"

"He's quite right, actually."

Adelaide slumped in her seat, ignoring the seat's loud complaint. "*Et tu*, Isobel?"

"Set your anger aside a moment and think," Isobel urged. "Upholding your innocence in this may not serve you in the long run. Certainly not if you have any intention of marrying Mr. Brice. In the eyes of society, you're either a victim or a woman of loose morals, and you'll never be anything else. Unless, of course, you *had* meant to meet him in the garden. If the two of you *had* been holding a clandestine courtship that you always intended to bring to light—and to the altar—then you are no longer a tragic figure, but—"

"Merely a woman of loose morals," Adelaide muttered.

"A woman swept away by the dark thrill of a secret romance," Isobel corrected. "The ladies will still tsk behind your back, but their tongues will taste of envy."

"That is quite an image."

"Isn't it just?"

"Smears a bit when one takes into consideration I might not marry Mr. Brice." She'd decided to, but Isobel wasn't aware of it. Adelaide thought it best to wait until the particulars were settled before making any sort of announcement.

"I think you should," Isobel said. "He is prodigiously handsome."

Adelaide gave her a bland look. "An agreeable countenance is not a sensible reason for marriage."

"Love is the only sensible reason for marriage. But as that's not an option for you at present, you might as well take the next best thing." Isobel shrugged. "Entirely up to you, of course."

Her sister would choose now, of all times, to attempt a bit of pragmatism. "Oh, very well. Let him in."

"Excellent." Isobel bobbed once on her toes in a disgustingly chipper manner then strode back to the parlor doors. She looked at them, sighed, and began the process of wrenching them open. "We should just remove the bloody things," she muttered.

Adelaide opened her mouth to berate Isobel for swearing, then snapped it shut again when Connor's large hand appeared in the meager space Isobel had managed to create.

"If you would back away, Miss Ward . . ."

Isobel did as suggested, crossing the room to stand next to Adelaide. A moment later, both doors flew open with an angry shriek of old wood and rusted hinges. Adelaide jumped at the sound and sight, half expecting the doors to explode into splinters under the strain.

Still intact, they came to a screeching, shuttering stop to reveal the foyer, and Connor Brice standing in the doorway with his legs braced apart. He wore tan breeches, a green coat several shades darker than his eyes, and a smile. *That* smile. The terrible, beautiful, inviting smile that had been the start of her undoing.

"Your sister is right," he announced. "You should remove the doors."

She curtsied out of habit, and, admittedly, a little out of the pleasure to be had in spiting his attempt at familiarity. "Good morning, Mr. Brice. My sister and I are grateful for your assistance and shall take your advice under advisement."

If he was put off by her cool tone, it didn't show. "It was my pleasure to offer both."

Brushing off his coat, he stepped into the room. A floorboard in need of replacing groaned under the weight of his large frame. Adelaide wished the house would finally make good on one of its threats and the floorboard would buckle. It would be immensely satisfying to see Connor Brice take a tumble.

It was a childish and petty wish, but she didn't much care. She had to marry the blighter; she didn't have to like him. She didn't even have to be nice to him.

Sadly, the floor held. Fortunately, another possibility occurred to her.

"Won't you have a seat?" she offered, gesturing to the cherrywood chair before the settee. She threw a hard look at Isobel, warning her to say nothing.

No one sat in the cherrywood chair. There was no one left alive who could even remember someone having ever sat in the cherrywood chair. It had been rickety and unpredictable when she'd been a child, and—spared from the woodpile for sentimental reasons of unknown origin—consigned to the attic as a result. Its entire purpose now was to provide a surface on which to place a book, or George's spoon, or anything else that was lightweight and sturdy enough to survive the likely event of the chair giving out.

But if Connor insisted on staying . . .

He eyed the chair dubiously. "I'll stand. Thank you."

Blast.

Stifling a sigh, she gave up the hope of seeing Connor tumble. It was tempting to think of another trap—heaven knew, the possibilities in her home were endless—but they'd never get around to the business at hand that way. And she very much wanted to get to the business at hand, and Connor out of her home, as quickly as possible.

"What may I do for you, Mr. Brice?"

"You may grant me the pleasure of a few hours of your time. I thought perhaps a drive."

"It is a lovely day for it," Isobel chimed before Adelaide could speak.

"I haven't a chaperone."

"I have a phaeton." He gestured to the window to where the open-air vehicle was waiting in the drive. "An acceptable conveyance of courtship, I believe. Shall we, Miss Ward?"

She couldn't see that she had any choice. There would be no time to stroke her pride before bidding it a fond farewell. She'd have to lay it at Connor's feet just as it was and hope there was something left of it when he was through.

"A short drive," she relented and headed for the foyer in search of her bonnet. "I want to return before George."

She wanted a readily available excuse to return to the house should a hasty retreat become necessary.

Isobel's voice trilled cheerfully at her back. "I'll see to George. No need to rush."

Adelaide crammed the bonnet on her head and spoke around a jaw clamped tight with frustration. "Thank you, Isobel."

"You're welcome. Do enjoy yourselves."

Unable to form a response, Adelaide swept past a smirking Connor and out the front door into the bright light of midday. Connor followed, closing the door behind them. He placed a gentle hand at the small of her back and ushered her toward the phaeton.

Attempting to ignore the warmth of his touch through her gown, Adelaide concentrated on the vehicle. Isobel was right; it was new, without a rough spot of wood or visible scratch on the black and gold paint.

"Is this yours?" she asked.

He nodded and assisted her onto the seat. "I had it commissioned upon my return to Scotland. What do you think?"

"I think you're dissembling," she replied smartly. "Your assets were seized by the courts."

He came himself onto the bench beside her. "You've been asking about me."

"I heard a rumor."

"There's truth to it," he confirmed. "As my elder brother, Sir Robert was allowed to take guardianship of my fortune during my imprisonment."

She thought that grossly unfair, as Sir Robert had been his accuser, but she felt no particular desire to express her sympathies to Connor. "Then how did you purchase this phaeton?"

"It was commissioned before my arrest." He started the horses off with a light flick of the reins. "Sir Robert wasn't given the bulk of my fortune, at any rate. Just a small part of the whole."

"You had funds hidden away," she guessed.

"I did." He smiled a little. "Sir Robert was aware of it, but he could never prove it."

"Were you given the rest back on your release?"

"Physical properties were returned to me intact. He'd

not been allowed to sell them. As for the rest, I was given what remained—all fourteen pounds."

She grimaced, all too familiar with the frustration of watching another fritter away the family fortune and being helpless to stop him.

"Was it a great deal of money?"

"Depends on your definition of a great deal. It was enough." He deftly steered them around a pothole. "You visited your brother."

It took a moment for her mind to wrap around the sudden change of subject. "Have you been spying on me?"

He had a roundabout way of denying the accusation. "I inferred from your willingness . . . more or less . . . to join me on this drive that you are no longer laboring under the impression I am a liar."

"Oh, I labor—"

"Allow me to rephrase. I inferred that your brother admitted to Sir Robert's role in his imprisonment."

Because he sounded too smug by half, she sniffed and replied in her finest you're-not-so-clever-as-you-imagine tone, "*Sir Robert* admitted to it."

He brought the horses to an abrupt stop and pivoted in his seat to pin her with a cold stare. Evidently, he was not impressed with her tone.

"You *confronted* Sir Robert?"

His voice was no less chilling for its softness, and his anger was no less palpable. The eerie stillness of his large frame spoke of a fury carefully tethered. She suspected it would be an awful sight to see that tether snap. And yet, she wasn't at all frightened. She wasn't nervous as she had been in the presence of Sir Robert's temper. Certainly, it was discomfiting to be the object of such an imposing glare, but she didn't feel threatened, or even particularly intimidated.

No, he didn't make her uncomfortable in the way Sir Robert did. But he made her uncomfortable in every other way.

"Naturally, I did," she replied with what she hoped was equal composure. "Did you expect me to condemn the man without giving him an opportunity to defend himself?"

"I expected you to have the good sense to keep your distance from the rotter." His eyes narrowed. "You won't see him again."

He attempted to round off this insulting and ridiculous bit of nonsense by returning his attention to the road, effectively dismissing her. As if the topic were closed. As if her own feelings mattered not a wit.

He lifted the reins.

She reached over and snatched the right one out of his hand. "You will not dictate to me, Mr. Brice. If I should fancy another visit with Sir Robert, I'll have it."

She didn't fancy another visit, but that was not the point.

He turned back to her, slower this time, and held his hand out for the rein. "That's dangerous, lass."

Having never before ridden in a phaeton, let alone driven one, she had no idea if that was true. But it didn't seem the sort of thing she ought to take a chance on. Feeling a bit foolish, she handed him the rein, and then a good piece of her mind.

"If you start this vehicle again, I shall have to insist you return me to my sister. I'll not be spoken to like a child, or as if our marriage was a foregone conclusion."

His lips twitched as he settled the reins in his lap. "But you'll adhere to your husband's dictates after marriage?"

She gave him a taunting little smile, and a lie. "You're not in a likely position to ever know."

"And Sir Robert is?" He shook his head, clearly not believing the lie. "Sir Robert is responsible for your brother's—"

"He had his reasons," she cut in. Those reasons were unacceptable to her, but that, too, was not the point.

Connor lifted one very arrogant, very irritating brow. "I should very much like to hear them."

"Yes." She shifted in her seat and returned his leveled stare with one of her own. "I imagine you would."

What followed was an exceedingly long silence accompanied by what could only be described as a childish battle of stares. Adelaide had never before considered herself to be of an obstinate nature—not an excessively obstinate nature, anyway—but she'd always known herself to be honest. And she could honestly say they were both being stubborn as a pair of mules. She was not, however, willing to admit they both had equal cause for such ridiculous behavior. Connor Brice was not her father, not her husband, and not her brother. If he thought himself due an explanation, he was sadly mistaken.

She rather hoped his error occurred to him soon. A contest of wills was a bit less comfortable than she might have imagined. She was twisted awkwardly at the waist, and an itch on her ankle that she'd been vaguely aware of during their short trip suddenly sprung to life, demanding her attention.

She tried rubbing her other foot against it, but the soft leather of her slippers acted like a breeze against a bug bite. The itching intensified. She tried shifting ever so slightly on the seat, but not only did that fail to alleviate the itch, it succeeded in positioning her so that a stream of sunlight broke through a small crack in the weave of her old bonnet and landed directly on her left eye. Now she was itching *and* squinting.

Oh, blast. This was dreadful.

Worse, she could see the growing light of humor on Connor's face.

Infinitely worse, she felt a matching spark of amusement.

Dear heavens, what sort of husband and wife were they going to make? He with no care for her, she with visions of torment for him, and the both of them impossibly stubborn.

"Go on and scratch, Adelaide. I'll try not to think the less of you for it."

She caved—but only, mind you, because he gave in first—and reached down and ran her fingers over the offending spot. It felt like heaven. "What is said between Sir Robert and myself is none of your concern."

"On the contrary, the actions of my future wife are very much—"

"I have not agreed to marry you."

"You can't still be considering Sir Robert."

"I am considering all of my options," she hedged, not quite ready to hand Connor his victory.

"He must have been very convincing in his excuses."

"Sir Robert is a most eloquent man."

Connor's response to this was to glare a moment longer, which she found quite gratifying, then turn to the road and start the horses moving again with a flick of the reins.

Little was said for the next five minutes, but Adelaide snuck the odd glance at Connor. She wanted to ask him what else he knew of Sir Robert. Were there other secrets? Had the baron entangled himself in other aspects of her life? But it seemed inappropriate to question one suitor about another. More important, it was impractical, as neither was apt to be a reliable source of information.

Chapter 12

Connor steered the phaeton onto a narrow road Adelaide knew well. It led north to the prison and the town of Enscrum beyond. But well before the prison, and the town, was Ashbury Hall, a vast estate that had been built by an eccentric and reclusive merchant more than three decades ago and abandoned a mere five years after completion when the merchant decided he'd rather be a recluse in a more hospitable climate.

The house and grounds, now fallen into disrepair, were little more than a mile from her home. As a child, she'd often snuck away to play in the overgrown garden and brave peeks through the windows with Wolfgang.

A year ago, she'd heard Ashbury Hall had been sold at last, and work had begun on restoring it to its former glory. The renovations had ceased abruptly for months and had resumed again a few weeks past. As they drew near, Adelaide saw that the stone manor had been washed and its wood trim scraped of old paint. But some of the windows remained boarded, the bare wood looked sad and weathered, and the grounds . . . Dear heavens, the grounds. They were a veritable jungle. Weeds of every variety stood knee to neck high, and a number of plants had escaped the gardens and looked to be making a dash for England.

She shook her head and was about to comment on the state of Ashbury's front lawn when Connor turned into the drive.

"What are we doing here?" The point of taking the drive had been to be seen together, a task that could have been better attended to by making a quick trip into the local village of Banfries.

Connor slowed the horses. "We are choosing a house."

"A house for what? For us?" She looked at the enormous manor, then back at him. "Oh, for pity's sake, you are not in earnest."

"I am, I assure you."

"Ashbury Hall is not a house. It is a gentleman's country estate." And it was not a viable choice of home. Aside from the fact someone else was already in possession of the place, he couldn't possibly afford such a property. She lifted her gaze to the heavens and prayed for patience. "Why must I be plagued by men who cannot manage their funds with a modicum of foresight and wisdom?"

He brought the horses to a stop a small distance from the house and turned to smile at her. "I was wise enough to pay a good deal less for it than it's worth."

"You . . . It's *yours*?" Good heavens, that couldn't be possible. "How is that possible?"

"You aren't aware of how property is bought and sold?"

"Yes, of course I am. I just . . ." She shook her head, bewildered. "Sir Robert stole your fortune. You were impressed. You were imprisoned—"

"Same thing, really. But Sir Robert stole only part, you'll recall. And I bought Ashbury when I bought the phaeton, before my arrest. Also before I bought my freedom."

Her eyebrows winged up. "You bribed your way free?"

"I'd say the funds were extorted, but I do so hate to fill the role of victim."

She gave him a mocking smile. "Yes, distasteful, isn't it?"

Grinning in response, he hopped down and came around

to assist her from the vehicle. She put her hand out, expecting him to take it, but he grasped her round the waist instead and gently lifted her off her feet as easily as if he were lifting a sack of grain.

Good gracious. Her hands flew to his shoulders for balance, and she felt the coil and release of muscle under her fingertips as he set her gently down on the drive. Unbidden, the memory of the last time he'd held her close filled her mind . . . the rough drag of lips, the drugging heat of his mouth, the way he'd banded his arms around her as if she was something precious, something he needed.

She'd never been held that way, never before known what it was like to have a man look at her . . . the way Connor was looking at her now. His eyes darkened and settled on her mouth, and the hands at her hips brought her closer with subtle pressure.

Adelaide leapt back and swallowed a yelp when the backs of her legs met with the hard wheel of the phaeton.

Good heavens, what was she thinking?

It didn't require much guesswork for her to ascertain what Connor was thinking. He'd dropped his hands, but his eyes were still fixed on her mouth. He looked tense, tightly coiled, as if he might pounce on her with the slightest provocation.

"I . . ." She searched for something, anything, to distract him. "Er . . ."

Eventually, she landed on, "Ashbury Hall!" For no other reason than that it was there.

Connor lifted his gaze to hers, finally. But his only response was to raise his eyebrows.

She resumed her search. "Um . . . Is it truly yours?"

His lips twitched, and he waited a beat before speaking. Just to let her know she wasn't fooling either of them.

"Truly," he said at last. "And I promise you, I can well afford its upkeep."

She considered that statement, and the man, and the fine opportunity to turn the focus further away from the tension between them.

"Why did it take you so long to gain your freedom?" With access to a corrupt official and the sort of funds needed to buy country estates, he ought to have been out in a day.

"In the English judicial system, even bribery is subject to the delay of bureaucracy." He lifted a negligent shoulder at her bland look. "It took time to access the funds without attracting attention. And the only obliging official of my solicitor's acquaintance was visiting his sister in St. Petersburg. Negotiations were slow."

"Bribes and negotiations have no place in a court of law."

"Such a moral creature," he teased. "How would we ever know who's guilty and who isn't?"

She ran her tongue over her teeth. "Lord Gideon interfered on your behalf at his wife's request, you know."

"Did he?"

"Your money may well have been wasted on your solicitor's obliging friend. It is something to consider." She wagered his pride would consider it for a long time to come.

She wagered badly.

Connor blew out a long, dramatic breath that was just a hair shy of being a whistle. "Lovely, generous Freddie. If I'd not been behind bars when we met . . ."

"Yes, some ladies have all the good fortune," she said dryly.

She wasn't honestly offended by the means of his release. She'd paid for Wolfgang's private room, hadn't she? And one couldn't fault the man for gaining his release through the same corruption that had unjustly imprisoned him in the first place. Provided, of course, it had been unjust. Lilly and Winnefred proclaimed his innocence, but what did they know of the man, really?

What did any of them know?

"Were you a highwayman?"

His smile didn't waver. "No."

She waited in vain for him to elaborate. He didn't, and she realized that was all the reassurance she was going to receive. It was galling to know she had no choice but to accept it.

"Lilly and Winnefred say Sir Robert fabricated the story. I am inclined to believe them."

"But only them," he guessed and offered his elbow.

She took it without thought. "Until given reason otherwise. Aren't we going to look at the house?"

He led her off the drive and onto a narrow path through waist-high weeds, and around a box hedge that hadn't been pruned in decades.

"I thought you might like to see a bit of the grounds first," Connor explained. "What do you make of them?"

She could make out a small pond in the distance—provided she walked on her toes—and, beyond that, the walled garden Wolfgang once utilized as a medieval fortress. If memory served, it had been England's last defense against the marauding Viking hordes.

She sighed and resumed a normal, ladylike walk.

"They're overgrown," she said. And then, at length, ". . . And beautiful." She'd always thought them beautiful, even in their wildness.

Connor frowned thoughtfully. "They need a gardener's touch."

"They need a plow," she replied. And peonies by the gate of the walled garden. Wouldn't that be lovely?

"The interior of the house is in better repair." He turned her down another path, one that looked to have been cleared all the way to the front door. "There are four wings and three floors plus the attic. It looks a bit coarse as yet, but the needed repairs are mostly superficial, and quite a few are already completed. The new windows will go in the day after tomorrow. Many of the rooms have furnishings, but I've an interior decorator coming from London to take care of the details."

She gave him a speculative glance. "You didn't bring me here to choose a home; you brought me here to boast."

"I was hoping to impress you," he admitted, unrepentant. "The choice of home is yours, Adelaide. This is merely one of your options."

"What are my others?"

"I've several similar properties. None quite so impressive in scale, but most are in better condition."

"Several?"

"I did tell you I was wealthier than Sir Robert."

"You also told me you were a guest at Mrs. Cress's house party."

"I never did," he protested, affecting the air of a man grievously insulted. "You erroneously inferred from my presence that I had been invited. I, you will recall, strove to correct the misunderstanding at the earliest opportunity."

She snorted at that. "You are many things, Mr. Brice. Honest is not one of them."

"Such venom," he taunted as they climbed the front steps. "And here I am, inviting you into my home."

She rolled her eyes when he turned his back to open the massive front door. Which, she could not help but note, failed to issue even the minutest of squeaks.

Connor waved her inside with a flourish. "Welcome to Ashbury Hall, Miss Ward."

She stepped over the threshold and caught her breath. "Oh, heavens."

Her voice was a mere whisper, and yet it all but echoed in the cavernous room. She walked across the great hall, awed by the dual staircases, with their wide, graceful steps and marble balustrades. She marveled at the towering domed roof. The sheer vastness of the space was overwhelming. Her entire home could fit into Ashbury Hall's entry.

That was, perhaps, a slight exaggeration, but the room was remarkable in size. And in its quietness. Where were the footsteps and voices, the everyday sounds one associated with a home?

Connor wasn't the sort of man who insisted his staff never be seen or heard, was he?

She turned around and found him leaning against the

door frame with his arms folded at his chest and his legs crossed at the ankles. He was watching her, not as he had on the drive, but with an intensity she nonetheless found unnerving.

"Is there no one here?" she asked, her eyes darting away. "No staff?"

"A few of the village women come to clean during the day. I believe they're in the attic at present. And I have men about after dark, but I've not obtained much in the way of permanent staff as yet. I thought to wait until you'd made a choice of homes. You may select something I own at present, or we can search for something new. A great deal will depend on where you'd like to settle. Or if you'd like to settle. We could spend the seasons in London and the rest of the year touring."

He was leaving it up to her. She didn't want to be pleased by the gesture or moved by his thoughtfulness. But she was. She couldn't help it. Even knowing that he likely made the offer for selfish reasons, she couldn't help but hope that some part of the man she had met in the garden remained in the man she would marry.

"I've always lived in Banfries," she said quietly. "I've never wanted to live anywhere else."

"Never?"

She shook her head without looking at him.

"Then Banfries it will be."

"I should like to travel," she said and discovered the dream was becoming easier to admit aloud. "I should like to visit the places we spoke of before. But I want a home, as well. I'll always want to come back here."

He tapped the wall. "Here, specifically?"

"We shall see," she replied primly. "Ashbury Hall certainly is . . . substantial."

"There's more to it than size. Have a look about. Explore a bit."

Why not? It was likely to be her home soon enough. "I believe I shall."

She took her time, wandering from hall to hall, room to

room. There were an inordinate number of halls and rooms. Tidy stacks of tools lined the walls, and here and there she saw a project still in progress—the piece of molding waiting to be refinished, a door off its hinges, and those boarded windows—but the vast majority of the worked appeared to have been completed.

It was, she had to admit, a sizable feat for Connor to not only have purchased the estate but have effected such a remarkable change in so short a time.

Some of the rooms were already furnished, and most of those furnishings appeared to be new. Everything appeared expensive.

Adelaide trailed her fingers along wainscoting as she walked down an upstairs hall. The wood was a rich, glossy brown and smooth to the touch.

She'd had such fantasies of Ashbury Hall as a child. It had been an enchanted castle or the haunted lair of a murderous ogre, depending on her mood. But seeing it now, from the inside, with its wood and crystal polished to a gleam, it no longer seemed a castle from a magical tale, just a large and opulent home.

Her fingers met air at the entrance of a lavishly appointed billiards room containing, not one, but *three* tables. Good Lord, she never aspired to this sort of opulence. She'd never expected a home of such vast proportions.

But, heaven forgive her, the mere thought of having it now made her almost giddy. It took very little imagination to picture herself in the library, reading a book by a roaring fire while George played on the plush carpet and Isobel's bubbling laughter filled the air. It took a little more effort to envision Wolfgang in his chambers, a snifter of brandy . . . No, a cup of tea in his hand and a contented smile on his face. But envision it she did. It was lovely.

"You're smiling."

Adelaide jumped and whirled at the sound of Connor's voice. He was standing not six feet away.

"You do sneak up on a person. I thought you were waiting downstairs."

"I was. Then I wasn't. Don't try to turn the subject. You were smiling."

"Perhaps."

"Because you like the house."

She did. Oh, she did. It occurred to her suddenly that Isobel had been quite wrong. She wasn't a martyr at all.

She was an adventuress.

"You're a breath away from laughter." He moved forward. "Admit it, you want this."

She bit her lip to make certain that breath didn't slip away. "Possibly."

He came closer. "Say the word and it's yours. Say yes and I'll give you anything you want. Everything your family needs. A permanent home. Fine gowns for Isobel and a proper education for your nephew." He moved nearer still. "You could see your brother walk free."

Anything you want. Everything your family needs.

They were one and the same for her. And well Connor knew it. It was then that Adelaide realized his purpose in bringing her to Ashbury Hall. It hadn't been to boast or impress her.

"It's bait," she muttered and stepped away from him.

"Beg your pardon?"

"This house. You're using it like a lure, a symbol of what I might have."

"If you like," he replied after a moment's thought. "All you have to do is reach out and take."

"And the moment I do, you'll swoop down on me like a hawk."

His smile brought fine creases to the corners of his eyes. "Hawks don't need lures. I believe you're mixing metaphors."

Nevertheless, a hawk is what he was. And in her mended gown and worn slippers, she felt very much the disheveled wren he'd called her the night of the masquerade.

A plain songbird in a raptor's nest. It was a fitting image. It was also unacceptable. She would not be snatched up like prey . . . Unless, of course, the bait was very alluring indeed.

"You've such an expressive face," Connor murmured. "What are you thinking, love?"

Her pulse surged at his easy use of the endearment. She tipped her chin up. "I'm wondering how much you're willing to sacrifice to have your revenge."

"What is it you want? Name your price."

Adelaide chewed on the inside of her lip, considering. Under the circumstances, "name your price" was a distasteful and debasing phrase. Only she didn't feel debased, particularly. Whichever suitor she might have chosen, her reasons for marriage remained unchanged. But it was only with Connor that she'd been able to speak of those reasons aloud. She didn't have to pretend an affection. She didn't feel obligated to bite her tongue when she wanted to argue, or swallow her reservations and hope for the best.

However objectionable the current conversation, the honesty of it afforded her a certain measure of relief and no small amount of empowerment. If she was going to allow herself to be lured into a snare, or bought like a side of beef at market, she damn well *would* have something to say about the price . . . or the bait. Damn it, she was mixing metaphors.

"I want the terms of marriage agreed upon in advance," she announced.

Connor inclined his head in agreement but said nothing.

"Well," she prompted after a moment's silence, "make an offer."

"As I said, name your price."

She bit her lip again and shifted her feet. "I can't."

"Why not?"

She tossed her hands up. "I don't know what you have."

"You've your brother's head for business, I see," he drawled before taking pity on her. "Very well. Ten thousand pounds per annum. How does that sound?"

"You have ten thousand pounds a year?" Good heavens, it was twice Sir Robert's income.

"*You* will have ten thousand pounds a year."

She smiled a little at the invitation to consider what was

his as her own. Sir Robert had never made such a gesture, but then, he only had half the income. Ten thousand pounds, however, though a highly respectable sum, seemed far less than what would be needed to own several properties like the one they were in now. He'd need . . .

Suddenly, Connor's emphasis of "you" took on another meaning. But it seemed so fantastical to her, so unlikely, she couldn't quite wrap her mind around even the possibility.

"When you say *I* shall have ten thousand pounds," she began slowly, "you do mean *we*. You are referring to a sort of . . . joint accessibility—"

"I am referring to an allowance. Your pin money, as it were."

"Good *heavens*." Ten thousand pounds was . . . It was . . . Well, it certainly wasn't *pin money*.

Her heart began to race as visions of what she could do with such a fortune danced through her head. Isobel could have the finest gowns. George would never know a day's want. Her home would be repaired and refurbished. Wolfgang would be freed of his debts. She could purchase a pianoforte for herself, or even travel. The bulk of the funds would be put away for safekeeping, of course, but a few indulgences here and there . . .

"Adelaide?"

"You could withdraw those funds," she said quickly, surprised she was able to snatch the concern from her whirlwind of thoughts. "As my husband, you could cut me off—"

"We'll draw up a legal contract."

"Contracts can be broken."

"They can, but it's more assurance than Sir Robert will offer you."

She couldn't argue with that. Or perhaps she could have, had her mind not still been occupied with the idea of having *ten thousand pounds*.

It was far more than she had ever hoped for, more than most people saw in a lifetime, and she blamed the shock of such a windfall for what next came out of her mouth.

"I want twenty."

She nearly swallowed her tongue. There was naming a price, and then there was asking for more than what could reasonably be expected to materialize. She had most certainly crossed the line.

Connor grinned. "Eleven."

"Nineteen," she shot back and rather wished she had swallowed her tongue in truth.

"Shall we save time and agree on fifteen?"

She couldn't believe what she was hearing. She couldn't believe what she was saying.

"Fifteen is acceptable, but initial payment will be rendered in full the day of marriage." She'd put it in her sister's name, or her nephew's. Whatever happened after, even if she never received another promised penny, her family would still have that fifteen thousand pounds.

"Agreed. Anything else?"

There were likely an infinite number of demands it would be wise for her to make, and an equal number of points on which an understanding should be reached in advance. Unfortunately, she had only the foggiest notion of what those might be. She'd never negotiated a marriage contract before.

And, oh, but it was difficult to concentrate when there was fifteen thousand pounds sitting on the table, figuratively speaking.

She walked a few feet away and back again. Difficult or not, she had to consider things carefully and thoroughly. No one else was going to take care of matters for her. She couldn't very well ask Lord Engsly and Lord Gideon to engage in this sort of bartering. Her knowledge of marital contracts might be limited, but she was fairly sure that, generally, a bride did not demand a lump sum of money be delivered on her wedding day.

And she was quite certain that the next concern that occurred to her was not one she wished Lord Engsly and his brother to address on her behalf.

She looked at Connor and found him waiting with an air of amused patience. She cleared her throat. "What of . . . er . . ."

He lifted his brows and bent forward a bit, waiting.

"Will you expect . . . ?" Lord, this was awkward. And ridiculous. If she could demand a price for herself without batting an eyelash, then she ought be able to reference the marriage bed without tripping over her own tongue.

She blew out a short breath and tried again. "A marriage is not a marriage, not a lawful one, until . . . That is, will you require . . ." She made a prompting gesture with her hand.

"To . . . go somewhere?"

"No, to . . ." Feeling increasingly foolish, she made an even more emphatic—and no doubt even less decipherable—prompting motion. ". . . To have a *lawful* marriage . . . ?"

"Ah." Understanding dawned on his face. "Yes."

Right. Well, that was to be expected, wasn't it? "I understand the marriage must be consummated, and I am willing to . . . do what must be done."

"You sound like a martyr."

"I don't. I merely wish to make clear the details of our contract." A hint of annoyance crossed his face. She ignored it. "I will agree to share a bed with you once a year."

"No."

Now she was growing annoyed. " 'No' is not a counteroffer, Mr. Brice."

"Connor. And 'no' means the offer was too insulting to dignify with any other response."

Was it? Well, how the blazes was she to know? She sniffed, because it seemed the only thing to do. "Well, it stands until you come up with one of your own."

"Fine. Ten times a day."

She gaped at him, shocked beyond measure. "Surely not. There is only one night in a day."

"I know."

Adelaide felt a moment's panic. She was at a terrible disadvantage in this negotiation, utterly in the dark in the private ways of husbands and wives. With her mother gone, and her friendship with Lilly and Winnefred not yet the sort that allowed for the discussion of such delicate matters, there was no one to whom she might turn to for guidance . . . No one but Connor.

"Is . . . ten times . . ." The heat of embarrassment and frustration filled her cheeks. Without realizing it, she leaned in a little and spoke in a lowered voice. "Is that *normal*?"

Connor blinked. For several long seconds, that was his only reaction. He stood mute and still as a statue. There wasn't a trace of humor on his features, nor anger, come to that. There wasn't a trace of anything that she could see. His face was a blank mask.

Good Lord, she'd shocked him stupid.

Adelaide straightened and twisted her lips. "The question hardly warrants that—"

"We'll discuss it later," he said suddenly, coming to himself.

His peculiar behavior deserved pondering, but his suggestion they revisit the conversation another time took precedence.

She shook her head in adamant refusal. "No. Not later. Now."

She sounded like George asking after a biscuit. She didn't care. Under no circumstances was she going to repeat this experience.

Connor stepped forward, took her by the elbow, and began to lead her down the hall. "Not everything needs to be decided today."

This from the man who'd proposed after a day's acquaintance? "But—"

"I've business to see to in Edinburgh this week. Take the time to think on matters." He stopped, turned, and pulled her into his arms. "And while you're thinking, keep this in mind."

His lips brushed across hers, soft and warm as the sun of spring. There was no hurry to his kiss, no demand, only patient invitation delivered with devastating skill. She accepted without thought, caught off guard by the sweetness of it, and before she knew it, her mouth was moving steadily under his. She leaned forward, gripping handfuls of his coat.

Connor pulled back. "Want more?"

She nodded. Shook her head. "I don't know. I don't like you."

"I know." Connor lifted a hand and trailed the backs of his fingers across her jaw. His face was so close, she could make out every shade of green in his eyes. "I want you," he said thickly. "I wanted you the first time I saw you. Even before I knew who you were."

Before he knew of her connection to Sir Robert? She pulled away and looked at him, the warmth of the kiss draining away. "Do you really expect me to believe that?"

"No." His mouth quirked with humor, but she wasn't sure if he was laughing at himself or her. "Which is why I'd never planned to tell you."

"And yet you just did." She shook her head. "You're very much like your brother, you know."

He winced. "Have I angered you again, or are you being unkind in retaliation for past slights?"

"I believe you'll say whatever you must to get what you want. Both of you." All of you, she amended, thinking of her brother.

"You were wearing a blue coat," he said quietly. "It was torn at the hem, and too thin for the weather. I could see the red in your cheeks and nose from the cold, and this . . ." He lifted a hand and toyed with a lock of her hair. "I could see it peeking out from under your bonnet. You bent to kiss your nephew's brow as you crossed the yard."

"You couldn't have known he was my nephew."

"I didn't. I assumed he was your son and you were bringing him to see his father, your husband—didn't stop me from looking for you every Saturday for almost six months. The hem was mended next I saw you."

"That proves nothing. You could have . . ." She trailed off as something he had said suddenly took on new meaning. "Six months? This past winter?"

He nodded. "And an ocean of grief I received from the other inmates for it."

A sick weight settled in her stomach. "Your interest was known."

"There's no privacy to be had in prison." His brow furrowed as he studied her face. "Have I offended you? Are you angry that I watched you?"

"No. Some. I . . ." She pressed her lips together and shook her head. Her anger didn't stem from that, directly. It stemmed from every lie, secret, and trap she'd fallen victim to—Connor's, Wolfgang's, Sir Robert's. She was naught but a marionette in their show, and every time she thought to have gained her freedom, discovered where all their nasty little strings were attached, she turned about and found another.

Anger boiled and swirled. It was too solid to see past, too thick to speak through. She decided not to bother trying to do either. If Connor wanted to wait for his answer, then wait he would. And Wolfgang, she decided, could wait for his freedom.

Sir Robert could wait in hell.

"I wish to go home."

Chapter 13

Connor knew that there were times when it was best to press, and times it was best to let things settle. He let Adelaide settle, making no attempt to fill the silence that accompanied their return carriage ride.

It cost him to do so. He wasn't blind to the fact that something was bothering Adelaide, nor that the change in her demeanor had immediately followed his confession. He'd like to think she'd been struck senseless by the sudden realization of her good fortune, but even he could not lay claim to that level of arrogance.

He wanted to demand an explanation for her sudden change of mood or provoke her until the line between her brows disappeared. But he didn't. He kept his peace as they came to a stop in her drive and issued only a few formal words of farewell after assisting her from her seat.

She mumbled something vaguely like, "Safe journey," and headed for the house.

Suppressing an oath, Connor climbed back onto the phaeton and started the horses off at a trot. Adelaide wasn't the only one in need of settling.

I want you. I wanted you the first time I saw you. Even before I knew who you were.

For the life of him, he could not say why he'd admitted to that, why he'd handed Adelaide what essentially amounted to a weapon.

He only knew that one moment he was enjoying the exchange, amused by the bartering, charmed by her incongruent mix of determined purpose and stumbling innocence. And the next moment, he'd felt like a jaded brute. Not exactly a novel sensation for him, but this time had been different.

He could still see the way the color had all but drained from her cheeks, then rushed back to leave her skin flushed.

"Is that normal?" she'd asked.

Bloody hell.

She'd unmanned him with that one question. Suddenly, she hadn't looked sweet and brave and charming. She'd looked afraid, and cornered, and very, very alone. Like a babe in the woods.

It pricked at him now that he'd bargained with her that he'd been amused at all. It irritated him that they'd spoken of contracts and the bedchamber in the same conversation.

He wasn't buying her like cattle. He wasn't purchasing the favors of a light skirt.

And he wasn't the sort of man who found pleasure in watching a woman struggling to find her way out of an untenable situation. He didn't kick at innocents. Certainly, when that innocence could be used to benefit, he took advantage. But he didn't kick.

He didn't want to be the sort of man who kicked.

Somewhere in that jumble of doubt and worry and guilt was his reason for spouting off at the mouth. He'd wanted to apologize. Or give her something. Or give her something back.

Which was patently ridiculous, he decided. He *was* giving her something. Fifteen thousand somethings, to be exact. There was no reason for him to feel as if he were gaining the better part of a bargain. And there was no reason he couldn't remember to hold his peace in the future.

Reasonably, if not wholly, satisfied with this line of logic, he set the matter aside. There were more immediate concerns that demanded his attention.

Not far from Adelaide's house, he slowed the horses and carefully maneuvered the phaeton off the road onto a flat, grassy area surrounded by a thick line of evergreens. Then he hopped down, leaned against the front wheel, and waited.

It wasn't long before the sound of old leaves cracking underfoot reached his ears, and a young man in peasant's attire emerged from the surrounding trees. Connor knew Graham Sefton to be four-and-twenty, a half inch shy of six feet, and currently the single most useful individual of his acquaintance. He'd been Sir Robert's man of all trades for three months, and Connor's for six.

A man met the most interesting fellows in prison.

Connor nodded in greeting. "What will you tell your master?"

Graham came to a stop before him and scratched a nose that looked to have been broken and reset more than once. For reasons that eluded Connor, women in the local village found the flaw, and the man, all but irresistible.

"Depends, don't it?" Graham remarked in a voice that held the hallmarks of a low birth softened by a late education. "You want him flapping like a fish on a hook or squirming like bait?"

"There's a difference?"

"There is." Graham grinned, dark eyes creasing in a faced tanned by both sun and heritage. "Give me the coin for a pint and I'll explain it to you."

Connor dug out payment and held it up, then away. "Explanation first, then we'll see."

Graham considered, then shrugged. "Bait knows he's done for when the hook goes through. The squirming's just the death throes. But a fish don't always know it's caught for good. Thinks all that flopping about on the line will earn his freedom. What's a bit of metal through a lip, after all. So, which will it be?"

The image of Sir Robert squirming was tempting, very tempting. But Connor knew he couldn't risk it. Sir Robert was unpredictable. The possibility of him directing his frustration at Adelaide was real.

"I want him confident. Tell him you witnessed an argument."

"And what was the nature of this argument?"

"You were too far away to hear. Tell him it looked as if I made an advance, and the lady rebuffed."

"Simple enough." Graham held out his hand and wiggled his fingers. "Do I have me coin?"

Connor tossed it to him. "You're a cheap traitor."

"Aye," Graham agreed with a wink, "but a loyal one."

*A*delaide didn't immediately go into the house. The moment Connor drove away, she turned her steps away from the front door and strode around to the relative privacy of a side garden. She followed a stone path that was rapidly disappearing beneath an onslaught of dirt and weeds.

A stunted but cheerfully blooming hydrangea caught her eye. She stopped to stare at it. She'd planted it before the death of her parents, and it survived and flowered, year after year, despite her neglect. Happy blooms, courageously thriving in the inhospitable world in which they had been so carelessly deposited.

She wanted to stomp on them. Just this once, she wanted to know the power of being the cause of havoc, instead of its victim. She turned away before the ridiculous temptation got the better of her.

If it was devastation she craved, she'd be better served by paying a visit to Sir Robert.

What a damn fool she was.

She remembered, perfectly, the day she had met the baron. It had been morning; she'd been on her way to town for bread, and she'd come across him on the road. His horse had gone lame—that's what he'd told her after he'd intro-duced himself and offered his company for the walk into town.

She'd known who he was. Her little corner of Scotland was not so rife with barons that she could overlook one liv-ing but a few miles away. But they moved in different cir-cles, different worlds, and they'd never spoken until that day.

Later, he called the meeting a wondrous spot of fate, a delightful sprinkling of serendipity. She'd thought the sen-timent rather sweet. She'd even felt guilty that she'd not been able to summon a similar enthusiasm.

What good fortune, he'd said. What fine providence. What grand luck.

What a pile of rot. Sir Robert had sought her out.

Adelaide didn't fully believe Connor's story of wanting her. She wasn't inclined to believe much of anything that came out of the man's mouth. But he'd not have lied about showing an interest in her during his imprisonment or being teased because of that interest. That was too easy a claim to verify or refute.

Just a few inquiries at the prison, that's all it would take. Sir Robert wouldn't have had to make the trip to the prison. His pocketed guards would have come to him with the infor-mation. And it wouldn't have taken months for them to do it.

Apparently, it *had* taken him a month or two to figure out how to use Connor's interest to his own advantage, but then, he was an idiot. A nasty, lying, cowardly idiot.

They all were. She was furious with all of them. Sir Robert for his lies. Her brother for his lies. Connor for his lies . . . And his truths.

Oh, yes, that anger was present as well. It was irrational, unfair, and quite simply wrong, but in that moment, she didn't care. She was happy to shoot the messenger. She was willing to do most anything that might ease the painful, humiliating truth . . . She had fallen prey to not one, but two false courtships.

Good Lord, had she no gauge of character? Was there not a single man of her acquaintance who she'd not misjudged?

"Idiot," she whispered, uncertain, at this point, to whom she was directing the insult. It hardly mattered. It fit the lot of them.

She scrubbed her hands over her face, trying to settle her temper and clear her mind. One step at a time, she reminded herself. One choice at a time.

Only she hadn't a choice left. Her steps had already been mapped out for her.

So be it, she thought darkly and marched back to the front of the house. There would be no more excuses. No more delays. She would mail the letter to Sir Robert today. Now. And when Connor returned from Edinburgh, she would give him exactly what he asked for.

She would marry him and make his life a living hell.

She opened the front door, glanced into the parlor, and saw Isobel, fast asleep on their grandmother's old settee. Her arm was bent under her head, half hidden beneath a soft tumble of blonde hair. Her expression was one of innocent contentment. She made the very picture of peaceful repose. And it irritated Adelaide to no end. No adult member of the Ward family had any right to feel so bloody relaxed.

"We're to be rich!" Adelaide shouted and slammed the door.

Isobel jolted awake at the sound, nearly tumbling off the settee. "What? What?"

Slightly mollified by the sight, Adelaide yanked the ribbons of her bonnet free. "Fifteen thousand pounds a year. That is to be my allowance."

"Fifteen—? Beg your pardon?"

"We'll reside at Ashbury Hall."

"Ashbury Hall?"

"Are you a parrot?"

The remnants of sleep drained from Isobel's face. She eyed her sister warily as she rose to stand. "Your mood is very peculiar."

Her mood was *foul.*

"Well, it isn't every day a lady must forgo the affections of a coward for the fortune of a scoundrel."

The *pretend* affections, she amended silently.

"I see." Isobel gave her a bolstering smile. "It's to be Mr. Brice, then, is it? I must say, I am glad you've decided against the dragon—"

"I did not want to decide!" Adelaide threw her bonnet down on the foyer side table. "Why must I *always* be the one to make the decisions, Isobel? Why am I always the one to make the sacrifices?" She didn't want to be the one with the choices. She didn't want to be the one with the abysmal expectations. "I'm not the maiden of this kingdom, I'm its whipping boy! It's pathetic, ridiculous—!"

"No! No! No!"

George's angry shout cut Adelaide off mid-tirade. Horrified, she looked to the second-floor landing, where she found him peering through the bars of the banister, blue eyes wide with confusion and anger. Remorse gripped her like a vise. She hadn't seen him there. She'd been so swamped in her own resentment that she'd not even thought to look for him.

"Oh, Georgie, I'm sorry." She climbed the steps two at a time. "I'm so sorry. You're absolutely right. No more shouting."

"I just put him down for a rest," Isobel said. "I thought he'd fallen asleep."

Clearly he hadn't. A bit of shouting wouldn't wake George from a nap. Cannon fire wouldn't wake George from a nap. A more sound sleeper was not to be found in Scotland.

Adelaide picked George up and settled him on her hip. He felt soft and warm in her arms, his weight a familiar and comforting burden. "Did I give you a fright, darling? I didn't mean to. Aunt Adelaide is very naughty. And very sorry."

She brushed his curls back from his forehead and kissed his nose. That was all it took to appease him. His eyes cleared, he gave her a distracted kiss in return, and then he squirmed in her arms.

"Down."

Adelaide sighed and considered. She ought to put him back down in bed. Heaven knew, without a proper rest during the day, the boy became impossible by evening. But she wanted to coddle him a minute longer. He deserved a bit of coddling.

"Yes, I'll take you downstairs, but only—"

"Down!"

"You are not climbing down the steps, Georgie. Not until—"

He struggled harder, made an indecipherable statement of dissent, then broke into a loud, harsh, and entirely counterfeit cry.

Adelaide smothered a smile, carried him downstairs, and set him on his feet. The wailing ceased instantly, and he made a dash to the steps. She caught him up and twirled him around to provoke a giggle, and set him back down. She wasn't the least surprised when he charged right back to the steps. The child was nothing if not determined.

She decided to make a game of it and let him run, over and over again, for the steps. She chased after him, caught him at the last moment, and swung him up into the air. It did wonders for her mood to hear him squeal and shout with laughter, the sort that came straight from the belly.

Her arms began to ache after the tenth go-round, but she ignored them, determined that nothing should detract from those few minutes of silly, carefree pleasure.

Isobel's next words sliced through that pleasure like a hot knife.

"Sir Robert is here."

Adelaide picked a giggling George up and went to stand next to Isobel at the parlor window. Sure enough, there was Sir Robert striding toward the house from the old stables. Just the sight of him sent her blood to boiling all over again. Perhaps she'd made her promise to George in haste. Perhaps there would be just a bit more shouting.

Isobel looked to her, to the window, then back again. "I'll send him away."

Adelaide watched as Sir Robert stopped ten feet from the door to smooth his hair forward. It clung to his face in golden waves. Like butter on a misshapen piece of toast, Adelaide thought. *How* she loathed his hair.

"No. I'll speak with him."

Isobel eyed her with reservation. "Are you certain that's wise in your current mood?"

No, but she was certain it was going to be most gratifying. "Yes."

"He is a baron, Adelaide."

Which was why she would refrain from mentioning the bit about the buttered toast. She walked to the foyer. "Will you let him in, or shall I?"

With a shake of her head, Isobel followed and opened the door. Sir Robert stepped inside without showing even a hint of embarrassment at having arrived for a visit today after she had expressly requested otherwise.

"Ladies," he said smoothly and gave an eloquent bow. He flicked a glance at George. "Young man."

As always, he looked uncomfortable, and just a trifle put out, in the boy's presence. Adelaide was a trifle tempted to have the boy stay. Just out of spite.

"Take George upstairs, please, Isobel."

"No! No! Down!"

"Oh, yes, up," Isobel informed him. She transferred him from Adelaide's arms, adjusted her hold when he squirmed, then headed upstairs. "And this time, you shall sleep."

"No! Down! *Down!*" George demanded. When Isobel failed to comply, he broke into a howling wail that gained in volume and pitch with every step she took. The sound echoed in the foyer, floated down the steps, then faded when Isobel reached the nursery. Given the ferocity of his battle, Adelaide guessed he was but moments from succumbing to sleep.

Sir Robert shook his head and headed to the parlor without invitation. "We must see about procuring a proper nanny for that boy. He ought to be better behaved by now."

The slight fed Adelaide's anger. She no longer cared that he was a baron, that he held her brother's last debt. He could take his title straight to the devil. Grinding her teeth, she followed Sir Robert into the room and watched him fiddle with the sewing kit on the window seat. He looked sure of himself, perfectly confident in his right to be in her parlor, touching her things, criticizing her nephew.

It would be a pleasure to disillusion him. "George is the very definition of civilized . . . compared to some."

Sir Robert looked up and frowned. "I cannot fathom what you mean by that."

"You've lied to me."

"Are we back to this—?"

"You said Mr. Brice's awareness of me was a result of our courtship. But you know full well his interest preceded your own."

"He told you that? And you believed him?" He closed his eyes on a sigh, and when he opened them again, they were filled with condescending patience. "Of course you did." He reached for her hand. "My darling girl, you are too generous of nature for your own good. You would believe the best of anyone, wouldn't you? Even the cad—"

She snatched her hand away. "Why not pronounce me a twit and be done with it?"

"I beg your pardon?"

"Tell me, Sir Robert, what color is my winter coat?"

"Your coat?"

"My *winter* coat."

His expression was one of perfect bafflement. "I . . . It's . . ."

"You don't know, do you?" She tilted her head, smiled sweetly, and mocked his patronizing tone. "Of course you don't. Our courtship began in the spring."

"What has that to do with anything? What nonsense has he put in your head?"

"There was no nonsense. Just an image. A perfect image of me in my blue winter coat."

"He could have learned the color of it from anyone."

Connor could have, but not about the torn hem. That mishap had occurred on the road that morning and been repaired when she'd returned home.

"He learned of it with his own eyes."

Sir Robert blew out a long breath. "Perhaps you are right. And I confess, I would be much relieved to see the proof of it. I have regretted, *bitterly* regretted, bringing you to the attention of that scoundrel. If, by some twist of fate, he had set his sights on you before we met, it would do a great deal to ease my burden—"

"Oh, stop," she snapped, disgusted with him. "Have the decency, at least, to admit to a lie when you've been caught in it. Even your brother has managed that much."

Sir Robert pinched his lips. "Do not compare me with him."

"How could I do otherwise, when your motivations for marriage have been the same all along? There was no twist of fate," she said bitterly. "He took an interest in me, and you learned of it and began a courtship for the purpose of thwarting him. It is as simple and infantile as that." She made a derisive sound in the back of her throat. "The pair of you, like five-year-olds fighting over a marionette, when all they really want is to hit each other on the nose."

"Marionette?" Sir Robert shook his head. "Adelaide—"

"It is Miss Ward until such time as it becomes Mrs. Brice."

He looked as if she'd slapped him. "You can't mean it."

"I assure you, I do."

He opened his mouth, closed it, and shook his head again as color began to crawl up his neck. "You're being unreasonable."

And there was that condescending tone again. It fed her temper like a fan to flame. "And you are being an ungracious loser. The game is over, Sir Robert. Mr. Brice is the victor."

"I don't lose to the likes of Brice," he snapped and reached out to grab hold of her wrist.

"Let go," she gasped. "Let—"

"He's a bastard," Sir Robert snarled. "The illegitimate son of a grasping whore."

"Let *go!*" She twisted her arm and yelped at the feel of his fingers digging cruelly into her skin. Spurred by pain and fear, she clawed at the restraining hand until it released her.

Sir Robert swore and moved so quickly, she didn't recognize his intention until it was too late. He caught her across the cheek with the back of his fist, and the force of the blow sent her reeling into a side table. Her hip slammed against the wood, and her feet tangled beneath her. Blindly, she reached out for something to hold on to and caught the edge of a picture frame on the wall behind the table, but it wasn't strong enough to hold her weight. She, the picture, and the table crashed to the floor.

The pain was shocking. Disoriented, she shoved wildly at the debris from the table and scrambled to move away. There was a flash of movement, Sir Robert's dark form was in front of her . . . And then it wasn't.

Isobel was there, their father's old dueling pistol in hand. Sir Robert was on the floor. For one horrifying moment, Adelaide was certain her sister had killed the man. But that didn't make sense. There hadn't been a shot.

She struggled to think clearly through the pain, to hear over the roar of blood in her ears. Isobel grabbed her hand and pulled her to her feet. The room tilted briefly before righting itself.

"Take this." Isobel pressed the gun into her hand. "Take it."

Adelaide grasped the weapon without looking at it and shoved Isobel behind her. Her focus was on Sir Robert. Slowly, he gained his feet, a thin stream of blood trickling from his temple. Adelaide blinked at it. Not a wound from a bullet, she realized. Isobel must have hit him with the gun.

Oh, thank you, God.

"Bitch," he snarled and took a lurching step toward them. "I'll—"

"Out!" She lifted the gun, aimed it straight at his heart, and prayed she had the courage to use it. "Get out!"

He came to an unsteady stop. Feral eyes darted from her, to the gun, to Isobel, and back again.

"You'll regret this," he spat at last and stabbed a finger at them. "You mark my words, you will regret having crossed me."

She regretted having ever crossed paths with him. There were a thousand insults she wanted to hurl at him, an ocean of threats and promises of retribution. She bit them back. They would only tempt him to retaliate, and she wanted him to leave. It seemed an eternity before he obliged. With a final curl of his lip, he turned and strode away.

When the front door shut with a bang, Adelaide sank to the floor. Isobel followed, wrapping her arms tight around Adelaide's shoulders.

"Are you all right? Did he hurt you terribly?"

Yes, and yes, Adelaide thought. Her cheek throbbed with every wild beat of her heart. But she would live. They were all safe. Rather than answer, she reached up and gripped her sister's hand.

Adelaide would never be sure how long the pair of them sat in a daze amidst the glass and broken wood, their silence broken only by their labored breathing, the howl of a building wind, and the familiar creaks and groans of the house. It might have been two minutes; it might have been half an hour. But eventually, her pulse began to slow, and the sick fear in her belly abated.

Isobel let go of her shoulders. She drew the gun away and turned it over in her hand, studying it with a rare furrow of concentration across her brow. "Do you know why you're the one to always make decisions?"

Adelaide closed her eyes. She didn't want to think of that now. "Isobel—"

"Do you?"

Adelaide sighed. "Because I am the eldest."

"No. It's because you're the bravest of us."

"I'm not."

"Every time you make a choice, it's for all of us. And every time you make a decision, you take the risk of being wrong." She ran her finger along the pearl handle. "I can't do that. I'm not brave, like you."

"You're the bravest person I know. You would emigrate to the Americas given half the chance. You would explore the wilds of Africa, seek adventure after adventure, and—"

"I would do those things alone. It's a sight easier to take risks when one need think only of oneself. There's so much less to lose if one makes a mistake."

"Wolfgang had plenty to lose. He hadn't any trouble taking risks or making mistakes."

"Yes, because he hadn't the courage to think of anyone but himself. He hasn't the spine to hold himself accountable for those mistakes. But you . . ." Isobel lifted a hand and brushed gently along Adelaide's back. "You think of us all the time. You'll always hold yourself accountable."

"I'm scared all the time."

"Well." She gave Adelaide two soft pats. "I never said you were confident. I said you were courageous."

Adelaide smiled, then winced when her cheek protested.

Isobel returned her attention to the pearl handle. "I'm sorry I made you take the gun."

She made a soothing noise. "It's all right, Isobel. You—"

"It's not. It's not right that you should have to make all the decisions. I'll try to be more helpful in the future."

"I'd like that."

"May I start now? Excellent. I have decided you shall not marry Sir Robert." Isobel shook her head, her blue eyes filled with wonder. "I have *never* seen you so angry."

"I've never been so angry." Adelaide blew out a long breath. "I'd have shot him, Isobel, and that's the truth of—"

"No, you wouldn't have."

She frowned, a little insulted. "I most certainly would—"

"The pistol's not loaded."

"What?" She snatched the gun away, checked for herself, and saw there was no shot or powder. "Did you know that when you handed it to me?"

Isobel shook her head. "I didn't think of it. I forgot we'd unloaded it when—"

"When I'd thought to sell it," Adelaide finished for her, remembering. Worried two women living alone might have need of protection, she'd changed her mind and sold their mother's emerald earrings—the last of her jewelry—instead. "What would we have done if he'd charged?"

Isobel produced a hopeful smile. "Swung hard?"

Adelaide snorted. "You tried that."

"I didn't. That is . . . I didn't swing as hard as I could. I meant to, but then I panicked and—"

"You hit him hard enough. You saved me. Thank you."

Isobel shrugged as if mildly embarrassed. "What will you do now? Even a baron is not allowed to assault a woman in her own home."

Not allowed and susceptible to the consequences were two different matters. She could go to the authorities, press charges, but nothing would come of it but a public trial in which a dozen character witnesses would pronounce Sir Robert the most honorable of barons, and she a common woman who'd been caught cavorting with a criminal at a house party.

Knowing inaction would frustrate Isobel, Adelaide skirted the question. "I'll think on it. For now—"

She broke off at the unmistakable whoosh and thump of George sliding down the steps on his backside.

With a smothered oath, Adelaide scrambled to her feet and rushed into the great hall. She found George a quarter way down the steps.

Had he not fallen asleep straightaway, after all? Had the noise woken him? Had he seen . . . Surely not. Surely he would have made his presence known before now. And he didn't look upset or frightened. He looked fascinated, his wide blue eyes scanning the wreckage of the room.

"Naughty. No, no."

Behind her, Isobel laughed softly. "From the mouths of babes."

Adelaide climbed the steps, lifted him into her arms, and cradled him against her chest. The feel of him, warm and loose from sleep, quieted a thousand screaming nerves.

His small mouth turned down at the corner, George reached up and touched her cheek. "Ouch?"

"A small one, love." She hid a wince at his probing and kissed the tip of his index finger. "It doesn't pain me."

"Fall down?"

"That is one way to put it." She smiled a little at his blank expression and carried him down the steps. "Yes, I fell down. But it is over and done with, and now I shall have a spot of tea, and you shall have a little milk and—"

A loud bang on the door nearly scared her out of her skin. George chuckled at her sudden jolt, while Isobel peeked through the window drapes.

"It's a stranger. I think. He does look a mite familiar." Isobel scrunched her face. "I think I've seen him in the village once or twice."

As long as it wasn't Sir Robert, Adelaide didn't much care who it was or why and how Isobel had seen him. "Please just send him away, Isobel."

"Yes, of course." Isobel hurried over and opened the door partway, blocking his view to the inside. "Good day, sir. May I—"

"Everything all right, miss?"

Isobel visibly startled at the question. "Er . . . Yes . . . Yes, everything is perfectly well. I'm sure I don't know why—"

She broke off when the man reached out and very gently nudged her head out his line of sight and took a quick look at Adelaide.

Isobel shoved his hand away. *"I beg your pardon."*

"Right. Thought the bugger looked a mite off. Beggin' pardon, miss." And with that, he spun about and strode down the path.

"Sir? Sir!" Isobel threw a bewildered look over her shoulder. "He's not answering." She looked back at the man. "Sir! He won't even turn around . . . Now he's gone off the drive . . . Right into the woods. Who the dev . . ." She turned and flicked a glance at George. "Who the deuce was that?"

Adelaide started to shake her head, then stopped when

its pounding protested the movement. "I don't know, perhaps he was passing by on the road and . . . I don't know. Did he harm you?"

"No, not in the least. But why would he look and then run away?"

"I don't know," Adelaide repeated. And quite frankly, she didn't much care. In comparison to the rest of the day's events, daft men who went about knocking on doors seemed of little consequence.

"We'll worry if anything comes of it." She shifted George to her other hip when he poked experimentally at her cheek. "We've more pressing concerns at the moment."

The splintered wood and broken glass needed to be cleared away before George cut himself. She wanted a cool rag for her cheek. And someone needed to go to town for shot and powder.

Chapter 14

*I*t was a simple matter to repair the parlor—a few sweeps of the broom, a trip to the attic to store the damaged painting, and the task was complete.

Repairing peace of mind did not come so easily. Overnight, Adelaide's cheek went from red and swollen to red, black, blue, and swollen, and every time she caught sight of her reflection the next day, she was hounded by questions of what if and thoughts of what might have been.

What if she had never gone to Mrs. Cress's house party? She might have married Sir Robert without an inkling of his true nature. What sort of life would that have been for George?

She'd brought a monster into his world. She'd very nearly made him a permanent resident. It was an unforgivable error.

Despite George's complete lack of interest in her ouch and the events surrounding it, she felt an overpowering desire to coddle him. She even went so far as to have Isobel purchase a strawberry tart for him while she was in town buying shot and powder. It was a rare treat in the struggling household.

Adelaide handed it to him in the dining room as the late afternoon light filtered through the drapes. And she watched, delighted beyond measure, as his eyes widened and his plump little fingers curled around the fruit-filled sweet.

"Biscuit!"

"No, it's not a biscuit, darling. It's a tart. Will you say that for me? Tart."

"Biscuit!"

She didn't have the heart to argue with him. "Yes, all right. Enjoy your . . . sweet."

Isobel stepped up beside her. "You shouldn't feel guilty for a mistake you might have made."

"It's not guilt," she lied. "It's a celebration. The dragon has been slain. The fair maiden emerges victorious."

Isobel turned and grinned at George. "A party, is it?"

"Biscuit!"

"So I see," Isobel exclaimed. She turned her head at the sound of hoofbeats thundering up the drive. "It appears we're to have guests for our celebration."

Adelaide groaned and took George's free hand, leading him into the parlor. One day, she thought, why could she not have one day without a visitor? After her brother's removal to prison, their fair-weather friends had dropped away like flies. They'd gone weeks, months without a caller. Suddenly, everyone in Scotland wanted a word with the Ward family.

Isobel brushed aside a drape. "It's Mr. Brice. I thought you said he'd gone to Edinburgh."

"I did. He had."

"Well, he's here now," Isobel pointed out—uselessly, in Adelaide's opinion—and strode to the door. She opened it before Connor could knock and gifted him with a wide smile. "Mr. Brice. A pleasure to see you."

Connor strode inside, and Adelaide admitted that—her

wish for a day of solitude notwithstanding—it wasn't altogether terrible to see him.

His clothes were dusty and wrinkled from the road, his thick blond hair tousled from the wind. He looked like a man who'd ridden hell-for-leather across half of Scotland. It suited him, Adelaide thought. That edge of wildness would sit poorly on most men, but it suited Connor Brice.

He gave a short, impatient bow to Isobel. "Miss Ward. Where is your sis—?" He broke off as his gaze landed on Adelaide.

Wary of strangers, George ducked behind her skirts and threw an arm around her leg. It was the only movement in the room, one she doubted Connor noticed. His gaze was focused on her bruised cheek.

A taut silence descended, and tension became a living, breathing entity in the room as she waited for his reaction. But Connor said nothing. He didn't need to; the searing heat in his eyes spoke volumes.

Adelaide strove for a way to relieve the mounting pressure. "You've returned early," she remarked and thought her voice sounded uncommonly loud. "Did you encounter trouble?"

Connor didn't immediately answer. His gaze traveled slowly from her cheek to her eyes. "You might say that."

"Yes, well . . ."

Adelaide felt George shift behind her for a peek of their guest. Connor's eyes darted to her skirts, and his demeanor underwent a miraculous change. The line across his brow disappeared, and his expression cleared as he entered the parlor and—to her shock—knelt down.

"Is that an infant hiding behind your skirts, Miss Ward?"

George stepped out from his hiding spot and scowled. "No! Not infant!"

"Yes, I can see that now."

"Mr. Brice, my nephew, George Ward."

His store of courage spent, George sidled closer to her

skirt and gripped his pastry so tightly, thick globs of strawberry filling oozed between his fingers.

"Manners, Georgie," she chided. When that failed to elicit a response, she gave him a gentle nudge forward.

To her surprise, George threw her a mutinous look before facing Connor. Round shoulders rose and fell with a heavy sigh before he extended his arm and held out his pastry to Connor. His fingers opened around the remains, pulling free with a loud slurp.

"Share."

It was the single most reluctant offering Adelaide ever had occasion to witness. Her first instinct was to laugh and reassure George that sharing was not the good manners she'd been referring to, but curiosity kept her quiet. She wanted to see what Connor would do.

To his credit, Connor blinked at the mess once but otherwise remained stoic in the face of such an appalling present.

"That is . . . very generous." He blinked again, then dragged his gaze to George's face. "But perhaps, in exchange for the treat, you might take your aunt Isobel outside for a time. We'll consider it a favor between men."

George dropped his hand, sent her a bewildered look over his shoulder, then turned back and said, "Peas."

Connor opened his mouth . . . and closed it. "I was certain that would work." He stood and studied the child before him. "What does he mean, 'Peas'?"

Adelaide's laughter blended with Isobel's. She couldn't say for certain why she found Connor's bafflement so endearing. While she pondered the idea, Isobel crossed the room and swept George into her arms. "It means he likes peas. Give him a few more years, Mr. Brice, and your sort of flattery will have him eating out of your hand. Come along, poppet. Shall we go into the garden and see what creatures are about?"

"Beetles!" George wrapped one arm around Isobel's neck and crammed a large bite of his treat into his mouth. "Eewels! Eewels! Eewels!"

Adelaide smiled at the pretty, albeit messy, picture her sister and nephew made as they headed off for adventure.

"Your experience with small children is limited, I see," she said to Connor. And still, he'd made more of an effort in two minutes than Sir Robert had in four months. That was very promising. She leaned down to brush sticky crumbs from her skirts. "He is a little shy. Unaccustomed to seeing strangers in the house, I suppose. And he needs a proper nanny. I fear he might be—"

"Look at me."

Compelled by the low vibration of fury in Connor's voice, Adelaide straightened and caught her breath. There was no bafflement in his features now, none of the warmth he'd shown George. He lifted his hand and brushed his fingers along her jaw below the bruise. She wasn't sure what affected her more, the exquisite tenderness of his touch or the roiling violence in his eyes.

"It's true, then," he whispered and let his hand fall.

"I . . . I'm fine. It's over." She looked for a way to change the subject. "You've not told me why you returned early."

"Did you think I'd stay away after hearing of this?"

"You heard . . . In *Edinburgh*? Good heavens, the ton must be starved for good gossip indeed—"

"I didn't make it to Edinburgh. Word reached me en route. I've had my men keep an eye on you."

"Oh." She thought it rather sweet that he'd been concerned enough to watch out for her. "Well, if you knew it was true, why did you come to check?"

"I like to make sure I've all the facts before I shoot a man."

And with that, he turned about and headed for the door.

"What?" Adelaide blinked at his back, twice, before moving to intercede. "No! For pity's sake, not this again."

She raced forward, grabbed hold of his arm, and pulled. Connor didn't throw her off, but he didn't stop either, merely dragging her along.

"Connor, stop. Please. Be rational."

"No."

"Remember your quest for vengeance." She tugged on his arm again. "A single shot and it's done? What sort of revenge is that?"

"Expedient."

"But it's not what you've planned." He'd never expounded on his plans, so she had no idea if that was true, but it seemed a reasonable assumption that if a quick murder were Connor's intention, Sir Robert would be dead by now.

"Plans change."

Desperate, she jumped in front of him. "I will agree to marry you if you will cease this—"

He stopped at the edge of the parlor and looked down at her with a frown. "You have to marry me. You haven't another choice."

"I do. There are other gentleman in this world aside from yourself and Sir Robert." Pity she didn't happen to know any.

"I compromised you."

Sensing an opening, she jabbed a finger into the center of his chest. "Yes. *Yes*, you most certainly did. And if you have a duel with Sir Robert now, and you miss and he does not, I will . . ." She trailed off, surprised by what she'd been about to say.

I will be left alone. But that didn't make any sense. She had Isobel and George, and Wolfgang, if one was willing to stretch the definition of good company.

"You'll what?" Connor prompted.

"I . . . will . . . be left without a wealthy husband," she improvised.

"How touching," he said dryly and gently moved her aside. "I don't miss."

She jumped in front of him again and put a restraining hand against his chest. "Then you'll end on the gallows, or be forced to flee the country, and I will still be left without a wealthy husband. You *owe* me a wealthy husband."

Connor's lips thinned into a line. He looked to the door, to her, and back again. She could feel his body hum with frustration, like a bow drawn taught and lightly plucked.

With bated breath, she waited to see if a seemingly logical, and indisputably obstinate, man could be persuaded by such a ridiculous argument. Owed a wealthy husband, indeed.

"Fine," Connor relented at last. His eyes came back to her face and stayed. "I'll not demand a duel. I'll not kill him."

"Thank heavens." She let her hand fall.

He raised his hand and cupped her face. "I will never do this," he said gruffly. Lifting his eyes from her cheek, he caught her gaze and held it. "I would never raise my hand to you."

Adelaide said nothing. Words came easy to Connor; changes of mood came swiftly. But there was no doubt he meant what he said now, and she believed him . . . for now. She had no fear of him or his temper. Not once had she felt threatened in his presence. But her faith in his promises was limited. Only time would tell if she'd misjudged another aspect of his character.

She nodded, but lest he should begin to think she had reverted to blindly accepting everything to come out of his mouth, she added, "If you do, it will only be once."

He wasn't pleased with the response. Dropping his hand, he scowled at her. "You'll believe me."

He wasn't predicting the future, she realized. He was issuing a command. She would believe him *now.* It was so *un*believably absurd that she broke out into laughter.

Connor didn't appear the least amused. "This is not a laughing matter."

"It is," she assured him. "It most certainly is."

How like a man to presume he could demand trust from a woman. How like one to take offense when that woman refused to cooperate.

"Adelaide—"

"Oh, stop glowering." Her laughter faded, and she was within an inch of following it up with a sound lecture. *You'll believe me . . .* Honestly. But she was more than a little weary of arguing, of being angry. She had a lifetime to spend with this man. She could spend it hoarding her resentment, finding fault with everything he said and did, and plotting vengeance for what had occurred at the house party, or she could make some effort to be civil . . . and, perhaps, plot a bit when he wasn't around.

"As it happens, I do believe you."

J do believe you.

The tight knot between Connor's shoulder blades loosened but failed to disappear altogether. It didn't worry him overmuch that Adelaide wasn't sure of him in a general sense. A little time and some careful maneuvering would remedy the problem. But the idea that she might fear him in a physical sense, that she suspected him capable of striking a woman in anger, that was intolerable.

He'd never raised a hand to a woman. Never. Oh, he'd wanted to. There had been the boardinghouse mistress in Boston who'd taken the rent he'd risked life and limb to steal and kicked him out on the street, and the urchin who'd stolen the bread he'd bought with a hard day's honest wages. God knew, he'd had the opportunity to retaliate for both insults with his fists. He'd never laid a finger on them. He'd be damned to hell before he laid a finger on Adelaide in anger.

His eyes tracked over the angry bruise on her cheek.

He'd be damned if he didn't lay fists on Sir Robert.

Rage was a towering flame inside him, blistering his skin and threatening to consume his control. He banked it through a well-honed force of will and let it simmer below the surface. Later, he would let it spill over, when it was Sir Robert, and not Adelaide, who would suffer the burns.

He strove for a lighter tone. "I'd not thought Sir Robert would make it so easy for you to decide in my favor."

Her eyes darted away. "I didn't decide because of this. This is because I had decided."

"Had you?" It gave him a ridiculous amount of pleasure to hear her say it. "Dare I ask why?"

She looked at him again and gifted him with an adorably cheeky smile. "The fifteen thousand pounds."

"Naturally."

He didn't believe it. That she would marry for money, he never doubted, but she hadn't chosen him because he had *more* money. Sir Robert's income was sufficient to see her family comfortably settled, and she would have been content to accept sufficient, if it had been offered by the better man.

Damn if he didn't like knowing she'd thought him the better man, even before Sir Robert had betrayed his true nature. But knowing for himself and hearing her admit it were not the same thing.

It was ridiculous that he should need the words from her. *He* knew, didn't he? Clearly, she knew as well. There was no reason for the obvious to be said aloud. And yet, he couldn't stop himself from asking to hear them.

"I would like the truth, Adelaide. If you could see your way to giving it."

Chapter 15

$\mathcal{A}$delaide considered Connor's request and the manner in which it had been given. There was a new kind of hesitancy in his voice, something she'd not heard from him before. If she'd not known better, she might have called it uncertainty. She knew better. Men like Connor were never uncertain of themselves. They were confident to a fault.

She was tempted to repeat her insistence about the fifteen thousand pounds, but in the interest of beginning their new life on a more affirming note, she decided to try for a bit of honesty.

"I chose you because you told me . . ." She trailed off and reconsidered her words. Almost, she'd said she'd chosen him because he'd told the truth. Which was perfectly absurd. "You told *more* truths than Sir Robert. You said you'd taken notice of me before you knew of the baron's courtship." She nodded once. "That was the truth."

It wasn't the only reason, or even her first reason, but it was the one that carried the most weight with her now. After her temper of yesterday had passed, she'd looked beyond the tangle of lies and latched onto that one truth.

Connor had wanted her, just for her. Only until he'd found other reasons to want her, of course, and it hardly excused him from having played merry hell with her reputation. But still . . . He'd wanted her, and that was something.

"You believed me." Connor didn't sound stunned, exactly, but there was an unmistakable note of surprise.

Good heavens, he had been unsure. Amusement tugged at her lips. "Yes."

"And do you believe he stole my inheritance and sold me to a press-gang when I was a boy?" he asked, a hint of eagerness in his tone.

She remembered the fury and violence in Sir Robert's eyes. "It is possible."

"And tossed me in prison and made another grasp at my fortune when I returned?"

"Yes, of course." She'd believed that from the start.

Now he was just looking smug. "And that I have, in fact, saved you."

Insomuch as a gentleman could save a lady from a burning building *after* he had set it on fire. She opened her mouth to inform him of Sir Robert's own plan for revenge but thought better of it at the last moment. Connor may have noticed her first, but it didn't follow that his first thoughts had been of marriage. Would his offer stand if he learned Sir Robert had never really cared for her? That there was no revenge to be had in marrying her? She wanted to think it would. She wanted to believe he would keep his promise. But she couldn't be sure.

"You provided a viable alternative," she replied.

His mouth turned down at the corners. "An equivocation, but I'll accept it."

"Generous of you."

He didn't smile as she'd hoped. His gaze was steady and intense, his voice soft and even. "You'll be Mrs. Brice. You will not regret it."

For the life of her, she couldn't tell if he was making a promise or delivering an order. She nodded, thinking it was an appropriate response either way.

"You'll not see him again," Connor said.

She nodded with more enthusiasm, not caring if it was an order or a promise, so long as it was true.

Connor caught her chin gently and brushed a whisper-soft kiss against her lips. "Until tomorrow," he murmured. Then he dropped his hand, spun on his heel, and strode toward the door.

"But . . ." They had more to discuss—more details and negotiations to work through. There was still that awful matter of *how many times a day.* "Where are you going?"

He threw a sharp smile over his shoulder. "To not kill Sir Robert."

*T*here were quite a few things a person could do to a man without killing him. Arms and legs could be broken, or even removed. A body could live without all its limbs. A body could live without a number of things—the eyes, nose, ears, and tongue.

Connor hadn't included mutilation in his original inventory of ways Sir Robert would pay. But he was a flexible man, and he'd always meant for the list to be open-ended.

He took dark pleasure in adding to that list now, carefully selecting each gruesome punishment. It gave him something to do while he waited in the dark alley between Banfries's tavern and the mews. He needed something to distract himself from the image of Sir Robert lifting his hand to Adelaide, and visions of divesting Sir Robert of the offending appendage almost did the trick. Almost.

The fury he'd kept carefully concealed for Adelaide's sake had boiled over the moment he'd walked out her front door.

The bastard had used his fist. His *fist.*

So, it would be the hands first. He'd break each finger individually. The tongue next. A fitting price for the lies that had spilled from Sir Robert's mouth. Then . . .

He turned his head at the sound of the tavern door swinging open and laughter pouring outside. When Sir

Robert and his man stepped into the alley, the list was forgotten. Connor forgot everything but his fury. The urge to attack clawed at him, but he waited, letting the rage build higher, until the men were in the dark of the alley. Then he stepped from the shadows and reached his quarry in three purposeful strides.

He gave Sir Robert time to defend himself—he gave Sir Robert time to try, anyway—but the man just stood there, immobile but for the widening of his eyes.

Those eyes snapped shut when Connor's fist connected with flesh. Connor found satisfaction in the throb of his hand. He found greater satisfaction in hearing Sir Robert grunt with pain and watching him fall back against the wall.

Sir Robert's fingers scrambled for purchase on the bricks. He succeeded in keeping himself more or less upright and stumbled over a pile of refuse, into the center of the alley. He spun around, his face a mask of fear, rage, and blood from a missing tooth.

"Help me, you fool!" He shouted at his man.

Connor stayed the man with a quick shake of his head and a simple flick of the hand.

At the sight of his companion backing away, palms out, Sir Robert pulled a small knife from his coat, let out a shout of fury, and charged at Connor. He swung his arm in a wide arc. It was almost too easy for Connor to dodge the attack, knock the knife away, and land another blow. It was just as easy to step out of the way of Sir Robert's swinging fist, then step back in again to catch his adversary in the gut.

When Sir Robert let out a sharp wheeze and doubled over, Connor grabbed him around the throat and shoved him straight again. There was no pleasure to be had in punching the back of a man's head. But there was quite a bit to be found in the sound of Sir Robert's nose breaking on the next punch.

Sir Robert crumpled to the ground, a bloody, groaning heap.

Connor battled the urge to follow him and pummel with

his fists until the groaning stopped . . . Or the vision of Adelaide's bruise faded from memory. Whichever came last.

Instead, he kicked the knife and sent it skittering over the cobblestones to bounce off Sir Robert's knee.

"Care to try again?" he taunted. He hoped Sir Robert would take the bait. Nothing would give him more pleasure than an excuse to break his promise.

Sir Robert's groaning faded. His fingers curled around the knife, and he struggled to his knees.

"You'll hang for this," he rasped.

"They don't hang commoners for brawling with your type, only killing them. And I've not laid a hand on you." Connor made a show of brushing a bit of dust off his coat. "In fact, I spent the night at home, nursing a brandy."

"I have a witness," Sir Robert barked, his voice gaining strength.

"Do you?" Connor dug a sovereign out of his pocket and tossed it at Sir Robert's man. "What did you see here?"

Graham Sefton snatched the coin out of the air. He studied it, a line of concentration across his brow. "It's not right, a man telling what he knows for a bit of coin. Ought be speaking the truth for its own sake." He tossed the coin back to Connor. "And it weren't fair, I tell you, the way those footpads laid into my master. Two of them, there were, and the elder was a brute of a lad. At least ten years of age."

"You . . . The two of you . . ." Sir Robert glared at Graham, his skin turning nearly as red as the blood on his mouth and chin. "You traitorous filth! I should have known better than to hire your kind!"

"Aye," Graham agreed with a pleasant nod. "You should have. I might have run off with your silver. Or slit your throat in your sleep . . ." He cocked his head. "Thought about doing both, truth be told."

"I get his throat," Connor said mildly. "It was my fiancée he laid hands on."

"Miss Ward?" Sir Robert threw his head back and let loose a short, raspy laugh. "That's what this is about? *Miss*

Ward? Oh, Christ, this is priceless. You think you've won. You think you've landed me a terrible blow, but you've accomplished *nothing* but to tie a noose round your own neck."

He wiped the blood from his nose with the back of his hand and managed to gain his feet. "I never wanted the bitch. I'd not have given her a second glance if it hadn't been for you. Poor Mr. Brice," he crooned in a singsong voice. "Unjustly accused. Locked away without cause. Fated to spend every Saturday watching, *pining* for just a glimpse at his fair maiden. My *God*. So tragic. So *romantic*." His rapidly swelling lips curved into a gruesome smile. "Such a pleasure to steal her out from under your nose."

Connor was careful not to react. He wanted to believe Sir Robert spoke out of shredded pride and spite, but he couldn't.

Bloody, buggering hell. He was responsible for bringing Adelaide to Sir Robert's attention.

"Even more pleasure to be had in watching you fail," Connor returned with false calm.

"I'll have her yet!" Sir Robert's voice rose in pitch and volume. The humor in his eyes vanished. "I'll have her when she's tired of you. When she's itching to have a man and not a bastard boy. And then you'll know. You'll *know* what it's like!"

"What what is like?"

"To be passed over!" He was near to screeching now, his voice strained and scratchy. "To come second! To have your life ruined—" He took a breath, then another, visibly calming. He pointed the blade at Connor. "—because of a *whore*."

Connor could all but feel the hate coming off of Sir Robert in waves. It coated his skin and slithered into his pores. He took a menacing step forward and bared his teeth. "Come within a mile of Miss Ward again, and I'll cut your heart out with that knife."

"You can have her," Sir Robert spat. "For now." And with

that, he spun on his heel and loped off unsteadily toward the mews.

Connor watched him go as Graham strolled over and let out a long, low whistle. "Mad as a hatter, that one."

"No." Connor rubbed the back of his hand across his jaw. "Just mad enough to be dangerous."

"He'll clean his house of staff now."

Connor nodded. "Do you know which are to be trusted?"

"Don't know but one or two in the lot who wouldn't be happy to find other employment."

"They have it. At Ashbury Hall."

"Will you still be getting married?"

He spoke without hesitation. "Yes."

"You're a good man."

He wasn't, particularly. He was selfish, and greedy, and territorial. It was a pity Sir Robert hadn't fancied himself in love with Adelaide, and it infuriated Connor to know he'd been the reason Sir Robert had sought Adelaide out. But neither of those things altered the pertinent facts. He'd wanted Adelaide, and now she was his. She would always be his. That was what mattered.

Graham sniffed and cocked his head. "Connor?"

"Hmm."

"Can I have the sovereign back?"

Chapter 16

Connor called on Adelaide the next morning. He didn't mention where he'd gone the night before, and Adelaide didn't ask. As far as she was concerned, what was done was done. She was more than ready to put the distasteful events of the past week behind her.

That's not to say she forgave Sir Robert for his actions, nor intended to forget the humiliation she had suffered because of Connor. She simply saw no benefit in dwelling on her anger, not when there was so much else to occupy her time and thoughts.

Wedding plans, for example, took up an inordinate amount of time and energy. A circumstance she attributed to Connor possessing an inordinate amount of stubbornness.

He wanted the efficiency of an elopement. She wanted to wait for the banns to be read. He suggested they compromise with the purchase of a special license. She called it an inexcusable waste of money and refused to admit the truth of why she wished to wait. No bride, no matter how steeped in pragmatism, wanted the memory of her wedding day to be marred by a bruise the size of Inverness-shire.

To distract him from that argument, she started another. She wanted a small ceremony. He insisted it would be a grand affair.

She thought to wear a simple muslin dress. He offered to pay for a gown made of the finest silk.

She reminded him a lady did not accept articles of clothing from a gentleman. Not even her fiancé.

He offered her the fifteen thousand pounds in advance so she could purchase the items herself.

"She accepts."

This immediate response came from Isobel, who had been entertaining George with a tugging match over an old apron and watching Connor and Adelaide argue across the dining room table for the last half hour—an exercise she gave every appearance of enjoying.

"Do I, indeed?" Adelaide inquired. She might have, actually, if she'd been given the opportunity.

"Yes." Isobel turned to her with twin flames of mischief and excitement in her eyes. "I am fully willing to bear the consequences of this decision."

"Selfless creature," Connor murmured with appreciation.

"Beetles!" George dropped the apron and ran to Connor. "Beetles! Beetles!"

"Not that sort of creature, lad. Look, look what I've brought for you." He pulled a clean handkerchief from his pocket, set it on the table, and unwrapped it to display its contents for George.

"Biscuits!" George snatched one from Connor's hand and held it up for Adelaide to inspect. "Biscuit."

"It certainly is. Gingerbread, by the looks of it." And there appeared to be three more just like it in the handkerchief. She smiled at Connor as George tottered off to play with a step stool against the wall. "It was very kind of you to think of him."

"Not at all. I wasn't certain if he cared for gingerbread, but I thought—"

He broke off when George shoved the step stool into Connor's leg and, biscuit caught between his teeth, scrambled his way onto Connor's lap.

George turned about, nestled his back against Connor's chest, and went about the messy business of eating his treat.

Connor went very still and stared at the top of George's head. "Er . . . Is this safe?"

A choking sound came from Isobel. Adelaide forced a bland expression.

"Yes. Small children have been known to sit on a lap or two and emerge from the experience unscathed."

"Right . . . Right, of course." He neither sounded nor appeared particularly convinced. He lifted his hands to George's shoulders, as if afraid the boy might tumble off without warning, then seemed to change his mind. He gripped the table edge instead, neatly boxing George in between his arms. "Right."

Adelaide smothered a laugh, fearful she would break the sweet spell of the moment. This softer, less confident side of Connor was still new to her. She'd caught a glimpse of it when he'd asked for the true reason she'd chosen him, but seeing him with George . . . This was another level of endearing.

It wasn't every man who would allow—however reluctantly—a child to climb onto his lap. Most gentlemen of her acquaintance would balk at such a familiarity. Few would have been so charmed, or so transparently ill at ease.

She wondered if there might be something redeeming in Connor Brice. Something more valuable than a promise of fifteen thousand pounds a year.

Isobel, though clearly amused, was evidently not contemplating the possibility of Connor possessing more than one virtue. "We were discussing funds made available in advance of the wedding?"

"Right. You'll need a bit to keep you over until the paperwork is complete." Connor hesitated, then let go of the table briefly to once again reach into his pocket, this time pulling out what looked to Adelaide to be a veritable mountain of banknotes. He stretched over George and placed them on the table. "Two hundred pounds should be sufficient, I think."

Adelaide couldn't believe what she was seeing. Two hundred pounds, sitting pretty as you please on her own dining room table. It was exactly one hundred seventy-three pounds more than what was left of her savings.

"Good heavens."

"Two hundred pounds?" Isobel snatched a note off the table and turned it over, her face a picture of wonderment. "Do you always walk about with this many pound notes on your person?"

Connor lifted a shoulder. "More or less."

"Oh, I *shall* like having you for a brother-in-law."

Connor laughed and winked at her, a small and wicked gesture that was certain to elevate Isobel's estimation of him. Isobel had a keen and worrisome fondness for rakish behavior.

"Now, if we've settled everything," Connor said, looking to Adelaide, "I thought we might indulge in a picnic."

Adelaide scarcely heard him, so occupied was she with staring at the banknotes on the table. Oh, the things she was going to do with that money. Clothes, decent food, a tidy sum set away in the likely—and in her experience, it was always likely—event of a calamity.

"Adelaide?"

"Hmm?" She glanced up to find Connor and Isobel staring at her expectantly. "A picnic. Yes."

She dragged her attention away from the money, took mental inventory of the pantry and larder, and concluded that, unless Connor was partial to stale bread and cold porridge, a picnic was out of the question.

"I don't know that it would be possible today. Perhaps day after tomorrow?" When she'd had a chance to spend a bit of that that two hundred pounds.

"It's doubtful what I've packed in the carriage will keep until the day after tomorrow."

"You brought the picnic along?" She smiled, pleased with the small act of thoughtfulness. "In that case, I should be delighted to attend."

"I'll watch Georgie," Isobel offered, rising from the table.

At the sound of his name, George glanced at Isobel, grinned, and reached for another biscuit.

Connor eyed the top of his head speculatively. "Lad, do you think you might hop down, now?"

George bit into his treat, giving no indication he'd even heard, let alone meant to honor, Connor's request.

Connor reached for George's shoulders as he had earlier and, once again, pulled his hands away at the last second. He looked to her. "Could you—?"

"Fetch my bonnet and gloves?" she cut in, deliberately misunderstanding. "Yes, of course."

She jumped up from the table before he could protest and went into the foyer, where she made a show of picking her bonnet off the side table and fidgeting with the ribbons. Then she ever so subtly shifted to the left for a better view of the dining room.

Isobel didn't bother with subterfuge. When Connor looked to her, she merely smiled and shook her head. "Pick him up and set him down, Mr. Brice. He'll not bite . . . Not anymore."

"Right."

Connor stared at George for a moment longer, clearly trying to decide how best to go about dislodging the child from his lap without having to actually pick said child up. At long last, he took the handkerchief holding the last biscuit off the table and held it out to the side, well out of George's reach.

"Here you are, lad." Connor shook the handkerchief. "Wouldn't you like another? Come here, then. Come and get them."

A snicker emerged from Isobel. Adelaide rolled her eyes and abandoned all pretense of disinterest. "George is not a puppy, Connor. He'll not—"

George turned onto his belly, slid off Connor, and tottered over to grab the biscuit.

"Oh, for pity's sake." Fighting a laugh, Adelaide set the bonnet on her head. "That is not how one reasons with a child."

"George thought it quite reasonable," Isobel pointed out. "We should give it a go when he makes a fuss over wearing his Sunday clothes."

"No." She turned to George, who ignored her in favor of the last biscuit. "Do you see what you've begun? Where is your pride, young man?"

Connor stood, looking enormously pleased with himself. "There's no loss of pride in refusing to do something for nothing. The boy shows good sense."

It was an offhanded compliment—and likely intended in defense of his own behavior more than George's—but, all the same, Adelaide liked him the better for having said it.

She smiled and gestured at the door. "Shall we, then?"

*U*pon stepping out her front door, Adelaide noticed three things in quick succession. First, that the weather was unseasonably cool, quite perfect for a summer picnic. Second, that the carriage and four sitting in her drive looked as new as most everything else Connor owned, and finally— and most notably—that there were two men sitting atop the vehicle . . . one of whom she recognized.

"Good heavens."

She grabbed hold of Connor's arm and pulled on it until he bent down to give her his ear.

"What—?"

"That man," she whispered in a rush. "On your carriage next to your driver. He came to my door. He came to my door and then left without saying a word. The day Sir Robert was here. He knocked, looked in, and—"

"Ah. Yes, I know."

She pulled back to gape at him. "How could you possibly—?"

Green eyes sparkled mischievously in the sunlight. "I told you I had men watching."

"Yes, but . . . You meant that literally?" She dropped his arm and glanced over her shoulder to where she and Isobel had watched the man disappear into the woods. "He was *literally* watching us?"

"Settle your feathers, wren." He laughed and ushered her toward the carriage. "Graham was watching the house and grounds, not peeking into windows." He glanced sideways at her bruised cheek, and a hardness flashed over his features. "I should have let him peek in the—"

"No," she cut in with a severe look. "You most certainly should not have."

She settled into the forward-facing seat and took a moment to appreciate the vehicle's interior of plush leather and richly grained wood. It wasn't proper for her to be riding in a closed carriage, but she couldn't bring herself to care. In a few weeks, they would be married, and it was unlikely anyone would be about to see her, at any rate.

Connor took the bench across from her and gave the roof a quick rap with his knuckles. The carriage started with a soft jolt.

"Are you angry?" Connor asked. He didn't look worried by the idea, merely curious.

"No, I'm not angry." She thought about that. "Exactly. I am little perturbed. Was it necessary to leave a man, *that* man, creeping about my woods?"

"Yes."

She looked out the window, a disturbing thought occurring to her. "Are there still men creeping about my woods?"

"No one at present."

That was not a full answer. "Do you trust him? This Graham—?"

"Sefton. I trust he wants the considerable amount of coin I pay."

She slumped in her seat. "You're not going to give a direct answer to any of my questions, are you?"

Connor reached over and tipped her chin up with his finger. "I mean to keep you safe. If that requires hiring a man or two to keep an eye on you when I can't, so be it. Are you going to fight me on this?"

Strictly speaking, that wasn't a direct answer to her question either, but it was hard to take offense at the sentiment.

"I don't wish to fight with you," she replied, choosing her words carefully. "But I would very much appreciate it if you would inform me in advance of such matters."

He frowned thoughtfully and let his hand fall. "I can do that."

"I might have slept better these past few nights knowing there was a guard about."

"And I should have thought of that," he said softly.

Willing to accept that as a kind of apology, Adelaide shrugged. "No harm done, really."

He studied her face. "You haven't been sleeping well, have you?"

"Not really." Not since before the house party. That seemed ages ago. "Kind of you to mention how noticeable it's become."

His lips twitched, but his voice was gentle. "We've a drive yet. Close your eyes and rest a bit."

Surely, he was jesting. "I can't sleep with you sitting across from me, watching." No one could sleep like that.

He left his seat and settled beside her. "How's this?"

A thousand times worse. Their legs and arms were brushing, and she could feel the heat of his skin permeating the layers of clothes between them. The scent of him tickled her nose, and she knew that if she turned her head so much as a fraction to the side, she would be all but kissing him. It wasn't an altogether unappealing notion, but liking the idea and instigating the act were two different animals.

She stared straight ahead and tried to think of something else.

"Do you know—" She stopped to clear her throat. "I'm not all that tired, really."

"I see." And from the sound of it, he most certainly did. "Try to rest anyway. Just for a little while."

Feeling foolish, she scooted away from him, leaned against the side of the carriage, and closed her eyes. It would never work, she thought. She'd never be able to fall asleep with Connor sitting *right there*.

Chapter 17

Adelaide woke curled up against Connor like a sleeping kitten. His arm was around her, anchoring her to his side. Her feet were wedged up in the seat next to her, her head nestled against his shoulder, and her hands . . . Good Lord, her hands were in his lap.

She snatched them away and righted herself so fast it made her head spin.

"I . . . I didn't . . . How did I . . . ?" She swallowed the question as sleep retreated and her mind cleared. "Never mind."

If she'd cuddled up to him in her sleep, she didn't want to know.

"My apologies," she mumbled. He would tease her now. Lord knew, he'd yet to pass up an opportunity to poke at her dignity.

But he surprised her by gently capturing a lock of her hair that had been pulled from its pins during sleep. "Don't apologize for this. You were tired." He rubbed the strand of hair between his fingers a moment, a crease forming between his eyes. Finally, he tucked the strand behind her ear and let his hand fall away. "That was my doing."

She opened her mouth, intending to argue, but then she realized he was quite right. It was, at least in part, very much his fault.

Too groggy to give the matter any more attention, she glanced out the window and asked, "How long was I asleep?" It felt as if it could have been days. Surely it had been at least half an hour. Why hadn't they arrived? Growing concerned, she turned from the window. "Where are we going?"

"On a picnic," Connor reminded her. Then he grinned and added, "in England."

Which was highly effective in banishing the remnants of sleep.

"*England?* You're not serious." She stared at his grin a moment longer. "You *are* serious."

"I am indeed. We're—"

"Stop!" She half stood and stretched up to pound on the roof. "Stop the carriage!"

Laughing, he took hold of her fist and brought it down. "What are you doing?"

"I'm stopping the carriage." She'd rather thought that was obvious. "I can't go to England." She'd rather thought that was obvious as well. What wasn't obvious was why he continued to laugh.

He tugged on her hand, toppling her off balance and onto his lap. "You look a picture, half awake and rumpled—"

"Let go." She struggled against him. How far had they come? How long *had* she been asleep? "Turn the carriage around. I have to go back. Isobel will be in a panic."

"Isobel knows where we are. I spoke with her when you went into the kitchen to fetch the apron for George."

"You did? She knew?"

"Yes, and I am to tell you . . . Quit squirming, love . . . Thank you. I am to tell you that you are not to argue, not to worry, and not to forget to bring her back a memento."

Her eyes narrowed. "You just made that up."

"Only part. She does want the memento."

That did sound like Isobel. "I cannot take a trip to England. I have duties, responsibilities—"

"We're not going to London. We'll be back by nightfall."

"Oh. Just for the day?" She sighed an enormous breath of relief. "Why didn't you say so?"

"How long do your picnics generally last?"

Embarrassed that she'd failed to put two and two together, she pressed her lips shut and refrained from comment.

"Besides," Connor said, his voice turning low and wicked, "I like seeing you flustered."

"I . . ." She trailed off as she became increasingly aware of her position on his lap and of the strong arms that held her close and the hard thighs beneath her legs. His mouth was mere inches from hers, and his green eyes swirled with the unmistakable lights of laughter and desire.

He held her with such care, just as he had on that first night in the garden—as if she was special, as if she was something he treasured.

Suddenly, she had the compelling need to be bold, to be courageous in the way she remembered from childhood, before responsibility had pushed dreams aside.

Without another thought, she leaned forward and kissed him. It was little more than a soft, untutored press of her lips to his, but it was exciting to her—a thrilling and liberating act.

Better yet, Connor seemed to appreciate her effort. He smiled against her lips and murmured approvingly. And then he was kissing her back, taking her mouth with devastating skill. He teased her with small, artful nibbles that sent her pulse racing and drugged her with long, deep tastes that made her fingers curl into the fabric of his coat.

She heard herself gasp and felt his breathing quicken and his hand settle at her hip. And then . . .

The carriage slowed and bounced over a rut, jarring them apart.

Connor swore.

Adelaide ignored both interruptions and leaned forward again. She wanted more. She wanted everything. But Connor thwarted her by taking her face in his hands and pressing a kiss to her brow.

"The carriage, love."

Yes, she thought dimly. They were in a carriage. She sought his mouth again. "Hmm."

"It's slowing. No, sweetheart . . . God, you taste good . . . No, we're here."

"Here?" She pulled back and blinked at him, feeling like a half-witted owl. The sound of the wheels became muffled as they rolled onto grass and, finally, the meaning behind the words seeped in. "Oh, *here*. England!"

"Yes." Connor smiled ruefully as the carriage came to a stop. "What fine timing."

Poor timing or not, Adelaide was suddenly eager, even anxious, to greet the next stage of her adventure. This was, without question, the most wonderfully exciting day she'd had in years. Pushing herself off Connor—who objected with a mild grunt—she threw the carriage door open and hopped down without assistance.

"Where are we?"

"About a half mile past the border," Connor replied, following her. "Or, if you prefer, slightly more than twenty miles from your home."

Her smile was slow, and matched a growing warmth in her chest. "You remembered."

"Of course I remembered." He gestured at the scenery. "What do you make of it?"

"It's . . ." She looked away and took in the rolling hills and fertile farmland broken by dark stands of woods. A delighted bubble of laughter filled her throat. "It's the same. Entirely the same."

"But it's England."

"Yes, it's England." It was new. It was more than twenty miles from her home. It was something she'd wanted and nothing like what she'd expected. It was brilliant.

* * *

C onnor unpacked what was, to Adelaide, a perfect feast. Chicken and lamb, fresh bread and potatoes. There was watered beer, wine in a carafe, and apple slices for dessert. All were spread on a blanket, and in short order, she and Connor were sharing a meal on a gentle hill that overlooked the English countryside.

"What will you do with that fifteen thousand pounds?" Connor asked conversationally. He was reclining on his side, his long legs crossed at the ankles and his weight propped up on his elbow. The prone position ought to have made him seem less substantial, but to Adelaide, he looked like a Titan in repose.

"Find a nanny for George, to start," she replied. "Perhaps even a tutor. I fear he is behind in his education."

"He's two."

"Almost," she corrected and shrugged. "His vocabulary is not what it should be, I think. Isobel and I have tried—"

"He's a fine boy," Connor cut in, his authoritative tone suggesting she not argue. "A sharp lad. And he's fortunate to have you. Did something happen to make you think otherwise? Did someone say—?"

"No," she said softly. Sir Robert was the only person to have disparaged either of them, and his opinion mattered not a jot. Connor's quick defense, on the other hand, meant quite a lot. More than the money and Ashbury House. Those were necessities. If he wanted her for a wife, he had to provide them. But faith in her and an affection for George—those were things he gave by choice.

Oh, yes, she thought, there was something redeeming in the man before her. And perhaps there was something to be made from their union.

"Adelaide?"

Connor's voice brought her back to the moment. "I worry, that's all."

"Well, don't. Tell me what else you'll do when you're wealthy."

"Well . . ." She frowned absently. "Isobel needs new gowns, as do I. Our home could do with a new roof, and doors, and—"

"You're speaking of the small again, the mundane."

"They're not mundane to me," she muttered, feeling a little put out.

"Those are things you need. What do you want?"

"I want the things I need."

"But now you can want more. Be imaginative," he insisted. "What will you do when your responsibilities are met? You'll have thousands of pounds left. What will you do with them? And do not tell me you plan to put every penny into savings."

"Not every penny," she grumbled.

"Creative, Adelaide. Try—"

"I should like to take George shopping," she cut in, surprising herself. She'd not realized until that moment how much she wanted the chance to spoil her nephew. Oh, wouldn't it be lovely to shower him with toys and treats? Evidently, Connor didn't think so. He looked a bit pained at the idea.

"What?" she demanded. "Why are you looking at me like that?"

"Most boys aren't fond of spending time in shops with their aunts."

"They are when they're shops like Mr. Fenwick's bakery," she replied smartly. "I'll let him buy anything he wants. Everything he wants. All he'll need to do is point his finger. And I'll not make him save the treats either. He may eat whatever he likes."

"He'll make himself sick, a boy that age."

"Much you know of it. You thought he could be bribed with a bit of flattery. George has the constitution of a bull. He'll tire out before he can do himself harm." She could picture him now, sticky with sugar and fast asleep on the pile of new toys she intended to buy him.

"What else?"

Warming to the exercise, she grinned and reached for a

slice of apple. "I'll take Isobel to the bookseller's. She has a great love for the written word. And she'll have new watercolors and brushes. The finest to be found in town."

"You could have finer delivered from Edinburgh or London."

"Then that's what I'll do. She can use the ones from Banfries until they arrive."

"And then what will you do?"

And then . . . Well, then it was Wolfgang's turn, wasn't it?

"I'll pay Wolfgang's debts, of course, and . . ." She wasn't sure what came after that. She wasn't sure there was anything that could be done for her brother.

"You won't be paying your brother's debts," Connor said. "That's for me to handle, and I am doing so."

"You are? But—"

"Sir Robert is one of the creditors. I won't have you dealing with him." He gave her a hard look. "The matter is not up for debate."

"Far be it from me to keep you from spending your own money on my brother's debts." She wasn't a compete twit, for heaven's sake. "I was only wondering . . . How long will it take to free him, do you think?"

"Sir Robert will try to make things challenging, I imagine. But there's only so much he can do. Another day or two, no more."

"Oh." She bobbed her head but couldn't force herself to take a bite of her apple. Her appetite was greatly diminished.

Connor dipped his head to catch her eye. "What is it?"

"Would . . . would you think less of me if I told you I am not eager to have him home?"

"No, a shared parentage does not always guarantee affection. I should know."

"It is not the same as with you and Sir Robert. You never really knew your brother." To her way of thinking, Sir Robert had betrayed blood but not family. "You certainly never loved him."

"No. I never did." He paused as if picking his words carefully. "Would you like me to wait to pay Wolfgang's debts? There are excuses—"

"No. No, of course not. I don't want him to rot away in prison." But neither did she want his animosity to rot away the first bit of happiness the family had found in years. "Perhaps a commission could be purchased for him."

Connor shook his head. "I offered. He declined."

Adelaide's mouth fell open. That Wolfgang should not take advantage of the opportunity was disappointing, but hardly shocking. That Wolfgang had been offered the opportunity without her knowledge was astonishing.

"You went to see him? You spoke with him?"

"We had a discussion, of sorts, yesterday. I offered to buy him a commission, and he sent his regrets by missive today. He was decidedly unimpressed by my visit and my offer."

Adelaide grimaced, imagining the kind of insults her eternally ungrateful brother had likely tossed about. "You should not have gone to the prison without me."

His lips twitched. "Yes, Mother."

She sighed and wished she could pace. "I didn't intend that as a scolding. But you've already taken on the responsibility of Wolfgang's debts. You shouldn't be saddled with his anger as well."

All signs of humor fled from his face. "That's for you to carry?"

"I'd just as soon not," she assured him. "I only wish . . . I don't know how to help him. I've tried everything, but somehow . . . I so often make mistakes."

Connor set down a glass of wine and looked at her with a kind of impatient puzzlement. "How can such a capable woman have so little appreciation for her own worth?"

"I've appreciation. But I've . . . I have no training for this." She shook her head, frustrated that she couldn't find the words to make him understand. "It was always assumed I would either marry a gentleman of modest means or remain a spinster with a modest income. My mother saw that I was given the skills necessary to thrive in those conditions. I know how to needlepoint and paint in watercolors and organize a dinner party. But I know nothing of business or how to keep a reckless brother *out* of business. I was never taught how to be the head of a household."

"And yet you've filled the role admirably for a number of years."

She'd filled it, at any rate. "I don't know that I've done it admirably. I . . ." She took a breath, surprised at what she was about to admit. "I've been resentful of the responsibility."

"Who wouldn't be?" Connor asked, his impatience clearly outpacing his confusion. "No one wants to be made captain of a sinking ship."

She frowned a little, not sure if she cared for the analogy. "I don't know that we were sinking, exactly . . . Yes, all right, we were sinking."

"And though you weren't trained as an officer, you have nonetheless succeeded in pulling yourself, your sister, and your nephew off the boat and onto solid ground." He wiggled his finger in the general vicinity of his chest. "Fertile ground, if I may say so. A veritable paradise. An Eden beyond the wildest imaginations—"

"Yes," she cut in, laughing softly. "I get the general idea."

"Good." Connor reached for his wine again. "Don't discount what you've accomplished, Adelaide. It's not your fault Wolfgang refuses to abandon ship."

A small part of her wondered how much she had actually accomplished and how much had simply fallen in her lap. But most of her wanted to believe in what Connor said.

"Perhaps you're right." She took a small bite of her forgotten apple. "Perhaps I will enjoy being captain of Ashbury house."

"She's a worthy vessel. But I'm afraid she already has a captain."

"You?" She thought about that, then shrugged. "Very well, then. Admiral Ward has a nice ring about it anyway."

"Admiral Brice sounds even better."

"Too late, you already chose the rank of captain."

"It will still be Admiral Brice, Mrs. Brice."

"Oh. Right." That was going to take some getting used to.

"And I shall be Supreme Grand Admiral of the Fleet."

"You can't . . ." She burst out laughing. "That is not a real rank."

He plucked the apple from her fingers. "It will be once I'm emperor. Do you know, I believe I'll raise your George as my successor. It might be wise for me to have an ally about when you begin your campaign for revenge. You do still plan on making my life a living hell?"

She pretended to reflect on the matter. "I think . . . Not *every* aspect of your life. Not the parts we are to share as husband and wife. I wouldn't want to bring hell down on my own head."

"Trust me, love, there is no sweeter place to raise a little hell than in the parts we are to share as husband and—"

"That is *not* what I meant."

"I know. It wouldn't have been half as amusing if you had." He appeared singularly unimpressed with her withering glare. "So, what should I be expecting, exactly? The occasional pocket of hell? Small projectiles of damnation?"

She stole the apple back with a smug smile. "You will have to wait and see."

Connor studied Adelaide's face carefully. She was smiling and laughing now, but the shadows under her eyes persisted. The one on the right blended seamlessly into the healing bruise on her cheekbone, and both were in sharp contrast to skin that had been leached of color by worry and exhaustion.

He hated seeing it. He hated having to wait to do anything about it.

An image of Gregory's wooden carving entered his mind. Quietly brave, that's how he'd once seen her. Stubbornly courageous seemed a more accurate description now. Courageously stubborn was even better. Resentful or not, she was accustomed to having the final word in anything and everything that touched the Ward household. She was (and would no doubt continue to be) unyielding in her defense of that duty, in her right to retain both the pleasure and weight of leadership.

It wasn't his intention to take the first away from her, but she'd have to learn to share the latter. He wasn't going to stand idly by while his wife bowed lower and lower under the burden of her own family.

They'd be his family too, soon enough.

Sooner, if the extra pounds he'd passed on to his solicitor had anything to say about it.

Connor watched as Adelaide popped the last bite of apple in her mouth and reached for another slice. It had been a very long time since he'd been part of a family—a traditional one. He had Michael and Gregory, but the bonds that held him and his men together were not the same as those that came with marriage, and neither were the expectations.

He experienced an unfamiliar twinge of uncertainty at the thought of some of the intangible expectations he was facing. Until now, he'd given them very little thought, concentrating instead on what he wanted from Adelaide and what he could easily provide in return. He wanted Adelaide to wife, and he could provide her with the security of his name and his wealth.

But there was more to being the head of a household than the supply of provisions and a surname. Ideally, a lady with even a thimbleful of blue blood would marry a man who was a gentleman by birth. Barring that, she'd marry a gentleman by nature.

Connor knew full well he was neither. According to his father, a gentleman never wavered from his dedication to honesty, integrity, and courage. He had abandoned the first two before the age of twenty.

Then again, fidelity had been conspicuously absent from his father's list of gentlemanly attributes. And there were any number of men the ton considered paragons, and whom Connor wouldn't trust with the care of his boots.

His brother came to mind. Like as not, there was no such creature as a true gentleman, only those who could play the part well and those who could not.

There could be no doubt the late baron would consider his younger son a failure in the role, but Connor shoved aside both his uncertainty and the old, unwelcome lick of shame. He wasn't marrying his damn father. The only expectations and ideals that need concern him were Adelaide's. And like every other gentleman in existence, he could meet the ones that suited him, and he could fake the rest.

Chapter 18

The trip home proved to be as diverting for Adelaide as the roadside picnic. For three hours, she and Connor kept up a lively, rambling conversation.

He asked about her parents and about what she'd been like as a little girl. He teased her mercilessly when she admitted to once having a great affection for mawkish poetry and entertained her with stories of his travels abroad.

He was charming and attentive, and for that brief period of time, she forgot to think of lies and debts and quests for vengeance. Connor was once again her secret gentleman from the garden; that was all that mattered.

Before she knew it, the carriage had rolled through Banfries . . . And then right past her house.

"The driver seems to have forgotten where I live," she said to Connor.

"I'd like you to meet someone at Ashbury Hall, if you've no objection. It won't take long."

It was growing late, already dusk. A visit to Ashbury Hall meant she likely would not return home until well after dark. A lady did not go about with a suitor after dark. Then again, a lady also did not go riding about in closed carriages. In for a penny, in for a pound, she thought.

"I've no objection. Who am I to meet?"

"My men."

She assumed he was referring to Michael and Gregory, the men who had come from Boston with Connor and shared a prison cell with him in Scotland. It occurred to Adelaide that those men were probably the closest thing Connor had to true family, and yet she knew nearly nothing about them.

"I should very much like to meet them."

In comparison to her first visit, Adelaide found Ashbury Hall to be a hive of activity. There were two footmen waiting to assist her from the carriage, a butler to open the front door, and a maid waiting to take her bonnet.

Her eyes grew wider with every member of staff she ran across, and by the time the housekeeper arrived in the front hall to assist the maid, who looked a trifle lost in her new home, Adelaide wasn't sure if she wanted to gape or laugh.

"Mrs. McKarnin?"

The housekeeper, a tall, thin woman with a mop of white hair hidden under a cap and a bright smile spread across her narrow face, gave a low curtsy. "As you see, Miss Ward. Good evening to you, Mr. Brice."

Adelaide chose to gape, and did so until the housekeeper left the hall with the maid. She'd met Mrs. McKarnin several months ago, when she'd been Sir Robert's housekeeper. She'd recognized the footmen, butler, and maid for the same reason.

She turned to Connor. "Did you steal Sir Robert's staff?"

"Nothing of the sort," he assured her briskly. "They were free of Sir Robert's employ when they were hired this morning."

She watched as another familiar footman walked by. "What, all of them? Today?"

Connor gave a small, dismissive shake of his head. "They're well rid of him."

"Yes, they are, but how on earth . . . ?" Laughing, she held up a hand. "Never mind. I don't wish to know."

"Excellent. I don't want to tell you."

Unable to determine if he was in earnest or not—and loath to admit she couldn't tell—Adelaide refrained from further comment and allowed Connor to usher her into the front parlor, a room she felt to have more in common with Ashbury's great hall than any parlor she'd ever seen. It, like everything else in the house, was immense in proportion and luxurious in decor. The upholstery and drapes were a lush green velvet, the fireplace marble, and the carpet thick enough to swallow her shoes. The Great Parlor, that's what it ought to be called. In fact, all of the rooms at Ashbury ought to begin with a similarly descriptive title. The Grand Music Room, the Colossal Library, the Lesser Yet Still Unnecessarily Oversized Family Parlor.

She stifled a giggle and turned at the rise of voices coming down the hall.

"Stand still, damn you. It's only a bit of—"

"Stay away from me with that. I've not put powder on my head in thirty years, and even then it weren't on purpose. Scuffle with a magistrate—"

"Are you wanting the lass to think we're savages?"

"I'm not wearing it, and that's that."

A moment later, a generously proportioned middle-aged man and an elderly man with too much powder in his hair appeared at the open doors. Both were garbed in gentlemen's clothes, and both gave the impression of being decidedly uncomfortable in the attire. The younger man was stretching his neck as if he might work it free from the constricting cravat, and the older man kept jerking his head to the side, leading her to the assumption that either the hair powder was irritating him or he was possessed of an unfortunate tic.

Connor introduced her to the elderly man first. "Miss Ward, may I present Mr. Gregory O'Malley. Gregory, Miss Ward."

Gregory came forward and executed a surprisingly jaunty bow for a man of such advanced age. Then he straightened and smiled at her. "Will you be forgiving an old man for frightening you, lass?"

Oh, dear. The poor man had grown a little daft in his old age. "You haven't frightened me, Mr. O'Malley."

He beamed with obvious approval. "Sure and I didn't. You see, boy? Spine."

She had no idea what he was talking about, but he was clearly pleased with her, and she was inclined to be pleased with anyone who referred to Connor as "boy" and got away with it.

The second man stepped around Gregory with a limp and ran a smoothing hand down his coat.

"Miss Ward," Connor offered. "Mr. Michael Birch."

"A pleasure," Adelaide murmured. The surname rang a bell. She looked closer. "Have we met before?"

"Not proper. But I'd wager you burnt a hole in the back of my head when you was in the garden."

The back of his head . . . In the garden . . .

It came to her then. Mr. Birch, her obstacle at Mrs. Cress's house party, was the same Michael of whom Freddie had spoken.

"You?" Aghast, she looked from Mr. Birch to Connor. "The two of you?"

"The *three* of us, lass," Gregory corrected.

Connor cleared his throat. "Gregory was the gentleman in the hall."

"The gentleman . . . I . . . You . . ." She glared at Connor, then Michael, then Gregory O'Malley with extra heat because she'd felt a little sorry for him a moment ago.

The old goat wasn't daft at all.

Disappointment twisted in her chest as she realized she'd found yet one more string, one more deception. Until now, she'd retained the hope that some part of that night in the garden had been real. She'd known Connor had sought her out, of course, but she'd not realized just how much of their first meeting had been staged. Now she couldn't help but wonder if every part of it had been an act, and if she would ever be more to Connor than a useful toy.

To her eternal horror, she felt a lump form in her throat and the burning threat of tears. To cover it, she planted her hands on her hips and turned her anger on Michael and Gregory. "The *nerve* of you, sneaking about a lady's home, uninvited. Conniving to compromise an unsuspecting woman. Grown men behaving like callous youths. You should be ashamed of yourselves. Both of you."

They didn't look ashamed, particularly. Michael was grinning. Gregory was rubbing his hands together enthusiastically. "Aye. Spine."

"Aye."

Adelaide tossed her hands up. "Oh, for pity's sake. You cannot—"

"Have a seat, Adelaide," Connor suggested softly.

She shook her head without looking at him. She was reluctant to meet his eyes, afraid of what she might see there. Was he laughing at her? Was he feeling proud of himself for having maneuvered her so cleverly?

"I prefer to stand," she replied coolly. What she truly preferred was to concentrate on her anger. Also, she wanted to deliver a proper set-down to Gregory and Michael, which was fairly difficult to accomplish from a seated position.

"We'll discuss it later," Connor murmured. "Privately. Have a seat, wren. Please."

Finally, she forced herself to look at him, and she noted with relief that he didn't appear amused or proud of himself. Unfortunately, he didn't appear especially ashamed of himself, either. His expression was guarded, his green eyes carefully shuttered, and she realized there were to be no answers or apologies while his men were present.

She looked back at Gregory and Michael. They grinned in unison. Clearly, there was also nothing to be gained from them.

"Very well," she replied with as much dignity as she could muster.

Defeated, she took a seat on the settee, and for the next half hour, she listened to Gregory and Michael talk and laugh, swap barbs and insults. It seemed bizarre to her that they should carry on so, as if they were all old friends sharing pints and conversation round a table at a tavern. And it was further distracting to have Connor seated next to her. His arm was draped over the back of the settee, and every so often, his fingers brushed along the nape of her neck, or toyed with a loose lock of hair. His touch sent warm chills along her skin, and she was torn between wanting to move away and wanting to lean into him like a purring cat.

She stayed perfectly still and tried to focus on the conversation. Gregory, she learned, was the third son of a failed Irish jeweler. Michael had been born to parents in service to a prominent English family, and orphaned before the age of ten. They'd met as sailors aboard a merchant ship and, after a particular grueling voyage from London to the Americas, agreed to pool their savings and become Boston businessmen.

"What sort of business?" Adelaide inquired.

Michael gave her an odd smile. "We was what you might call . . . purveyors of fine art."

"You sold art?"

"Aye," Gregory said. "But we weren't what you'd be calling successful. Not until we met our Connor."

"How did you meet?"

Connor pulled his hand away from her neck. "I don't think—"

"Caught the boy trying to lift my purse," Michael explained cheerfully.

"What?" She turned on the settee. "You were a pickpocket?"

"No, I worked on the docks . . ." Connor shifted in his seat. It was a small movement, but she saw it. "But I may have picked a pocket or two when an opportunity presented itself."

"Did opportunities often present themselves?"

"Define often."

It seemed best to reply with silence.

He shifted again. "Now and then. I hadn't the training or practice to be confident in the game."

Michael laughed. "There's the truth of it. I've known East End doxies what weren't so grabby as you."

"Remember you're speaking to a lady," Connor said before looking to Adelaide. "They put me to work. I ran errands in exchange for food and lodging. Later, when I'd proven I could be trusted, they made me a partner."

"Selling art?" Somehow, that didn't seem right. The savings of two sailors couldn't possibly have been sufficient to enter into such a business, and Connor had made no mention of his interest in art when she'd spoken of Isobel's painting. "What sort did you—?"

Connor rose to his feet. "It's growing late. We should get you home. Gentlemen, you'll excuse us."

Michael leveraged his considerable girth out of his chair. "But we were just getting—"

"Another time."

The men were slow to leave, mumbling their farewells and dragging their feet across the carpet. Michael turned around at the door and spoke in a tone that approached, but didn't quite reach, apologetic.

"For what it's worth, miss, I never were inside the bird's home."

It took Adelaide a moment to realize they'd gone back to the topic of Mrs. Cress. "Oh, for the love of . . . You were on her grounds, Mr. Birch. And Mrs. Cress is not a *bird*." A silly, gossiping biddy, but not a bird. "She is—"

"*Good night*, gentlemen." Connor's hard tone cut through the men's amusement like a knife. Unfortunately, the effect proved temporary. Adelaide could hear them laughing seconds after they walked out the door.

She ground her teeth a little at the sound. "You keep interesting company, Mr. Brice."

"They meant no offense, Adelaide."

"Was everything about that night a lie?" She cut in, uninterested in listening to a defense of his men. It was Connor's behavior for which she wanted an explanation. It was his apology she'd been waiting to hear.

"Not a lie, exactly," Connor hedged. "A ruse. There is a difference."

By no stretch of imagination did that qualify as an explanation or an apology. "There certainly is. A ruse requires a multitude of lies."

"I had no other choice," Connor replied patiently. "I'd only just gained my freedom, and you were all but engaged. I thought there wasn't time for a traditional courtship."

"Well, we'll never know now, will we?" She folded her arms over her chest. "I want to know what else has been kept from me. What else should I know—?"

"Nothing. There is . . . Well . . ." He offered her a sheepish smile. "I might have had a hand in stalling your brother's creditors in their attempts to seize your inheritance."

Her heart executed a quick and painful somersault. "There was an attempt to take my inheritance?"

"Also, I might have had a hand in keeping that information from you."

She digested that disturbing news in silence.

Connor lifted a shoulder. "It was just a bit of lost paperwork here and there. A way to stall things until I could gain my release. If you had lost the inheritance, you'd have put every effort into bringing Sir Robert up to scratch."

She would have, without question. His reasons for interfering made perfect sense—from the standpoint of a man intent on stealing his brother's almost-fiancée. But there was no reason for him to have hidden the trouble from her. No reason at all . . . except to shield her from worry. It had been an act of thoughtfulness. A rather misguided and inexcusably high-handed act, but a thoughtful one all the same.

"You should not have kept information related to me and my family to yourself. It was wrong of you, and I'll not tolerate such overbearing behavior in the future." She sniffed, made a show of brushing a few wrinkles from around her waist, and mumbled at the floor, "But I thank you for your assistance."

"You're welcome." He didn't mumble at all.

She dropped her hands and straightened to give him an exasperated look. "You are fundamentally incapable of issuing an apology, aren't you?"

"Not fundamentally, no." A thoughtful furrow formed across his brow. It looked at odds with the spark of humor in his green eyes. "Deeply suspicious of the purported wisdom of admitting to fault, however—"

"Oh, never mind." A reluctant laugh escaped. "Is there anything else? Any other secrets I should be made aware of?"

"No. There is nothing else you need to know."

"Are you certain?" she asked, her tone mocking. "You haven't any other nasty siblings? You're not married? You're not wanted for murder in the Americas?"

"No." He ran his tongue along his teeth. "Not murder."

"Oh, my—"

He laughed and stepped forward to sweep her into his arms. "Holy hell, you're gullible."

"This is *not*—"

He bent down and gave her a brief but heated kiss. "Be easy, wren. To the best of my knowledge, and much to my regret, I have only the one brother. I've never had a wife, and I am not wanted for a crime in any country. It was only a jest."

"It was in poor taste," she grumbled. "I want your word there have been no other, and will be no other, deceptions."

He brushed the backs of his fingers across her jaw, a quizzical expression on his face. "Do you trust me to keep it?"

"No, not entirely." He'd given her reason to like him, even to be grateful, but she'd be a fool to forget where she, and her trust, fell on Connor's list of priorities . . . Well below his plans for revenge. "But I should like it all the same."

He let her go suddenly, and a humorless smile pulled on his lips. "Very well. You have it."

* * *

Two days later, Connor took a seat behind his desk in the Ashbury Hall study and frowned at the pristine mahogany surface. The desk was new, just arrived from the cabinetmaker. The wood was waxed and polished to a glassy shine. Nearly every piece of furniture, every inch of the house, looked the same. He could practically see his reflection in the library shelves.

Ashbury Hall was ready; the repairs were nearly complete. The servants' quarters were full of Sir Robert's former staff. All that was left was for Adelaide to arrive and decide what final decorative touches to put in place. Everything was as it should be. All was going according to plan.

So why the blazes did he feel so dissatisfied? Why was he being plagued by thoughts of one little lie?

There is nothing else you need to know.

It wasn't even a real lie. Adelaide did not need to know that Sir Robert had never cared for her, that the only reason he'd taken an interest in her at all was because . . .

Connor swore ripely . . . Was because of *him*.

That was the truth. He knew it, and had no intention of telling Adelaide. He was lying by omission.

As a rule, lying in any form didn't trouble him overmuch. Needs must, and all that. But this was different. It *felt* different. He'd made a mistake not keeping his interest in Adelaide secret. It was a carelessness that had cost Adelaide dearly, and for that she deserved an apology. Offering one, however, would only serve to ease his conscience, not give her peace of mind.

Adelaide loathed Sir Robert and didn't give a damn for his opinion of her, but no one, *no one*, wanted to hear they'd fallen prey to a false courtship, twice.

Not *exactly* twice, Connor amended. However unconventional, however far removed from the ideal, his courtship was legitimate. Unlike Sir Robert, he wanted Adelaide. The fact that Sir Robert hadn't was an insult that would never reach her ears.

This was, at best estimate, the fourth time Connor had arrived at this conclusion. And still he remained dissatisfied, and still the lie niggled at him.

Which was his fault entirely. Sometime in the past week or so, he'd let Adelaide get under his skin.

After a moment's reflection, he decided this assessment was not entirely accurate. Adelaide had gotten under his skin months ago. Somehow, she'd worked her way deeper. She was in his blood.

And why the devil wouldn't she be? Lord knew, she was everywhere else. She dominated his thoughts, invaded his dreams, and featured prominently in every one of his waking fantasies.

Something had to be done about those fantasies. Visions of her and him engaged in the most delightful—and, admittedly, improbable—activities popped into his head at the most inconvenient times. Just that morning, he'd been going over the books with Michael one minute and envisioning Adelaide in the next . . .

Connor tilted the chair back on two legs, propped his feet on the desk, and stared at the ceiling.

She'd been in the walled garden at Ashbury Hall, if he recalled correctly, wearing her wren's mask and not a stitch more. A blanket was spread on the ground, and her lips were parted in a seductive smile. She was waiting for him. Only him.

Her thick chestnut locks fell loose around her bare shoulders. He brushed a strand aside and bent to taste the salt of her skin. The shiver that passed over her tickled his lips. The soft intake of her breath turned him to stone. When she lifted a hand to touch, he captured it and held it down.

He wouldn't let her take, not right away. He'd keep her still, standing just as she was, as he explored every luscious curve, every soft plane. When she trembled, when her knees buckled, he would lay her on the blanket and continue the sweet torture. When she moaned for him, he'd let her touch. And when she cried out his name, he'd slip between the soft cradle of her thighs and . . .

The chair slammed to the floor with a crash.

"Bloody, *bloody* hell."

It was damn distracting. And it made him feel like a randy teenage boy.

How the devil was he to manage a proper revenge when every time he tried to plot, the lie he'd told Adelaide niggled at him and an image of her stripped bare and smiling at him filled his head.

He could work around the guilty conscience. There was no plotting round a naked woman.

"Begging your pardon, sir."

Connor looked up to find an elderly man with a baritone voice and more white hair than a footman's wig standing in the open doorway. His new butler. Devil take it, what was the man's name? Jenkins, Jones . . .

"Jennings." That was it.

"Yes, sir." Jennings held up a folded note. "A missive has arrived for you, sir."

Connor accepted the letter, read the contents, and grinned.

Chapter 19

*W*olfgang Ward was returned to the bosom of his family with nothing but the clothes on his back and the hostility he'd wrapped around himself like a cloak.

Adelaide stood with Isobel and George on the front steps of their home and watched her brother climb from Connor's carriage.

He looked terrible, far worse than he had the last time she'd seen him. Adelaide didn't understand it. How could her brother have grown more gaunt and look even more haunted? Angry and indignant, she understood. Wolfgang had never responded well to having his wishes denied. But the family's new circumstances, *his* new circumstances, ought to have provided him with some peace of mind. He was free of prison, debt, and Sir Robert.

Why did he look like a man still caged?

She scowled at him as he strode away from the carriage without a word to the driver. Angry and indignant or not, he should have passed on his thanks to the driver for the lend of Connor's vehicle. Lord knew, he'd not pay his thanks in person or think to send a note.

Reaching the steps, he greeted Isobel with an embrace and George with a bright smile and his favorite game of tickle the infant. For Adelaide, he had only a perfunctory kiss on the cheek and the words, "I'll speak with you in the parlor."

Hoping to get over and done with whatever unpleasant business he had in mind, Adelaide followed her brother inside and watched as he took in his home with a slow sweep of his eyes, before marching into the parlor, where he opened a cupboard in search of brandy. He made no comment on how much further the house had deteriorated during his absence. Not a single word was spoken about the missing furniture and decor.

"If you are looking for Father's decanter," Adelaide said evenly, annoyed by his lack of interest in the family home, "it was sold two months ago."

Wolfgang swore lightly and tapped the cupboard shut with his finger. "Never mind, I'll drink the swill at the tavern. We need to discuss what's to be done next."

"About what?"

"Your engagement." He caught his hands behind his back. "I've given this some thought, and I have decided it would be best if you broke it by letter. No need to bring an ugly scene—"

"Break it?" she interrupted. "Why ever would I do such a thing?"

"Because you've no reason to keep it." He spoke as if the answer were obvious and she a trifle dense for not having figured it out on her own. "Our debts are paid, Adelaide. We've the inheritance, and the money Mr. Brice—"

"The inheritance is nearly gone. And that is quite beside the matter. I did not engage myself to Mr. Brice for his fortune." She would marry him for his fortune, which was entirely different. The latter was a reasonably acceptable means of providing for one's family. The former spoke of thievery and deceit. "What you are suggesting is wrong in every sense of the word. I'll not do it."

"It's done all the time. Ladies break engagements left and right these days—"

"They don't take money, Wolfgang. An engagement is not something one can let out for a fee and then insist on having back."

He made an impatient gesture with his hand. "Well, what do you suggest? You can't mean to go through with the marriage. You're the grandniece of a count. You can't go about marrying just anyone."

"Our great-great-great-uncle by marriage was a count, Wolfgang. That means nothing. And I do mean to go through with it. I am happy to go through with it." She reached up and pinched the bridge of her nose. Lord, how he exhausted her. "Mr. Brice has the means and desire to provide for this family. *Your* family," she emphasized, dropping her hand. "We were but a few short months from the poorhouse. Does that mean nothing to you?"

"Sir Robert would never let it happen." Growing visibly agitated, Wolfgang began to pace in front of the fireplace. "Christ, what a mess you've created. He'll not let this slight go lightly, you know. But if you were to make a gesture now, he might—"

"*Sir Robert?* You're angry because I . . . ?" She shook her head slowly, shocked by the words, appalled at his callousness. "How can you champion him now?" she asked on a horrified whisper. The bruise on her cheek had not yet fully healed, and already her brother was willing to forgive and forget. "How can you defend him after everything that has happened?"

Wolfgang sighed heavily. "I am not defending him. He should not have raised his hand to you. It was wrong of him to do so." He spoke as if being forced to recite a technicality. As if Sir Robert had done nothing more nefarious than steal a bite from their larder. And wasn't she being awfully silly to make such a racket over the matter?

Shock drained away to be replaced by a wave of cold anger. "That you would brush aside the insult so easily speaks worse of you than—"

"Do you think you'll receive better from Brice?" His voice dripped with scorn. "He's a bastard, Adelaide."

"Mr. Brice is . . ." She wanted to say he was good and honorable, but that didn't make any sense. He'd lied to her and compromised her on purpose. It was difficult to argue the good and honorable in that. "He is the acknowledged son of a baron, the man who paid your debts, and the man who will be my husband. You will show respect."

Wolfgang's lips thinned into a pale line. "I'll pay him back, but that's all I'll do."

She almost laughed at the outlandish statement. It was just like Wolfgang to make such an impossible promise.

"Oh, do let me know when hell has frozen over," she drawled. "Until then, for the sake of your family, and the coin for that brandy you're wanting, you'll keep a civil tongue in your head. Am I understood?"

She didn't expect to be understood and wasn't the least surprised when Wolfgang leveled a long, ugly glare at her, then exited the room without another word.

*A*delaide avoided Wolfgang for the next twenty-four hours, a remarkably simple exercise, as he'd taken himself off to the tavern moments after their argument and had not returned home again until dawn.

Now it was early afternoon, he was still in bed, and she was taking a few moments to tend the hydrangea she'd nearly flattened, and trying very hard not to worry herself over where Wolfgang had gotten the money for drink.

Isobel, like as not. He'd probably told her he meant to buy new clothes or have a pint in celebration. Fortunately, although Isobel was susceptible to the pleas of a sibling, she was neither a fool nor particularly generous. She'd not have given Wolfgang more than a few shillings. Which he'd no doubt succeeded in turning into a hundred pounds of debt in the course of an hour.

"You don't have to do that now." Connor's gruff voice fell on her back. "We'll hire a gardener."

Straightening with a small start, she turned and saw he was standing directly behind her, holding a thick stack of papers on top of a large tome. His approach had been muffled by the hum of a light breeze.

"Good afternoon, Mr. Brice." She peeled off her gloves and smiled. "I like to garden, you'll recall."

"So you've said." He frowned a little. "I assumed that meant cutting flowers and . . . what have you."

"I enjoy all aspects." Even the repetitive work of weeding was rewarding. She tilted her head at him, wondering if the sight of his future wife digging in the dirt had somehow offended him. "Does that bother you?"

"No." His face cleared, and he gave a quick shake of his head as if dismissing the idea. "Not if it gives you pleasure." He shifted the papers in his arms and handed her the tome. "Here, I've brought you something."

Happy with his quick acceptance of her hobby—and, naturally, with his offer of a gift—she took the book with a smile.

"What is it? . . . An atlas?" She turned it over in her hand, studying the fine leather binding. It was a thoughtful, if somewhat odd, present. "This was very kind of you. Thank you."

"The atlas is not the surprise. It's a tool. I want you to decide where you would like to go on our tour of Europe." He reached over and tapped the book. "A bridal tour. That's the surprise."

Stunned, she looked at him, the atlas, then him again. "Really? Do you mean it? We can go anywhere I like?"

"Everywhere you like. Make a list."

She laughed, delighted with the suggestion. She'd made a hundred lists in the past. With pen and paper, when she'd still had the funds for them, then mental lists later—one for bills, one for debts, one for supplies she couldn't buy, another for repairs she couldn't afford. Not for the life of her could she remember the last time she'd made a list for fun.

Everywhere she'd wanted to go. The possibilities were limitless. Well, not entirely limitless. She couldn't take a full year as her parents had done. There was George to consider, and heaven knew, her brother couldn't be left unsupervised for so long a time. But she could take a month or two, perhaps even three. Three months of travel to any place she liked. She could scarce believe it.

Excitement and longing hummed through her veins. "I want to go to Prussia and France."

"That's a start. Where else?"

"Oh, I don't think there will be time for anyplace else."

"We can take all the time you like."

She shook her head. "I can't leave George alone for too long."

"Why should we leave him? Traveling is a fine education for a young boy."

"He may come with us?"

"Certainly, as long as we take a nanny along as well." He lifted a hand to brush a loose lock of hair from her shoulders. "I don't fancy competing for your time or fishing him out of a canal in Venice. And I imagine Isobel will want the freedom to explore a bit without having a child in tow."

"Isobel may come as well?" She realized she was more or less echoing everything Connor said, but she couldn't help it. It was all so extraordinary. He was handing her another dream. More, he was fulfilling the dream her mother and father had never been able to see materialize. The Ward children on tour . . . Most of the Ward children, she amended.

"What of Wolfgang?"

"He may join us, if he likes."

Given her brother's sour disposition of late, she rather hoped he wouldn't. But at the same time, he couldn't be left to his own devices for any length of time.

"I don't know that he'll agree to join us."

"Then he won't," Connor said dismissively.

"Wolfgang cannot be left unattended for—"

"Unattended?" His brows winged up. "Is he an invalid?"

"Very nearly," she grumbled. "He makes terrible choices. I don't know if he's capable of making good ones."

"He's capable. We will do what we can for him, but he's a grown man, Adelaide. You cannot stop him if he is determined to make himself miserable."

"I know, but I have to try." Frowning, she looked down and nudged a rock with her toe. "It's not just himself he injures. There's Isobel and George—"

He cut her off by capturing her chin in his hand and lifting her face to his. "Your fate is no longer tied to your brother's. Do you understand?"

Adelaide considered it. A part of her would always be tied to Wolfgang, because a part of her would always hope to see the boy she'd loved become a man of whom she could be proud. Though it pained her, she wouldn't sever that tie if she could. Who would look for a lost boy, if not his family? Who would mourn his loss?

But Connor was right from a financial standpoint. The days of fearing complete ruin were over. Nothing Wolfgang did now could change that.

"Yes, I understand." She reached up, took his hand, and gave it a gentle squeeze before letting go. She let go of her sorrow along with it. Now was not the time to dwell on the heavy matters of the heart. It was a lovely day, a beautiful day. And she had a trip to plan.

"When shall we leave?" she demanded, growing excited. Directly after the wedding? Or should they take a week or two to settle into Ashbury Hall?

"When I've done with Sir Robert."

That was not the answer she'd been expecting.

Hadn't Connor said he had his own list? A long list of treats in store for his brother, or something along those lines? How long? How many weeks or months, or even years, would it take to check the items off on that list?

She struggled not to let her disappointment show. He'd never promised her a trip. He'd certainly never promised a trip taken in the immediate future. Eventually, he would take her, and that was more than she'd ever thought to ask for.

"Well," she said in what she hoped was a passably cheerful voice. "I shall have some time to plan, then. Is there someplace you'd like to recommend?"

"I remember Vienna being agreeable in the fall. Isobel would enjoy Rome, I imagine."

"You've been those places as well?"

"My mother took me to Vienna when I was a child. I was in Rome two years ago on a matter of business."

She tilted her head. "What is your business, exactly?"

"I've more than one, but the bulk is shipping. Goods from the Americas, silk from China—"

"China? You've been to China? How on earth did you go from escaping impressment to traveling the world?"

He shook his head. "Another time."

"But—"

"I've something else for you." He handed her the papers.

Distracted from the inquiry, she took them with a baffled smile. "More presents? What is all this?"

"The contracts. Your fifteen thousand pounds. A few other items of business."

With a gasp, she bobbled the atlas in an attempt to get a better look at the papers. "How on earth did you get these so quickly?"

"It wasn't easy." He reached out and retrieved her book before she could drop it. "The special license alone cost more than—"

"Special license?" She dug through the papers, realized she had no idea what a special license looked like, or why she needed to know, and stopped in favor of gaping at Connor. "But we don't need a special license. We agreed to wait for the banns to be read."

"Yes, because you didn't want to be married by the blacksmith." He jerked his chin toward the papers. "Now we don't have to."

There had been a host of reasons to wait. She tried to remember them now as her heart galloped. "I . . . I don't have a gown. Isobel and I went to the modiste only yesterday."

"Wear the gown you had on when we met. Marry me today."

"No." She couldn't believe what she was hearing. "No, that was a ball gown. And I need to review the contracts and—"

"So review them," he suggested easily.

"What, now?"

"As good a time as any."

She shook her head. "I don't know anything about the law. A solicitor—"

"If I wanted to cheat you," Connor cut in with a hint of impatience, "I'd have seen to it the contract was too complicated to decipher, then I'd simply pay whichever solicitor you hired to say everything was on the up-and-up."

"Not *everyone* is susceptible to bribery," she grumbled.

"No, just enough to keep things moving along nicely," he said cheerfully. "Let's move this courtship along—"

"But you wanted a grand affair. You wanted an acre of flowers and your bride in the finest gown." She'd assumed he'd meant to make a great show of his victory over Sir Robert.

"I'll buy you a hundred fine gowns and watch you tend the garden." He smiled when she did. "I wanted to elope first, you'll recall."

"Yes, but I . . . I've made plans." Most notably, the plan to marry in a few weeks. "I cannot—"

"Change them. Every day you put it off is a risk, you know. I could be thrown from a horse on my way home, or change my mind and run off to Australia with the widow McClary tomorrow."

Mrs. McClary was old enough to be his grandmother. "She wouldn't have you. She's more particular in her taste than I."

While he chuckled at that, she considered his argument. What he said did make a sort of sense. He could change his mind. If he discovered the truth of why Sir Robert had courted her, he might very well change his mind. Then she would be out the fifteen thousand pounds as surely as if the contract was a lie, *and* she would be out of a husband.

Connor must have sensed her resolve was wavering. He set the atlas and papers on the ground and stepped closer, until the scent of him filled her senses. The fingers he trailed gently along her cheek were warm and lightly calloused. "Ashbury Hall is habitable now. All but the interior designer, architect, and a few craftsmen are gone. Most of the new windows are in. There's furniture, staff, a nursery all set up for George. I've a gardener—"

"You made up a nursery?"

"Were you expecting otherwise?"

"Well, no." Or possibly yes. She wasn't sure what she'd been expecting, but she'd not have been surprised if he'd not thought of George's needs. "It's only—"

"Everything is ready," Connor said softly. "Why wait?"

She thought through the matter with a mind for what was best for herself and her family, but quickly realized that, barring Connor taking a tragic fall from his horse, her decision would make very little difference in the long run. Whether she married Connor today or married him in a few weeks time, the end result would the same.

Except that, if she waited, there would no longer be a decision to make. She would wake on her wedding day knowing her only options were to arrive at the chapel and say her vows or send her family to ruin.

But today . . . She could marry by choice. It was an exceedingly loose definition of choice, a razor-thin veneer of control, but it was enough to bring a smile to her lips.

She could marry Connor today because she wanted to marry Connor today; there didn't need to be any other reason. There didn't have to be strings or expectations. She could do exactly as she liked.

"I want to change," she announced. "I want Isobel and George to be in attendance." She gathered up the stack of papers and all but shoved them into his chest.

"And I want you to sign the contracts."

Chapter 20

At the age of thirteen, Adelaide had briefly fancied herself in love with young Paul Montgomery, the son of a local farmer, and for three long weeks she had hounded her mother for the details of her parents' wedding day. Had there been music and flowers? Had she felt like a princess in a gown of silk and lace?

Her mother had answered with patience and humor. What she remembered was excitement, and nerves, and a great whirlwind of activity. The details would forever remain a blur.

Adelaide anticipated a similar experience on her own wedding day. Only there wasn't much in the way of activity. The only whirlwind was George, who strenuously objected to having to bathe and wear Sunday clothes on a Friday and made his displeasure known by leaping out of the tub and streaking about the house while screeching at the top of his lungs like a soapy, irate piglet.

It took a solid half hour to catch him, rinse off the soap, and wrestle him into his clothes.

There was little to be had in the way of excitement after

that. Unlike her mother, Adelaide wasn't in love with her bridegroom. She was, at best, cautiously fond of him.

She thought perhaps she might be a little excited, but it was difficult to determine the exact cause of her racing pulse and trembling hands. It could just as well have been nerves. Unable to identify the source of her anxiousness, she set aside the question of how she felt and focused on what needed to be done.

Practicality. That's what her wedding day was filled with.

She washed; she changed. Word was sent to Wolfgang at the tavern. No one expected a reply.

Connor left for Ashbury and returned with his carriage a few hours later to whisk them all to the small chapel where Adelaide had attended services all her life. She knew every detail of its one stained-glass window, and the backs of the pews she knew as well as the back of her own hand. The vicar was the same man who'd baptized her as an infant and patted her back years later when she'd been sick on his son.

Now she was standing before him at the altar as he spoke of fidelity and the sanctity of holy matrimony. He said something about wives and masters, as well. She pretended not to hear.

Another step, she reminded herself as her world spun. This was all merely one more step, and it had been her choice.

She said her vows. Connor said his. Isobel clapped when the vicar pronounced them man and wife. George bumped his head on a pew and howled. Michael Birch and Gregory O'Malley signed as witnesses.

And she was married. Just like that, she had a husband, a new life.

It was done.

"Well," she heard herself whisper in a daze. "Well."

Connor's large hand settled on her back, and his low laughter floated over her head. "Ready to leave, are you?"

She wanted to take offense at his amusement, but the presence of his touch and voice were welcomed anchors in her spinning world. Slowly, her mind began to clear as he ushered her outside into fresh air and the last light of evening. She felt nearly coherent when she thanked Gregory and Michael for their assistance and then climbed into the carriage with her family and Connor. And by the time they were rolling down her drive, she fancied herself quite . . . Well, herself.

She'd scarcely heard the words Connor had spoken to her at the altar, but she understood what he was saying to Isobel now. They should pack tonight, as he meant to send for the family tomorrow. Thinking that made perfect sense, she nodded as the carriage rolled to a stop in front of her home.

Isobel hopped out, scooped up a fidgeting George, and headed for the house. Adelaide rose from her seat, intending to follow. Should she pack her ivory muslin gown, she wondered, or had it become so discolored as to be unsalvageable?

An arm looped around her waist before she could so much as poke her head through the door.

Laughing, Connor pulled her back inside and onto the bench beside him. "Where do you think you're going, love?"

Stunned, she stared at him. "I . . . You said you'd send for us tomorrow. After we packed. You said it not two minutes ago."

"I said I'd retrieve the Ward family tomorrow—" He reached over and closed the door. "—Mrs. Brice."

It was then that she realized that she wasn't quite as clearheaded as she'd imagined. *Of course* he'd not meant for her to return with Isobel and George. Because she was his wife now. Because this was their wedding day. Because, oh, good heavens, it *wasn't* done.

Alarm shot through her at the belated realization that there was more to becoming a wife than going through the motions at a chapel. There were . . . other motions. Secret, wicked motions of which she had only the vaguest understanding.

"I . . ." Her eyes shot to the door again, and if the carriage hadn't begun moving at that very second, she may well have made a second attempt at escape.

Evidently, her thoughts were plain to see, because Connor slipped an arm under her knees and hauled her into his lap. Her alarm spiked to near panic. Did he mean to have it done in a carriage?

But that particular terror was short-lived. Connor gave no indication of taking premature—in her opinion—advantage of his marital rights. He pressed her cheek to his chest and draped his arms loosely about her waist. She felt his chin brush the top of her head.

"You'll not regret today," he said softly and moved his hand in gentle circles against her back.

Clearly, he wanted to soothe her. She wanted him to be successful. She feared they were both bound for disappointment.

She was surrounded by the scent of him, vividly aware of the hard beat of his heart and the latent power in his muscular frame. He was so much larger than her, stronger than her, and undoubtedly more knowledgeable of what was shared between husbands and wives.

She could think of nothing but him, of what he would do, and of what a shortsighted fool she'd been to ask her mother about her wedding day when she ought to have asked after the wedding night. Not her mother's wedding night, specifically, she was quick to amend—no one should be made to suffer the details of one's parents' wedding night—but *a* wedding night. She ought to have asked her mother what happened on *a* wedding night.

She wondered if she could ask Connor, and then wondered if asking was really necessary. While there were a good number of details that were unclear to her, she wasn't completely ignorant of the subject. The fundamental mechanics were known to her . . . somewhat.

Maybe she should have spoken with one of the village women, or even Isobel, whose insatiable curiosity had probably led her to acquire a book on the subject. Did they produce books on the subject? Blast, she ought to have asked someone about that.

Connor's lips brushed her hair. "Don't think so hard, sweetheart."

"I'm not."

A soft laugh rumbled in his chest. His thumb sought the inside of her elbow, stroking the delicate skin. "Close your eyes, wren. Relax."

She took a slow breath and concentrated on the gentleness of his touch and the careful, almost sheltering way he held her. It helped, a little. She wasn't relaxed when they reached Ashbury Hall, but neither was she quite so tempted to make a dash for home.

It also helped that the staff was not lined up for a formal welcome. In her opinion, the potential awkwardness in such a scenario was mind-boggling.

Thank you all for such a warm and generous welcome. As we all are perfectly aware, my first act as mistress of the house shall be to bed your master. Do excuse.

Good heavens.

Mrs. McKarnin and a maid were the only servants waiting inside. "Shall I take your gloves, ma'am?"

"What? No!" Adelaide grimaced when the housekeeper's eyes grew wide. "I beg your pardon, Mrs. McKarnin. What I meant to say is, thank you for the offer, but I shall retain my gloves for now." No article of clothing would be removed until such time as it became absolutely necessary. The fact that this was absolutely ludicrous was something she chose to ignore.

Mrs. McKarnin's expression softened to one of understanding. "As you like, ma'am. Is there naught I might do for you?"

"There is. Might I . . ." *Ask you some wildly inappropriate questions?* ". . . have a small glass of wine?"

Connor stepped up beside her. "I'll see to it, Mrs. McKarnin. Thank you."

He placed a warm hand on her back and urged her forward with subtle pressure. Adelaide had no choice but to follow where he led—across the great hall, up the stairs, and down the hall of the family wing. But to her surprise, Connor led her not into the master chambers but its adjoining sitting room. It was relatively smaller in size and less imposing than the rest of the house. The colors, mostly blues and greens, were softer here, the centered chaise lounge and set of upholstered chairs were feminine in design, and the wood in the room was stained a golden brown that glowed in the flickering candlelight.

She watched as Connor crossed the room to pour a small glass of Madeira at a sideboard and wondered if he'd had the room finished with her in mind. Then she wondered if he'd be willing to trade a night's reprieve for the chance to outfit his sitting room however he liked.

Oh, for pity's sake, she thought with a huff. Her fear was pushing her past ludicrous and straight into cowardice. With a long, steadying breath, she released the death grip she had on her skirts and gave herself a stern lecture.

She was being a ninny. Women became wives every day. Presumably, no one had ever died of the affliction. So, what was there to fear, really? A few moments of embarrassment and discomfort, that was all. Hadn't Connor bartered for ten times a day? It must go very quickly indeed if one could fit the deed in ten times a day.

Probably it was like the birds she'd spied in her mother's garden. A bit of flapping about and it was done.

"How bad could it be?"

Connor turned from the sidebar, a small glass in hand. "Beg your pardon?"

"Nothing," she chirped and forced her face into serene lines.

Expression tender, Connor crossed the room to her. "I don't want you to be afraid, Adelaide."

"I'm not."

He handed her the Madeira and said nothing, which was tantamount to calling her a liar.

"Very well," she conceded, "I am perhaps a little nervous. But I imagine it's rather like pulling a thorn from one's finger. The anticipation is worse than the deed. Grit one's teeth, a quick tug, and it's over and done."

"Over and done," he repeated.

"Yes." She nodded once, then reconsidered and grimaced. "I didn't mean to make that sound quite so much like I was anticipating an injury." Now that it was brought to mind, however, an injury did not seem outside the realm of possibility. "I'm sure it will be lovely." No, she wasn't. "But as we never got around to concluding the matter before, you should know . . ." She drank the contents of her glass in a single swallow. "I'll not do this ten times a day."

"Ten times . . ." Connor blinked, then closed his eyes on a groan. "Oh, hell."

"Oh, hell" was not the response she'd been hoping for. "I am willing to negotiate. A little."

Connor opened his eyes, took the glass from her, and set it aside, all without saying a word. Then he took her hand and spoke in a tone of patience, sympathy, and regret. "Adelaide. Sweetheart."

"Oh, dear."

She wanted to snatch her hand back and use it to cover his mouth. Nothing good ever came from a tone like that. It was the sort one used to deliver the news of illness and death and—

"I was jesting about the ten times."

"Oh." Well, that wasn't too terrible. She didn't care for having been the victim of his jest, but it was a relief to know she'd not be expected to—

"It's not like pulling out a thorn," Connor explained.

Relief vanished. She knew it was too much to hope that he meant it wouldn't hurt. "It's not done quickly, is it?"

His mouth curved. "Not when it's done well."

"Let's do it poorly," she suggested.

"You won't like it done poorly."

She was afraid she wasn't going to like it done any way. "Couldn't we try?"

Connor sighed. "You're afraid now."

"Well, I wasn't when I thought it would all be done in a rush," she muttered.

"There will be a rush."

"I don't understand—"

"Never mind." He brushed the hair back from her face. "Do you trust me, Adelaide?"

Oh, dear, not this again. "If you're asking if I trust you to make a fair job of . . ." She waved her hand in the direction of the chambers. ". . . *that*, then I suppose I really haven't a choice."

There was a pause before he said, in a very dry tone, "You make me feel like a king."

"Would you prefer I be dishonest?"

"Let's try this again," he suggested, a heartbeat before he slipped a hand behind her neck and brought his mouth down on hers.

Instinctively, she wedged her hands up between them. They fluttered indecisively, then settled on his coat lapels as his lips moved over hers with gentle, coaxing pressure. For a moment, she was reminded of their first kiss in the garden when he'd tempted and teased her into a willing submission. But it took only another brush of his lips, another careful sweep of his tongue, for the comparison to fade away. This kiss was nothing like any that had come before. There was no demand, no maneuvering. He kissed her not with determined patience, but with a tenderness that seemed infinite.

A heavy warmth settled over her tingling skin and seeped inside, stealing the strength from her limbs. She let herself lean against him, and his arm slid around her waist, pulling her closer so he could take her weight. His mouth left hers to trail feather-soft kisses across her cheek. He pressed his lips to her temple and tasted the sensitive skin along her jaw.

She shivered when he reached the delicate lobe of her ear, then gasped when he tugged gently with his teeth.

Connor whispered against her skin, "You like this part, don't you?"

"Yes."

He toyed with her now, finding the spots along her neck that made her tremble. "The rest is just like it . . . Only more . . . Let me."

She felt herself give a shaky nod, and in a single, fluid motion, he swept her into his arms.

Dimly, she was aware of being brought into the bedchamber, of more glowing candlelight and the faint crackle of fire. Her world dissolved into a languid series of sensations—the slide of her feet to the floor, the pressure of his mouth on her neck, the thick silk of his hair in her fingers. As the warmth progressed to heat, she grew restless, anxious for the next touch, the next shivering pleasure. But Connor remained relentlessly, maddeningly slow in his seduction. He undressed her leisurely, stopping to taste and touch every inch of newly exposed flesh. Gently, he drew her trembling hands away when she tried to help, tried to make him hurry.

"This way," he whispered and swallowed her whimpering protest with his mouth. "My way."

Despite the warm air in the room, she knew a moment's chill when he slipped her chemise over her head. Connor laid her on the bed, and the chill was banished by the hard heat of his body settling over hers. The feel and scent of him enveloped her . . . The faint aroma of sandalwood, the soft bristle of the hair on his chest, the heat of his hands as they glided over her skin.

He brushed her thigh and sought the heat between her legs. She squirmed beneath him, caught between desire and embarrassment.

"Connor . . ."

"Shh, love . . . let me."

She stopped struggling and gasped at the first smooth glide of his fingers. Deftly, he stroked and teased until the pleasure turned into a delicious ache, and the ache became a desperate need. She moaned and strained beneath him, grabbing at his shoulders, his hair, any part of him she could reach. Connor dipped his head to draw a nipple into his mouth, and suddenly the need was pleasure once more—a great solid wave of it that drew every muscle of her body tight as it crashed over her and left her dizzy and panting in its wake.

On a shuddering sigh, she lifted her lids and found herself staring into Connor's hooded green eyes. They were dark with passion, glittering with triumph, and filled with warmth.

His hands slid under her knees. "Put your legs around . . . that's it."

He shifted his weight and pressed into her slowly. There was pain, but it was slight. It did nothing to diminish the extraordinary feeling of Connor's body moving over hers or her desire to rush headlong into the next sensation, the next wave of pleasure. Until he muttered something against her hair and pushed himself inside her with a long, determined thrust of his hips.

Suddenly, the moment was no longer quite so enchanting.

She dug her nails into his shoulder and cried out. "Oh! Ouch!"

Connor went perfectly still but for the heavy rise and fall of his chest. "I'm sorry. Darling, I'm sorry. It had to be done."

Done was exactly what she wanted to hear, and exactly what she intended to be. She shoved at him. He wouldn't budge.

"Connor—"

"Lie easy, sweetheart." He bent his head and brushed his lips across hers. "Lie easy and wait. It will get better. I promise."

He kissed her again, slow and deep, and the pain ebbed into mild discomfort. His hands skimmed over her skin, reigniting fires that had been doused. They were flickering sparks at first, then little flames that licked and teased and finally burst into life. Cautious, she ran her hands up the hard bands of muscles in his arms, and down the smooth plane of his back. She heard the rough catch and release of his breath, and she felt the violent beat of his heart against her palms.

Connor trailed kisses up her neck, across her jaw. "Better?"

"Yes." The discomfort was all but gone, replaced by the inexplicable need to move. "I think . . . I want . . ."

"I know." Carefully, he withdrew partway, then slid inside again.

"Oh."

His lips curved in a wicked smile. "Better?"

She couldn't answer. He moved again, beginning a steady rhythm of gentle invasion and retreat that robbed her of speech. The ache and need returned, different this time. Tentatively, she arched up to meet him and was rewarded with a low masculine groan. Connor dropped his head, burying his face in her hair. His movements grew faster, more forceful, and still they weren't fast enough, or slow enough, or something. She needed *something*.

"I need . . . Connor, I need . . ."

"Shh. I know."

He reached down to stroke her where their bodies were joined. Pleasure broke over her, wave after astonishing wave of it. And just as she began to surface, Connor gathered her close, thrust deep, and shuddered in her arms.

Chapter 21

*A*delaide opened her eyes and squinted against the early morning light that snuck around the edges of the drapes. Not quite half awake, she rolled onto her back to escape the glare and stretched the aching muscles in her legs. The softness of new linen caressed her bare skin. She nearly moaned with appreciation . . . Until she remembered *why* she was bare-legged in a bed covered with soft linen and not tangled up in her scratchy wool blanket and perfectly ancient night rail.

She was married. She was a wife.

She rolled her head on the pillow and found Connor fast asleep beside her.

Good God, she had a husband.

A bubble of laughter formed in her throat, the sort that came when one teetered between outrageous delight and outright panic. She swallowed the laughter and the panic. The first because she didn't wish to wake Connor, and the latter because she recognized it as illogical and useless.

The next step, that was what she needed to think of now. Only she ran into a spot of difficulty concentrating on the next step. It was far more interesting to focus on the step she'd taken last night.

Her wedding night had been a whirlwind of discovery. What they'd done . . . What *she* had done . . . Wanton did not begin to describe her behavior. Probably, she should be ashamed. At the very least, she should feel embarrassed. She didn't. She felt deliciously wicked, enormously pleased with herself, and wildly curious about the man sleeping next to her.

Connor was her husband. She'd married him and shared a bed with him. And yet she knew so little about him.

Her gaze trailed over his prone form, searching for details. He slept on his stomach, his arms under the pillow and legs sprawled out—taking up far more than half the bed, she noted. Dark blond lashes, thick and long enough to ignite a silly spark of envy in her, rested on skin pale by heritage and lightly tanned by the sun. He had a tiny scar at the hairline, and a large one that started at the base of his left shoulder blade and formed a two-inch, jagged trail down his back before disappearing under the sheet. She frowned at it, wondering what sort of injury had caused it, and how terribly the wound must have hurt. It was a stark reminder to her that he'd not always had soft sheets to sleep on, that his life had been bleak for a time.

Dark images filled her mind. There were an infinite number of ways the injury may have occurred. Connor had been little more than a boy when he'd been impressed. And while her knowledge of maritime life was limited in the extreme, she'd heard a tale or two of the awful things that could occur aboard a warship.

The scar might be from a captain's whip or a shipmate's knife. Connor might have been wounded in battle, or—

"Guarding my sleep, love?"

Connor's voice, gruff from sleep, banished the disturbing thoughts. Her gaze snapped to his face, and she found his hooded green eyes studying her as closely as she'd been studying him.

Suddenly embarrassed, she cleared her throat and picked a spot on the wall behind him to stare at. "Certainly not."

"Relieved to hear it, as that's my duty." He rolled over and absently dragged a hand through his hair before crossing his arms behind his head. "What were you thinking just now? I could hear the wheels and cogs turning in your head."

"I was wondering how you'd been hurt," she replied, seeing no need to lie. How was she to learn more about him if she never asked? She shrugged when his eyebrows winged up. "You've a scar on your back."

"Ah. A fall from a horse in my youth. I took a tumble down a rocky slope."

"Oh." That . . . was not what she had envisioned.

Connor laughed, reached up, and pulled her down on top of him. "You were expecting a different story."

"I thought . . ." She twisted to keep from elbowing him in the ribs. "You were impressed."

"I was." He settled her against his side, his arms wrapped loosely around her shoulders. "There's more than one sort of injury, sweet."

And more than one kind of scar, Adelaide thought. She squirmed a little, trying to find a position that would allow her to see his face, but it wasn't possible to do without either throwing his arms off or acquiring a kink in her neck. Giving up, she rested her cheek against his hard chest.

She wanted to ask him about the sort of scars he had but thought it might be a topic better suited for another time. Perhaps when they were more accustomed to one another.

"How did you go from being impressed to having all this?" she asked instead.

His arms tightened around her. "Well, I saw it, decided I should have it, compromised it in a garden, and that was—"

"That is not what I meant." She laughed. She lifted a hand and gestured at the room. "I mean, *all this*."

"Yes, I know." She felt him shrug. "I've a head for the shipping business."

"But how did you go from impressed to shipping?"

"Luck, hard work, determination. Mostly luck."

She stifled a sigh at his evasiveness. Connor was not the sort of man one could press. Which was unfortunate, because she was the sort of woman who couldn't refrain from pressing.

"Might you be a bit more specific?"

"Another time." In a quick, sure move, he rolled her onto her back and ranged himself over her. Sharp green eyes searched her face. "How do you feel this morning?"

"Oh, quite well." She liked the feel of him pressing her into the mattress, his legs tangled with hers, and his strong arms bracketed on either side of her like a protective cage. Suddenly, she felt better than well. She felt . . . interested. With a shy smile, she put her arms around him and let her fingers drift over the warm skin and taut muscles of his back.

Connor made a low hum of appreciation, and she watched, fascinated, as his eyes darkened with desire. Lowering his head, he took her mouth in a long, languid kiss.

Pleasure settled over her, seeping into her blood, but just as it began to grow, Connor pulled away. "Enough," he said thickly. "That's enough, sweet."

Her hands stilled. "Why?"

"Because . . ." Hooded eyes fastened on her mouth. His chest rose and fell raggedly. "Because . . . Damn it, one more."

He took her mouth again, deeper and harder this time, as if he were trying to draw something out of her. Wanting to help, she shifted and felt the heavy heat of his arousal brush against her stomach.

Connor pulled away with a groan. "Holy hell, that's enough. It's too soon."

"Too soon?" she echoed in a daze and glanced at the window. "Because it's morning, do you mean? Is . . . Is it not the done thing?"

He blinked once, then quickly turned his face away . . . But not before she saw the smile.

"Are you laughing at me?" she demanded with mock outrage.

His shoulders shook.

"You are!"

"God, yes, I'm sorry." He faced her, his handsome features lit with a combination of laughter, arousal, and affection. "It's too soon after your first time, sweetheart. That's what I meant."

"Oh." She blushed a little and tried to hide her disappointment. "Are you . . . quite sure?"

"As I've never been a maiden, myself . . . No, I'm not sure." He pressed a quick kiss to her lips and with a small, rueful groan left the circle of her arms. "But we'll not risk it."

He rolled from the bed and padded, with a remarkable lack of self-consciousness, across the room to a wardrobe. Adelaide couldn't help but stare—at the powerful legs, the tawny skin, and the firm muscle of his buttocks. Mostly she stared at his buttocks. For reasons that eluded her, she found his backside absolutely riveting. And she was more than a little sorry when Connor slipped his arms through the sleeves of a robe, depriving her of the view.

"Shouldn't I have a say in what can be risked?" she asked, gathering the counterpane around her.

"Certainly," Connor agreed easily. "And though I'll not change my mind, I've no objection to hearing a beautiful woman beg for—"

"Never mind," she drawled and rolled her eyes when he laughed.

Keeping a firm hold on the counterpane, she slipped her feet off the bed and retrieved her chemise from where it had been left on the floor the night before. She felt silly dragging the blanket along like a queen with a train, but there was deliciously wicked, and then there was parading about the room without a stitch of clothing. In her mind, the line between the two was quite distinct.

It took some doing, but she eventually succeeded in pulling the chemise over her head without letting go of the counterpane. When she emerged from the material, she found Connor regarding her with baffled amusement.

"Was that really necessary?"

"Yes." Refusing to feel foolish over something as perfectly natural as modesty, she dropped the counterpane and worked her arms through the sleeves of her chemise.

"You might have asked me to turn my back," he pointed out. "Or for a robe."

"Well, if you're seeking to help, you may assist me into my gown."

He obliged, helping her into the dress and working the buttons up her back with the deft efficiency of a lady's maid. Adelaide thought it might be best not to dwell on how he came by such a skill.

She rubbed her palm along the muslin at her waist. It was the same gown she'd been married in, and the same gown she'd been wearing the first time she'd seen Connor in the light of day. It felt strange to be wearing it now.

"Connor?"

He brushed her hair over her shoulder and pressed his lips to the base of her neck. Her skin prickled and warmed.

"Hmm?"

"Why did you marry me?"

His mouth stilled against her neck. "You know why."

"You told me it was for revenge. And you've told me you wanted me."

"So I did." His breath was warm and moist against her skin. "So I do."

"Either one of those . . ." She licked her lips and wondered if it was the sensations he was stirring in her or her own nerves that had caused them to go dry. "Both of those could have—"

"Been had another way," he finished for her. The heat of his mouth disappeared from her neck, leaving the spot he'd kissed damp and chilled.

"Yes. It would have been just as devastating to Sir Robert if you'd made me your mistress."

Taking gentle hold of her arm, he turned her about to face him. His eyes searched her face but betrayed nothing of what he was thinking. "Would you have agreed to become my mistress?"

Not initially, she thought. But once she'd learned of Sir Robert's true nature . . . If it had been the only way to save her family . . . She didn't know.

"No," she said, simply because she thought it was expected.

He nodded once, his expression inscrutable. "There you are."

She wasn't sure what answer she'd been hoping for, but clearly "there you are" wasn't it. A large, uncomfortable knot formed in her chest. The cold at her neck spread, seeping under the skin.

Forcing a smile and brisk tone, she stepped away from him, needing distance. "Well, that makes sense, doesn't it?"

"Adelaide—"

"Do you know, I think perhaps I'll take a stroll in the garden this morning. We'll not have such fine weather for much longer, and it seems a pity not to take advantage of every—"

He caught her arm before she could reach the door. "Are we having an argument?"

She closed her eyes on a sigh. She didn't want to argue anymore. She'd had enough anger and ill will to fill a lifetime. He'd not lied about his reasons for wanting marriage, and there was nothing to be gained from condemning him for those reasons now.

"No." She turned on her own and met his eyes. "There's nothing to argue about. I want a walk, that's all."

A crease formed between his brows, but he nodded and let his hand fall away.

Adelaide made herself smile once more before taking her leave.

For nearly an hour, she wandered about the grounds of

Ashbury Hall, taking in what progress had been made in taming the lawn and gardens and allowing the easy exercise and soft morning air to settle her worries, or at least brush them away for a time.

A gardener was already in residence, and she knew an architect had been hired and plans were being drawn up for the gardens. They were large plans, elaborate plans. Ashbury Hall was a grand manor, and it would have the grounds to match.

She walked along the south side of the house and found that a small section of the garden had already been cleared of weeds and turned over. There was enough room for a small fountain. A few stone benches would be lovely there as well, she mused. The light was perfect for dahlias. She'd never tried to grow them before, but—

Connor's voice pulled her from her musings. "Do you like the spot?"

She glanced over her shoulder and smiled, pleased to discover her walk had been effective in relieving her of her odd mood. "I'm sure it will be a fine garden."

"It's yours."

"Yes." She looked around her, studying the grounds. She was mistress of Ashbury Hall now, though that fact seemed distant and surreal to her. "There's quite a bit for the architect and gardener to see done, but—"

"No, I mean . . ." He gestured at the tilled earth. "That. On this side of the house. It's yours."

"The dirt?"

Connor lifted a fist to his mouth and cleared his throat. Then he tugged a bit on his cravat. Then he caught his hands behind his back as if suddenly aware that he was fidgeting.

She stared at him with wonder. My goodness, she thought, was he embarrassed?

"I had work begin on it yesterday," he explained. "When I returned to retrieve the carriage. I thought you might like to have a part of the garden all your own. To do with as you liked."

The last of the chill that had come upon her in their chambers melted away. She wasn't sure if Connor was trying to spoil her, bribe her, make amends, or all three. But she was quite certain she liked it. Whatever his past misdeeds, and whatever his motivations now, he was trying to make things comfortable between them. She rather thought that ought to count for something.

She stretched up and placed a chaste kiss on his cheek. "Thank you."

"You're welcome." He slipped a hand around her neck and pulled her mouth to his for a long, searing kiss that left her breathless and overheated. "Thought it might be wise to take advantage of our privacy, while we still had it," he said when at last he released her. "I've sent a carriage to fetch your family."

"Oh." She blinked, trying to see past the haze of passion. It didn't work.

But then she heard Connor say, "Wolfgang means to come."

Which was quite effective in dousing her ardor.

"Oh." She managed a half smile when Connor chuckled. "How can you be certain?"

"I spoke with him about it at the prison."

"What did you say?"

"That a move to Ashbury came with an allowance."

"Bribery again?" That didn't surprise her as much as why the bribe had been made. She'd have thought Connor would pay good money to keep Wolfgang out of his home.

"A compromise," Connor countered. "He needs funds. I want to keep a close eye on him until we can be sure he's spending those funds wisely."

"You didn't tell him that, did you?" She could only imagine her brother's reaction to such a slight.

"Give me some credit, love. I told him his family needed him." He kissed the top of her head and toyed with a lock of her hair. "And that he'd find his childhood home a mite inhospitable once repairs began on the roof."

"Repairs?"

"They begin next week. The parlor doors are to be replaced

immediately." He gave her a pointed look. "And that cherry-wood chair is going into the fire."

She broke into laughter and thought, oh, yes, he was try-ing. "I should have guessed you'd known what I was about. We can't burn it. It's an heirloom."

"The attic then," he agreed easily and bent to give her another quick kiss. "I'll leave you to your walk."

She almost asked him to stay but bit back the request at the last second. She no longer wanted a walk or needed to clear her thoughts, but she did want just a moment more of solitude.

After he disappeared into the house, Adelaide made a slow survey of her surroundings, seeing it all in a different light. This was hers. The house, the grounds, the plot of dirt, and the fifteen thousand pounds in the bank—they were all hers.

For years she had been weighed with the worries of what would become of her family. For weeks she had faced an unknown and unexpected future. Now that future had arrived . . . and it was wonderful. She was safe. They were all safe. There would never be a poorhouse, never be another creditor at her door. Isobel would have new gowns, new books, a world of opportunities opened to her. George would have a proper nanny, the finest tutors when the time came, and all the biscuits he could eat. And Wolfgang . . . Wolfgang would come around. She was sure of it.

For the first time in longer than she could remember, she felt free—well and truly free. A giddiness washed over her. She heard her own laughter echo back from the woods across the lawn. And like a small child at play, she threw her arms wide and spun in circles.

Connor watched Adelaide spin in the garden. From his position in front of the window in his second-floor study, he could make out the twirling folds of her skirt and the strands of auburn that sunlight wove into her hair. The soft lilt of her laughter filtered through the glass and soothed the tightness in his chest.

The night before had been his every fantasy come to life, but the morning had not gone quite as he'd hoped.

There you go.

In retrospect, that had not been his finest display of charm. But holy hell, the woman liked to press.

How had he been injured? How had he gone from impressment to shipping? Why had he married her? Why had he not made her his mistress? The questions, and the patient way she had pressed for answers, had unnerved him.

She wanted him to share.

Unfortunately for the both of them, sharing was not something he did well. Connor made it a point to avoid contemplation of his shortcomings, but of his myriad forms of selfishness, he was perfectly aware. He was generous with money and goods because he could afford to give them away without risk or inconvenience to himself.

But Adelaide, he was afraid, wanted him to give a piece of himself. It was an expectation he wasn't sure he could fill, or fake.

He didn't know how to be generous in that way. It had never been required of him. He'd not been raised with siblings. His parents, though he knew they loved him, had been reserved in their affections. The mistresses he'd had over the years had been content with his time and expensive trinkets. And his men . . . Well, they were his men. Mostly they spoke of women, drink, and their desire to stick Sir Robert's head on pike.

No one had ever asked more of him than he'd been comfortable giving.

For now, Adelaide seemed appeased by his gift of the garden. And perhaps that would be the key to keeping her happy, keeping them both happy—bribery, distraction, and careful distance.

He hoped it would be enough. He hoped she'd not ask so many questions.

Because, God's truth, he wasn't sure she'd like the answers.

Chapter 22

If Adelaide's wedding night had been a whirlwind of discovery, the first week of marriage was an education.

The day after the Wards' arrival, Connor took all but Wolfgang—who chose to remain in his chambers—into town so Adelaide could fulfill her wish of spoiling her nephew and sister with sweets and art supplies. As Adelaide had predicted, George fell asleep before he could make himself ill. Isobel took her paint and easel outside and, for the next six days, spent every hour of sunlight in the garden, hunting for blooms to paint.

Adelaide found pleasure in her own hobbies. She began the delightful task of planning her own garden, and in a moment of rare spontaneity, she asked the stable master to teach her how to ride. But with so many other duties requiring her attention, it wasn't often she found time for herself.

Major repairs on the house had been completed, but there was still some work to be done, and the decorator seemed to need her approval for every new drape and scrap of wallpaper he wished to order. The staff required the more mundane, but no less time-consuming, sort of directions always needed for the daily management of a large home. New clothes had to be purchased for the entire family. Letters had to be written to Lilly and Winnefred. A nanny had to be found for George, and she'd hoped to draw Wolfgang out of his bad temper by involving him in the process, but he demonstrated a distinct lack of enthusiasm for the task.

"What the devil do I know of nannies?" was his response. They were, in fact, the only words he spoke to Adelaide in the course of the week. He kept to his chambers in the day, and the town's tavern at night.

At Connor's urging, she let the matter go without argument. If Wolfgang wished to lick his wounded pride with a bitter tongue, he was welcome to do it alone.

And really, George didn't need a nanny right this moment. He was thriving in his new home, and there was no shortage of people willing, even eager, to watch over him in the interim.

The staff and residents of Ashbury Hall were enamored with the child, none more so than Michael, Gregory, and Graham. They lavished attention on the boy and seemed especially fond of picking him up and tossing him in the air like a sack of flour. Adelaide nearly fainted the first time Gregory did this, but the old man caught George without so much as a grunt for the effort, proving he was stronger and quicker than he appeared.

It was strange sharing a house with grown men to whom she was not related, and who were neither staff nor guests. Connor treated Michael and Gregory like family, but while Adelaide came to enjoy the men's easy smiles and gentle bickering, she still didn't fully trust them.

The air of secrecy surrounded them. And Connor. And a good portion of everything they did.

Connor spent hours every day behind the closed doors of his study. Sometimes he preferred his own council, but typically he met with his men and the low murmur of male voices would drift into the hall and down into the front parlor. For reasons she neither understood nor cared to examine too closely, Adelaide found the sound agreeable and often created excuses to sit in the parlor when the men were above stairs. Though their words were unintelligible, it was easy to distinguish who was speaking when. She listened for the distinct and familiar cadence of Connor's deep voice.

Adelaide wondered if she would not be so inclined to listen for the sound of him if only he were more readily available in the flesh. And by that, she did not mean available for concerns of the flesh. Connor was certainly accessible for that. Every night, as it happened. And every morning. She was fairly sure he'd become available during the day given half the provocation. He was, in that regard—and to her unqualified delight—unfailingly attentive.

In fact, he was attentive in all regards . . . when he was around. He rarely missed breakfast or dinner, but often the noon meal and tea. If she stopped him in the hall to ask a question, or brought a concern to his attention before bed, he listened carefully and offered thoughtful answers or sound advice. If she wanted to ask him a question while he was with his men, however, she had to wait. Connor didn't expressly ban her from his study, nor forbid her from interrupting, but given his tremendous need for revenge, she imagined any disruption would be poorly received.

She wasn't sure how she felt about the arrangement. She had no reason for complaint. Connor wasn't neglecting his duties as a husband, and yet she couldn't help but feel a sliver of discontent every time he disappeared into his study with his men. And the grim smiles of satisfaction she saw on his face when he emerged again only increased her unease. Because, really, "grim" was not a word that should be applicable to any aspect of a marriage in its first week.

But more than that, she was afraid for him, of what risks he might be taking. How far was he willing to go in his hunt for revenge, and what if the search led him back to prison or, God forbid, to the gallows? What if it led to nothing at all? How long would he dedicate his life to vengeance, to the exclusion of nearly everything else . . . including her?

She tried reminding herself that she'd known from the start where Connor's priorities lay. She'd entered into marriage knowing full well what to expect. But none of these were effective in softening the troubling truth.

For the first time, in a very long time, she hoped for something more.

Marriage to Adelaide was all that he had hoped. Connor arrived at this conclusion as he walked down the second floor of the family wing.

In fact, marriage was more than he had hoped. He'd imagined it would be a pleasant and satisfying state of affairs. What he'd not expected was the sheer convenience of it all.

What color fabric did he want for the sitting room drapes? Ask my wife.

Should it be lamb or beef for dinner? Ask my wife.

A dispute between the maids? A problem with the gardener? A yen for a beautiful woman in his arms? They were all issues Adelaide was available to address at a moment's notice.

Bloody brilliant institution, marriage.

In truth, his one and only disappointment was that Adelaide's accessibility had failed to improve his ability to concentrate. He needed only to catch a hint of her scent in a room or hear the lilt of her laugh through a wall and his thoughts veered toward the extra hour he'd enjoyed in bed with her that morning, or the delights of the night to come, or the possibility of an afternoon steeped in pleasure—he'd not tried that particular convenience as yet, but he did like thinking about it.

He began to think of it now, and had just arrived at the particularly agreeable bit in which Adelaide crooked a finger at him, when a soft sniffle and small movement in an open doorway caught his attention. Turning, Connor spied George sitting on the floor in one of the extra family bedchambers. His eyes and nose were red, and fat tears slid down his cheeks.

Something akin to fear skittered up Connor's spine. He ruthlessly shoved it aside. Children cried. It was just something they did. There was no reason for panic. No reason at all, he silently repeated as he stepped forward, then back, then forward again. And he repeated it yet again after he finally managed to cross the room, only to stand and stare helplessly at the top of the boy's head like a towering idiot.

"Don't do that."

In deference to the child's age, Connor issued the order in what he measured to be a gentle tone of voice. Evidently, the child did not agree. George looked up, widened his eyes, and burst into an earsplitting wail.

"Good God." Connor wiggled his jaw, half expecting his ears to pop. "Don't do that either."

He crouched down, which seemed to have a calming effect on George, who traded his wails for sobs. Emboldened by the small victory, Connor took a deep breath, reached out, and gave the boy a bolstering pat on the arm.

George slumped to the floor like a deflated soufflé.

Mother of God.

Now there was reason for panic. He gripped George by the shoulders and quickly tried to right him again. George crumpled back to the floor.

He tried again with the same results. "Bloody hell. Sit up."

Wincing, he berated himself for the slip of tongue. First he'd knocked the child to the ground. Now he was swearing at him. Well done.

Where the devil was his staff? Where the devil was Adelaide?

"Stop this . . . George . . . This is no way to behave. Do you want the maids to think you're an infant?"

The sobbing came to an abrupt stop. Slowly, and to Connor's considerable relief, George pushed himself into a sitting position and sniffled loudly. "Not infant."

"Certainly not," Connor was quick to assure him. In truth, he was prepared to agree with anything the boy cared to say. Anything at all. So long as it kept the crying at bay. He put his hand out to pat the child, then quickly snatched it back. "Not an infant."

George sniffed loudly and tilted his head in a quizzical manner. "Naughty."

"Are you referring to me or yourself?" He shook his head at George's blank stare. Odds were he meant the swearing, and the sooner that was forgotten, the better. "Never mind. What's put you in such a state?"

When that failed to produce an answer, Connor tried rephrasing. "What's wrong, George? . . . What is the matter?"

Nothing. The child just sat there, staring at him with big, wet eyes, sopping cheeks, and an objectionable amount of fluid leaking from his nose.

Connor tried enunciating each word slowly and carefully as he pulled out a handkerchief and mopped George's face. "Why . . . are . . . you . . . ?" He stopped, a disturbing thought occurring to him. "You haven't . . . You're not still in nappies, are you?"

"Ouch," George said all of sudden. He threw his elbow up, nearly catching Connor in the chin, and pointed to a patch of skin on his forearm.

Connor pulled back and stared at the spot. He couldn't find a damn thing wrong with it, which left him guessing at what he was supposed to do next. But at least it wasn't a dirty nappy.

"I see," he lied.

Oh, hell. Was he supposed to kiss it? He hoped, *fervently* hoped, he would not have to kiss it.

"Kiss."

Damn.

"It appears to be a mild injury, George. Why don't we find your aunt—?"

George's lips trembled. *"Kiss."*

Connor kissed it and was rewarded with a wide grin from George.

Well . . . there you go, he thought. That wasn't so difficult. Nothing to it, really. And since no one had been about to witness the moment, nothing lost.

"Well done, Connor."

He turned, slowly, and found Adelaide standing in the doorway, her soft brown eyes laughing.

"How long have you been standing there?"

"Not long."

But long enough, he imagined, to have spared him the indignity of playing nursemaid. "You might have said something."

"Yes." Her lips curved up. "I might have."

Gaining his feet, he sent her a surly look. "Am I this irritating when I'm being smug?"

"Twice as," she assured him.

"Excellent."

Adelaide laughed softly and crossed the room to George. She scooped him up, planted a kiss on his arguably injured elbow, and then gave him a reprimanding scowl. "Do you know why you have an ouch, darling? Because you were poking about in here instead of sleeping in the nursery as you were told."

Connor doubted the boy fully understood what was being said. But the word "sleep" seemed to hit a chord.

"No! Down!" He squirmed in Adelaide's arms, but to no avail.

"Oh, yes. Down."

Ignoring the new round of wails that followed, she walked over and tugged on a bellpull. Connor glowered at the rope. Why the devil hadn't he thought of the bellpull?

He was still glowering a moment later when a maid answered and relieved Adelaide of her loud burden.

"You're still not entirely comfortable with him, are you?" Adelaide asked after the maid left.

The comment made him feel unaccountably defensive. "I am fond of him."

"Yes, I know. I didn't mean it as a criticism." She walked over to the bed and leaned against one of the posters. "Merely an observation. Didn't they have small children in Boston?"

"Yes." He wanted to roll the sudden tension out of his

shoulders. "But they were different. They weren't quite so . . ."

"Quite so what?" Adelaide prompted.

His, he thought. They weren't quite so *his*. "Innocent."

"All children are innocent."

"You've not been to the back alleys of Boston."

"All children," she repeated, and then studied him with a quiet intensity that made him uneasy. "It must have been hard for you there. You were hardly more than a boy yourself."

The tension grew, pulling taut. "I was a teenager, not a child."

"Debatable," she murmured. "How old were you when you met Gregory and Michael?"

She asked the question casually, but he knew she was pressing for information about his past. "Still a teenager."

"You don't remember, exactly?"

He remembered; he just didn't want to encourage the line of questioning.

"I was nine months past my fifteenth birthday when I escaped the ship," he replied stiffly, hoping a quick response would put an end to the topic. "And four months past sixteen when I met Gregory and Michael. Life before them was difficult, but life after was not. I had food, shelter, and two savvy adults looking out for my welfare."

"Will you tell me what it was like in the press-gang?"

"No." *Hell, no.*

"Why not?"

"Because you can imagine it for yourself." The hardships and deprivations impressed sailors experienced were hardly secret. There was no shortage of other men who were willing to speak of the constant hunger, the brutal cold of winter and stomach-churning heat of summer, the endless hours of hard labor, and the biting humiliation of knowing you were as expendable as the powder stuffed into the cannons. If she wanted specifics, she could find them somewhere else.

"You don't like to speak of it," she guessed.

"Remembering is not always best." He'd come to terms with those dark months and banished the fear and nightmares that had plagued him for years after his escape. Damn if he would invite them back so her curiosity might be assuaged.

He waited for an argument, but she surprised him by nodding as if she understood. "Will you tell me of Boston, then? Of you and Gregory and Michael?"

Bloody hell, she was like a dog with a bone. "You want to know what sort of business we ran," he guessed.

She tilted her head at him. "Is there a reason I shouldn't know?"

He could name any number of reasons, but none that would put her off for the next thirty to forty years of marriage. He rolled the tension out of his shoulders and decided he didn't care what she knew. There was nothing he'd done in Boston that he wouldn't do again. He'd never killed anyone, never stolen food from the mouths of babes. He wasn't ashamed of his past.

If Adelaide didn't care for the answers to her questions . . . Well, there wasn't much she could do about it now, was there? She'd signed the contract, said her vows, and taken her fifteen thousand pounds. It was too late for second thoughts.

Adelaide watched with uneasy fascination as the man she'd witnessed kissing a little boy's ouch transformed into the remote, apathetic man she'd met in the widow's cottage. A coldness settled over his face as he moved to lean a hip against a writing desk and fold his arms over his chest.

"Forgeries," he said suddenly and gave a careless lift of his shoulder. "We made forgeries."

Her eyes widened. She'd expected something a mite untoward, not wholly criminal. "You said you weren't wanted for any crime in any country."

"I'm not. We were never suspected of wrongdoing, let alone charged."

"Oh." She blew out a short breath, with the ridiculous hope it might ease the tight knot in her belly. "Well, what sort of forgeries did you make?"

"Deeds. Wills. Even a marriage certificate once." Another shrug. "Whatever the customer was willing to pay for."

"Did . . ." She swallowed past a ball of fear in her throat. "Did you forge money?"

His mouth hooked up in a patronizing smile. "That's counterfeiting, love. Different skill, entirely."

She gave a small, breathless laugh. "Needleworking and horsemanship are skills, Connor. Forgery is a crime."

In some cases, like counterfeiting, it was a hanging offense. The thought of Connor being dragged back to prison and then onto the gallows made her mouth go dry and her stomach roll. Hoping to relieve the discomfort, she straightened from the poster and walked to the nearest window.

"You're pale," Connor said, sounding more angry than sympathetic.

"Well, what did you expect?" She pushed the window open and let the fresh air cool her skin. "This is disturbing news."

"It's too late for you to back out of this marriage." His voice took on a hard edge. "I won't allow it. Do you understand?"

She turned to face him, stunned not by his sudden anger but by the whisper of fear she heard beneath. At first glance, he looked to have not moved an inch. But upon closer inspection, she saw that he'd lowered his head, just a little, and his fingers were digging into the fabric at his sleeves.

"I have no intention of backing out of this marriage," she said carefully, certain her words were important, even if she wasn't certain why. He had to know she wouldn't leave. For pity's sake, she'd married him after he'd broken into Mrs. Cress's home—which occurred very shortly after he'd been cleared of charges of highway robbery—for the express purpose of stealing another man's intended through trickery and deceit. What was a bit of forgery tossed into that unholy mess?

"But you'd like to," Connor guessed with a sneer.

"What I would like is for you to cease making assumptions long enough for me to get a thought in edgewise," she snapped, losing patience.

His lips curved up, but there was no humor in the smile. "What is it you want to say?"

"To know, actually. I want to know if that is how you acquired your entire fortune." Is that where her fifteen thousand pounds had come from? Is that how he paid her brother's debts and bought manors like Ashbury Hall? "Are you still making forgeries?"

"You can rest easy, wren. We made a small profit as criminals, but it was shipping that built our fortune. I've not sold a forgery in more than a decade."

Oh, thank heavens. "Why did you stop?"

"We were careful, but there is always risk. Once we had the funds to invest in other ventures, it made sense to be rid of the risk. Simple as that."

She found herself picking at the folds of the drapes and forced herself to stop. "You are very cavalier about it."

"Why shouldn't I be? I don't regret my actions." He studied her a moment, then straightened and moved toward her. "And I'm not inclined to act the remorseful sinner for your benefit. I'd not be a legitimate man of business now if not for the profits I turned as a criminal. I did what was needed to secure my fortune."

She wasn't sure if she agreed with that assessment, but he didn't give her an opportunity to comment one way or another. He stopped just inches from her, his tall frame towering over her.

"It's your fortune as well, you'll recall," he reminded her. He lifted his hand and trailed a finger along the green velvet trim at the neck of her gown. The dress was new, expensive, and purchased with Connor's money. "Willing to give it up now that you know the unsavory truth of its origins?" He let the back of his hand brush across the sensitive skin at her collarbone and gave her a cold, mocking smile. "What say you, Mrs. Brice? Shall we hand it all to charity in the name of making amends? Or do you suppose you could scrounge up the fortitude to stomach my ill-gotten gains awhile longer?"

Adelaide studied him with curiosity. With every second that had passed, every word that was spoken, he'd grown more callous, more contemptuous. He wanted her anger, she realized. He wanted her to proclaim him a hopeless rotter and toss her hands up in defeat. And she might have obliged him, if she'd not heard the fear in his voice only moments before.

Holding his gaze, she reached up and placed her hand over his, trapping it in place. "May I ask why you are going to such pains to be offensive?"

"Merely reminding you who it is you married."

"I know who I married. I watched him wipe the tears from a little boy's cheeks not ten minutes ago."

A wariness settled over his features. "Is that who you think I am?"

"It is part of you."

He slipped his hand out from under hers. "The part you like."

"I like it better than this."

He caught and held her chin; his eyes burned into hers. "I am not ashamed of *any* part of who I am, nor anything I've done."

"I can see that." There wasn't a hint of remorse in him, not one iota of regret, but there was still the fear.

It dawned on her then that it wasn't his own judgment that he feared. It was hers. She remembered something he'd said to her the first night they'd met, when she'd admitted that she was willing to marry a man for his fortune.

"Perhaps the shame is that you were given no other choice," she said quietly and waited while the anger in his eyes faded and the grip of his fingers relaxed. And then, because she wasn't quite generous enough to absolve the man of *all* his sins, she added, "In Boston."

Connor blinked and released her. "In . . . I beg your pardon?"

"You *should* be ashamed for what you did at the house party."

Astonishment, and the first light of humor, crossed his features. "So, my misdeeds were perfectly acceptable, so long as they didn't touch you and yours, is that it?"

She pretended to consider. "Yes, I believe so."

He ran the back of his hand over his jaw, eyeing her with frank amusement. "Well, well, Mrs. Brice. How self-centered of you. I'd not have guessed you capable of it."

"We all have parts," she said softly.

Slowly, his humor faded. His gaze drifted from hers and landed on a distant spot on the floor. After a long moment, he whispered, "I suppose we do."

She'd rather see him smiling, but this new pensiveness was an improvement over his earlier mood. For now, it would have to be enough.

Believing he might like to be left alone with his thoughts, she ran a hand down his arm before stepping away.

"Shall I see you at dinner, then?"

He gave a small nod without looking at her, and she turned for the door. She had one foot in the hall when his voice fell on her back.

"My father caught a poacher on the grounds once."

Slowly, she turned around again and found him standing, still as a statue, staring at the same spot on the carpet.

"I was twelve, nearly thirteen," he continued. "He handed the man over to the magistrate, who sentenced him to two years on a prison hulk, at my father's request."

She stepped back into the room, drawing the door closed behind her. "That seems severe."

"My father could have had him shot. He fancied himself a compassionate man." He moved, finally, but only to turn his eyes toward the window. "I remember . . . He sat me down in the library and explained to me that there was room in the world for mercy, but none for leniency. He told me that a demonstrable lack of morality was indicative of a weak mind. Thieves like the poacher were to be pitied for their inferior make, but not coddled lest they fail to understand the purpose of the punishment and revert to their shameful ways."

"He was wrong," she said quietly.

"He was, and a hypocrite to boot, as his own life was hardly free of iniquity." He was quiet a long moment before, at last, he turned and looked at her. "I loved my father."

And he would have remembered every word of the lesson, Adelaide thought as her heart twisted. Even after he'd known those words to be false, they would have retained the power to turn every bite of stolen bread into sour paste and every successful illegal endeavor into a bitter accomplishment.

She ached for him, unable to imagine what that must have been like, having to choose between the fear of hunger and the fear of shaming a lost, beloved father. She wished she had the words to soothe away those memories, wished she could assure him with some confidence that his father would have been proud of the man he'd become. Failing those, she wished she could go back and give the baron a piece of her mind.

Because none of those were possible, she did the only thing she could think of. She crossed the room, laid her hand on his chest, and stretched up to press a soft kiss to his lips.

"I'm not ashamed of you," she whispered. And then, because the want to see him happy again was almost painful, she patted his cheek with exaggerated condescension. "But you are exceedingly inferior of mind if you honestly believed I would give up this gown."

Connor's smile was slow and accompanied by a wolfish gleam in his eyes. His hand slid around her waist, pulling her close. Her heart skipped a beat. "What are you doing?"

"Proving you wrong." Still grinning, he bent and gently nipped her earlobe. "You're giving up the gown."

"What? No." She laughed with both excitement and nerves as she pushed at his chest. "We're not in our bed-chamber. We can't—"

"Your sister is in the garden. Your brother is in town, and George is in the nursery."

Her eyes darted at the door even as she shivered with pleasure from the feel of his mouth moving over the sensitive skin of her neck. "But . . . the staff—"

"They won't intrude." He paused to linger at the juncture of her neck and her collarbone, something that never failed to weaken her knees. "Not if they want to keep their positions."

"Oh . . . Oh, but—"

He silenced her next protest with a two-pronged approach. First, he stepped away to lock the door (a task he accomplished with commendable speed), and then he returned to take possession of her mouth with a long, lush kiss. She gave up the fight without further ado.

In truth, it had been only a halfhearted argument. She didn't want to stop. Not really. If she could, she would draw out the delicious sensation of building passion forever.

Possibly not forever, she amended as his mouth settled over hers for an even deeper taste and pleasure built to a dizzying level. Restless, she moved against him, her fingers seeking the buttons of his waistcoat. There was too much between them, too many layers of clothes, and she sighed with satisfaction as Connor stripped them away with quick and clever hands. She forgot her fear of discovery and heard herself moan when his tongue found the heat of her breasts.

She forgot everything when she was with Connor like this, everything but the pleasure of the moment and the building anticipation of what was to come. There were no secrets or bargains when they made love, no revenge and no fifteen thousand pounds. There were only expectations she knew would be fulfilled, and promises she knew would be kept.

She didn't feel like a means to an end when he laid her down on the bed. She felt like a cherished lover, a beloved wife. There were no thoughts of marionettes as she drew her hands boldly over the long line of his back and watched the fire leap in his eyes. She was powerful here, an equal to him in every way. It hadn't taken her long to discover that with a careful brush of her fingertips, she could turn Connor into a man of wild demand. Or she could sap the strength from his limbs and draw a helpless moan from his lips. The choice was hers.

She chose demanding, reaching between them to caress his manhood with a brashness she'd not have imagined herself capable of only a week ago. The harsh groan that tore from his throat fed her own desire, and as his mouth and hands moved over her skin in rough insistence, she became just as helpless as Connor, just as lost to the demands of her body . . . and his.

In the mad rush to completion, she felt only the shameless joy of abandonment and the sweet thrill of knowing there was nothing Connor kept from her, nothing he held back. And in the warm glow of satisfaction that followed, she knew the rare pleasure of absolute contentment. For a little while at least, there would be no need to hope for something more. Connor's arms were tight around her, and the hard pound of his heart sounded beneath her ear.

In that moment, everything was exactly as it should be.

Chapter 23

*A*delaide maintained a buoyant mood for exactly thirty-two hours. Which was how long it took for Wolfgang to seek her out in the library and say, "I need money."

Adelaide didn't bother to look up from the small writing desk where she'd laid out the plans for her garden. She'd known it would only be a matter of time before Wolfgang came to her with the demand for more funds.

"Dare I ask why?"

"What does it matter? We're flush now, aren't we?"

They were, she thought, and she meant to keep it that way. She dipped her nib in the inkwell. "What is it for?"

"It was just a game of cards. I hit a run of bad luck."

"You were gambling?" Hardly an unusual pastime for a young gentleman, but in the past, Wolfgang had always preferred his wagers hold at least the taint of business. "This is a new vice. How much?"

"Four thousand."

She felt the pen slip from her fingers. "You're jesting."

Please, please, merciful Lord, let him be jesting.

"I'm not."

"How . . ." She rose from her seat and wondered that her legs didn't fold beneath her. "How could you? . . . So much . . . In a single night?"

She'd heard of men losing entire fortunes in a single game, but those stories came from the gambling hells in cities like London. There was nothing like that in Banfries or any of the nearby villages.

Wolfgang's bony shoulders rose and fell dismissively. "I've told you, I had a run of—"

"That is not a legitimate excuse!" Sucking in a gulp of air, she pushed past him and began a fast pace in front of the fireplace. "Oh, damn you. *Damn* you, Wolfgang. That is nearly a third of what I have."

"It's not," Wolfgang scoffed. "Your husband's flush."

Disgusted, she stopped and jabbed her finger in the general vicinity of Connor's study. "Well, if it's his money you're after, go and ask him for it yourself."

Isobel's voice chimed from the doorway. "Ask who for what?"

"Never you mind," Wolfgang snapped. "This is between Adelaide and—"

"Your behavior affects us all," Adelaide cut in. Ignoring his mutinous expression, she waved Isobel inside. "Our brother lost four thousand pounds playing cards last night."

"What?" Isobel paled, her eyes widening a second before they narrowed on Wolfgang. "You *liar*. There's not gambling such as that to be had in Banfries."

"Apparently, there is," Adelaide muttered.

"There can't be," Isobel insisted. "There's no one in our village who could afford to play. No one . . ." She trailed off and stepped back from Wolfgang as if physically repulsed. "Wolfgang, you *didn't*."

It took Adelaide a moment to follow her sister's line of thought. She almost wished she hadn't.

It couldn't be true. It couldn't possibly be true.

"Sir Robert?" She saw Wolfgang's eyes dart away, and

she knew it was true. "You lost the money to Sir Robert?! Oh, how could you? How could you possibly be so . . . so *stupid*?"

Wolfgang opened his mouth, but she silenced him with an angry swipe of her hand through the air.

"I don't care!" If he'd owed the money to someone else, anyone else, she might have seen her way to helping him. But, by God, she'd not help him with this. "I don't want to hear your excuses. I'll not hear one more ridiculous, selfish, infantile justification from you. He'll not have the money from me. Do you understand? Sir Robert will not touch one penny of what's mine."

Wolfgang's lips thinned into an angry white line. "You know what will happen if I don't pay."

"Prison again?" Isobel guessed, not sounding the least sympathetic. "Consequences are something to be considered before one acts like a selfish twit, not after. This is a mess of your own making. You may see your own way clear of it."

Wolfgang didn't take his gaze off Adelaide. "I won't go alone."

A shiver passed over her skin. "What does that mean?"

His lips thinned briefly. "A boy belongs with his father, don't you think?"

Isobel's gasp blended with her own. It was not unheard of for children to live in debtors' prison with their parents. But she'd never met a man willing to subject his child to such a fate out of spite. She would never have guessed Wolfgang to be that sort of man.

"You cannot mean it," Isobel whispered.

"I do."

Adelaide shook her head. "What's happened to you? What have you become?"

"A man," Wolfgang bit off. "A grown man bloody tired of taking orders from his own bloody sisters."

Isobel spun to face her. "Fetch your husband. He'll not stand for this."

Adelaide swallowed hard. She couldn't go to Connor now. He was with his men in the study.

Wolfgang sneered. "Oh, by all means, bring the matter to the attention of Mr. Brice. No doubt he'll be keen to keep me under his roof after learning of this."

Isobel shook her head in denial. Adelaide remained utterly still, rooted to the spot by shock and heartache.

Sensing victory, Wolfgang sniffed and shot the cuffs of the coat she'd paid the tailor for only days before. "If I am forced out of this house for any reason, then I take George with me. Understood? Have the money ready before the end of the week."

He walked past them, back straight and eyes fixed on the open door.

"Wolfgang Ward," Isobel called out. She waited for him to turn around, then she lifted her chin and spoke the words Adelaide had long feared resided in her own heart. "You are *not* my brother."

A hint of something that might have been pain crossed his face, but it disappeared as quickly as it had arrived.

"End of the week," he repeated and left.

What followed was a long, painful silence broken only by the sharp retort of Wolfgang's boots echoing down the hall. The sound faded, then disappeared.

"What will we do?" Isobel whispered at last.

"I don't . . ." Adelaide shook her head helplessly. She didn't know. She couldn't think. They were supposed to be safe now. George was to have a nanny, and toys, and treats, and—

"I won't let him take George. I won't. I *won't*." The sharp note of panic in Isobel's voice yanked Adelaide from her stupor.

"No, we won't," she agreed, careful to keep her voice calm and even. "We'll think of something. Right now . . . Right now, I need you to speak with the staff. See if they've heard rumors about where Wolfgang was last night and who else was—"

"What good will that do? We know—"

"We know only what he told us. Maybe there were witnesses to the game. Maybe there are whispers of cheating. I'd not put it past Sir Robert. Every bit of information helps."

"You're right." Isobel nodded her head vigorously as if trying to convince the both of them. "Of course you're right. I'll see what's to be learned."

Isobel spun about and dashed out the door, leaving Adelaide alone in the library with her fear. Shoving it aside, she slipped off her shoes and began to pace again with brisk, purposeful strides.

She walked for what felt like hours, until the heels of her feet grew tender and her legs began to throb. It was easy to ignore the physical discomfort. The turmoil in her heart and mind all but drowned it out.

She had to make a decision. She had to make the *right* decision. She couldn't afford to make a mistake. But no matter how she turned the puzzle, no matter from which angle she looked at the problem, she couldn't come up with a solution.

If she paid the price and kept silent, George would be safe. But only until Wolfgang made his next demand. She didn't doubt for a moment that there would be a next demand, and a next, and a next. Eventually, her funds would be gone and she would have to turn to Connor for more. He would toss Wolfgang out, and Wolfgang would take George with him.

If she refused to pay the price and told Connor, Wolfgang would be forced to leave, and he would take George with him.

If she refused to pay the price and kept silent . . . That wasn't even possible. Wolfgang would leave with George, Connor would want to know why, and—

"Is there a reason you're wearing a hole in my new carpet?"

She swallowed a yelp of surprise at Connor's voice and whirled around to find him standing in the doorway with a ledger in hand and a curious expression on his face.

"I . . ." Her mind went blank. She couldn't think of an excuse for why she was pacing, and wasn't sure if providing one would be the right move or a terrible mistake. At a complete loss, she stood still and mute and simply stared at him.

Connor strode inside, tossing the ledger down on a chair without looking. "What is it?"

She continued to stare at him as he crossed the room and came to a stop before her. Her eyes traveled over his familiar features. This was the man who'd brought George gingerbread cookies. This was the man who'd let George sit on his lap and kissed George's imaginary ouch when he'd thought no one was looking. Surely George meant enough to him . . . Surely *she* meant enough . . .

"I have a dilemma," she blurted out.

"I see," Connor said carefully. "And what is the nature of this dilemma?"

"It's . . ." It was unthinkable, impossible. That was its nature. She shook her head, unable to remember a time she had been so afraid. To her shock and horror, she burst into tears.

Connor reared back at the sight. "Here now, don't do that."

If she'd not been so miserable, she might have laughed. He looked and sounded as dismayed as when he'd faced a wailing George.

"I'm sorry." She swiped her hands across her cheeks. She never cried. Even when her family's circumstances had been at their lowest, she'd kept a level head. "I'll stop," she assured him, but the promise came out a choked sob. "I need . . . a moment . . . that's all. I need . . ."

Connor made a low sound in the back of his throat, and suddenly she was in his arms, her cheek resting against his shoulder. He rubbed her back, kissed the top of her head, and murmured something unintelligible into her hair.

She cried harder. She didn't mean to; she simply couldn't seem to find a way to stem the flood of misery, and the more she tried, the worse her sobs became. Connor mumbled something else, something that involved the word "tell," or possibly "hell," and lifted her into his arms.

Vaguely, she was aware of him moving, of him taking a seat and settling her in his lap. He held her there, stroking her hair, whispering comforting nonsense until the misery receded.

Connor fished a handkerchief from his pocket and gently mopped her cheeks. "Better?"

She sniffled and took the handkerchief from him. "No, of course not."

Crying never solved anything. She'd succeeded in making herself stuffy and exhausted, nothing more.

"It will be, once you talk to me." He pressed her cheek back to his shoulder and brushed his chin across her head. "Tell me what's wrong, love. I'll fix it for you."

"I don't know that you can." Or that she should risk asking it of him.

"Why not? I . . ." He trailed off and went eerily still. "You're not . . . You're not unwell, are you?"

"No, not at all."

His arms tightened around her briefly, and his breath escaped in a long exhale. "What is it, then?"

She shook her head in an effort to clear it. Where to begin?

"Is it a friend, sweetheart? Has someone passed?"

"No. No, it's nothing like that. No one is sick or dying—"

"Then I can fix it."

Despite everything, a watery laugh sprung from in her throat.

"You find that amusing?" Connor asked.

"I find your arrogance *astounding*." And oddly comforting. It was easier to believe in someone when he believed in himself. She lifted her head to look at him. "Will you promise me something?"

"Anything."

He hadn't hesitated, and she took strength from that. "I want you to promise George will stay here with us."

He pulled back, visibly startled. "Is that all? Why would you think—?"

"*Promise* me." She knew it wasn't fair. She knew she wasn't being rational. But everything in her told her that if Connor would only say the words, then they would be true. "Promise me Georgie will stay. Say it. You have to—"

"Shh." He kissed her brow, her cheeks. "I promise George will stay. All right?" He waited for her unsteady nod. "Good. Now tell me what this is about."

She licked lips gone dry and prayed she was making the right decision.

"It's Wolfgang," she began and, for the next few minutes, described the horrible scene that had taken place with her brother. It was both awful and relieving to go through it, as if she were both reliving and distancing herself from the heartbreak at the same time.

Connor listened without interruption and without any visible reaction. When she was through, he simply nodded and tucked her head beneath his chin.

"All right. Let me worry about it now."

She sighed heavily, wishing it was that easy. "It's not a burden I can hand to you like a picnic basket."

"Sure it is. You say, 'Husband, will you take care of this for me?' Then I say yes. Then you trust me to see it done."

Her lips curved in a tired smile. "Husband, will you take care of this for me?"

"Yes." Connor tipped her chin with his finger. "Do you trust me?"

How many times had he asked her that now, she wondered. The first time had been on the night she'd met Michael and Gregory. She'd been sure of her answer then. It was remarkable how much could change in so short a time.

"I came to you, didn't I?" she hedged.

"That is not an answer." He took her face in both hands and held her gaze. "Do you trust me, Adelaide?"

A number of responses came to mind, all involving a positive response and a qualifier.

I trust you right now.

I'm trusting you with this.

I trust you to help.

None of those truly answered the question, and none of them answered how she truly felt.

She studied his face as she contemplated her next words. They were so close together, she could feel the warmth of his breath on her lips and see the annoyance and determination in his green eyes. It took her a moment to see beyond those to what lay beneath. There was worry there, she realized. There was fear and vulnerability. He wanted her trust. More, he was afraid she wouldn't give it.

It would have been a simple thing to tell him that he might have considered that possibility before compromising her in Mrs. Cress's garden. She could wound him with a single sentence. It wouldn't be as dramatic as taking an army of lovers, but it would still be revenge, and a fitting one.

She couldn't gather up so much as a kernel of enthusiasm for the idea. If she'd retained any lingering thoughts of vengeance after their courtship, they were gone now. And heavens, it felt so good to know she'd let go of that anger. Wonderful and liberating and—

"*Adelaide.*" Connor spoke her name like a warning.

Oh, yes, he's worried.

She smiled, which did a fair job of surprising him. Then she took his face in her own hands and kissed him soundly on the mouth.

"Yes," she declared after she'd released him. "I trust you."

A weight slid from Connor's shoulders.

I trust you.

He wasn't sure why he'd needed the words so badly, or why Adelaide felt the need to proclaim them as she had . . . But he had needed them, and he'd take them any way she cared to offer. Besides, this new mood was a sight better than seeing her in tears. A flogging round the fleet would be better than seeing Adelaide in tears.

"Well," Adelaide said bracingly. "What shall we do about this mess?"

Her voice was brisk, but he could still see the shadow of worry in her eyes. It fed the outrage that had been steadily growing since the moment she'd began to tell him of Wolfgang's threats. Careful to keep that anger safely hidden beneath the surface, he brushed a wisp of hair from her cheek and wished he could brush her fear away as easily.

"We've until the end of the week." He pressed a kiss to her brow. "Give me a day to consider the options."

Chapter 24

Connor didn't need the day to think over his options. He knew exactly what needed to be done.

First he coaxed Adelaide into lying down in their chambers for a spell . . . Well, initially he coaxed, then he demanded, then he pled, then he tried all three simultaneously and that seemed to do the trick.

She muttered and grumbled, but nevertheless crawled under the covers and promised to remain there for at least an hour. Which left Connor free to seek out Wolfgang in his chambers.

He didn't bother knocking, simply took the key from the housekeeper and let himself in.

"Good evening, Mr. Ward."

Wolfgang stood by a washstand with a pair of gloves in hand, apparently under the impression he was free to go out for the night. "Hell, man, don't you know how to knock?"

"Yes." Connor stepped inside, closed the door behind him, and crossed the room, taking dark satisfaction in watching the nerves jump in Wolfgang's eyes.

"You've something to say?" Wolfgang asked, sticking his chin out like a surly child. "Spit it out, then."

"We're to be frank, are we? Excellent." Connor leaned a hip against the washstand. "I don't like you. The only reason I've not been rid of you is because your sister retains some affection for the boy you once were. Until late, I saw no harm in that. And so, out of deference to my wife, I have been patient, even lenient, with you."

Wolfgang tossed his gloves aside and curled his lip. "I never wanted your—"

Connor reached out, grabbed Wolfgang by the throat, and in the space of a heartbeat, had him pinned against the wall.

"That leniency is at an end."

Wolfgang gurgled a protest and clawed at the choking hand. Connor ignored both. "You used your son as a threat?"

It wasn't possible for Wolfgang to respond. It wasn't necessary either. Connor only asked as an excuse to prolong the conversation, and therefore the pleasure of squeezing the bastard's throat. He wanted to keep squeezing, wanted to watch Wolfgang's eyes roll to the back of his head. Take George, would he? Hurt Adelaide, would he?

"I will send you to hell before you cause one more second of heartbreak in this family. I will eviscerate you. Do I make myself clear?"

He loosened his grip to give Wolfgang the chance to nod, but the young man was either too stubborn or too stupid to take advantage of the opportunity.

"You can't," Wolfgang rasped. "Adelaide hates me, but she would never consent to physical—"

Connor squeezed and leaned closer to whisper, "Adelaide would never know."

He waited for the awful light of understanding to dawn on Wolfgang's face. There were all sorts of tragic accidents that could befall a man—a tumble from a horse, a sudden meeting with a speeding carriage, an unfortunate hunting accident. Connor had no intention of arranging for any of these to happen, but it served his purposes to have Wolfgang believe otherwise.

"Now have I made myself clear?" He loosened his grip once more.

"Yes," Wolfgang choked out. "Yes."

"Excellent." Connor released him and watched him slide down the wall into a gasping heap on the floor. "Why do you owe Sir Robert four thousand pounds?"

Occupied with coughing and wheezing, Wolfgang didn't immediately answer. His bulging eyes darted away, an unmistakable sign of an impending lie. Connor flexed his fist, persuading him to rethink the decision. "Why?"

"Letters," Wolfgang finally spat, and the admittance acted like the release of a cork. The fight simply drained out of him. Closing his eyes on a groan, he let his head fall back against the wall. "He has letters."

"What sort of letters?"

"Oh, Christ," he moaned. "They're from me . . . to Lord Stites."

Connor knew the name. "You dallied with the son of a duke?" Not a wise decision but more common than some imagined.

Wolfgang rolled his head back and forth. "No. He took funds from his father. At my suggestion."

"For what?"

"A financial scheme." A broken laugh spilled from his lips. "He loved the idea. He salivated over the notion of cheating his own father out of money."

And the letters, no doubt, spelled out every sordid detail of the crime. Idiot boy. "How much?"

"Ten thousand. We were to have five each. He kept it all."

"How did Sir Robert obtain the letters?"

"I don't know." Wolfgang's lids flew open. "What does it bloody matter? I stole from a duke. Do you know what that means? Do you realize what will happen to me when he discovers the truth?"

Given the involvement of the duke's son, Connor imagined Wolfgang's punishment would be swift and silent. A quick deportment or sudden disappearance were the most likely outcomes.

Pity he couldn't count on it being the first.

He watched the young man's chin sink to his chest and resisted the urge to tip it back up again with the toe of his boot. "You're a foolish, selfish arse, Wolfgang, but for the sake of your family, and your neck, you are going to pretend otherwise for the next twenty-four hours and do exactly as you're told. Understood?"

Wolfgang nodded weakly.

"Good. Stay here; talk to no one."

Wolfgang looked up, a small spark of hope on his haggard face. "You're going to give Sir Robert four thousand pounds?"

"I'm going to retrieve those letters," Connor corrected. "And you are going to accept the commission I offered."

Wolfgang nodded again, this time with more vigor. "I wanted to. When you—"

"I don't give a damn what you want. Just do as you're told." Through with the conversation, he turned on his heel and headed for the door.

"Brice?"

"Bloody hell, what now?"

Wolfgang surprised him a little by lifting his face and making eye contact. "I wouldn't have taken George. I know what I am, but . . . I'd never have done that to my own son. Adelaide has to know that."

"She does. She knows I'd never have allowed it." And with that, he left the room in search of his men . . . and the damn letters.

He found the first already in the study, holding a good-natured argument with Graham over which of the local tavern wenches would be most likely to win at a footrace, and whether or not the lasses could be persuaded to give the contest a go. He persuaded them to drop the topic.

Discovering the whereabouts of the letters proved nearly as easy. Connor didn't even have to bribe the information out of Mrs. McKarnin. Her gratitude for her new, and considerably more lucrative, position at Ashbury Hall was all the motivation she required.

"Articles of business are kept in the study," she informed them. "Personal correspondence is stored in a wooden box next to the bed. The baron never varied from his system of organization."

"Thank you, Mrs. McKarnin."

"My pleasure, sir."

Graham turned to him after Mrs. McKarnin's departure. "Blackmail is business."

"Aye," Michael agreed. "Who's to fetch the letters, then?"

They all volunteered, and a lengthy debate ensued, all three men of the opinion that none were as fit for the task as himself.

Michael insisted that as a reformed thief, he was clearly the most qualified.

Gregory pointed out that Michael hadn't picked a lock in thirty years, and if anyone was to risk his neck for a bit of paper and ink, it ought to be the man with the least to lose and the most to gain. He was old. He was tired. If he ended on the gallows, so be it. It wasn't every day a worn-out old criminal like himself knew what it was to be a hero to a lass. He wanted that, just once, before he died.

It was a moving, albeit maudlin, sentiment.

Graham followed it up with an offer to see the job done for fifty pounds.

Connor leaned back in his chair. "It's for me to do."

This announcement was met with loud complaints from Gregory and Michael. Graham spoke over them.

"What's the nature of these letters?"

Connor considered his answer. He'd been circumspect in his telling of events. Sir Robert had letters that Adelaide wanted returned, that was all he'd offered. He didn't like keeping secrets from his men, particularly from Gregory and Michael, but he disliked the idea of Adelaide being the last to learn of her brother's crimes even more. He'd inform her of the truth once he could assure her the letters no longer posed a threat. Then he would tell his men . . . Possibly. He'd see how she felt about it.

"Their nature is personal," he replied.

Michael slammed a fist on the desk. "You letting your wife send personal letters—?"

"No." He slanted Michael a withering glance for the insult. "They're letters she wants. The contents would be of embarrassment to the family."

"And Sir Robert knows it, does he?" Gregory demanded. "Been holding it over her head?"

"Over Wolfgang's."

"Ah." Michael shared a knowing nod with Gregory. "That explains a thing or two, don't it."

Graham rose from his seat. "A moment, lads."

"Bring us beer," Michael tossed at him before turning to Connor. "Look here, boy, there's no sense in you being the one what sneaks into Sir Robert's. You've never done the thing."

"Aye," Gregory agreed. "And you've a family to be thinking of."

Connor decided to let them argue a bit longer. They'd abide by his decision in the end, but there would be less grumbling in the long run if they felt they'd had their full say on the matter first.

Five minutes of heated debate later, the door opened and Graham crossed the room to toss a stack of letters on the desk. "These them?"

The room fell silent. Connor grabbed the top one and scanned the contents. "Bloody hell."

"Is it them?"

"Yes." He tossed the letter with the others and eyed Graham speculatively. He wasn't sure if he wanted to grin or shout at the man. "How did you get these?"

"Usual way. Saw the box weeks ago, thought the contents might be worth something." His mouth hooked up. "And they didn't get checked so often as the silver."

"Are these all of them?"

"Aye, and I want a hundred pounds for 'em."

Connor didn't take offense at the sudden rise in price. It was business. "I'll give you the fifty and won't break your neck for not having turned them over earlier."

"Seventy-five and I'll slip word to Sir Robert's new valet that someone ought check the box."

"Done."

Connor flicked a glance at Gregory and Michael. After more than a decade of working together, a single pointed look was understood as readily as a verbal order. They rose together and left the room in silence, closing the door behind them.

Graham looked from the door to Connor. "If you're thinking to snap my neck after all, you'll find it's got more steel than most."

"I'll not snap your neck. The deal is done." He leaned back in his chair. "You've made a tidy profit these last few months."

"Man's got to live."

"If he wants to live here, he's got to mind the silver."

Graham smiled at that and shook his head. "If I'd been after harming you and yours, I'd have used those letters same as Sir Robert."

"Why keep them secret?" Connor asked, tapping the letters.

Graham shrugged. "I figured if the boy didn't know the letters were about and you didn't know the letters were about, then the lass didn't know they were about. What was the point of bringing 'em to light?" A scowl settled over his face. "A girl don't need to know every foul deed her brother's done."

"You could have destroyed them," Connor pointed out.

"Aye, but this particular brother . . ." Graham narrowed his eyes and gave a quick shake of his head. ". . . I don't trust. Never know when a bit of leverage might come in handy. You aim to use it?"

"No. I've my own means for keeping Wolfgang in line." Financial manipulation and, failing that, brute force.

"I'd wager you do. Are we done?"

Connor jerked his chin in agreement. "We're done."

As Graham let himself out, Connor flicked the edge of one of the letters and swore. Bloody hell, they were going to break Adelaide's heart.

Chapter 25

Adelaide told herself she wasn't heartbroken—no more so than she'd been an hour before, anyway. There was only so much grief she was willing to bear for Wolfgang, and the last of it had disappeared when he'd threatened to take George. She was done with him.

She accepted the letters and Connor's explanation of their contents with quiet resignation and watched them burn in the fireplace. When they'd gone to ash, she turned to Connor, wrapped her arms around him, and held tight until the heartache she refused to acknowledge was eased.

Wolfgang left Ashbury Hall at dawn the following morning. He was to go south, to another of Connor's holdings, and wait there until he received word of his post.

His departure was a subdued event. He looked in on his sleeping son, nodded to Isobel in the hall, and walked to the waiting carriage with Adelaide. At her request, Connor and his men stayed away. There was no sense in forcing polite good-byes. No point in pretending the departure was anything other than what it was—a banishment.

He offered an apology. A single, softly spoken "I am sorry," before he climbed inside the carriage and shut the door.

Adelaide believed he was, but whether he was sorry for the sake of his family or sorry that he'd made himself so miserable, she didn't know. And because she couldn't know, she made a conscious decision to leave the question alone and concentrate on what was right before her.

George was safe, Isobel was happy, and Wolfgang's carriage was rolling away. He would start a new life far away from them all.

A hesitant smile spread slowly across her face as she turned away from the drive and walked into the house. With every step she took, she felt another weight slip from her shoulders, and the last of the marionette strings snap free.

She intercepted a maid carrying a fussy George in the great hall. The young woman cooed patiently, bouncing him gently on her hip.

"He woke up a mite cross, ma'am. I thought a walk about—"

"I'll take him." She transferred George onto her hip and brushed a hand over his disheveled hair. "Will you bring a small glass of milk to the parlor, please? And a plate of those pastries Cook made yesterday."

"The pudding filled, ma'am?"

"Yes, please."

She felt like indulging. She wanted to pamper herself and spoil George.

"Let's be a trifle reckless," she whispered to George as she carried him into the parlor. She set him down on the plush carpet and watched him dart to the settee and shove his hands between the cushions. "There's no spoon in there, darling. But just you wait, I've something even better coming for you."

When the pastries arrived, Adelaide cut them into thirds while George slurped down his milk. She wiped pudding from her fingers, took a slice for herself, and set the plate on the floor for George. Then she watched with tender amusement as he hunkered down on his haunches in front of the offering.

"Biscuits!"

"Biscuits, indeed."

She took a seat next to him, uncaring that she was setting a terrible example by eating sweets on the floor with her fingers. A few moments of silliness would hardly ruin the child, and it was such a joy to watch him giggle and squirm and reach out to squeeze the creamy white pudding from one of the slices.

"Ooooh. Beetle."

"Beetle? . . . Oh, ew." She laughed and ruffled the silken curls of his hair. "No, it is not a squished beetle. It's . . ." She took a bite of her slice and made a humming noise. "Mmmm."

George mimicked her by cramming half the remains of his pastry into his mouth.

"You may have two," she informed him, knowing full well he had no idea what that meant. It didn't matter; she liked saying it.

Connor's teasing voice floated overhead. "He'll be fat as his namesake within a year."

A pleasant shiver chased over her skin as he stepped up behind her, so close she could feel the heat of his powerful legs against her back. She had the passing thought that it was a pity she'd not had the foresight to agree to his original demand of sharing her bed ten times a day.

"He'll not," she said pertly, tilting her head back to give him a smile. "And he's not named for the Prince Regent. He's named for his mother's father." Who had been, now that she thought on it, a bit round about the middle as well. "Perhaps you're right."

She reached to put the plate of pastries away. One was more than plenty, really.

"Leave it." Connor stepped around and bent down to take the plate from her. "Spoil him awhile longer if it gives you pleasure."

He set the pastries back down, took her hand, and drew her to her feet. Worried green eyes swept over her face.

"How are you?"

"Fine. Quite well, considering. I feel . . ." She closed her eyes on a happy sigh as he traced the line of her jaw with his thumb and brushed a feathery kiss across her cheek. "I feel myself. I feel more like myself than I have in ages."

She felt his lips curve against her skin. "Have you been someone else?"

"No. And yes. Parts," she reminded him and smiled sheepishly when he pulled back to look at her with a curious expression. "I used to enjoy being carefree, even a little reckless. When circumstances changed for my family, I set those parts aside. I suppose I forgot about them." Because she'd had no other choice, she thought. Careless, reckless individuals did not make for ideal heads of households. "I think I've begun to remember them."

"Am I to understand that you are not the woman I thought I'd married?"

"You'll find your bride was far more biddable than your wife."

"If I had a pound for every new husband to have heard those words . . ." He smiled when she laughed, and he tapped her chin lightly with his finger. "You were never that biddable, love."

"Perhaps not," she agreed. But she had been more cautious, less interested in taking risks, being silly, and exploring the world around her. Which reminded her . . . She glanced out the window toward the stables as Connor bent down and helped himself to a small slice of pastry.

"So you're feeling reckless," he said and ate half the pastry in single bite.

Oh, drat. In light of what she was about to ask him, reckless had not been a wise choice of words. "Not reckless, really. More . . . Responsibly adventurous." She smiled at him sweetly as he polished off his food. "May I ride your stallion, Midas?"

Connor stared at her, swallowed, and said, "You may."

"Really? When?"

"When I am dead, buried, and in want of your company."

"Ah." She tilted her head. "That was very nearly romantic."

"You're welcome." He smiled mischievously as she laughed, then jerked his chin in acknowledgment of the footman who entered. "What is it, John?"

"Begging your pardon, sir. Mr. O'Malley, Mr. Birch, and Mr. Sefton have sent me in search of you, sir."

Connor dismissed the footman with a quick nod, bent down to give her an equally quick kiss, and walked out of the room.

Adelaide frowned at his retreating back, then at the empty doorway, then at George.

"Was I just dismissed?"

George grabbed his second pastry, squeezed mightily, and looked mildly disappointed when the folded end piece failed to produce a gush of pudding.

"Take a few bites, darling, then it will mush." She glanced at the door and tapped her foot. "Do you know, I believe I was dismissed."

Connor might as well have nodded at her and kissed the footman. Just like that, she and her questions had been put aside. If she wished to continue their discussion, she could do so after he'd finished meeting with his men.

To the devil with that, she thought. She wasn't staff, and she was heartily sick of being put behind his men . . . and Sir Robert. No one should have to come after Sir Robert.

"We'll just see about this," she muttered.

Mind set, she scooped up George and his pastry and chased after Connor.

The heels of her half boots cracked loudly in the hall, a quick staccato that pulsed in time to her rising temper. Thought she'd been unbiddable before, did he? Thought he was the only one with moods and parts? Oh, she'd show him unbiddable. She'd show him a mood.

She caught him with one hand on the study door. "Not your stallion, then. Another."

He didn't start—as she'd rather hoped would be the case—but merely paused and lifted a brow. "Beg your pardon?"

"I want another horse to ride," she ground out. Honestly, the conversation was less than thirty seconds old. Just how easy to dismiss was she?

"Ah. Right. So choose another. We've a dozen mounts." He opened the door and stepped into the study.

Determined not to be brushed aside twice, she took a steadying breath and followed. Gregory, Michael, and Graham sat around the desk arguing and digging through a veritable mountain of papers. Their conversation came to an abrupt halt at her entrance.

Good, she thought. Let *them* wait.

"We've several horses suitable for pulling carriages, along with one stallion and one old nag," she pressed, shifting a squirming George.

Connor walked around to the back of the desk and shook his head at Gregory, who'd reached out to put the papers away. He turned back to her. "Why can't you ride the nag?"

Gregory withdrew his hand, shrugged, and resumed his argument with Michael and Graham. It was irritating, trying to carry on a conversation with Connor when there was another conversation being carried on two feet away. It was particularly annoying that Connor appeared to be giving both equal attention.

"I have been," she said, raising her voice over Gregory's. She dodged a careless swing of George's pastry-filled hand. "But I should like something that can go faster than a plod. Why on earth do you even own an old nag?"

"I thought George might like to sit her in a few years." He turned to Michael. "That's not the baron's seal." He turned back to her. "You've funds of your own. Buy a horse if none of those in the stable suit you."

"I don't know the first thing about purchasing a horse. Do stop waving your hand about, George. It's food, not a sailboat."

"The stable master will advise you."

"Where's the map?" Gregory asked.

"The stable master has advised me. He suggested I ride the nag."

Connor pushed a paper toward Gregory. "I'll speak with him."

"I don't wish for you to speak with him."

"Not that map. The other one."

"There is no another one," Graham put in.

"I wish for you to speak with me about what sort of horse I ought to buy."

"I'll be happy to, as soon as I'm done here."

"I would rather you set this aside—"

"This one has black ink. I want the one with blue—"

"George, will you *please*—"

Too late, she recognized her error in bringing George into the study. His fingers squeezed the half-eaten pastry, and an enormous glob of pudding shot out of the center. Adelaide watched in helpless horror as it sailed toward Connor's desk and a piece of paper she was almost certain Gregory had referred to a moment ago as "the key." It landed with a thick splat, and Adelaide swore she could feel the force of its impact under her feet. Or perhaps that was the shock of her heart colliding with her toes.

Oh, no. Oh, *no*.

She stared, unblinking, at the mess, and knew with awful certainty that everyone else in the room was doing the same. The men said not a word, moved not an inch. Even George seemed to understand the enormity of what had just occurred. He'd gone stiff and still as a tin soldier in her arms.

Slowly, and with great reluctance, she dragged her gaze up to face Connor, but he was still looking at the desk. She searched for something to say, some way to fill the terrible silence, but nothing seemed adequate. What if the damage was irreparable? What if the paper was irreplaceable? It had to be important. It wouldn't have been on top otherwise. Her heart threatened to beat its way out of her chest. Revenge was Connor's world; it was all he wanted, everything he had worked for. And she'd let a toddler drown it in pudding.

"Connor, I—"

She broke off with a start when Connor moved. Very quietly, and very deliberately, he dipped his finger into the center of the goop, taking away a sizable amount. His eyes lifted to George's. And then, to her absolute astonishment, Connor stuck the finger in his mouth and pulled it out again with a small pop.

"Manna from the sky," he said and winked at her.

George couldn't have understood the words, but he knew that eating fallen food—with one's fingers no less— was the height of silliness, and a definitive naughty. Or he simply liked the popping noise. Whatever the cause, he threw his head back and roared with laughter. He trembled and shook in her arms, his small body struggling to contain the magnitude of his glee.

That alone was enough to turn Adelaide's heart over, but what struck her deepest, what took her breath away, was the expression on Connor's face. He looked enormously proud of himself. Proud, delighted, and a little bit stunned. All because he'd made a little boy laugh.

And in that moment, Adelaide fell hopelessly, irrevocably in love.

The realization was stunning, and for a woman already contending with a considerable stun, it proved debilitating. Her heart galloped, the air backed up in her lungs, and her mind turned to mush.

She could do nothing more than look at Connor and make the patently absurd offer of, "I'll clean it."

Connor shook his head and pushed the paper to Michael. "I'll send a letter to Lord Gideon at Murdoch House today, and we can visit tomorrow. I wager he has a horse to suit you."

Horses? He wanted to speak of horses?

"I . . . Thank you. I'll just . . ." She backed away, hiding a wince when Connor came around the desk to gently take her arm.

"I am sorry," she whispered, as he led her to the door. "Truly, I am. I know how much this matters to you. I'll get you another."

"You don't know what it is."

"It's the blue map," Gregory muttered from his seat.

Oh, she wanted to sink into the floor and take what remained of George's pastry with her. "I am sorry. So very—"

Connor gave her a gentle nudge, gently propelling her over the threshold. She'd have taken the opportunity to bolt, but his next words, spoken softly, stilled her feet.

"Do you know the real reason I didn't make you my mistress, Adelaide?"

Was there a false one? She shook her head.

"For the same reason I'm not angry about the pudding. You matter."

And after imparting that astounding bit of information, he closed the door.

Adelaide stared blindly at the wood grain in front of her until George grew impatient and began to fuss. Slowly, she began to walk down the hall.

You matter.

It was hardly a declaration of love, and heaven knew, she could have done without having it punctuated with a door shut in her face—but still . . .

You matter.

It was lovely. The initial panic she'd felt in realizing her feelings for Connor slid away. Uncertainty remained, but it was tempered with hope. Connor might not love her, but she mattered, and that was a fine start. It wasn't foolish to believe a fondness might grow into something more. It wasn't imprudent to have fallen in love with a man who cared for her. It was dazzling and exciting.

She felt bold and reckless and brimming over with hope . . . Until she spoke to the housekeeper nearly eight hours later and discovered no missives had been sent to Lord Gideon at Murdoch House.

Connor had forgotten. She'd tried not to draw any conclusions from the news. After all, he was not the first person on earth to have forgotten something. Life was rife with distractions. Only last year, she'd carried a squirming, squalling George halfway back from the village before remembering she'd left Isobel waiting at the butcher's. In truth, she'd only remembered then because she'd reached into her pocket for something with which to distract George and pulled out one of Isobel's hair ribbons.

Everyone was susceptible. Everyone needed a reminder now and again. She'd remind him when he came to bed, he'd be suitably contrite for having forgotten, the letter would be sent, and that was that.

She fell asleep waiting for him, and she awoke alone the next morning with only the vaguest memory of him crawling into bed with her during the small hours of the morning and crawling out again at dawn.

It was disappointing, but she refused to give up faith. Connor would remember, she was sure.

But as the hours passed and Mrs. McKarnin began to deliver the news—in increasingly sympathetic tones—that still no missives had been sent to Murdoch House, Adelaide's patience began to wane.

She found reasons to pass—or to be perfectly accurate, stomp—by the study door. But her efforts were for naught. All she heard were voices pitched low in anger and the single phrase, "The bugger's run off to devil knows where!"

Oh, she hoped he had. She hoped Sir Robert had fallen into a bog somewhere or taken it upon himself to emigrate to Australia. She was tired of the shadow he cast over their lives and more than ready for Connor to let go of the past and see what was right before him.

It was high time they all ceased tying themselves into knots over Sir Robert.

By noon, when it had become apparent that Connor did not intend to take her to see Lord Gideon's horses, she decided it was also high time she stopped waiting on Connor Brice to remember she mattered.

Chapter 26

The bugger had run off to Edinburgh.

Connor left his study with the thrill of the hunt still coursing through his veins. It had taken the better part of thirty-six hours to track down Sir Robert. Nearly two days of frustration and a fortune spent on bribing Sir Robert's new housekeeper. The woman wouldn't think of betraying her new master . . . for anything less than a hundred pounds.

Connor couldn't help but admire the woman's gall, and he'd paid the price without bothering to barter. Now everything was set, and with a perfection that he could not have planned. Sir Robert's flight to Edinburgh was a welcomed bit of serendipity. The man sought refuge amongst his own kind. He would dine and dance with Scotland's elite, gathering his peers around him like stones in a defensive wall.

What a sight it was going to be, to watch those boulders come crashing down on his head.

Connor grinned. Almost, *almost* he had reached his goal. A few more weeks and he would be done with Sir

Robert . . . Maybe two months . . . Six at the most . . . He'd revisit his timeline after Edinburgh.

For now, he wanted to savor the pleasure of impending victory with a glass of brandy and the company of his pretty wife.

The first could be had without difficulty. The second was nowhere to be found—a state of affairs Connor had trouble accepting. How could she not be home? What the devil was she doing, running about the countryside by herself? Granted, she wasn't alone in the strictest sense of the word. According to his butler, Mrs. Brice had taken a maid, a driver, and a pair of footmen. But she wasn't with *him*, and that was the pertinent point.

Connor had grown accustomed to knowing where she was every minute of the day. Even when he sequestered himself away with his men, all he needed to do was inquire after her whereabouts.

The missus is gardening. The missus is in the nursery. The missus is on the veranda with Miss Ward.

He liked that. He liked knowing he need only look out the window to see her or walk down the hall to speak with her. He liked having her at hand. And wasn't the convenience of having a lovely woman at hand supposed to be one of the benefits of taking a wife?

She bloody well wasn't at hand now. And it was damned inconvenient. Worse, not a soul was willing to tell him where, exactly, she'd run off to or how long she intended to be gone. That they *knew* was obvious. That they were unwilling to tell him was equally clear.

Don't know, sir.
Couldn't say, Mr. Brice.
She's gone out.

This last came from Isobel, who then proceeded to shut her chamber door in Connor's face.

He stared at the wood, torn between bewilderment and a rising temper. Eventually, the latter won out.

Enough was enough. He lifted a fist and pounded. "I

damn well know she's gone out! Where? What the devil is going on here?"

The only response was the sound of a key turning in the lock. It sent his blood to boiling. Damn if he'd be locked out of a room in his own bloody house! He spun on his heel, intending to find the nearest bellpull and ring for assistance in taking the door off its hinges, but the soft jingle of keys snagged his attention.

"Mrs. McKarnin!"

The housekeeper stepped out of a nearby room and eyed him with poorly concealed distaste, as if he'd stuck his foot in something foul and, like a good and loyal servant, she was doing her utmost not to notice.

Had *everyone* turned against him? "It's a bloody insurrection."

"Beg your pardon, sir?"

"Nothing." He stuck his hand out and wiggled his fingers. "The key to Miss Ward's chamber."

She took her sweet time, retrieving her enormous ring of keys from her apron pocket, flipping through the keys, studying each one individually.

Connor tapped his foot, ground his teeth, then tapped his foot some more. "Before nightfall would be—"

"I don't appear to have it on my person, sir."

He dropped his hand. "What do you mean, you don't have it?"

"I remember now. I put it away for safekeeping. What if someone should get hold of the ring, I thought? What if that someone should have wicked intentions?" She sniffed and gave him a long, pointed look. "All precautions must be taken to protect a lady's virtue."

"Oh, for the love of . . . I'm not going to ravish my sister-in-law. I merely want a word."

"I shall look for the key."

He'd wager a thousand pounds she intended to look for it until Boxing Day. He'd wager a thousand more the damn thing was on her ring.

"Mrs. McKarnin!" He counted to ten as she turned around, then ground out, "Where is my wife?"

"She's gone out, sir."

He counted to fifteen. "Where?"

"It was not my place to ask, sir."

Twenty. "Did she give any indication as to when she might return?"

So help him God, if she failed to answer—

"Before dark, sir."

His jaw relaxed, just a little. "Thank you. I'll take the *Review* in my study, now . . . No, the parlor."

The parlor had more comfortable seating. It also happened to have windows facing both the front drive and the stables, but he refused to acknowledge this as his reason for the change of plans. A man had a right to sit and read the *Edinburgh Review* on his own damn settee.

He neither read nor sat. He tried, several times, but each time he settled in to read, he was beset with worry. What if Adelaide's carriage had met with mishap? What if Sir Robert hadn't left for Edinburgh as they'd thought? What if two footmen hadn't been sufficient? And each time, he rose again to pace off the restlessness. Three hours later, when the carriage finally rolled down the drive, he was near to climbing the walls.

"About bloody time."

He marched out of the house, down the front steps, and waited, hands caught behind his back, for the carriage to stop and Adelaide to emerge. He wasn't going to shout. He was not going to put himself in the position of having to apologize for losing his temper.

"Where the hell have you been?" He'd apologize later.

Adelaide flicked him a glance as she withdrew her hand from the assisting footman's grasp. "Mr. Cawley's farm."

Surprise temporarily pushed aside temper. "Why the devil did you go there?"

"Because there is where the stable master suggested I look for a suitable mount."

"A suitable—?"

"He has a fine four-year-old mare. Miss Crumpets. A stupid name for a lovely horse."

She headed for the house and would have walked right past him without another word if he hadn't turned and fallen into step beside her. Her cold manner both baffled and unnerved him.

Cautious now, he slanted a look at her. "Did you purchase her?"

"I did not." She kept her gaze straight ahead as she walked inside.

"Why not?"

"Mr. Cawley would not sell her to me."

"Why?"

"Because he was uncertain as to whether my husband would approve." She tossed her reticule on a side table with more force than necessary. "He says he will not sell the mare to me without your consent."

"I see." He felt inexplicably guilty all of a sudden. As if he needed to apologize on behalf of his entire gender. "I'll speak with him."

She rolled her eyes and brushed past him, but he caught her arm and turned her about again. Her color was high, her eyes flashing.

"Are you angry with me?" What did she have to be angry about? He'd been the one pacing in the parlor for the last three hours.

"*Of course* I am angry with you," she snapped. "It was an insulting and completely unnecessary experience. One I would not have had to suffer if you had sent a letter to Lord Gideon and taken me to Murdoch House as promised."

"Letter?" His mind went blank, then . . . Horses. Letters. George's mishap with the pastry. He dropped her arm. "Oh, hell."

"You forgot entirely, didn't you? Completely dismissed it. I don't know why I . . ." She pressed her lips tight, shook her head, turned, and headed up the steps.

Connor watched her until her small form disappeared. It wasn't hard for him to finish her sentence . . . *why I bother . . . why I expected better.* He didn't need the exact words to understand the sentiment.

An unforgiving weight of guilt, and something that edged perilously close to fear, settled in his chest like a block of ice. Uncomfortable with the sensations on every possible level, he scowled at the stairs and decided that what he *really* didn't need was the bloody sentiment.

So, he'd made a mistake. It was just one sodding mistake, not a statement of his character as a whole . . . which was, granted, a bit murky about the edges, but holy hell, he was only human. He ought to be forgiven the odd mistake.

And he ought to be trusted to make up for that mistake. Hadn't he made up for everything else, even the things that hadn't been mistakes? Hadn't he given her a fine home and a fortune to spend, a picnic in England, and a brother free of debt and out from under Sir Robert's influence?

He damn well had.

And yet she didn't know why she bothered? Didn't know why she'd expected better? Well, if a reminder was what she needed, he was happy to oblige.

Fuming—and comfortable with that sensation on every level—he stormed across the great hall and up the steps. He took them two at a time and came to an abrupt halt halfway up the staircase.

This . . . was not a wise course of action.

Holy hell, what was he thinking to do? Demand an apology? Demand she trust him? He'd done that already. Obviously, it failed to take. Itemizing the things he'd done for her and her family was not going to change that. Moreover, he'd not done those things out of guilt or to gain her trust. He'd done them because . . . well . . . because he had, that's all. He'd wanted to. No need to go dissecting the matter.

He rolled his shoulders, inhaled deeply, exhaled slowly, and resumed his progress toward their chambers. This misunderstanding had been blown entirely out of proportion. She'd read far too much into a temporarily forgotten letter, and he was reading far too much into a half-finished sentence. For all he knew, she'd meant to express her regret at not having trampled Mr. Cawley under Miss Crumpets' hooves.

This was a small row, the kind husbands and wives were wont to have on a regular basis. He wasn't an expert on these sorts of disagreements, but he was fairly certain they all played out the same. The husband displayed a suitable level of contrition for *one* mistake, and the wife forgave him. Because she trusted him. It was as simple as that.

Feeling settled and confident, he entered their chambers and softly closed the door. Adelaide stood looking out the window. She failed to acknowledge his presence with so much as a flick of her eyes.

He caught his hands behind his back. "Adelaide, I apologize."

She nodded without turning her head and offered no forgiveness.

He decided a bit of resistance was to be expected. He took a step forward. "Let me make it up to you."

"You may speak with Mr. Cawley, if you like."

Oh, he intended to have a conversation with Mr. Cawley. One the man would not soon forget. "I can manage better. What do you say to a fortnight in Edinburgh?"

Finally, she glanced at him. "Edinburgh?"

It was a brilliant idea, if he did say so himself. He could be present to watch Sir Robert fall and placate his wife at the same time. Even better, he'd have her all to himself. "We'll go shopping, to the theater." Spend the week in bed without fear of interruption from her family or his men. "Whatever you like."

She looked caught between hope and doubt. "Do you mean it?"

"I'd not suggest it otherwise."

"And when would we have this fortnight?"

"Next week."

She worried her lip. "Could we leave sooner?"

"I've some business to conclude first." The trap was set for Sir Robert, but he wanted to make certain, absolutely certain, of the details before that trap was sprung.

"What sort of business?"

"A bit of this and that. I've the final plans for the garden to review, and I've something in store for Sir Robert I think you'll—" He broke off when she lifted a hand.

"It doesn't matter," she murmured. "This trip, it will be just the two of us?"

"Absolutely," he replied and meant it. Gregory and Michael would be in town for part of that time, but he'd make certain they understood he and his wife were not to be disturbed. If they needed him, they could send a note. "What do you think?"

She gave him a hesitant smile. "I think I should like a trip to Edinburgh."

He closed the distance between them and ran his fingertips along the underside of her jaw. He was fascinated with the skin there . . . soft, fragile, and infused with her scent. He couldn't resist bending his head for a quick taste. "Am I forgiven?"

A shiver ran through her. "I suppose . . . I suppose it was just an honest mistake."

*A*delaide believed those words as she said them, and she believed in the sincerity of Connor's apology and promise to make amends. And yet a niggling discontent weighed on her shoulders for the rest of the evening and night. By morning, it had grown as thick and heavy as the blanketing fog outside.

Hoping to shake free of the mood, she excused herself from breakfast and went for a stroll in the cool, damp air. She wandered aimlessly along the trails that had been cut through the overgrown garden and tried to sort her disjointed thoughts and feelings into some semblance of order.

It wasn't difficult to pinpoint the cause of her unsettled mind. She'd forgiven Connor. Again. Was this to become a habit, she wondered, with Connor charming her one day, disappointing her the next, and she forgiving him every time? Where was the line between reasonably understanding and utterly spineless? And why the devil was she the only one stumbling between the two?

Because she was the only one in love, she thought with a sigh. It was wildly unfair.

If only she had a better sense of how he felt. He'd said she mattered, and she believed him. But matter had a vague and varied definition. Revenge mattered. So did routine bathing. Did she fall somewhere in between?

She didn't want to fall in between. She wanted to be first. She wanted to matter above all else. She wanted to know what steps she needed to take to see that happen.

"There's a long face."

Startled, Adelaide turned at the sound of Gregory's voice. He was sitting not six feet away on a bench, whittling a weathered piece of oak. Lost in her thoughts and the thick fog, she'd nearly walked right past him.

"Mr. O'Malley." She chuckled softly at herself. "I thought you were in the study with my husband."

Gregory shook his head and shaved off a long sliver. "He's seeing to business in the library this morning. Reports and manifests and all manner of paperwork I've no interest in." He patted the seat next to him with the handle of his knife. "Have a seat, lass. Tell me what's troubling you."

"Nothing is troubling me," she murmured, even as she took the seat.

"Aye, there is. You've had a row with your husband."

Her lips twisted in a combination of humor and chagrin. "You shouldn't listen to staff gossip."

"You had a part of it out on the drive," he reminded her. "You've not come to an understanding?"

"We have. He apologized."

"Well now, that's good. That's fitting. Have you forgiven him?"

She absently brushed a thick wood shaving from the bench. "Yes."

"And are you regretting now that you have?"

"No. He was sincere in his apology." She watched him

shape the top of the stick and found there was something soothing in the sure and steady pass of his knife over the wood. "He was very quick to offer it as well."

Gregory made a noncommittal sound in the back of his throat, which Adelaide would have paid dearly to be able to translate into something useful. It was ridiculous, perhaps even a little sad, that she should be seeking insight from one of Connor's men. But, damn it all, there was no one else to ask. There was no one else who knew Connor so well, or for so long.

"He's very charming, don't you think?" she commented casually. "When he wants to be."

Gregory glanced at her, his bushy white brows lifting. "Tangled you up some, has he?"

"No—"

"Sure and he has. You're wanting to paint a picture of him, but he won't stand still."

"I don't need a picture," she replied defensively. She had a picture. She just wanted a few of the smeary bits tidied up for her, that was all. "I know who Connor is."

Gregory considered her a moment before returning his attention to the wood. "Could be you do."

"I only wonder . . ." She bit her lip, struggling between her pride and the desire to understand. "He was so quick to apologize, and that ought to be commended, but I can't help feel he simply didn't want to dwell on the matter."

"Don't know as the boy's capable of dwelling on that sort of thing."

Her mouth fell open. "Are you saying my husband is witless?"

"I'm saying he's a man. And selfish. The boy's always been selfish—"

"That's not true," she said, though she knew quite well that it was. She was in love with Connor, not blind to his faults. It pricked at her, however, to hear someone else point them out.

"Raised the pampered prince, then left a pauper? Either

one of those are enough to be turning a man's thoughts to what's best for himself."

"He thinks of you," she pointed out.

"Sure and he does. Love the boy, don't I?" Gregory carved a notch into the wood with the tip of his knife. "A body can be good one day and bad the next."

She reflected on that in silence for a moment before asking, out of curiosity, "And do you love him on the days he's bad?"

"I do, but his selfish streak suits me, as I've one of my own I'm not of a mind to be giving up."

She thought of the way Gregory played with George and the story of how he'd met Connor. "I don't think you're selfish either."

"Ah, now you're wanting to paint a picture of me." He pointed the stick at her. "It's single-minded, you are."

"I'm not," she insisted. "Certainly not so much as Connor."

"Oh, aye. Determined, our Connor is, but I'd not be calling him single-minded. Too much of his time is spent looking about the edges of things, finding the ins and outs and ways around. A man's needing to be flexible, after all, if he's wanting to be both good and bad."

And a woman in love with such a man would need to learn flexibility as well, she thought. "Are you flexible?"

"Nay, lass. Old is what I am, and resigned to my faults."

She heard the thread of amusement in his voice and wondered if the entire conversation was little more than a diversion for him.

"I don't believe you."

Gregory chuckled. "You, not seeing the forest for the wood. Connor, not seeing the wood for the forest. I'm thinking you're either the perfect match or you'll be after murdering each other in your sleep."

She understood the second half of that comment well enough, but the first baffled her. "I don't like riddles."

And she didn't like tying herself into knots in front of a man who may, or may not, be having fun with her. She didn't like tying herself into knots, period. Moreover, it wasn't fair to Connor. He'd offered a sincere apology, and she'd accepted. It was wrong of her to go about grumbling and doubting his motives now. Forgiveness was granted or it was not. There was no in between.

She inhaled deeply through her nose and rubbed her hands up and down her thighs in brisk manner. "Do you know, I think this weather has made me maudlin."

Gregory bobbed his head, seemingly content to let her change the subject. "Aye. Fair gray out."

"I suppose we've been spoiled these past weeks, but I do hope our blue skies return for a time. Connor is taking me to Edinburgh next week." She felt a rush of pleasure and excitement at the thought of the upcoming trip. Another reason, she thought, to cease questioning Connor's motives. Another sign that he was trying. "I've never been to a proper town before. I can scarcely wait."

"Aye." A grim smile spread across his wrinkled face. "Looking forward to it myself."

Pleasure drained so rapidly, it felt as if someone had reached inside her and torn it free.

She knew that smile. She'd seen it on Connor and his men countless times. It was the same smile they wore when they emerged from a long session in the study. There was only one reason for Gregory to be wearing it now.

"Sir Robert is in Edinburgh, isn't he?" she asked.

"Sure and he is," Gregory replied easily. He glanced up from his work in the ensuing silence, took one look at her face, and sighed. "You didn't know."

"No."

"Ah, well." He transferred his knife to the hand holding the wood and patted her arm with the other. "Good and bad, lass. Good and bad."

Chapter 27

Gregory insisted on walking her back to the house, and he kept up a steady stream of chatter along the way. Very little of what was said registered with Adelaide, and she scarcely noticed when he left her in the front hall. She walked to the library in a kind of determined daze and found Connor sitting at a writing desk stacked with papers and books. He gave her a distracted smile.

"Good morning, Adelaide. I thought you were——"

"What was your purpose in planning a trip to Edinburgh?" she heard herself ask.

"Beg your pardon?" He frowned when she refused to repeat the question, and his eyes took on a wary glint. "You know the purpose."

"I know what you told me, and I know what Gregory told me. He'll be joining us. Michael too, I presume."

"Ah." He set his pen in its holder and rose to come around the desk. She couldn't see a shred of wariness in him now, not a hint of shame that he'd been caught in a lie. If anything, he looked relieved. "Is that what this is about?" He cupped her shoulders with his hands. "Sweetheart, Gregory and Michael will not be joining us. They'll be in town, yes, but—"

"Why?"

"Sir Robert is there. We've something in store for him."

The explanation was provided without hesitation, and it occurred to her that Connor could have demanded his men's silence if he'd wanted to keep his true reasons for going to Edinburgh a secret. He didn't look guilty or ashamed, because he hadn't been trying to lie. In all probability, the idea of doing so hadn't even crossed his mind.

Perversely, that made her feel worse. It snatched away the comfortable shield of righteous anger that had begun to fill the hole in her chest and left her with only hurt. She didn't want lies, of course. She wanted honesty from him in all things. But would it have been so difficult to have at least thought of her feelings? Of how an invitation produced as an afterthought might look to her?

"I thought it was a trip for us. I thought you planned it for us, and that it would be about us, and we'd—" She pressed her lips together to stem the rapid flow of words. There was a telling tremor in her voice that embarrassed and frightened her. She hadn't confronted him with the intention of pointing out the heart on her sleeve. And yet she couldn't seem to make herself leave. She wanted something from him. A sign, a reason to hope . . . Anything.

A furrow appeared between his brows. "It is is for us—"

"It's not," she whispered. "It has never been about us. It has always been about your revenge." Their courtship, their marriage, their daily lives—everything had been based upon, or was arranged around, Sir Robert.

"Revenge?" He rubbed her shoulders. "Adelaide, it's just a spot of business. It makes sense. If we're to be there, anyway—"

"Then you might as well placate your wife by bringing her along?" She snorted and grabbed hold of the sliver of anger his words afforded. "Efficiency, thy name is Connor Brice."

"That is not—" Connor broke off and swore at the sound of a soft knock on the door.

A footman entered, carrying a silver tray with a letter on top. "Missive's come for you, sir."

Connor's hands slid away, leaving her cold. He accepted the letter and dismissed the footman with a nod. And as he read the note, his lips curved into that awful, grim smile.

The sight of it filled her with a profound sense of defeat. "I'll not go to Edinburgh with you."

Connor looked up in surprise. "Why not?"

She gestured angrily at the letter in his hand. "Because I've no interest in sharing the experience with Sir Robert."

"What . . . Because of the note?" His expression was one of bewilderment heavily weighted with frustration. "It's only a note. One note." He held it out to her. "You can read it, if you like. We can—"

"I don't want to read it," she snapped. "I don't care what it says."

"You don't . . ." Astonished, he dropped his arm. "How can you not care?"

"This is your quest, Connor, not mine. Sir Robert has never been my obsession."

He looked at her as if she were a stranger. "You don't wish to see him pay? Is that what you're saying?"

"No—"

The flush of temper crept up his neck as he closed the distance between them. "Do you want me to forgive him? Let him walk away?"

"Of course not."

"Well, what the devil do you want?"

"I want you to not care so much. Why must your life be centered around Sir Robert?"

"Because he's a right bastard who has to pay—"

"Then toss him on a ship bound for Australia and have done with it!" She threw her hands up. "For pity's sake, how much of yourself will you give to him? How long will you set aside everything else in your life and—"

"You . . . That's what you mean, isn't it? How long will I set *you* aside?" A hardness settled over his features, and his voice turned cutting. "And I deserve that, do I? Have I been a poor husband, Adelaide? Neglectful of you? Cruel to you?"

"No, of course not. I'd not have—" She snapped her mouth shut before she could finish the thought. She'd not have fallen in love with a cruel man.

"Then what the *hell* is your objection?" he growled.

His green eyes were sharp with anger and swirling with confusion. And why shouldn't they be? Adelaide thought. She was poking and prodding and hinting, but never landing the point. Ultimately, she was trying to expose his heart while she guarded her own. It wasn't fair to either of them.

Taking a deep breath, she held his gaze and spoke softly. "I object because it hurts to see you deny yourself happiness in the pursuit of vengeance. I object because it hurts to be part of the life you reject. I want a real marriage with you. I want . . ." *I want your love,* she thought. She tried to say it, but the words tangled with the ball of fear caught in her throat. "I want a marriage that has nothing to do with Sir Robert and revenge."

Connor's eyes went flat, and for several long moments, he said nothing, gave nothing of his thoughts away. When at last he spoke, his voice was cool and faintly mocking. "We had a bargain, Mrs. Brice. I have my revenge, and you have your fifteen thousand pounds. Are you attempting to renegotiate?"

She hadn't thought of it that way, and though the idea of relinquishing her fortune frightened her, it was a fear she was willing to face. Connor was worth it.

"Yes. Yes, I am."

A flash of surprise and fear crossed his face. He shook his head slowly. "Too late; you took the money."

"You may have it back. I would like for you to take it back. I would like our marriage to be like any other. I would like you to . . . to look forward instead of back."

He balled the note in his hand and tossed it at the hearth with an angry flick of his wrist. "Is this a test, Adelaide?"

She shook her head. Strangely, the more agitated he grew, the more reassured she felt. He'd not be in such a temper unless at least some part of him was tempted by what she offered.

"No," she said. "It is an offer."

"The money in exchange for letting Sir Robert go free?"

"No. You may have your revenge. I've no protest against seeing Sir Robert get his comeuppance. I welcome it." Slowly, she reached out and placed the flat of her hand against his chest, and felt the brutal pound of his heart against her palm. "But you can no longer define yourself and your life by it. It can no longer come first. Your anger and your revenge can no longer—"

"Do I come first in your life?" he asked caustically.

Be reckless, she told herself. *Be hopeful. Expect more.*

"Yes." Her voice came out remarkably strong and clear. "I love you. There is nothing I would not do for you."

He shivered at the words. She felt the tremor pass under her fingers. But he said nothing, and simply stared at her for what seemed an eternity. Finally, he reached up and pulled her hand away.

"Then allow me this," he said and let her go.

*F*or a long time after Adelaide's departure, Connor remained in the library, going through every word of their argument. At least, he tried to go through every word. His mind kept returning to same spot, the same moment.

I love you . . . There is nothing I would not do for you.

Her admission had hit him like a blow to the chest. He'd never known such an instant, irrational, and painful bliss. He'd lost his air, lost his sense of balance. He'd damn near lost his mind. Almost, he'd agreed to her terms. In the first moments after she'd said the words, he'd been willing to agree to anything, anything at all, just to hear her say them again. Fortunately, that moment of lost control had shocked some sense into him.

Bloody hell . . . Let Sir Robert go? Was she mad? He'd waited fifteen bloody years—no, not waited, *worked*—he'd *worked* for fifteen bloody years to see the bastard pay. And she expected him to toss it all away because of three little words?

Well, not toss, he allowed. She'd not asked him to give it up entirely. *Have done with it.* That had been her suggestion. As if he and Sir Robert were engaged in a minor quibble. Didn't she understand the enormity of what had been done, the importance of what needed to be done? How could she claim to love him and not bloody understand?

Suddenly in need of company who had no trouble understanding, Connor left the library in search of his men. Gregory and Michael knew what it meant to seek revenge. They'd not wanted it for as long, but they'd always understood.

He found them in their usual chairs in his study, and after pouring himself a large drink, he took his own seat and explained his situation . . . In part, anyway. He skirted around a few details of the argument, and Adelaide's confession of love he kept to himself, but the basics were relayed.

As he unburdened himself, he began to feel better. His men would stand behind him, offer a bit of well-meaning, if useless, advice, and otherwise prove their loyalty to him and the revenge they'd all worked so hard to obtain. Comradery always helped to put a man at ease. He sure as hell hoped it would ease whatever nasty bit of unpleasantness was chewing on the inside of his chest.

He rubbed at it without realizing and took another long drink of his brandy before finishing up his recitation. "I told her no, naturally. I'll make it up—"

"Devil's the matter with you?" Michael demanded.

Connor blinked at the outburst and set his drink down slowly. "Nothing is the—"

Gregory looked at him as if he'd grown a second head. "Putting aside your own wife?"

"I've not put her aside."

"Aye, but you've put her *after*." Michael shook his head in disgust. "A man thinks of his family first."

Gregory nodded and lifted his glass in agreement. "His children, if he's having any. Then his wife, then everything else."

"Priorities, boy."

"I know what my priorities are." Damn it, this was not what he'd come to the study for. "Sir Robert—"

"Ain't going nowhere," Michael told him, before leaning back in his chair, his round face tightening into a challenging expression. "More'n what might be said for your wife."

"She's upstairs," Connor ground out. "Not missing."

"For now."

"For good," he snapped. Whatever was gnawing on his chest clamped down with iron jaws. "She's not going anywhere."

Michael mulled that over a bit before asking, "What if she did? What if she went missing?"

The jaws gnashed and ground. "She'll not."

"But if she did," Michael pressed. "If she decides she don't want a husband what puts her last. What then? Would you look for her?"

"I don't put her last." He reached for his glass, discovered it empty, and swore. "And of course I'd bloody look for her. What sort of question is that?"

Gregory shared a quick look with Michael. "Aye, but would you be looking for her if your brother went missing as well?"

"If he kidnapped her?" That question was more ridiculous than the last. He'd never let it happen. "What—?"

"Not kidnapped," Michael cut in, rolling his eyes. "Gone missing at the same time. Adelaide's left you. Sir Robert's gone off to hide in the laps of luxury and a pretty tart."

Connor pinched the bridge of his nose and prayed for

patience. "If there is a point to be made by these questions, make it now."

"Who are you going after?" Gregory huffed with impatience. "Your wife or Sir Robert?"

"Both." He'd find Adelaide, lock her in their chambers, then hunt down the baron.

Michael swore and tossed his hands up in defeat. "Boy's friggin hopeless."

Gregory muttered something about wood and forests. "Now listen carefully, lad; you know what's being asked of you. Which are you wanting more, your wife or your revenge?" Gregory jabbed a finger at him in a rare show of temper. "And don't you be telling me both. You'll answer the question as I put it to you, or I'll be taking a strap to your hide. Not so bleeding big I can't beat some respect into you."

Connor struggled between his threatened pride and the respect Gregory demanded. He itched to call Gregory on his bluff—*Try it, old man*—and knew damn well he'd cut out his own tongue before it could form the words.

Pushing away from the desk, he rose to pour himself another drink at the sideboard.

He wasn't the one being unreasonable. They wanted a simple answer to a complicated question. That wasn't the way the world was fashioned. Nothing was black and white. There were no absolutes, no definitive rights or wrongs. But if they wanted an empty, useless answer, they could have it.

Did Adelaide mean more to him than his revenge, or didn't she?

He forced himself to contemplate the notion of failing in his revenge. Sir Robert deserved to hurt. He deserved to suffer for every stolen coin, every second of hunger, every moment of fear and cold and misery. And Connor very much wanted to be the cause of that suffering, not just for himself but for Adelaide and his men.

That played into the question, didn't it? It damn well should. How could he want Adelaide and not want to butcher the man who'd hurt her?

"Sodding black and white."

"What's that, boy?"

"I'm thinking," he snapped over his shoulder.

Though it chafed, he pushed aside the matter of what was owed to Adelaide and his men and imagined how he would react if Sir Robert disappeared in the night, never to be seen or heard from again. He'd be furious. Without question, he would gnash his teeth over the loss of vengeance for a good long while. But eventually . . . Eventually he would learn to live with it. He'd not be happy about it, but, probably, he could learn to be happy without it, or at least around it. He'd survive.

Satisfied with the conclusion, he took a drink of his brandy and turned his thoughts to Adelaide.

If something happened to Adelaide . . .

The teeth in his chest tore viciously.

If she went missing . . .

His stomach twisted into a sick knot.

If she were never seen or heard from again . . .

The brandy turned to acid in his throat.

He set his drink down with a hand that shook. Holy hell, he couldn't even get past the question. He couldn't bring himself to think of what his world would be like without Adelaide. He'd all but torn his hair out when she'd been gone for half a day. How could he even fathom a lifetime without her? How could he contemplate what it would be like to live, day after day, without seeing her smile, hearing her voice, feeling her warm and safe in his arms?

He needed her. It was as plain as that. He wanted revenge. He craved it. But Adelaide, he needed. It was a terrifying and humbling realization.

The thirst for vengeance, he understood. It involved cause and effect. It had a definable beginning, middle, and end. Vengeance was due because Sir Robert had destroyed a part of his life. The thirst would be quenched when the favor had been returned. It was simple, quantifiable, and most important, manageable. The nature of the revenge, the steps between beginning and end, the length of time it took to reach the goal, those were entirely up to him. Even the depth to which he wanted his revenge was, to a degree, within his power to alter.

But this need for Adelaide, he had no power over that. Because unlike a desire for vengeance, what he felt for Adelaide could not be quantified, managed, or defined. Unlike vengeance, love was not something he could control.

Connor closed his eyes and swallowed a groan.

Bloody, bloody hell, he was in love with his wife.

Every fiber of his being rejected the notion. He despised not being in control. He had no experience with love. This sort of love, anyway. He wasn't a stranger to other sorts. He'd loved his mother and father, and though wild horses come from an icy hell couldn't drag the admission from his mouth at present, he loved Gregory and Michael. The first had been the love between child and parents. It came naturally and existed simply because they existed. Gregory and Michael— well, that was nearly as easy. They were the same as him. They wanted the same things, held the same expectations.

But this, what he felt for Adelaide . . . It was an altogether different sort of love. It was enormous, overwhelming, dangerous. It had the power to strip him of his pride and required he give over a part of himself, even all of himself.

"Son of a bitch."

"Come to a decision, have you?" Michael's cheerful voice grated.

Connor forced himself to turn and face his men.

"Yes," he said. "I want Adelaide more. She means more." She meant everything.

Michael nodded, then shrugged. "Then show her."

Despite the fear churning in his system, Connor chuckled. *Show her.* What a charming bit of advice from a man whose only known romantic gesture was to slip his favorite Boston barmaid a crown before he left for Scotland. Several times her usual fee.

"It's not that simple," he muttered. He'd given Adelaide fifteen thousand pounds. He sincerely doubted she'd be moved by a tumble and a coin.

Even agreeing to limit the time he spent on planning

revenge would likely prove inadequate now. He imagined offering his heart, laying open his soul to Adelaide, and watching her toss it aside.

Then allow me this.

Guilt flooded him and was closely followed by the fiery lick of panic.

Oh, hell. Oh, hell.

"I need to think."

He'd apologize. He'd take the words back. He'd make it up to her.

Vaguely, he was aware of returning to his seat. Mostly, he was focused on how futile and trite it would be to make yet another apology. He'd hurt her more than he could hope to make up for. Why the devil should she accept his apology now? Why would she even believe it? She'd offered him everything, more than he'd ever thought to hope for, and out of fear and selfishness, he'd tossed it all aside as if it meant nothing.

His eyes landed on the piles of papers upon his desk, and, suddenly, the panic began to retreat in the light of a new determination.

She'd offered more than he'd asked for. He could do the same.

He lurched from his chair. "Right. The plan is off. We're done."

"What?" Michael threw a startled glance at Gregory. "The plan . . . Entirely, you mean?"

"Now lad," Gregory said patiently. "I don't know as you're needing to go so far as all that."

"We were thinking you might scale back a hair," Michael explained. "Maybe take an extra hour here and there—"

"We're done." He grabbed a small stack of papers at random. "Destroy the rest. All of it. Do you understand?"

The men exchanged another glance.

"Aye."

Chapter 28

Adelaide huddled in front of the fire in the master chambers. She wasn't sure how long she'd been there, curled up in the chair. An hour . . . two? She barely remembered leaving the library, or asking one of the maids to light the fire. Time turned murky and sluggish. The better, she supposed, to draw out every long second of her misery.

Her heart ached like an open wound, and twice now, she'd crawled into bed, hoping to escape in sleep. But each time she'd closed her eyes, she saw Connor smiling at that bloody note and felt him letting her go, and her heart broke all over again.

She tried to rationalize the hurt away, tried to defeat it with common sense. Her anger and disappointment were unreasonable. She and Connor had married out of convenience. He'd never agreed to put her first. He'd never promised to love her.

It was foolish of her to have hoped for or expected more than what she was owed—his name and fifteen thousand pounds a year.

The lump in her throat broke free on a sob.

Foolish or not, she'd never wanted anything, hoped for anything, so desperately in her life as to hear Connor return her love. And she'd never been wounded so deeply as she'd been by his cold rejection.

Then allow me this.

Oh, God, it was more than heartache . . . It was the humiliation of knowing she wasn't what Connor wanted, and the fear he might never have what he needed to find peace. What if revenge brought only a hollow victory? What if Sir Robert slid out of reach altogether?

She wiped her sleeve across her wet cheeks and wondered how she could stand it—watching Connor suffer, knowing there was nothing she could do to help him, nothing she could offer that might bring him some measure of happiness.

The tears welled up again, but she sniffled and held them back as the door creaked open behind her. Thinking it was a maid come to tend the fire, Adelaide lifted a hand to stay her.

"Forgive me, but I'd like to be left alone, please."

"I know." Connor's voice settled over her softly. "I'm sorry . . . Will you look at me, Adelaide?"

She shook her head. She was shivering, and her eyes felt swollen and sore. She wanted time to pull herself together. "I wish you'd go away."

"I know," he said tenderly.

She heard the soft pad of his footsteps on the carpet. "Connor, please—"

"I've brought something for you."

He was standing behind her now, close enough to reach out and touch, and yet she'd never felt so distant from him. "I don't want anything. I don't need gifts."

"This one is for both of us." His arm came around the chair, and in his hand he held a thick stack of papers. The top one was a badly stained map, hand-sketched in blue ink.

Bewildered, she stared at it. "I don't understand . . . Do you want my help?"

He came around the chair slowly and made a low sound in his throat when he saw her face. With a carefulness that held her enthralled, he crouched before her and gently rubbed his fingers along the drying tear tracks on her cheeks. His green eyes trailed over her features, as if he was memorizing every detail. "I don't deserve you."

A frown tugged at her brow. "That's not true. I never—" She broke off when he stood, papers in hand, and stepped purposefully toward the fire. His intent was clear as day. "Wait! What are you doing?"

He gave her an incredulous look over his shoulder. "It's not obvious?"

She rose from the chair on legs that shook. "You can't. It means everything to you."

"No. It does not."

He lifted the hand holding the papers.

"Stop! No." She shook her head. "I don't want this. You'll regret it. You'll come to—"

"The only thing I regret," he said evenly, "is having waited so long."

"Wait!"

He dropped the arm again with a beleaguered sigh. "You're not making this any easier, sweetheart."

"I know. I'm sorry. But if you do this . . ." Then he would have nothing of his revenge, she thought, not even the sliver he'd thought he'd already obtained. She licked lips gone dry. She'd never imagined it would come to this. "I should have told you, but I was afraid you wouldn't . . ." Her hands clenched in the folds of her skirt. "You exacted no revenge on Sir Robert by marrying me. He never wanted me. He was never in love with me. His reasons for courting me were no different than your own."

He held her gaze a long, long moment, his expression unreadable.

"Yes. They were," he said at last and tossed the papers into the flames.

Adelaide stared at them in wonder, and as the edges of the paper blackened and curled inward, hope unfurled in her heart. "You knew?"

Connor turned from the fireplace. "Yes."

"And yet you . . . ?"

"I wanted you," he said softly. "That was never a lie."

The hope grew and was joined by a glowing warmth of pleasure that stole away her shivers. "You've let your revenge go?" Her voice was whisper soft. "Just like that?"

A part of Connor wanted to say yes . . . just like that. It would make Adelaide smile. It would answer the hope he could see lighting in her eyes. It would also be a lie.

"It's not all of it," he told her reluctantly. "Sir Robert invested a fair amount of money in a business venture that was designed to fail. If he's not heard of it by now, he will soon enough."

"Designed by you?"

"Yes. I can't take that back, Adelaide. I wouldn't even if I could. I'll not leave him with the resources to be a threat."

She blew out a shaky breath and, to his profound surprise, smiled in obvious relief. "Oh, thank goodness."

"You approve?"

"Yes, of course. I never wished for Sir Robert to go unpunished. I only wanted . . ."

"For me to have done with it," he finished for her.

"Yes."

"I am done with it." The promise was remarkably easy to make. Turning to stare into the fire, he watched as years of work turned to ash. He waited for a sense of regret that didn't come. "Two of those were deeds to sugar plantations that don't exist. Some were forged letters. Missives from Sir Robert to a fictional gentleman by the name of Mr. Parks. They detailed the baron's distaste for a number of prominent members of society and outlined his future plans for a few of their wives and daughters. Gregory and Michael were set to see them delivered into the hands of Edinburgh's elite tonight. And there were other papers, other . . ." He trailed off and shook his head. "I planned his ruin. Utter financial and social ruin."

"But you no longer want it," Adelaide said softly.

He turned to give her a rueful smile. "Oh, I want it."

Evidently, Adelaide didn't see the humor. "I didn't mean to deliver an ultimatum. I never intended—"

"I know."

"I don't want you to—"

"I know." He moved to her, wanting to reassure, needing to be close. He trailed his fingers along her jaw and outlined the soft shell of her ear with his thumb while she watched him through soft brown eyes. God, she was beautiful.

The words he wanted to give her caught in his throat. He'd never said them to another soul. Not to his parents, who'd practiced moderation in all things, including the sentimental, and not to his men, who would be no less mortified to hear them than he would be to speak them.

"I . . ." The hand at his side clenched as he struggled. "I . . . I don't want it as much as I thought . . . I don't need it . . . I need you."

That wasn't what he wanted to say. It was less than she deserved, and so he slipped his arms around her and bent his head to take her mouth. It was easier this way, to show her what he felt rather than speak the words. It had been easier from the start. How effortless it had been to allow a kiss, a trip to England, a plot of tilled land to speak for him.

What a simple thing it was now, to share the contents of his heart in the context of their lovemaking. Every brush of lips and tender caress was designed to please Adelaide. Nothing was withheld from her. There wasn't a thing she could demand that he wouldn't want to give. Everything she desired, everything she asked of him, he could grant without reservation. Without fear of failure.

He could see the desire grow in her eyes as he undressed her in slow stages, pausing to taste every inch of bared skin. He heard the sound of her pleasure when he took his time in the places he knew she liked best. He could feel the heat of her need after he had tormented them both beyond endurance and, at last, slipped inside her.

And when she found her release in his arms, he knew he'd made her happy.

He prayed that, for now, it would be enough.

Chapter 29

The following day brought an uncommonly strong wind that swept away the fog. To Adelaide, the garden was no longer a gloomy maze but the reckless wilderness she had come to love. As she moved along one of the paths, she wondered if she could coax Connor into leaving a part of it just as it was now.

Probably she should have thought to make the request yesterday afternoon . . . or last night . . . or this morning. There had been no end of promises made in the last twenty-four hours. Pledges whispered by the glow of firelight, confessions made in the soft light of dawn.

Connor had teased and tormented, thrilled and delighted until she'd agreed to his every demand. She'd never leave him. She would always love him. And in return, he'd promised to always take care of her, always listen, always be available.

He hadn't promised her love, but it seemed a reasonable expectation. One she decided to hope for, but not to press him into meeting. He'd accepted her love, and in return, he'd given her . . . *I need you.* That was enough for now.

Smiling, she turned down a path that led to the house. Connor should be finishing up his correspondence by now, she thought. And, if not, she'd convince him to set it aside. Graham had taken Isobel and George into Banfries. And Gregory and Michael had left the day before for—as they had put it—a round of carousing, and had yet to return. She wanted to take advantage of the relative privacy while they had the chance.

But it would have to wait a minute more, she realized when she spotted the gardener's cottage through a clearing. Someone had left the door open. Renovations on the small stone building had only just been completed. Broken windows had been replaced and crumbling mortar repaired. The interior was given a good scrubbing and fresh coat of paint. The head gardener was beside himself with excitement at the prospect of moving out of the servants' quarters and into his tidy little cottage.

He'd not find it tidy for long if people went about leaving the door wide open on blustery days.

Changing her direction once again, she hurried toward the cottage, turned a corner in the path around a hedge, and ran headfirst into Connor.

His low laugh floated over the wind as his hands came up to steady her. "Easy, sweetheart."

Grinning, she stretched up to kiss his cheek. The faint scratch of stubble tickled her lip. "I thought to come and find you in a minute."

"Now is better." His hands slid down her arms, and he took one of her hands, twining their fingers together. "Walk with me."

Anywhere, she thought. "Connor?"

His thumb brushed gently over her skin as he started them forward on the path. "Hmm?"

"I was wondering, must all the garden be landscaped?"

He frowned thoughtfully. "Aren't gardens landscaped by definition?"

"I suppose," she conceded. "But wouldn't it be nice to leave a piece of it as it is now? Just as we found it?"

"We'll leave the whole of it alone, if that's what you want."

"No, Ashbury should have—Oh, look!" She released his hand and rushed ahead of him toward a patch of blue-bells that were thriving amongst a tangle of weeks outside the gardener's cottage. "This is why we should let part of the garden be as it is," she called over her shoulder. "There are treasures in here."

Delighted, she bent down for a closer look. They weren't in bloom, but come next spring—

A flash of movement in the cottage caught her eye, and she straightened, expecting to see a maid with cleaning supplies. But it was Sir Robert who stepped through the open door, a pleasant smile on his face and pistol in his hand.

"Afternoon, Mrs. Brice."

Later, Adelaide would be unable to recall her immediate reaction to the sight with any clarity, but what she could remember would make her blush with embarrassment. She gave a small cry of alarm, and then she went perfectly still, the thick and icy grip of fear freezing her helplessly and uselessly in place.

A gun. He had a gun.

"Adelaide, back away." Connor's calm and steady voice cracked the ice.

She risked a glance over her shoulder and realized with a sinking heart that he was a good ten yards behind her.

Sir Robert shook his head. "She stays where she is. Or better yet . . ." His smile grew into a chilling grin. He transferred his aim from Connor to Adelaide. "Come here."

Connor's voice snapped like a whip. *"No."*

Adelaide was in full agreement. There was no telling what Sir Robert would do if he had hold of her, but kidnapping seemed a very real possibility. She shook her head at Sir Robert. She'd rather be shot in her own garden than dragged off someplace else and shot there.

Smile faltering, Sir Robert swung the weapon back on Connor. "Come *here*, or I'll blow a hole through his gut."

Oh, God. Oh, God. He meant it. She took a hesitant step. She'd rather be dragged off someplace else than see Connor shot in the garden.

Connor moved forward. "Adelaide, no."

"Ah, ah, ah." Sir Robert waved the gun. "You move, she dies. She doesn't move, you die. Are we clear?"

Adelaide moved forward, keeping her eyes trained on the gun. Sir Robert grabbed her arm and yanked her forward the last few feet. For one brief second, she thought she might have been in a position to reach for his weapon, but the opportunity was gone almost before she'd recognized it. Sir Robert spun her around, splayed his fingers on her waist, and rubbed his thumb back and forth in a revolting mockery of a caress. "Told you I'd have her eventually."

The taunt was for Connor. Somehow, that infuriated her more than the indignity of Sir Robert's touch. She'd not miss the next chance to try for the gun, she thought with dark determination. She'd not miss the chance to shoot him.

There was no visible reaction from Connor. His voice was low and eerily calm. "Let her go, Robert. This is between you and me. She has nothing to do with it."

"Neither does this gun. All the same, I believe I'll keep both for the time being."

"What do you want?"

"Oh, all manner of things," Sir Robert replied cheerfully.

"Our feud is over. Let—"

"Oh, is it?" Sir Robert's voice became needling. "Because you say so? Because you've had your fun destroying what's mine, and now you want to be done before—?"

"I haven't destroyed you. But I will. Harm a single hair on her head and I'll—"

"What?" Sir Connor snapped. "What will you do? You've ruined my name. Stolen my life." He pitched his voice higher when Connor shook his head. "Don't deny it. Don't you dare deny it. I know it was you behind the sham investments. And you who sent those letters."

"What letters?"

"What . . . *What letters?* Dozens of them! Bloody hundreds!" Sir Robert's chest rose and fell against her back like an overworked pair of bellows. "A mob formed outside my door. I had to crawl out a window. A window, you bastard. I barely escaped Edinburgh with my skin. I can never show my face in society again. Every husband, father, and brother in Britain wants a piece of my hide. I can't go home, and now I haven't the funds to go anywhere else. So tell me, please, what worse could you do?"

Adelaide's mind whirled. He'd learned of the fictional investments. But husbands and fathers? The forged letters Connor had told her about? It couldn't be true. Connor had burned those. He'd burned everything. She'd watched him. With a bone-chilling wash of dread, she realized it didn't matter what she'd seen, what she knew. Someone had sent letters, and Sir Robert would never accept a denial of guilt from Connor.

Connor obviously reached the same conclusion. "I'll give you the funds to—"

Sir Robert's arm tightened around her waist. "Oh, you'll give me more than that."

"I've two hundred pounds in my pocket. Let Adelaide go and you can have it. I'll see you make it safely out of the country. Anywhere you want to go."

Sir Robert fell silent, and Adelaide held her breath. Maybe he would take the offer. Maybe he was considering the wisdom of retreat. Maybe—

"Who the *devil* keeps two hundred pounds in his pocket?" Sir Robert's voice was a strange mix of bafflement, amusement, and disdain. "Idiot mongrel."

"Take the money," Connor pressed.

Sir Robert snorted. "Live off your largesse? My every move subject to your will? Even if I were fool enough to take you at your word, I'd not debase myself with your brand of charity. I'd rather hang for a murderer. At least I'll have the pleasure of watching the grief in your eyes as I swing."

"You won't hang," Connor said. "Your title will see to that. You'll spend the rest of your life in prison or a madhouse."

The gun swung toward Connor. "Then we finish this now."

Adelaide jerked in her captor's arms. "Take me with you!"

"Adelaide, don't be a fool," Connor snapped.

She ignored him. She had no intention of being foolish. She had no intention of going with Sir Robert, if she could help it. But she had to buy them time.

"He'll do anything you say," she rushed on. "Give you anything you want if you have me. He'll be completely under your power. Not for a few minutes, but as long as you like. You don't have to be locked away, and you don't have to take his charity. He'll pay any price you name."

"He'll hunt me down."

Connor's face was murderous. "I'll *slaughter* you, you—"

"Is he smarter than you, then?" Adelaide goaded. "Faster, stronger—?"

The gun nudged to her temple. "Shut up!"

She squeezed her eyes shut. "Think. What would be worse for him, my quick death or a lifetime of wondering?"

She prayed that he would take the bait. And failing that, that her death would be quick and painless and, most important, give Connor the opportunity to rush Sir Robert, or hurl a rock, or dive for cover. Something, *anything* that would save him.

"There's twine in the cottage," Sir Robert said suddenly.

Adelaide's eyes flew open, and she heard the harsh release of her own breath. She'd done it. She'd bought them more time.

Sir Robert jerked his head at Connor and began to edge them both away from the door. "Fetch it. But keep your distance."

Slowly, cautiously, Sir Robert moved them in a wide arc until their position and Connor's were reversed. Connor disappeared inside the cottage and reappeared a minute later with a ball of twine in hand.

"Toss it here and back away," Sir Robert instructed.

Connor lobbed it underhanded. It hit the ground with a soft thud, rolled, and stopped a few feet in front of her. He took two steps back then, but he was a little closer now, five yards away instead of ten. It wasn't much, but it was something. She prayed it would be enough.

Sir Robert's arm slipped from her waist. He pulled the gun from her temple and used it to gesture at the twine.

"Pick it up."

It was the chance she'd been waiting for. Without hesitating, she shifted her weight, shoved away the arm holding the gun, and rammed her shoulder into Sir Robert's midsection as hard as she could. She heard his grunt and felt him stumbling away from her. The gun went off, and the sound was deafening, like a physical blow. Adelaide staggered back as Connor rushed by her in a blur. He plowed into Sir Robert at full speed, hurling them both into the ground.

Sir Robert struggled to get out from under Connor's weight. He swung the gun up, but Connor caught his wrist and gave it a brutal twist. Sir Robert's mouth opened in a shout a second before Connor wrenched the gun away and brought it crashing down on the man's skull.

While Connor made swift work of tying the unconscious baron with the twine, Adelaide stood where she was, trembling from head to toe. There was a high-pitched whine in her ears, and the acrid smell of burned powder hung in the air. She barely noticed either. Her attention focused on Connor. He was alive. He was safe. And he was shouting something at her.

"Are you hurt?! Adelaide, are you hurt?!"

She shook her head. "No, I'm not hurt."

But for some reason, her hand crept to her side, just above her hip. She felt something thick and warm against her fingers. Dazed, she looked down and saw red bloom through a tear in the lavender silk of her gown. A mist formed over her vision, her knees gave out, and suddenly she was seated on the ground.

"I don't feel it," she heard herself say. "Shouldn't I feel it?"

Connor yanked the last knot tight and rushed to her side. She noted in a detached sort of way that his face was ashen as he took her shoulders and gently laid her down.

His hand shook as he reached out and pressed his palm against the wound. Hard.

The mist cleared, ripped away by the sound of her own scream.

Now she felt it.

She'd never known anything like it, the hideous mix of tearing and burning, as if someone was ripping at her with a glowing hot poker. And for a moment, she lost all reason. Nothing existed but the need to escape the pain. She struggled to get away, digging her heels into the earth, shoving at Connor with her right hand. She tried pushing him away with both, but lifting her left arm sent new waves of agony along her side and panic coursing through her veins.

Connor kept the pressure steady. Bending over her, he caught her flailing hand and pinned it to the ground. "No, sweetheart . . . I'm sorry . . . Darling, don't . . . Breathe through your teeth."

That last order was so outrageous, so preposterous, it actually succeeded in cutting through a layer of panic.

"Breathe . . . through . . . *my teeth*?"

"Try . . ." His breathing ragged, he arched over her protectively. A tremor racked his frame as he bent down to crush his lips to her brow. "Please. For me."

She tried, for him. With her eyes locked on his, she sucked in air through her nose and pushed it out through her teeth.

"Slowly," Connor said. His breath was hot and soothing against her skin. "That's it . . . That's it, love . . . Is it getting better?"

She offered a jerky nod. Her side hurt like the devil, but it was getting better, and with every slow exhale, the pain dulled a little more.

"I'm sorry," she choked out.

"No. *God*." He crushed his lips to hers. "It's all right. It's all right, now. Just keep breathing . . . That's it . . . Keep going . . ."

Releasing her, he drew away to inspect her injury. She felt his hand lift from her side and heard the rending of fabric. To distract herself, she studied the locks on his bent head, the details of each golden strand and wave. The pain receded further, until it was a throbbing ache instead of a shearing burn.

"It's a flesh wound," he whispered raggedly. "It's only a flesh wound."

She took immediate exception to that.

"It's *my* flesh," she ground out. There was no *only* about it.

Connor flashed her a wobbly grin. "Don't you trust me to take care of it?"

She wanted to smile back but couldn't quite summon the courage or the strength. Risking a peek at her side, she caught a glimpse of angry red flesh before Connor covered her injury with a makeshift bandage fashioned of his handkerchief and a strip from her chemise. "It's not . . . mortal?"

"No, sweetheart." He leaned over her for a quick soft kiss even as he divested himself of his coat and laid it over her. "It missed the vitals. You've lost some blood, but it's slowing."

She wanted to ask what the vitals were, exactly, and how could he be so certain they'd escaped damage, but she was distracted by the sudden arrival of several armed footmen.

" 'Ere they are!" One of them shouted. "Gardener's hut!"

Within moments, the housekeeper, butler, and several more armed footmen had joined them.

"Dear heavens, what's happened?"

"Is that Sir Robert?"

"Told ye there were a shot!"

"Oh, missus—!"

Connor brought silence and order with a few short commands. "Jennings, fetch the physician. Bernard, the magistrate. I want two guards on the baron. Mrs. McKarnin, have bandages, hot water, and honey brought to the master chambers. And brandy. A bottle of it."

He slipped an arm under her knees, the other around her shoulders, and carefully lifted her in his arms. Careful or not, the movement was jarring, and she bit the inside of her cheek to keep from crying out. Connor's manner was brisk and efficient, but there were deep lines of strain on his face. She hated seeing them.

"Connor—"

"Shh." He headed for the house without a single backward glance for the baron. "Close your eyes. Rest."

Rest? Her heart was still pounding, her mind a morass of questions and lingering terror. And she had a hole in her side. It would be months before she would be able to close her eyes and rest. But to please him, and comfort them both, she wrapped her arm around his neck, laid her cheek against his shoulder, and watched the steady throb of his pulse in his neck.

"Connor? The letters Sir Robert—"

"Rest."

"I don't want to," she said softly. "I want to hear your voice."

His arms tightened around her. "You're in pain. You need—"

"Not so much now," she said, thinking it was only a small lie. Her side throbbed mercilessly, but it was still an improvement over those first awful moments. "The letters Sir Robert spoke of . . . I thought you'd burned them."

He hesitated before answering. "I did. Some of them. I . . ." He trailed off, and something akin to a growl issued from his throat.

"What?"

"I didn't burn everything. Hell, I didn't burn half. I thought I'd only need a few so I could . . ." Color crept up his neck. "I burned them as . . ."

"As what?"

"A gesture." The color spread a little further. "I wanted to make the gesture. It was symbolic . . . Gregory and Michael were to dispose of the rest."

"Oh. I see." Obviously, Gregory and Michael went through with their own plans. "Were there really hundreds of them?"

"No," he said, as he brought them through a side door into the house. "A couple dozen. Doesn't matter. Even one was enough."

Chapter 30

Conversation ceased as Connor carried Adelaide through the house, up the stairs, and into the master chambers where he laid her gently on the bed. Maids and footmen darted in and out of the room, carrying bandages, scissors, water, extra blankets, and wood. Connor replaced the blood-soaked handkerchief with clean linen. A maid lit a fire in the hearth, while the housekeeper and cook held a murmured debate over whether the honey should be applied to the bandages before or after the physician had the opportunity to examine the injury.

Adelaide found the busy activity oddly soothing, until someone mentioned the word "sepsis."

"Out!" Connor bellowed, his face bleached of color. "Everyone out!"

The staff hurried to obey, setting down their burdens and scurrying out the door. Over the shuffling of feet, Adelaide heard the slam of the front door and the pound of boots on the stairs.

"Connor!"

"Lad!"

She stifled a groan. Michael and Gregory were home, and their timing could not have been worse.

"What's all this?" Michael called out. "Where's the boy, then? He'll want to hear—"

"Aye, from me," she heard Gregory say. "*I'll* be telling him."

"The hell you will. He'll hear it from me, or—"

Connor marched to the open door. "I've heard!"

Though Connor blocked most of her view into the hall, she could make out the edge of Michael's round form and Gregory's bony side as they came to a stop.

"What's this ruckus for? The wife abed? Why—"

"She's been shot, you—"

"Shot?!" both men exclaimed at once.

"I'll be quite all right," Adelaide called out, mostly for Connor's benefit. "It's only a flesh wound."

"A flesh wound, is it?" She heard a pair of relieved exhalations, something about spine, and then, "Who shot you, lass?"

"Sir Robert," Connor bit off.

A brief silence followed.

"Ah."

"Hell."

"You went through with it," Connor snarled. "You delivered those damn letters."

"Sure and we did," Gregory agreed.

Michael's voice turned defensive. "The rotter tossed us in prison. What did you expect?"

"I expected you to follow my bloody orders!" Connor roared. "I told you to destroy the papers. I told you Adelaide wanted me done with it. You said you understood."

"And so we did," Gregory replied.

"A man ought be putting his wife first," Michael agreed.

"Then why the devil—?"

"Well, she's not *our* wife, is she?"

Gregory peered over Connor's shoulder. "Would you be caring for more than one husband?"

"Thank you, no."

"There you have it, lad." Gregory's wrinkled hand pounded on Connor's shoulder. "She's yours, entirely."

"Demands and all."

"She didn't demand . . ." Connor dragged a hand down his face. "Go. Just go. I'll deal with you later."

"But what happened to—"

Connor slammed the door shut, then swore viciously when a soft knock sounded not five seconds later. "I bloody well told you—!"

He swung the door back open to reveal a young, wide-eyed maid holding a bottle of brandy and two glasses. "Beggin' pardon, sir," she said nervously. "Mrs. McKarnin said I should bring this straightaway. But if you're not wanting—"

"No. I want it." He took the bottle, ignored the glasses, and muttered something Adelaide very much hoped was an apology. The maid bobbed a lightning-quick curtsy and dashed away.

Adelaide studied Connor's face as he turned. Color had returned, but it wasn't what one might call a healthy hue. It was too dark, and steadily growing darker. He slammed the bottle down on the writing desk and began a steady pace at the foot of the bed. Hoping the exercise would serve to settle his temper, she decided to keep quiet for several minutes. She changed her mind when he began to flick dark glances in her direction every fifth step or so.

She lifted a hand to gesture at the brandy. "What are you going to do with that?"

"Drink it."

"Right from the bottle? Fine nursemaid you'll be then," she teased, hoping for a smile. "Will you at least share?"

"No." He all but snapped at her. "You'll have laudanum."

A little indignant, she frowned at him and plucked at the counterpane. "Are you angry with me?"

"No . . . Yes . . ." He spit out a word she'd never before heard and therefore assumed was highly profane, and then he stalked around the bed to crouch over her, his hands gripping the pillow on either side of her head. *"Take me with you?"*

"Oh. That." She offered him a weak smile. "I didn't mean it."

His eyes narrowed. "And did you *mean* to step in front of a bullet?"

"Certainly not." She'd meant to step in front of the gun. She distinctly recalled hoping bullets would not come into play.

Apparently, Connor failed to see the distinction. His face took on a tormented expression. "It was for me to fight him. For me to protect—"

"You were too far away. There was nothing you could do. And—"

"There was. I needed more time, that's all. I—"

"Isn't that what I gave you?"

There was a long, long moment of silence in which a muscle in Connor's jaw grew increasingly more active.

"Yes," he finally bit out. And it was amazing, really, how much reluctance could be fit into a single word. "But I'd have come up with it on my own. You had no business—"

He broke off, his entire body tense and straining, and then, suddenly, the fight went out of him. The anger drained from his face, and a rush of breath spilled from his lips.

"Oh, God." A deep groan rumbled from his chest and he bent his head, resting his forehead against hers. "I thought I'd lose you," he rasped, closing his eyes. "I thought . . ."

"I thought the same." She ran her palm up to stroke the knotted muscles in his neck. "But here we are."

And it seemed wondrous that they should be so, glorious that she could feel his breath, strong and sure against her skin. Closing her eyes, she let herself steep in the miracle of both. Connor was alive. He was whole and hale and safe. She couldn't ask for more.

*S*he might have been killed.

Connor struggled with the emotions warring inside him. There was anger, relief, and regret. But first and foremost, there was fear. Over and over again, he saw Adelaide stumbling back from Sir Robert. He watched helplessly as she collapsed to the ground, the bright stain of blood seeping through her gown.

He'd never known such fear; not in the darkest hours after his parents' death had he ever felt terror like this. He couldn't be rid of it, couldn't shove it aside or blanket it with anger. He could feel himself shake with it even now.

"I want to . . ." He wanted to wrap her in cotton batting and lock her away. More, he wanted to erase her own memories and spare her every second of fear, every heartbeat of pain.

"I'm sorry." His voice shook. "Adelaide—"

"Shh. You're not at fault."

"If I'd stopped it all earlier. If I'd made it clear to Gregory and—"

She gave a small huff of annoyance. "If Sir Robert had not hit you over the head with a dueling pistol and delivered you to a press-gang. If your father hadn't neglected his wife and child. If—"

He shook his head. "I should never have begun this. It was my fault Sir Robert took notice of you. I should never have brought you into it."

"I'm grateful you did. I'm so grateful to have found you." She brushed her hand through his hair. "I love you."

A shiver of pleasure raced over him, followed by a steely determination. What was done was done. He couldn't change the past, couldn't retrieve what had been stolen from him, erase who he'd been, or ignore what he'd done. But he could learn from his mistakes. He could treasure what he had now. Careful so as not to jar her, he settled his weight on the mattress, then took her face in his hands.

"You asked me why I compromised you, why I married you, and why I burned those papers. And I've given you . . ." He'd given her vague answers and half-truths. He wanted her. She mattered. He needed her.

"I love you," he whispered. "I love you with . . ." He faltered. "I love you more than . . ." He stumbled again. "Hell."

He couldn't find the right words. He'd thought they would come once he got out the hardest bit, but now everything else seemed trivial and inadequate. And nothing, not even those hardest words, seemed capable of expressing the immeasurable contents of his heart.

He took her hand and pressed it to his chest over his heart, willing her to understand.

"I love you." He kissed her softly, brushing his lips across her cheek, her brow, her lids. "I love you." He took her mouth hungrily, pouring every ounce of himself into the kiss.

"I love you," he whispered. "I don't have any other words."

Eyes bright with unshed tears, Adelaide framed his face with her hands. "They're all I need. They're everything I've ever hoped for."

Turn the page for a special preview of
Alissa Johnson's next historical romance

Practically Wicked

Coming soon from Berkley Sensation!

$\mathcal{L}$ ife was best experienced through a thick layer of fine drink.

Inferior drink might do in a pinch, but Maximilian Dane was certain that nothing accompanied an evening of debauchery with the demimonde quite so well as several goblets of excellent wine at dinner, followed by a glass, or two, of expensive port in the billiards room, followed by a liberal tasting of superb brandy in the card room, followed by any number of flutes of champagne in Mrs. Wrayburn's ballroom, followed by . . . whatever it was he had poured in the library. He recalled an amber hue and delicate bite. He also recalled forgoing the actual pour and drinking straight from the bottle.

In hindsight, that may have been a mistake.

Because at some point following that final drink, he left the library in search of . . . something or other, and rather than finding his way back to the ballroom where this something was most likely to be found, he had landed here—in a quiet, unfamiliar room illuminated by only a spattering of candles, and seated in a plain wooden chair before a plain wooden table, which had both initially appeared to be adequately sized for a man of five-and-twenty, but, upon his sitting, had proved to be entirely too near to the floor. His legs were bent at an angle he suspected would be impossible were it not for the limbering quality of all those glasses.

"What in God's name is the matter with this furniture?"

"Lord Highsup cut the legs off for me when I was six," a woman's voice explained. He liked the sound of it, lower than one expected from a woman and warm like the fine drink from the library.

He looked up from the golden wood grain of the table and squinted until the form sitting across from him came into focus. His companion wore a night rail and wrap. They were white, ruffled, and provided a sharply contrasting background to the dark braid of hair that fell over her shoulder and ended just below a well-formed breast.

"You're not six."

"Indeed, I am not. How astute of you to ascertain."

"Plenty tart, though, I see. Who are you?" He threw up a hand, narrowly avoiding a thumb to the eye. "No . . . No, wait. I know. I never forget a lady." Leaning closer, he took in the young woman's pale gray eyes and delicate features, along with her rigid posture and indifferent expression. "You . . . are Miss Anna Rees, the Ice Maiden of Anover House."

There was a slight pause before she spoke. "And you are Mr. Maximilian Dane, the Disappointment of McMullin Hall."

"Ah . . . *Not*"—he informed her with a quick jab of his finger at the ceiling—"*anymore*. At half past seven this morning, or somewhere . . . thereabouts, I became *Viscount* Dane . . . the Disappointment of McMullin Hall."

"Oh." Her tone softened as the meaning of his words set in. "Oh, I am sorry."

" 'S neither here nor there," he assured her with a clumsy sweep of his hand. "Speaking of which . . . Where is here, love?"

"Anover House."

"Yes, I know. Lovely party. Where in Anover House?"

"The nursery."

"Ah. That would explain the miniature furniture, wouldn't it?" He shifted a bit and grimaced when he caught the side of his ankle on the table leg. "Bit long in the tooth for the nursery, aren't you?"

"It was the nearest room, my lord. You—"

"*Don't*," he cut in sharply. "Don't call me that. I've hours yet."

"Hours?"

"Until everyone hears, until everyone knows I am Lord Dane." He curled his lip in disgust. "Until I have to be a bloody viscount."

"Very well. Mr. Dane, then. If you would—"

Something about the way she said his name sparked a memory.

"Mrs. Cartwell," he said suddenly and made a failed effort at snapping his fingers. "*That's* why I came upstairs." The reasonably attractive and exceptionally accommodating widow Cartwell had invited him to her guest chambers. He'd stopped in the library for that last drink, something to further blur the face of his brother, and then . . . he'd become a bit turned around. He gave Miss Rees a quizzical look. "Came down the wrong hall, did I?"

"If you were after Mrs. Cartwell, yes. She is a floor below."

"I climbed an extra set of steps?" Strange; he'd not have thought himself capable. His legs felt like pudding. "Huh. And how is it I came to be in your company?"

"I was in the hallway. You waved, tripped, and landed at my feet."

He closed his eyes in thought, found it made the room spin unpleasantly, and let his gaze drift over Miss Rees's face instead. He recalled now, smiling at the pretty lady, losing his feet and finding them again with the lady's assistance. She smelled sweet and flowery, like sugar biscuits and roses. "So I did. What the devil did I trip on?"

"I couldn't say," Miss Rees replied and rose smoothly from her chair.

In a display of coordination that surprised him, he reached forward and took hold of her wrist without falling out of his seat. "Where are you going?"

"To ring for assistance." She tugged at her wrist, but he held on with a gentle grasp. He liked the way the heat of her skin seeped through the cotton and warmed his palm.

"Don't. I don't want help. I don't need it." And the moment she rang for it, she'd leave. He wanted that least of all. The ballroom below was filled with ladies like the widow Cartwell—worldly women clad in silk, rubies, and the promise of sin-filled nights. But it was the prim little creature before him now who intrigued him. "You've a different sort of promise."

"I beg your pardon?"

He shook his head, lightly so as not to lose it entirely. "Never mind. Don't ring for help."

"You cannot stay here in the nursery, my lord, and—"

"Mr. Dane," he reminded her. "Why not? Are there children about?"

Surely not. Surely no one, not even the most depraved friends of Mrs. Wrayburn, would be so ridiculous as to bring a child to one of the woman's parties.

"No, but—"

"Then we'll stay. Sit," he pressed again. He considered and rejected the idea of tugging her back onto her seat. His current level of coordination was unpredictable at best. He wasn't looking to do the woman an injury. "Talk with me."

"I can't. It isn't proper."

He snorted a little in response. As far as good society was concerned, the words "proper" and "Anover House" were mutually exclusive. "What do we care for proper, you and I?"

"I care," she replied, and he watched with fascination as her already rigid back straightened just a hair further. "My mother would most assuredly care."

"Then she ought to have had the sense to move you out of the house by now."

If he remembered correctly, rumor had it Mrs. Wrayburn had, in fact, tried to marry her daughter off on more than one occasion, but Miss Rees was content to stay as she was—a reclusive and spoiled young woman, and a burden on her overindulgent mother.

Well, the little darling could indulge someone else for a change.

"I want you to stay," he informed her. "And now that I'm a viscount, I'm fairly certain you have to do as I say. Sit. Talk."

Unless he was very much mistaken, her lips twitched with amusement. "No."

This time, when she pulled at her wrist, he had no choice but to grant her freedom or risk being yanked from his seat.

He squinted at her willowy arms. "Stronger than you look."

That dubious compliment earned him a bland expression. "I daresay a kitten would give you trouble in your current condition, which is why I need to ring—"

"That's insulting." Quite possibly true, but nonetheless insulting. "Unless you are referring to one of those giant breeds of cats? Tigers and such? They have exceptionally large kittens."

"Cubs, Mr. Dane. And no, I was not."

"Then I'm insulted." He made a show of slumping in his chair, but when that failed to lure out a smile, he tried another tack. "Before passing along your next barb, you might consider taking into account the sad, *sad* nature of events which has led to my weakened state."

"I beg your pardon?"

He wondered if he was, perhaps, not expressing himself as clearly as he imagined. "There's been a death in the family, you'll recall."

It was unforgivable to make mention of his brother's passing in such a careless manner, and he might have felt a little guilty for it, were he not so damnably angry with his brother just now. And so gratified to see Miss Rees's expression soften once again. And so stupendously drunk.

But softened or not, Miss Rees appeared implacable in her resolve to leave. "Please understand, Mr. Dane, I am most sorry for the loss of your father. However—"

Baffled, he straightened in his chair. "My father?"

"The gentleman from whom you've inherited the viscountcy."

"Ah, no. My elder brother, Reginald. My father shuffled off the mortal coil years ago." He gave that additional thought. "Maybe only two. Strange, seems longer. And not long enough." The viscount's baritone voice had grown happily dim in his memory.

"I am truly sorry for the loss of your brother," Miss Rees corrected patiently. "However, I cannot continue to keep company with you in here, like this. I may not come from good ton, but I am an unmarried young woman, and, as a gentleman, you—"

"Good Lord, child, where did you acquire the impression I was a gentleman?"

"Very well," she conceded. "As a *viscount*, you are expected, at the very least, to make a show of adhering to the strictures governing a gentleman's behavior, and as such, you *must* respect my wish to not risk being seen in—"

"Oh, for God's sake," he groaned, "just *go*."

A lecture of what he *must do* was the last thing he wanted to listen to at present. He'd done nothing but follow the mandates of others for the first four-and-twenty years of his life. It had been an appalling experience. He had discovered in the year since that it was far better to be a disappointment than a pawn. Better still if he didn't have to suffer through someone else's long-winded opinion on the matter.

Miss Rees glanced at the bellpull, then back to him. "Will you allow me to ring for—?"

"No." If he couldn't sit with the pretty lady, he'd sit alone for a bit and find his own way back downstairs.

"As you like," she murmured, and she turned and walked

away with the flowing grace that had helped cement her nickname as the Ice Maiden.

"Like gliding on ice," he mumbled. "'S not natural."

Giving no indication of having heard the comment, she reached the door, paused with her hand on the handle, and looked back with a pleading expression. "*Please* allow me to ring for assistance."

"No."

"But I—"

"No."

A small crease formed between the dark arcs of her brows. "You can't mean to—"

"Unaccustomed to hearing the word 'no,' aren't you?"

Her lips thinned. "I ought to have left you in the hall."

"Regrets are like mistresses," he informed her.

"I . . ." Her hand dropped from the handle. "What?"

"Good men don't have them."

She blinked at that, then broke into a soft laughter that sent pleasant chills along his skin. "That is the most ridiculous adage I have ever heard."

"I'm foxed," he pointed out and shrugged. "I'm cleverer when . . . Cleverer? Is it 'cleverer'? Or is it 'more clever'? Whichever. I'm brilliant when I'm sober."

"And less inclined to announce it, one might hope." With a resigned sigh, she reached for the door handle again, but this time, she locked the door and dropped the key in her pocket.

"You move like a queen," he said quietly as she crossed the room and resumed her seat in front of him. "On ice skates. What did you just do?"

"I locked the door."

"Yes, I know." He was drunk, not blind. "Why?"

"To avoid another inebriated guest stumbling in upon us by accident."

"You mean to stay?" he asked, not quite believing it.

Avoiding his gaze, she brushed a smoothing hand down the sleeve of one arm. "You won't allow me to call for someone else."

"And you aren't willing to leave me sitting here all alone? That is . . . unexpected." He leaned in for a closer inspection of her features. "Aren't you supposed to be frigid and uncaring?"

She looked at him, her eyes narrowing just a hair. "Aren't you supposed to be charming?"

He grinned at her, appreciating the sharp retort. "I'll have you know, I could talk the devil out of his tail."

"I'm not a devil, Mr. Dane."

"No . . . I believe you might be an angel."

"And I believe the reports of your charm have been grossly exaggerated."

"Was a bit trite, wasn't it?" He propped his elbow on the table, rested his chin in his hand, and studied her features at leisure. "There *is* something . . . otherworldly about you. The eyes, I think. But they're not angelic. They're fae."

"They're merely sober."

"Equally disconcerting. Why is it you never come downstairs with your mother? She throws wonderful parties. You'd enjoy yourself, I think."

"I doubt it."

"You're enjoying yourself now, with me," he pointed out. Reasonably, to his mind. "The ballroom is brimming with fellows just like myself."

"Inebriated?"

"Yes," he allowed. "Also, exciting and charming."

She eyed him with frank curiosity. "Is that what you're doing coming to parties like these? Dedicating your life to being exciting and charming?"

"I don't dedicate myself to anything," he assured her, lifting his chin from his hand. "Entirely too much work."

"Being a member of the demimonde isn't work? Drink and women and scandals." She shook her head lightly. "Seems prodigiously taxing to me. Why do you do it?"

"Because I can," he replied with a careless lift of one shoulder. "Because I'm not supposed to."

She digested that quietly a moment before speaking. "A

viscountcy comes with many responsibilities, I imagine. Will you change your ways now?"

"I have changed my ways, sweet. That is how I landed here. And I must say, misshapen furniture notwithstanding, I rather like where I am at present." He smiled at her and watched the faintest of blushes bloom on her cheeks. "How is it you knew of my nickname, but not that my brother was the viscount?"

To her credit, she merely blinked at the sudden change of subject. "When one spends little time outside one's rooms, one gains information in bits and pieces. I encountered your name and reputation in passing."

"Everything you do is in passing. A moment in the ballroom, a mere peek out of the opera box. I've never met the man to have spent more than thirty seconds in your company."

A flicker of unease crossed her features, but it was gone almost the instant it arrived. "Do you mean to brag to your friends to have been the only one?"

"And be banished from your mother's home?" He made a scoffing noise. "I'll keep the accomplishment to myself, though it will cost me. You're the subject of considerable speculation, you know."

"Am I?" She digested that behind a shuttered expression. "One would think people would have something more compelling to discuss than a woman of whom they know nothing."

"It's the mystery of the thing," he explained. "What will become of the spoiled, reclusive daughter of the notorious Mrs. Wrayburn? Will she follow in her mother's footsteps and become a member of the demimonde? Will she marry a tradesman with the fortune to keep her in silk and diamonds?"

"Perhaps I'm not as spoiled as people seem to think," she offered softly. "Perhaps I'll marry a pauper and reside in a cottage in the countryside."

"And live off your dowry?" He considered that. "Do you have a dowry?"

"You'd have to ask my mother."

"Hardly matters," he decided. "Who are you going to meet, peeking into ballrooms and parlors long enough to give us all a glimpse of your fae eyes and fine feathers, and hiding away upstairs for the rest of the night?"

"I don't hide," she replied, a whisper of defensiveness creeping into her voice. "And I've met you."

"I hope you're not expecting a proposal."

Her lips curved. "You're shortsighted to not consider the notion. You could do your duty to the viscountcy and shock good society in one fell swoop."

"That is an *excellent* point." Leaning toward her, he offered a lovelorn expression. "Will you marry me, Miss Anna Rees?"

"No, Lord Dane. I will not."

The quick rejection surprised him into sitting up. There wasn't a single unmarried woman of his acquaintance who would refuse an offer, even a drunken one, from a peer. "You would turn down the opportunity to be a viscountess?"

"Gladly."

He pressed his lips together in thought before asking, "Is it because I'm the viscount?"

"No; it is because I have no interest in being a member of either the demimonde or the beau monde. Or being married to either." There was a short hesitation before she spoke again. "I want the cottage in the countryside."

"Do you? Truly?" He'd never have guessed it. No one who had caught a glimpse of Miss Rees in her exquisite gowns and sparkling jewels, or listened to Mrs. Wrayburn wax lovingly on about her daughter's adorable demands for exquisite gowns and sparkling jewels, would have entertained the idea for even a moment. Miss Rees was more of an enigma than any of them had realized. "Fascinating. What else do you want?"

"From my life, do you mean?" One dark brow winged up. "Why on earth would I share my dreams with you?"

"You just told me of the cottage," he reminded her. "And I'm not out to have your secrets. Merely your interests. It's a way to pass the time. Unless you'd care to sit here in silence?"

"I don't . . ." She trailed off, looked away, and was quiet for so long, Max thought perhaps she had chosen to sit in silence after all. Which was all the same to him. There were worse ways to spend the evening than sitting quietly with Miss Anna Rees. He liked looking at her—the high plane of her cheekbones, the soft curve of her jaw. He wanted to reach out and trace the outline of her ear, maybe draw his finger down the length of her pale neck.

"I want a hound," Miss Rees said suddenly, and even with the layers of drink blurring his senses, he instantly recognized the twin notes of uncertainty and determination in her voice. It took him a moment more, however, to push through those layers and remember what they'd been talking about.

"A hound. Right. You want a hound. Like your mother's pug?"

"No, not a lapdog. A *hound*," she emphasized with a hint of excitement. "I want a sturdy sort of dog I can stroll with through a forest or have run beside me when I ride. Something not apt to disappear into a well or be trampled under a carriage."

He was suddenly reminded of the Newfoundland he'd had as a boy. Brutus. A hulking, slobbering beast of a thing. "I *adored* that dog."

"I'm sorry?"

He shook his head. "Nothing. Won't your mother purchase a dog for you?"

"A town house is no place for a large animal," she said quietly and began to trace a narrow scratch in the wood of the table with a long, elegant finger.

"Not a sporting dog, certainly. But something like one of those spotted coach hounds. They'd be happy chasing you and your mother through Hyde Park." He couldn't recall having ever seen the lady in the park, but surely she went out for fresh air now and again.

"I'll wait for a cottage."

"Why should you?" When she refused to answer, he dipped his head to catch her eye. "Your mother won't purchase one for you, will she?"

"It is her home," she said by way of answer and went back to tracing the scratch.

"I see," he said carefully, straightening. Perhaps Mrs. Wrayburn and her daughter were not as close as Mrs. Wrayburn had led her friends to believe. "I think . . . You're not at all what you seem, are you?"

Her eyes drifted up from the table. "Beg your pardon?"

"Am I slurring?" he asked and smacked his lips experimentally.

"Considerably, but it's the yawning that renders you unintelligible."

"Ah." He closed his eyes briefly and discovered the room still spun around him, but at a more reasonable speed than before. "God, I am tired."

"Is there no one I could fetch to take you home?"

The few friends he would trust inside his home were not the sort of men who attended parties thrown by Mrs. Wrayburn. He opened his eyes and gave her what he hoped was a wink, but, under the circumstances, might well have been a slow blink. "No one whose company I should enjoy so much as yours. Are you quite certain you won't marry me?"

"Yes."

"Pity," he replied and meant it. Once his position as Lord Dane became public knowledge, the freedom he'd enjoyed as a less-than-desirable match would disappear. No one was interested in marrying the dissolute younger brother of a perfectly healthy viscount. But a dissolute viscount . . . that was another matter. He was to be prime game for the unwed young ladies of the respectable set until he chose a bride. What fun it would be to disappoint them all by eloping with the lovely, fascinating, and entirely unsuitable Miss Rees. "If you should change your mind—"

"I'll not."

"But if you should, I promise you that cottage in the country."

A small smile curved her lips. "And the hound?"

"And the hound."

"And why would you do that, Lord Dane?"

"Everyone should have at least a piece of what they want." And the longer he sat there, staring into Miss Rees's fae eyes, the more he realized that what he wanted most at the moment was her. "I like the way you smile. It's tremendously sweet. And that little eyetooth, there on the right. It's a bit crooked. I find that beguiling."

"Beg your pardon?"

He realized he was yawning again. "Beguiling. Your tooth is beguiling."

"An entire ballroom of charmers just like yourself, did you say? I'd no idea what delights I was missing."

Suddenly he didn't like the idea of her mingling with other gentlemen. Particularly not the sort of gentlemen to be found downstairs. "I may have exaggerated the allure of the ballroom. You're far better off up here."

"I have always suspected."

"You're best off in my company." He wanted to prove it, but it seemed too much of a challenge at present. "I shall call on you tomorrow."

"You may have other duties to attend to tomorrow, my lord."

"Right. Next week, then. I'll call on you next week."

She made a humming noise in the back of her throat that he easily recognized as the sound of a woman humoring a man. His sister had been fond of employing it when they'd been younger and he would air his intent to defy their father.

"Got round to it eventually," he heard himself mumble.

"What was that?"

"I'll get round to it," he stated more clearly. "After this business with my brother."

Another noise, this time accompanied by a patronizing smile and slight inclination of the head. It mattered little to his mind. Next week would be soon enough to prove himself. Just now, he was too exhausted to even think about attempting to prove something. And too drunk. And much, much too angry at his brother for his last attempt at trying to prove something to someone.

"Do you know how he died, Miss Rees? My brother?"

She shook her head.

"A duel. A damned duel. And not even over a woman. Some ridiculous puppy accused him of cheating during a game of cards, and my idiot brother called him out. He's left a wife and four daughters alone, and the estate to a ne'er-do-well. And they'll say he died with honor . . . or defending his honor, I've forgotten which. At any rate, honor will be bandied about like a child's ball while the puppy abandons his ailing mother to run off to the continent, my nieces wail into their pillows, and the Dane estate crumbles into ruin." He tried lifting his hand for a toast before realizing he hadn't a glass, or the energy to lift it.

"To honor," he muttered.

"Lives are ruined in less savory pursuits than honor."

"No." He sighed and leaned back in his tiny chair. His head was so damnably heavy. "No, I don't think they are."

"Haven't you honor?" Miss Rees asked quietly.

He allowed his tired eyes to close, just for a moment, and sighed heavily. "To be honest, Miss Rees . . . I don't much care."